STONER
Shannon
Rise
2011

FOND DU LAC PUBLIC LIBRARY

# The Rise of
# Sekhmet

WITHDRAWN

D0861381

By: Shannon Nichola Stoner

Illustrated by: Karl A. Nordman

JAN 1 7 2014

Copyright 2011 by Shannon Nichola Stoner. Cover Art used with permission and is copyright by Karl A. Nordman

# The Rise of Sekhmet

## By: Shannon Nichola Stoner

## Prologue

This little amulet is all I have left to remember her. The circular tiger's-eye stone reminds me of her beautiful brown eyes. The way it glistens in the firelight is how I remember my lover's eyes as they gazed at me. This stone, beautiful and precious, was meant to be a good omen, an object to bring a blessing into our house. Instead, it is the lone survivor of a vicious attack by some unseen foe.

The tribe's settlement has been destroyed and all its inhabitants killed, including the woman I loved, my precious Zahra. Who could have done this? I stare into the crackling fire in disbelief. How could this happen? I lost my friends, the ones who took me in when my family rejected me because of the woman I loved.

Love in my family could be bought with money. The Al-Sakhir name was built on money and appearances. My family was part of the Nobility of Heliopolis, the social class who lived lives of luxury and extravagance. They prized their affluence above all else and remained ignorant of the needs of those who lived in penury. The Al-Sakhir family shared the beliefs of the rest of the Noble Class; those who were wealthy were superior to those who lived in poverty. Those who lived in poverty were expendable and were useful only to please the desires of the Nobility, a belief that cost a terrible price to the impoverished of Heliopolis.

It wasn't always this way. I had learned of the deeds of great pharaohs, kings who were loyal to the ideal that all people, of Common or Noble Blood, all contributed equally to the benefit of our beloved homeland. The rich and poor alike shared the same table, full of beer and lamb. The equilibrium granted to us by the gods has been upset. The nobles no longer share their lamb. They swat the poor from their chariots like flies attracted to a dead carcass. Beggar children walk aimlessly in the streets looking for food in a land of plenty.

Pharaoh Runihura has dismissed the old traditions in favor of his own decrees. The new pharaoh doesn't support the ways of his predecessors. Instead, he has turned the rich against the poor and treats the poor as objects for his pleasure. He believes in nothing but tyranny. The rich have turned a blind eye to the sufferings of the poor. The pharaoh has dismissed the needs of the lower classes, ruling over the lower classes with an iron fist. My father taught me as I suckled from my mother's breast that the lower classes were expendable, that they were no better than common dogs. The only tradition to remain unscathed during the new pharaoh's reign is to be poor was considered an offense, one that was punishable by death. There is no penalty for the murder of a commoner. People like my companion are considered nothing but prey for Pharaoh Runihura. His actions may not always be respectable, but is killing someone for sport to watch them suffer respectable?

As I think, the fire dances between my companion and me. Only the sound of him chewing on bread could be heard in the dark desert night. My brown eyes rise and look at him as I hear the sound of metal clanging. He's inspecting a bag full of treasures. He helped me in the desert on my way to Thraxis for supplies. He is a thief, vermin in the eyes of the Nobility and the pharaoh. I consider Azizi my friend and not some animal to whip for my own personal pleasure. I saved his life when he was left orphaned at the young age of five. We met among the reeds of the Nile when we were young children. He helped me find my way through the wilderness of the desert when I lost my way. This thief returned to the settlement with me and he witnessed the same horrors upon our arrival. My family would balk at such company, but I have always believed that those of the nobility could be just as corrupt as any petty thug. Evil and greed knew no social station. The pharaoh levies heavy taxes upon the poor while the rich lounge with their dates and tables full of meat. The rich enjoy their lives of luxury at the expense of the poor's suffering. The poor need to eat so they must do what they can to survive.

Rejecting these beliefs, I abandoned my noble family in the name of devotion and adoration of my Zahra, the daughter of a Bedouin tribal leader wandering the desert sands of Egypt. Now their camp lies in ruins. The cold desert night hides the black, ashy smoke as it rises from their destroyed campsite. The bitter smell of the smoke and burning flesh dissipated long ago.

The deepest wound of all is that my Zahra is dead. She was my love, the woman I worshiped, the mother of my unborn child. I could not find our baby among the dead.

The baby was gone, removed from its mother's womb and carried off. I searched all day, turning the bloating bodies on their backs, searching through the smoking embers of tents, sifting through the sands for signs of my child. In my heart, I hoped I would find my newborn.

After an entire day of searching, I found nothing.

The desert sands hold many secrets and only they were a witness to what had happened in my absence. The desert sands cannot tell me where the murderers went or where they have fled.

I never should have left my wife or her tribe, but my departure was necessary. We needed food and supplies. My wife needed medicine to help her through childbirth. Had I not left, maybe I could have defended the camp. I might have been able to fight off their assailants. There's also the thought that I could have been slaughtered beside her. At least there would have been a chance that I could have defended her. Maybe she would have survived. Had I been killed, we would have died together.

So many questions went through my head. Did the camp know they were going to be attacked and they sent me away for my own protection? Who would be so heartless as to tear an unborn child from its mother's womb? Who would benefit from the destruction of my wife and her people? Who is responsible for their deaths? Speculation is the only action I can now take, but it doesn't answer any questions.

One way or another, I will find who committed this atrocity!

I will not stop until I find her killer. Until I find my baby, I will not rest.

Zahra, I will not let your death be in vain. My heart feels heavy as I watch the fire and think of you. I do not regret loving you and I will never admit that I regret taking you as my wife before the Eyes of Rā and Aten. Please believe me when I say I love you and I will never let the memory of you pass from my mind. I will avenge your death, my wife, and I will not rest until those who have taken your life have given me their own in return.

Above me, the stars twinkle in the sky, silent witnesses to the atrocities of humanity and human cruelty towards his brother.

"Amsi, are you okay over there?" he asks me, breaking me away from my thoughts. My companion looks at me from across the fire. A single gold ring in his hand flickers in the fire light.

I try to smile, to show him I'm not as upset as I truly feel. "I'll be fine, Azizi."

"You should eat, my friend," he says as he hands me a piece of bread.

"I'm not hungry. I'm sorry."

The thief reclined on the sand looking up at the stars. He yawned and rubbed his eyes. "Tomorrow I'll take you to a place where you can forget everything."

I looked into the fire with a sigh.

How can I forget? Can it be so simple to forget the death of the woman for whom you renounced your family and inheritance?

There are some things that time cannot heal, but the feelings I had for my wife are eternal.

I lay on the desert sand, gAzizing once again into the blackboard of shimmering lights above. The moon looks down at me, offering a little light to the night in the barren land around my companion and myself.

Very few flora can flourish in the desert, but Zahra was my beautiful flower among the emptiness of the sandy wilderness. In a world of tedious obligations and outdated traditions, she was the one person who gave life to the world around me.

My eyes close slowly as I drift into sleep as I dream about the woman I loved and how our love withstood the tests of social class and family bonds.

# I

## A Child of Noble Birth

The hot Egyptian sun showed brightly on the gardens below. The farmers tilled the earth with their tools as sweat glistened on their bodies. Women with baskets gathered a variety of vegetables from the plants, along with the help of their young children. Men's songs rose into the air as their master watched them from above, fanned by a young slave boy and fed dates by his twin brother.

A young woman ran to his side and bowed her head. "My lord, your wife is close to delivering her child."

"Tell me when my son is born, Qamra," Kaemwaset said, keeping his eyes on the workers in the field below him. "Then I will come see him."

The woman bowed again and left quickly.

"My son will inherit all my lands and my fortune. To him will I give all my wealth and prosperity. In return, he will give me immortality. He will carry on the great legacy of the Al-Sakhir family name. He will be my greatest achievement."

A hot breeze swept through the single braid of black hair at the crown of his head. The thirty-year-old Nobleman smiled with pride down at his vast lands. His dark-skinned arms were decorated with gold bands and around his waist hung a kilt of fine, white linen.

"What if your wife has a daughter, my lord?" the slave boy asked his master as he fanned him.

"Then she will inherit all of my wealth and I will find a fine husband for her to oversee my property. I will find a man from one of the noble houses of Egypt to marry my daughter, watch over my abundant lands, and to produce strong, healthy children by my daughter."

The slave boy handed another date to his master quietly.

In the distance, the man could see more workers toiling on his land. Women were carrying water from the flowing Nile. Oxen were pulling carts along the road.

The sounds of Heliopolis carried on the wind. Merchants were calling out their wares to the shoppers mingled with the sounds of animals in the city and the songs of his slaves.

The Nobleman sighed with contentment as his workers continued to pluck fresh vegetables from his gardens and till his fertile land along the Nile.

A shadow was cast on him and he looked up. A bald, elderly scribe holding a scroll of papyrus bowed his head to him.

"My lord, I have news of the harvest," the elderly man said.

"How bountiful is my crop this year?"

"Very prosperous, my lord. As you can see, we have exceeded expectations with this year's crop."

Kaemwaset took the scroll in his hand as a faint cry of pain sounded within his home. He reviewed the crops, which had indeed exceeded what he had originally planned. "Rā has smiled upon us. The Aten and Rā have blessed my crop with their light and bounty. No doubt, the pharaoh will be pleased with our results."

"We have set aside twenty bushels of grain for our pharaoh."

"That will please our king. I wish to purchase more land along the banks of the Nile. If my lands can produce such bounty, adding more land could double its yield," Kaemwaset said as he handed the scribe the scroll.

The scribe took the scroll in his hand. "That land belongs to your neighbors, my lord. How much will you pay them for some of their land?"

Kaemwaset smiled at his scribe. "Who says I will pay them?"

"They will not give up their land for a small price. If people own land along the bank of the Nile, they consider themselves blessed."

"Don't you worry. I will work out all of the details after the pharaoh graces me with his presence. He should be arriving shortly. In the meantime, you may get back to your counting. I want every grain accounted for."

The scribe bowed. "Yes, my lord." The elderly man left, leaving Kaemwaset with his slave boy who continued to fan him.

The boy fed him another date as a cry of pain echoed from outside. Kaemwaset looked below to see his wife being lead into a tent below his balcony. Kaemwaset smiled proudly as he saw two women helping the crying woman walk.

"Soon my son will be born and he will be the heir to a great fortune. He will be great. He will build a shrine to me and give me immortality. My name will live forever while the pyramids and my bones have turned to dust."

Kaemwaset looked down the distant road and saw a group of chariots racing quickly. He stood up and stepped to the edge of the balcony. One of the chariot riders racing towards his home wore the crown of Upper Egypt on his head.

"Behold! Your pharaoh is arriving! Bow to him!" Kaemwaset yelled loudly to his servants below.

The workers laid their farming implements on the ground as they kneeled towards the road.

The pharaoh and four guards quickly approached the large house of the Al-Sakhir family. Kaemwaset turned towards the twin slave boys. "Nakia and Nassar, return to the fields and help the others."

The seven-year-old twins bowed and ran away quickly. Kaemwaset followed them into the house and down the stairs. His wife's cries of labor pain echoed through the outer garden as he emerged from the house. He stood waiting for the pharaoh to arrive as the ruler's chariot raced towards him.

The workers in the field remained bowed until the pharaoh's chariot stopped in front of their master.

The pharaoh stepped off of his chariot, along with his ten-year-old son, Runihura and his eight-year-old servant girl, Janani. The little girl held a large fan of feathers to shield the pharaoh from the mid-day sun.

Kaemwaset bowed in front of his pharaoh and the prince. "My pharaoh, you honor me with your arrival."

The pharaoh looked down at the Nobleman. The dark shadow of the middle-aged pharaoh was cast over Kaemwaset as Rā's light shown behind the pharaoh, making him appear otherworldly. "I have come for my payment, Kaemwaset."

The man stood up and looked at the middle-aged pharaoh. "I have twenty bushels of grain for you, along with more of my bountiful harvest."

"I have brought my son to see your prosperity. The earth god Geb has shown favor on your harvest once again, I see."

"Indeed, the gods have granted me abundance this year, my pharaoh. Rā has showered his light upon my fields."

The pharaoh nodded as he approached a pile of vegetables. He reached down and picked up a head of lettuce. He looked at the green leaves and smiled proudly. "It appears that the gods have given you their blessing." The pharaoh replaced the vegetable on top of the pile and returned beside his son's side.

"Runihura, the Al-Sakhir family is one of the wealthiest families living along the Nile Banks. His land produces much of the crop that we enjoy at the palace. I must say though, Kaemwaset, that some of your servants look haggard."

"The gods work hard to assure my bounty. My servants can return the favor by working hard to till my soil and harvest what the Aten and Rā have provided for our use."

The pharaoh nodded. "Do not overwork your servants, Kaemwaset. Remember, Kaemwaset, do not have more regard for the well-dressed and do not despite the one dressed in rags. Even the lowly peasant has his natural place in our society."

Kaemwaset bowed his head. "Of course, my pharaoh."

"The order of Ma'at must not become destabilized. It will lead to unrest and chaos. The gods will no longer grant us their peace and their blessing if we do so."

"I will not do so, my god-king."

"I require ten bushels of grain today. I will return for the remainder tomorrow at high sun. The supplies for my workers building my tomb have been depleted and they require nourishment. Starving workers cannot build a tomb and they will not build my tomb well if I do not provide for their needs."

"The promise of food keeps them working for now," Kaemwaset said. "I would not spend my afterlife in a tomb that does not reflect my greatness. Hunger is a great motivator." The Noble landowner turned to the people kneeling towards the pharaoh in supplication. "Return to my crops!"

The workers quickly returned to their feet and continued their labor.

The pharaoh looked in the direction of the birth tent where a woman's cries of pain echoed from within. "I worry about my tomb, Kaemwaset. I do not trust those who work in that village. I have sent my overseers to examine their work."

"If you don't mind my question, my pharaoh, what makes you suspicious of their behavior?"

The pharaoh's piercing dark-brown eyes looked at Kaemwaset. "The gods have told me not to trust them. My priests have told me that there will be a revolt."

"A revolt, my lord? When?"

"My priests have not been very precise when a revolt will be imminent. They have simply told me that the poor will rise up against their pharaoh, according to their prophecy."

Kaemwaset looked down at the young prince. "Has he studied the ancient texts? Does he know of the prophecy?"

Runihura looked up at his father questioningly. "Father? What prophecy?"

"I do not wish to worry you, my son. You will find out in time."

"Why would the people wish to revolt against you, my king?"

The pharaoh sighed and looked up at the sky. "I know not, Kaemwaset. I treat my subjects according to the will of Ma'at. I am just and fair. Let this be a lesson to you, Runihura: If you do control your subjects with injustice, your subjects will not give you the immortality you so desire. Your name shall be erased like the heretic Akhenaten. When you are pharaoh, my son, you will be the intercessor of the gods. When you proclaim falsehoods before Osiris in the Hall of Judgment and your heart speaks against you, your soul will be devoured by

Ammut and your obelisks shall fall into ruin. You will not be celebrated as a great king, such as me."

"You are a great king, my pharaoh," Kaemwaset said gracefully.

"I will be remembered as such. My tomb will be great and will tell thousands of generations to come that a great king rests here and will return once more to life! I want you to stand beside me, my son. I want you to be a great king! My lowly subjects build my tomb, but their work will survive for thousands of years."

Runihura looked up at his father and nodded. "I will be a great a pharaoh as my father."

"I will be your loyal servant," Kaemwaset bowed his head at the child. "I will tell my servants to prepare for your arrival tomorrow, my king."

"Very well. I will send my men to obtain the rest of the grain."

Kaemwaset turned as he heard footsteps behind him. A young woman held a baby in her arms, swaddled in fine, white linen. She bowed and offered him the newborn baby.

"Your son has been born, my lord," the midwife said.

Kaemwaset reached out for the infant with shaking hands. "The gods are truly great today!"

The Nobleman brought the newborn against his chest and looked down at him. "Rā has blessed my house with a male-child. My son, my heir, my key to greatness has been born!"

Kaemwaset turned towards the pharaoh. "My pharaoh, he will be your servant. He will be the head of my household and govern all of my lands when I begin my journey through the Underworld."

"I am impressed, Kaemwaset. The boy looks healthy. He will please the gods and be a blessing unto your family."

Runihura stood on his toes to try and see the baby in the man's arms. His father picked him up and held him in his arms so he could see the newborn infant.

Kaemwaset kissed the infant on the forehead. "This is the gift for which I have long waited."

"What shall you name him?" Atenhotep asked.

The infant brought his clenched hands up to his eyes to shield them from the brightness of the sun.

"His name shall be Amsi Al-Sakhir! He shall be known as the embodiment of power in the universe!" Kaemwaset held the infant up towards the sky. "Behold, Rā! Your faithful servant has been born! He will serve your glorious name and worship you every day of his life! He is the pride of my heart, my son and heir! Look favorably on him, great god of the sun, and bless him! Your servant will proclaim your glorious name as long as he breathes! Your faithful servant has arrived!"

## II

## <u>The Fangs of Apophis</u>

Pharaoh Atenhotep looked at the ancient text in front of him. His brow furrowed with worry over the future of his son. The texts had revealed that the peasantry would rise against a Tyrant Pharaoh. The ancient prophecy foretold of a cruel and barbaric ruler who would seek power through sorcery and witchcraft.

Atenhotep shook his head with dismay. Who would dare to defy ancient tradition? His son was a studious pupil of the ancient ways. He had heard tales of Pharaoh Khufu, a tyrant king in his own right who had severed a man's head to see if his magician could reattach it through magic. He had sworn never to become such a leader to his people when he assumed the throne when his father's Ka had crossed into the Afterlife.

Atenhotep had tried to instill the virtues of honor, justice, and piety in his son, the next pharaoh of Egypt. Under his reign, and the blessing of Re-Atum-Khepri, Heliopolis enjoyed economic and social prosperity. One of his provincial viziers had boasted to him that he had not scorned any of those who had worked for him. Nobody was in need of food or other necessities and that he opened his door to even the poorest of the poor. He had opened his home and had given food and shelter to those in a state of extreme poverty. His district was thriving and he was sending a Nubian caravan to send surplus crops to Heliopolis.

If the people were content with his rule, for what reason would they want to revolt? Had the prophecy already come to pass?

The pharaoh continued to read, unraveling the scroll to read more of the document. His fingers ran over a burned section of the prophecy.

"This was not done by accident. This was intentional vandalism," Atenhotep said. "Who would seek to gain from this?"

The door to his large throne room opened. Janani bowed as she entered the room, holding a tray of fruit and bread for her master.

"My lord, I have come to bring you your afternoon meal."

"Bring it here, Janani."

The little girl walked towards the pharaoh, her bare feet tapping against the polished floor. The golden necklace of the pharaoh hung loosely around her neck, patting against her bare chest. The side-lock of youth dangled from the top of her head and rested against her shoulder.

The little girl placed the tray on the table beside him. She obediently kneeled beside her master as she offered him a grape. With a smile and a quiet giggle, she popped the fruit into her master's mouth.

Atenhotep chewed the fruit and nodded. "This is very delicious, Janani. Good girl."

The girl smiled and bowed her head. "Are you suffering from the rays of Rā, my lord?"

Atenhotep rolled the scroll and shook his head. "No, my dear. I have read something which troubles me, so the rays of Rā do not concern me."

"Is it scary, my king?"

Atenhotep reached over and grabbed a slice of apple from the tray. "I'm not certain. What I need to know has been burned away by some person unknown."

Janani looked at the rolled up scroll. "I have seen Master Hakim looking at that scroll some time ago, my king."

Atenhotep looked down at the little girl and raised his eyebrow in curiosity. "The palace scribe?"

Janani lowered her head to avoid the gaze of her master. "Have I angered you, my king? I'm sorry."

Atenhotep reached down and tilted the little girl's face upwards. He looked into her deep brown eyes. "Where did Hakim take the parchment?"

Janani swallowed nervously. "Please forgive me, my Pharaoh! I should not have said anything!"

"Janani, what are you hiding?"

"Nothing, my king!" Janani exclaimed as she began to quiver in fear.

Atenhotep took a deep breath. "Janani, I am not angry with you. I'm not going to raise a hand to you. Where did Hakim take the parchment?"

"Master Hakim took the scroll to the Instruction Room to use for the prince's studies!"

Atenhotep looked at the scroll. It was possible that the scroll could have burned as it was held up to a candle to read. His son could have become careless and burned a part of the parchment.

"Why do you quiver in fear, child?"

"Master Hakim told me keep silent. I was bringing your clothes back after I cleaned them in the laundry when I saw him leave the Royal Library."

Atenhotep smiled at the child. "Janani, how long have you been here at my palace?"

The little girl rolled her eyes in thought. "I have been here for two years, my pharaoh."

"I have never raised a hand to you, have I?"

The child shook her head. "No, sir."

Atenhotep caressed the child's cheek. "You do not have to fear me. I told you that when you were first brought to the palace."

"Yes, my pharaoh."

The pharaoh smiled at her and took a piece of bread in his hands. "Thank you for telling me. You need not fear

Master Hakim. You are a very brave girl for telling me. Thank you, my little lotus flower."

The little girl smiled and blushed. "You're welcome, my pharaoh."

The king swallowed and took a piece of apple in his hands. "While I have my lunch, why not entertain me with some dance?"

The little girl bowed her head as the king began to cough. "Yes, my lord! Allow me to get Kek. He can play the reed to entertain your lordship while I dance for you!"

Atenhotep watched as the little slave girl scampered from the room. He reached for his wine and drank quickly. He closed his eyes as the room began to spin around him. The temperature in the room seemed to soar as he sat on his throne. He held onto the handles of his golden throne and looked at the plate of food beside him.

"Maybe the fruit was rotten," he said as he saw Janani lead Kek into the room.

Janani held clappers in her hand as the teen stood beside the king ready to play his reed. The little girl bowed as she saw her king waver in his throne. "My pharaoh, are you not well?"

Atenhotep shook his head as he held onto the side of the throne. "Dance, Janani."

Kek began to play the reed as the little slave girl began to dance. She clapped as she spun in a circle. Janani laughed as she leaped into the air, her long, black hair flying behind her.

"Keep playing, Kek! Louder!" Janani laughed as she leapt and spun in the air.

The reed player watched the girl as he played to the rhythm of her movements. He tapped his foot on the ground to keep a beat as he watched her play.

"Play so loud that Re would hear, Kek!" the child exclaimed, her white linen flying behind her as she clip-clapped her clappers.

Kek increased the volume and pace of his tune. The little girl quickened the pace of her dancing, laughing and smiling as she entertained her monarch. She skipped and jumped as she saw the pharaoh tilt in his throne to the side.

The little girl stopped jumping as Kek ceased his tune. "Did the pharaoh fall asleep?"

Kek stood in front of the throne and saw his king's mouth hung open, his body breathless. The teen held his breath. "Could it be?" The teen reached out towards the pharaoh's neck and pulled his hand back quickly. "The pharaoh has died!"

Janani gasped as she ran beside Kek. "No! No, he can't be dead!" Janani placed her tiny hand on his leg and looked into the vacant stare of her deceased master. "My king? My pharaoh? Master?" Janani began to cry as she clutched onto Kek. "What are we going to do, Keket?"

"We must get help! Janani, run for the physician! Get Kazemde!"

Janani ran from the room and returned minutes later with Kazemde, the royal physician. The doctor examined the king and placed a mirror in front of the monarch's open mouth. When he pulled the mirror backward, it was not foggy.

Pharaoh Atenhotep was dead.

The physician sent Janani to find the prince and to bring him to the throne room to see his father before the mummification process would begin.

Kek shook his head. "Janani wanted me to play for him," Keket said sadly. "I never thought that I would be playing the music that would lead him into the Land of Osiris."

"I'm sure you made his last moments of this world pleasurable, Keket. You are a wonderful musician," the physician said, placing a supportive hand on Keket's shoulder. "He was a wonderful king and will be missed by his people."

Janani lead Runihura, his tutor and High Priest, Hakim, into the throne room. Runihura walked calmly to his father's body slouched in the chair. He put his hand on his father's arm sadly.

"Father, I will miss you."

Hakim looked down at Janani. "Where were you and Keket when the pharaoh died?"

"I served the king his mid-day meal." Janani quivered under the strict gaze of the royal tutor. "The king wanted me to entertain him. I was dancing for the king! Kek was playing."

Hakim looked at the half-eaten plate of bread and fruit. "This was the pharaoh's last meal."

"The baker already had the tray ready for me when I arrived in the kitchen," Janani said.

Hakim turned to Keket. "Did you poison our king?"

Keket's eyes widened as he stepped backwards. "No! I would never harm the king! He pays me good money to entertain him! I'm just a poor musician!"

Runihura turned to Janani with a smile. "I guess you belong to me now."

Janani lowered her head. "I believe so."

"Leave. Remove my father's belongings from my new bedroom."

Janani swallowed hard and bowed her head. "Yes, my prince."

Hakim looked down at the little girl. "No. That is no way to address your new pharaoh."

Janani lowered her head and bowed before the ten-year-old Runihura. "Yes, my pharaoh."

The little boy reached for the gold necklace around Janani's neck. "Take this off. You are my property now."

Janani raised her head. She reached for the necklace that Atenhotep had placed around her neck slowly. That necklace marked her as his property. Since she had arrived at the palace, she always wore it around her neck.

Keket watched the little girl remove the necklace with a tear falling down her cheek.

"Janani, leave," Hakim said. "Follow your new master's orders."

Runihura stood in front of the little girl. "Do exactly as I say or I will beat you! Go remove my father's belongings from the palace! I have no need for them."

Janani bowed her head and rose to her feet quickly. Janani shot Keket a troubled look. The teen nodded to the slave girl solemnly. She ran out of the room quickly, leaving Hakim and Runihura behind with Keket.

Runihura looked at his father. "I'm going to miss my father, but I know this was for the best."

Keket looked down at the prince. "Your father was a kind man, my pharaoh."

"He will be sorely missed," the prince said with a smile. "But his death was not in vain. I am the new pharaoh!"

Hakim stood before Keket. "You murdered our king."

Keket shook his head quickly. "No, my lord! I did not!"

Hakim smiled as he quickly stabbed Keket in the stomach with a golden dagger. The teen musician let out a scream of pain as he dropped his reed. "No, but everyone will believe that you did."

Hakim removed his dagger as the teen dropped to his knees and held his stomach. He looked the prince in the eye as blood trickled onto the shiny, polished floor beneath. Runihura smiled at his victim as he quickly sliced the blade of a dagger across Keket's throat. The teen fell to the floor as blood pooled beneath him. Runihura watched as the dying teen breathed his last breath.

"Keket's blood will not be the first to spill onto the ground," Hakim said, satisfied that the teen had died.

"Give me my crown," Runihura said with a grin.

Hakim removed the double crown from Atenhotep's head and placed it onto the head of the prince.

Runihura smiled as he raised his hands into the air. "All hail the new pharaoh of Egypt!"

## III

### A Child of Penury

The man held his wife's hand as her cry echoed through the house. Her palms grew wetter as she perspired. She leaned over, kneeling on the floor, pushing as hard as her muscles would allow.

The two candles burning on a nearby table dimly lit the small home. On the family altar, statues of Tawaret, Bes, and Osiris stood behind the lit candles. The flickering lights cast shadows around them, barely illuminating the kneeling women and the ground below.

The midwife kneeled in front of her, waiting for the couple's first child to appear. "It will be over soon. May Tawaret protect her and her child during this dangerous time."

The man looked at his wife and handed her a cup of wine. "Drink this so that your pain will diminish."

The woman held the cup with a trembling hand and gulped it quickly. She dropped the wooden cup as another wave of labor pains wracked her body. "The child......why will he not arrive?"

The midwife lifted the woman's white kilt. "Your child is beginning to arrive, my lady."

"Khepret, be strong. Our child is almost born," the man said, holding his wife's hand.

The woman breathed heavily as the sharp pains spread through her body. She clutched tightly onto her husband's hand. She clenched her teeth against the pain as her body pushed hard. She let out a scream of pain as a drop of sweat fell onto the dirt floor below her. The woman's body trembled as a final scream of pain echoed through the mud-brick walls.

The midwife reached below the woman and caught the tumbling infant. The man held Khepret before she could fall onto the ground from exhaustion. He kissed her forehead and looked down at the midwife washing the naked infant.

The newborn let out its first wail as the midwife washed the naked baby in water. The mother and father looked down at the shivering, crying child and smiled.

"Our son has arrived," the proud father said with a grin.

The midwife cut the umbilical cord with a flint knife when the afterbirth had appeared. She wrapped the child in a thin blanket and handed him to Khepret. "The gods have granted you a male child who will bring glory and fortune to your house."

The baby clung to its mother's breast and began to suckle quietly.

"Thank you for helping my wife deliver our child, Aneksi."

The young woman smiled at the new father. "It was my honor to help your wife deliver her child. You have been kind to my family."

"I do not have much to give you. Heliopolis has fallen upon hard times. The great pharaoh has died and the new boy-king has increased our taxes in grain."

Aneksi watched the newborn baby in its mother's arms. "This child will be burdened by being the pharaoh's servant. I can only imagine what he will face when he works for the new god-king."

"Azizi may be the one to stop the tyranny of the pharaoh. He may be the key to saving Heliopolis," the father said as he looked down at his son.

"Those who stood up against the new pharaoh have faced very unfortunate ends. Their deaths were very violent."

Ghazi reached over and placed a gentle hand on the newborn boy's head. "I am surprised that the great pharaoh has died so suddenly. His heir is too young for the throne. I wonder who is eliminating resistance to this new king's reign." The man looked out of the single window in the home. The sound of horses echoed through the streets. "Soldiers! Get down!"

He ran to the candles and blew out their light. He ran to his wife kneeling on the ground and wrapped his arms around her and their new baby boy. Aneksi hid in the shadows, away from the moonlight coming into the room.

The horses had stopped and their loud, boisterous voices were heard laughing above the sound of cattle and clucking chickens.

"What are they doing here?" Aneksi asked, trembling in the darkness.

The men banged hard on the door of the house beside them. Azizi trembled in his mother's arms and began to whimper.

The door of the nearby house opened and the soldiers were heard drawing their swords.

"We've come for the rest of what you owe Pharaoh Runihura. Give us the rest of your stores of grain and we will spare your life," one soldier threatened.

Khepret held her baby close to her, shivering not from the pains of labor, but from fear of the pharaoh's soldiers. "What are we going to do if they come here?" she whispered to her husband, fear plain in her voice.

"Just remain still. I know that man paid his dues to the scribes. He does not owe the pharaoh any more grain," he whispered to her.

"I have given the scribes what they said I owe the pharaoh," the man protested. "If you take any more of my grain, my family will starve."

The soldiers were heard laughing above the man's pleas. "The pharaoh recognizes your efforts in building his father's pyramid, but you still owe him part of your wages in grain. Give them to us."

Khepret rocked the baby in her arms and kissed his forehead. "Don't worry, Azizi. They won't come here. Osiris, please protect us and our infant son."

Aneksi trembled in the shadows, muttering a prayer to Osiris under her breath. She clutched an amulet around her neck as she whispered her prayer to the God of Death to protect her and the inhabitants of the home.

"I have paid my wages to the pharaoh! Please believe me!" the man exclaimed nervously.

"If you won't give us your wages, we will take what we feel is equivalent to the value of what you owe!"

Khepret tensed as she heard the sound of the man scream. His pain-filled cry filled the night followed by the sound of breaking furniture and two women screaming inside the house.

Their screams filled the night, echoing through the streets of Heliopolis. The soldier's laughter echoed as they mounted their horses and rode away swiftly.

Aneksi slowly shifted towards the door. "I must go to my home to protect my children."

"I will pay you for helping us when we get our wages tomorrow," the husband whispered.

Aneksi nodded and slipped through the material that provided entrance to the mud-brick hut, running towards her home. "We are saved," she whispered as she slipped into the night.

Khepret cried quietly against the forehead of her new son. "Ghazi, what are we going to do? How can the pharaoh wreak such carnage on those who build his tomb for eternity? If the boy is this strong now, how will he be when he grows older?"

Ghazi held his wife in the dark of the single-room home. "Pharaoh Atenhotep was not such a tyrant. He respected those who built his tomb and plowed his field. He paid his servants well. The new order has ignored the old ways and rules with his fists and clubs."

The baby in the mother's arms fell asleep as the parents sat in the shadows, carefully listening for the sound of returning soldiers.

"We should leave Heliopolis, husband. Our son should not be raised here. He deserves to live safely elsewhere."

Ghazi stood up slowly and crept to the window. "Where else could we go, my wife?" The moonlight showered all around him as he approached the opening to the mud-brick home. He pulled the sheer linen aside and cautiously peered out of the window. The streets were being populated by the wary inhabitants of Heliopolis.

Mud-brick houses surrounded Ghazi's home. Small torches began to illuminate the sandy ground. Chickens roamed the streets, their feathers ruffled, and clucking from the earlier disturbance. Asses were tied to wooden stakes by rope, their hooves stamped on the ground while others bucked from the sounds of people screaming within the house.

Ghazi turned back to his Khepret. "The soldiers have fled. There's no reason to hide anymore."

Khepret stood up and watched her husband walk towards into the street. "You can't leave, Ghazi! What if those soldiers come back again?"

"I will not be long, my wife. I will return if I see them approaching the village again."

"Please be careful."

Khepret touched his face lovingly. "Osiris will protect me, my beautiful, just like he has protected us this night."

Ghazi slowly left his home and walked towards a crowd gathered beside his hut. The door bore a dent where the soldier had banged his heavy hand.

"What were the soldiers looking for? Why did they do this?" a middle-aged man asked from the back of the crowd.

"They claimed that Arentep owed the pharaoh more of his grain. Arentep said he paid the scribes what the pharaoh was owed."

One woman was heard screaming from inside the hut. "They're dead! They're all dead!"

"Arentep was diligent in giving the pharaoh his dues," Ghazi said sadly. "Those soldiers killed him and his family for nothing."

"I'm will not serve this pharaoh who does not treat his servants fairly!" one man growled angrily.

The crowd immediately tried to quiet him.

"Those soldiers are probably still lurking in the night," a young laborer whispered.

"Hetem, choose your words wisely or you will all condemn us to the fate that Arentep and his family suffered!"

Hetem scowled angrily at the crowd. "You are all cowards! Pharaoh Runihura treats us like beasts of burden and yet we continue to toil in the hot sun! I say we revolt!"

Ghazi looked into the night anxiously. The soldiers may have ridden away, but if they remained to indulge in the fear they created in the town, they would hear the raucous.

"Hetem, hold your tongue! The soldiers may hear you and then we will all be killed for your words!"

The tall, dark man's eyes scanned the crowd and saw fear. "Ghazi, we must act! The pharaoh must learn a lesson!"

A young Egyptian woman stepped out of the crowd and stood in front of Hetem. "Violence is not the way. Pharaoh Atenhotep would not approve of us behaving so irrationally."

"Atenhotep has crossed into the Underworld. He cares not for the trials of mortal servants now. We live in squalor while the new pharaoh sleeps in bed of down and fine linens! Water is our wine and the earth is our beds. We need to rise up, people!"

Ghazi put his hand on Hetem's shoulder. "We must be careful, Hetem. We are not fighters or soldiers. We are laborers. We do not have what the rich enjoy, but we do not need wine and fancy luxuries to be content with our lives."

"Ghazi's right, but it would be nice to have a little more on our plates at the end of the day," an older man said. "Under Pharaoh Atenhotep, our granaries were filled and there was plenty. Now, there are not so much as a spare grain."

"That is why we need to stand up to Pharaoh Runihura and his army!"

Ghazi shook his head. "I will do no such thing and risk the life of my newborn child."

The group murmured and smiled at the new father offering their congratulations.

"How can a child order such a senseless slaughter?" a young man named Garai asked as he stood in front of the crowd. "A child would not have ordered the slaughter of an innocent man who was faithful in paying his dues to the state! What does a child know of the burden of ruling a kingdom? It is his advisors who are to blame!"

"I do not wish to see my son impaled at the end of a soldier's blade."

"Did you see the body of Keket hanging in the district square? It is rumored he killed the pharaoh," one woman said as she looked around the crowd.

The tall Hetem crossed his arms defiantly. "It's only a matter of time before you become a casualty of the new pharaoh and his greed, Garai."

"The child of Pharaoh Atenhotep would not behave in such a cruel manner, Hetem! Pharaoh Atenhotep was a champion of his people, rich and poor alike! Arentep must have committed some other crime to be executed by the soldiers!"

"I heard he spoke against the new boy-pharaoh and that is why the pharaoh signed his death warrant," another man said calmly.

Hetem approached Garai angrily. "I am not going to wait to be slaughtered in my own home, Garai. And you, Ghazi, what if the new king decides to burst into your home and use your new child as target practice for his archery skills?"

"How dare you suggest such a terrible thing, Hetem!" Ghazi seethed.

"It will happen, Ghazi. Sooner or later, your child's life will be taken by the new pharaoh and you will be powerless to stop him." Hetem turned and angrily returned to his hut nearby.

The crowd lowered their heads as the dead were removed from the home.

"We must bury them," Ghazi said. "They have served Pharaoh Atenhotep well. Pharaoh Runihura will not be able to wash his hands free of their blood."

The crowd carried the bodies to the desert. Two men dug the pits in the sand and placed the bodies into the sand. Hetem's wife placed pottery and two of Arentep's tools. Sand was pushed over the bodies and the people returned to their respective houses.

Ghazi returned to his hut and watched Khepret standing over their son laying in a basket lined with cloth.

"Did the soldiers return?"

"No, you would have heard them if they did. Hetem was calling for violence against Runihura."

Khepret hugged her husband tightly. "I heard him."

Ghazi held his wife protectively against him. "I will protect you and Azizi. Azizi will grow up strong. Our son could be the one to bring pride to our city and defeat the tyranny of the pharaoh."

Khepret looked down at her infant sleeping in a basket. She smiled proudly at the new life she created with her husband, but deep inside her, she feared for him.

Ghazi released his wife and kneeled beside his sleeping baby boy. He placed his hand gently on his son's head. "Osiris, on this night your servant has been born. May he serve you well."

## IV

## <u>Parasite</u>

Kaemwaset relaxed as he rode in his carriage. Nakia held the reigns of the horse as his twin held a canopy of feathers over his master's head. Imani sat beside her husband, holding his hand tenderly. In her arms, the infant Amsi slept peacefully. Imani smiled down at her sleeping baby and caressed his cheek.

"Amsi will make our house proud, my husband."

Kaemwaset nodded. "He will prepare my tomb for eternity. He will be my legacy to our family. You have made me proud, Imani."

Nassar almost lost his balance as the carriage hit a bump on the road. "Nakia, be careful!"

"I cannot control where the rocks fall on the road, Nassar!" the twin exclaimed.

"Do not wake my sleeping child, you two!"

Nakia tensed as he quickly stopped the argument with his twin. "Apologies, sir."

Nakia watched as the gates of Heliopolis appeared before them. Beside the gate, he saw a crying woman mourning over the sand. He slowed the pace of the chariot as it crossed past the gate.

Kaemwaset's nose wrinkled as the carriage walked slowly through the streets. People were announcing their wares loudly. Some people sat beside the path, reaching up towards the carriage, begging for money or food.

"Please, kind sir! My baby is sick and I cannot feed him!" one woman pleaded as she held her hand to the carriage.

"I have not eaten in days, my lord!" another man pleaded.

Kaemwaset put his arm around his wife as the carriage ambled through the crowd. "Filth."

"Those poor people are starving, Kaemwaset. You should not be so cold."

Kaemwaset looked over at his wife. "These people are good for manual labor, Imani. They may come work at my estate if they need money. That is, if I feel like paying them they may work for me."

Imani saw a woman dressed with dirty linen standing in the crowd holding an infant no older than Amsi. The two women locked eyes as they passed each other. The baby in her arms began to cry. "Azizi, my son, do not cry." Imani watched the woman enter a mud-brick home as they passed.

"Amsi will never need to live the life of the poor. He will have all of his needs fulfilled. He will have money. He will have an estate that provides the temples and the palace with the best vegetables and meat in this district. Amsi will have a mansion worthy of the pharaoh himself at his disposal. Amsi will have slaves to care for his every need. We will find him a woman of noble birth who will bear him strong children. She will be a fertile field for him and will please him greatly." Kaemwaset smiled proudly. "My son will inherit my station as one of the most influential families in Egypt. He will serve the pharaoh and the sun god, Rā."

Imani jumped in her seat as the carriage suddenly stopped. Nakia tugged quickly on the horse's reigns.

"Why did you stop? We are not at the palace!"

Nakia turned his head. "A child ran in front of the horse, my lord! I didn't want to trample him!"

Kaemwaset grabbed Nakia by his side-lock of youth. "You do not stop in this district at all, do you understand me?"

"Yes! Yes!" Nakia screamed. "I won't stop!"

Kaemwaset released the child's hair. "Proceed to the palace and do not stop!"

Imani looked at her husband angrily. "Why do you treat Nakia so violently? He didn't want the horse to trample that child."

"That child could grow to be a tomb robber or a thief. The lower classes breed only lower types of people."

Imani glared at her husband. "That is absurd! These people have built pyramids for the pharaohs! They work in homes as servants. They are artisans. They are not all violent criminals."

"Nakia, if given the chance, would you rob a tomb or steal from the rich?"

Nakia shook his head. "No, my master!"

"Nassar," Kaemwaset said as he turned to face the twin behind him. "Would you murder for sport?"

Nassar bowed his head. "No, my master!"

"Nakia and Nassar are prisoners of war, my husband. They were not born in Heliopolis."

Kaemwaset nodded. "The barbarians who raised them are no better than the people in this district. We have saved you, Nakia and Nassar. You should both be grateful that we have civilized you."

Nakia lowered his eyes solemnly as he loosened his grip on the reigns. Nassar tightened his grip on the handle, his teeth gritting in anger.

"I'm certain Nakia and Nassar were happy in their village and would have become great men."

"They are my reward for providing the palace with sustenance for many years. I plan to keep them in my service, even after the death of the great Pharaoh Atenhotep."

Nakia's eyes wandered to the elevated platform in the district square. A body was hung on gallows. The corpse had been stabbed and its throat cut. Around the neck hung a sign that read 'Murderer of Pharaoh Atenhotep.'

Imani's eyes widened at the sight of the dead body. "That is Keket Ptah-Hotep! He killed the pharaoh?"

"Do you see, my Imani? These people breed murderers and deviant people. That is why we do not stop in this district. We could be robbed by even a simple toddler holding a piece of bread. Let that be a lesson to you, Nakia and Nassar. That will be you should you disobey my law."

Nassar swallowed nervously as he held the feathered canopy over his master and mistress' head. "Yes, sir." Nakia swatted a fly from his face as the carriage passed the hanging body.

Imani's eyes looked at the corpse as Amsi began to stir in her arms. The baby opened his eyes and began to cry. "Amsi, don't cry," Imani said tenderly as she brought the infant to her breast. The baby began to suckle on its mother as the carriage continued through the streets.

"My son is becoming impatient, Nakia. My son wishes that you drive the horses faster."

Nassar grabbed onto the carriage with one hand, knowing how fast his twin could drive the horses. "Go, Nakia!"

Nakia looked over his shoulder at his twin and hurried the horses. "Ga'Ewe!"

The horse trotted faster through the streets as Nassar held onto the carriage tighter. His twin had a way with horses. Nakia could handle the horses well for a boy his age and Nassar wondered how Nakia could anticipate their needs when they could not speak. He had heard from their mother when Nakia was born, the horses in their village became noisy and stomped their hooves on the ground. It was rumor within the village that the horses were rejoicing in the birth of their future caretaker.

Nakia smiled as the wind whipped through his single lock of hair. The streets became less populated and he enjoyed the freedom of the racing horse. The carriage continued towards the palace where closed gates awaited them. A group of peasants stood outside the gates, pleading for entrance. Two guards stood outside the palace gates.

"Pharaoh Atenhotep opened the palace festivities to everybody, rich and poor alike!" the man argued. "Why are we being denied entrance?"

"Because you are not fit to stand in the presence of the Almighty Pharaoh!" the guard proclaimed loudly. "You are only fit to kneel at his feet and beg like the curs you are!"

Nakia stopped the carriage, giving the horse's reigns a tug. His eyes looked around at the angry mob standing before the palace gates.

Kaemwaset stood behind Nakia. "I am Kaemwaset Al-Sakhir. I am here for the celebration of Pharaoh Runihura."

The guards bowed their heads reverently as they began to open the gate. "You may pass."

The one guard opened the metal gate to the palace as the crowd of peasants attempted to slip between the carriage and the gate. The other guard attempted to keep the commoners at a distance.

Kaemwaset returned to his seat in the carriage and leaned forward to Nakia. "Keep moving forward."

Nassar looked back as the carriage passed the gate. The guards pushed back the people with their swords and shields. People raised their voices in anger and protest as they fought for entry into the festivities.

"Pharaoh Atenhotep never turned the peasantry away from celebrations," Imani sighed. "Why would the new pharaoh prohibit the people from celebrating the life and passing of Pharaoh Atenhotep into the Land of Osiris?"

Kaemwaset smiled at his wife. "Because we are privileged, my wife. We will celebrate the departure of the Ka of Pharaoh Atenhotep and pay homage to our new glorious king, Pharaoh Runihura! He will be great like his father, Imani!"

Nassar kept his eyes focused behind him as he heard the screams of the angry people intensify. He saw people began to strike at the guards with their fists. One of the guards quickly sliced through one of the men fighting for entry. The child gasped and faced forward as he began to shake.

The carriage stopped as Nakia tugged on the reigns. Kaemwaset and Imani stepped off the carriage and looked at the palace before them. Torches lined the great palace. The gardens were illuminated by a large bonfire. Nakia turned and looked at his twin in the back of the carriage.

"Nassar? What's wrong, brother?"

"Nothing," the child swallowed nervously.

Kaemwaset looked at the twins. "Nakia, you will remain with the horse. You will not leave the carriage or you will not have dinner tonight. Nassar, you will follow me."

Nassar jumped from the carriage along with his twin brother. The twin hugged his brother tightly. "I shall return soon."

Nakia returned the hug quickly and watched as his brother lead the couple into the palace. Separation from his brother was never easy. The twins were inseparable. Pharaoh Atenhotep had given them to Kaemwaset on the condition that they were never to be separated. Much to their relief, Kaemwaset had continued to honor Atenhotep's condition.

Nakia couldn't help but wonder for how much longer Kaemwaset would keep his promise. Nakia watched his brother look over his shoulder at him. Nakia gave his brother a smile and a friendly wave goodbye. The little boy looked up at the two horses. Hadi looked down at the boy and back at his departing master. Hadi stamped his foot and shook his head.

Nakia reached out and pet Hadi's leg. "Don't worry, Hadi. The master will be back soon."

Hamza lowered his head and stared into the eyes of the little boy with his cold, untamable eyes. Nakia gave the wild, black beast a smile and pet his cheek as he began to shiver in the night. "It's cold tonight, Hamza."

The black stallion nuzzled Nakia tenderly with his nose. The little boy giggled. "You're a good horse, Hamza." Nakia kissed the horse on the cheek and smiled.

Nassar lead Kaemwaset and Imani through the garden path and into the palace. The child's eyes widened at the height of the ceiling and the polished floors. The walls were lined with torches and candles, casting shadows on the elaborate murals lining the walls and floors.

"Keep moving, Nassar," Kaemwaset chided the boy ahead of him.

Nassar walked faster to the end of the hallway where he was greeted by Kazemde and Janani. Nassar smiled at Janani and bowed his head to her. The little girl forced a smile at the fellow slave.

Kazemde reached for Kaemwaset's hand and gripped it firmly. "I honor you for coming to celebrate the passing of Pharaoh Atenhotep and the rise of our new king."

"Long live the name of Pharaoh Atenhotep and may he find solace in the Land of the Dead."

"His passing was untimely," Imani said as she held the baby in her arms. "With the passing of Pharaoh Atenhotep, our family celebrates the birth of our new child, Amsi Al-Sakhir."

Janani rose on her toes to try to see the infant. "Blessings to you," the little girl said.

"Thank you, Janani," Imani smiled. "I know the death of the pharaoh has saddened your heart. I hope you find comfort in the good deeds he has done for Egypt."

Janani lowered her head. "The pharaoh was a very nice person. I will miss him."

"We must offer our condolences to the new pharaoh. Nassar, accompany my wife to her seat and ready a tray of refreshment for us."

Nassar lead his mistress into the room. The large throne room was illuminated by torches. A group of musicians were in the corner playing flutes and lyres. A harp player lightly glided her fingers across the strings, playing with the melody of the other musicians. A group of dancers clapped their hands as they danced in a circle.

Nassar watched as nobles from across the land were holding out their cups for more wine. Dancing women circled in front of the new boy-king, skipping joyously. The slaves of the Nobles were filling their cups and serving them plates of meat and dates. Large plates of fish were presented before the plates of the nobles. Nassar's eyes widened at the sight of fish. He almost licked his lips with anticipation. He had hoped he would be able to partake of a piece and bring back a bite to Nakia.

Imani looked down at the child, mesmerized by the festive atmosphere. "Nassar? Shall we find a seat?"

Nassar looked up at his mistress with a smile. "Yes, my lady. I apologize."

"You find me a seat, my boy."

The child looked around and lead Imani to a seat. Imani sat with her baby in her arms. "Please bring me some fish, Nassar."

Nassar looked around and saw Janani enter the room. He ran up to her quickly and bowed his head. "Where may I get a plate of fish for my mistress?"

Janani lead Nassar to a large table full of duck, fish, and vegetables. The little boy's eyes widened at the feast before him. I've never seen so much food before! This is a feast fit for the gods! "Here you are. Do you need help carrying the plate?"

Nassar grabbed a small plate and placed some fish and some bread on the plate. "No, thank you. I can carry this."

"Where is Nakia?"

"My master ordered him to stay with the carriage."

Janani bit her lip nervously. "I hope he will be alright. It can get cold in the night."

Nassar nodded. "I know. I don't want his ailment to become worse than it already has become."

"I'll give you a jug of wine to carry to your mistress," Janani said.

"Thank you, Janani," Nassar said politely and carried the plate to his mistress.

Nassar kneeled before his mistress and held the plate. He bowed his head and placed the fish on the table before her. "Here is your food, my lady."

Imani reached down and took a piece of fish in her hand. She took a small nibble of the piece and smiled. "This is wonderful." The woman took a small piece and offered it to Nassar. "Take a piece, my child. You are little more than skin and bones."

Nassar's eyes widened at the gift. He looked up at his smiling mistress and sighed. "I cannot, my mistress. Kaemwaset will be furious that I have taken food from your stomach."

"If I offer it, I am giving it generously."

The slave boy smiled at his mistress. "Thank you! Thank you!" The boy took the piece and shoved it into his mouth quickly. He chewed with closed eyes and a sigh of relief.

"You must be hungry, my poor boy."

Nassar nodded quickly. "I am very much so, my lady. Thank you!"

Imani looked down at Amsi in her arms. "Let this be a lesson to you, my son. Do not bite the hands which feed you bread and offer you wine. They are not much different than you or I."

Nassar looked up as he saw Kaemwaset hovering above him. He quickly swallowed his food and let a little cough.

"Where is my wine, child?" Kaemwaset asked.

Nassar stood on his feet. "Yes, sir! I will get it now, sir!"

"Don't be such a lazy boy, Nassar, or your twin will catch himself a death of cold from waiting for us all night!"

Nassar nodded quickly and ran towards Janani. "I forgot my master's wine!"

Janani opened her mouth to respond when Pharaoh Runihura called her name loudly and angrily. "I'm sorry, Nassar." Janani ran to the pharaoh and kneeled at his feet. Nassar jumped when he heard the new boy-king scold his servant angrily and loudly.

He narrowed his eyes angrily and began to approach the furious king when another slave caught him by his arm.

"No, don't interfere, child!"

"But he's yelling at Janani for no reason!" Nassar exclaimed, pointing at the shaking girl.

"Nassar! Where is my wine, you lazy child?" Kaemwaset bellowed from across the room.

The slave boy pulled Nassar to a large barrel of wine. He scooped some into a jug and placed it on a tray. He placed two cups on the tray. "Take this to your master before he becomes unruly!"

Nassar sighed as he looked at Janani. He took the tray and walked towards his master and mistress.

"It's about time, Nassar. We would have received faster service if we were being served by a snail."

Imani rocked the baby in her arms. "Kaemwaset, let us try and enjoy the festivities tonight. Let us not raise our voices in anger at our little servant."

"This is how slow all of his kind move, Amsi. They are slow as snails and devious as snakes. Serve me my wine, boy!"

Nassar grabbed the large jug and struggled to pick it up. He slowly lifted the jug and tilted it to pour wine into his master's cup. Imani held her cup as Nassar poured the wine for her. He kneeled beside Imani as the new pharaoh took his place on the throne.

Hakim, the High Priest of Rā, stood beside the little pharaoh and raised his staff and his arm. "Ladies and Gentlemen of the Supreme Class! Tonight we are here to mourn the passing Ka of Pharaoh Atenhotep. May his spirit and his memory endure forever!" The men and women dressed in fine linens cheered. They raised their glasses of wine and screamed with joy. "Pharaoh Atenhotep was a wonderful man. A man of many great deeds! He was a man of great compassion and dignity. He freely gave of his wealth to help the poorest of Heliopolis. He was a man of war! Pharaoh Atenhotep expanded the boarders of our territory, conquering the heathen tribes to the south!"

Kaemwaset raised his glass with a cry of triumph as he looked at Nassar. "More wine, child!"

Nassar stood and poured another cup of wine for his master. Kaemwaset quickly brought the cup to his lips and began to gulp the precious wine.

"He provided great times of festival and gaiety for people from all strata of society!"

"Long live Pharaoh Atenhotep!" one of the slaves exclaimed, raising his fist in the air.

Hakim continued. "Egypt has greatly prospered under Pharaoh Atenhotep. Now his son Pharaoh Runihura shall ascend to the throne. His reign will be memorable like his father! He will bring Egypt into the age of new glory and new triumphs! Egypt will become the most powerful territory in the world! Egypt will experience power unimaginable now that Pharaoh Runihura has proclaimed by Ra to be the new pharaoh!"

"Long live Pharaoh Runihura!" Kaemwaset exclaimed, raising his cup again.

The slaves exchanged unsettled glances between each other. The men and women in fine linens raised their cups and called out with joy.

"Pharaoh Runihura shall bring Egypt into greatness once again!"

"May Rā bless Pharaoh Runihura!"

Amsi began to cry in Imani's arms. The woman held her son to her breast as he began to wail loudly.

"My son, do not embarrass me in front of our new king!" Kaemwaset cheered.

Imani rocked the baby in her arms and looked at Nassar. "Nassar, see if you can calm him."

"Don't give our son to that boy, Imani!" Kaemwaset growled.

"Nassar will not harm him."

Nassar stood before his mistress and took the baby carefully into his arms. "Don't cry, little master," the child said as he rocked the newborn carefully in his arms. *Nakia is so much better with children than I am. The master should have let me stay with the horses. At least then, my sick brother would not be outside with his bad lungs.*

Pharaoh Runihura looked at Nassar holding the baby in his arms. Nassar rocked the baby gently in his arms. "Why is a slave child holding a child of Noble Blood?"

Nassar turned and saw Runihura glaring at him. He looked around as the Nobility directed their gaze towards him. Nassar cradled the baby against his chest protectively. "My little master is crying."

Pharaoh Runihura stood. "Why are you holding him?"

"My mistress asked me to calm him, my pharaoh," the boy said submissively.

The new pharaoh laughed. "Do you see this, my people? This child is trying to show compassion, but we all know that those of his station do not possess the capacity for such an emotion." The crowd began to whisper among themselves. Pharaoh Runihura stepped down the five steps leading to his throne. "What is your name, slave?"

Nassar protectively held Amsi closer to his body. "Nassar Agangi of the Enzi tribe."

Runihura laughed. "So you are a member of the Enzi tribe who were conquered by my father!"

Nassar bowed his head. "Yes, my lord."

Pharaoh Runihura laughed. "I remember seeing you in Kaemwaset's fields. Do you serve him?"

Kaemwaset stood on his feet and bowed. "He is my servant, my great pharaoh."

"You let your dog of a slave boy hold your son?"

"I did not wish for my son to embarrass me in front of your great presence."

Pharaoh Runihura glared at Nassar. "Why do you hold that child of Noble Blood with such care? I know you wish to slaughter that child."

Nassar shook his head. "No! I do not wish to harm Master Amsi!"

"You bear the same violent blood as those who dwell in the streets of Heliopolis. You seek to spread disease among the Nobility, do you not?"

Nassar clutched onto Amsi. "No! I do not wish to make my Master Amsi ill!"

Pharaoh Runihura stepped closer to Nassar. "Do you wish to slaughter the family you serve in an attempt to free yourself from the bonds of slavery that are now fastened tightly around your neck?"

"No! I do not wish to see my master or my mistress die!"

Pharaoh Runihura glared at Nassar. "I can see you are now infecting that Noble child with your filth. You are a parasite on the backs of our people and do you know what we do with parasites?"

Nassar began to shake as he held onto the infant Amsi. He cradled the baby protectively against him, seeing rage and disgust in the new pharaoh's eyes. The slave boy swallowed nervously as he looked up at the other boy. With Amsi in his arms, it was unlikely that the pharaoh would strike him.

"You plan to murder your master in his sleep, sicken his family, and bring pestilence to his crops. Not only have you planned this, but the lowly peasants of Heliopolis seek to destroy the Nobility. All of you plan to bring the destruction of Heliopolis!" the boy-king exclaimed pointing towards the slaves. "This is what we must fight!" Runihura exclaimed, grabbing Nassar's shoulder. "This is the disease which festers in the streets of Heliopolis! They seek the destruction of our society! They seek to undermine our way of life! They do not know compassion! They know only lust for power! They only know of corruption! They only know debauchery! They do not seek to better themselves for the good of Egypt!" Runihura released Nassar. "We, my people, live privileged lives! Our society is built upon the backs of the poorer class! We are powerful! We are strong! We are better than these rats which run rampant in the streets of Heliopolis! The gods favor our sacrifices to them over the meager offerings of the poor. We feast on duck and fish. They feast on garbage! Osiris will grant us entry into the Land of the Dead and will welcome our Ka. We are *powerful*! We are *superior*! We are the Nobles of Egypt!"

The men and women raised their cups again, cheering the pharaoh.

"Let us celebrate the life of my father, who wanted Egypt to be strong! We can be strong, my people! My father's outreach to the lower classes was admirable, but he was wasting time scratching a non-existent itch. We must look after our own, my Superior Nobility! He believed in extending generosity to the poor and look at his reward!" Runihura glared at Nassar. "My father was murdered by swine like you!"

Nassar sniffled as a tear fell down his face. "I am not a swine. I am human!"

"You dare talk back to me, you heathen?"

"Your father murdered my mother and father!" Nassar exclaimed. "I saw your father's army kill them both! I watched them both die! My father was stabbed with a sword and my mother's throat was cut in front of me!"

"Nassar!" Kaemwaset growled as he stood from his seat. "How dare you yell at your pharaoh!"

"He is not my king," Nassar growled, holding Amsi close to his body with a glare.

Runihura laughed. "My people, do you see the lack of respect that flows through their blood?"

Imani raised her hand. "Nassar, come here."

Nassar ran towards Imani as Kaemwaset approached him. Nassar felt Imani pick him up and cradle him against her.

"Imani, put that child down so that I may beat some respect into him!"

"You have had too much wine, Kaemwaset. You will not harm the child," Imani said, petting the child's head.

Nassar held Amsi against him. "Don't hurt your son!"

"Do you think you can protect him from me, Nassar?" Kaemwaset asked, glaring at the child in Imani's arms.

"I do not want you to hurt Amsi."

Kaemwaset narrowed his eyes. "I would not worry about Amsi, Nassar. I would worry about your own safety and that of your twin brother."

"Kaemwaset, it is time we leave," Imani said, standing on her feet. She placed Nassar on the ground and watched the boy scurry behind her to hide from the fury of his master. Imani took the baby in her arms. "My pharaoh, I must take my husband home. He is full of spirits."

"I wish you well, Imani Al-Sakhir," Runihura said. "You should punish your slave boy for his disrespect."

"I will discuss this with him, my pharaoh."

Kaemwaset watched as his wife walked away, Nassar clutching tightly onto her robe. The boy turned his head anxiously and saw his master glaring at him.

Runihura glared at the boy walking away. "We shall teach that one a lesson, Kaemwaset. Bring him here at dawn."

"Consider it done, my lord."

Kaemwaset walked behind Imani, glaring at Nassar from behind. They arrived at the carriage finding Nakia sleeping. The boy's arms were wrapped around himself as he shivered in the cold night air. Imani heard the boy wheezing in his sleep as he laid in the back seat of the carriage.

"Nakia, open your eyes!" Kaemwaset bellowed as he punched the boy in the arm roughly.

The little boy jumped as his eyes opened quickly. His body tensed and shivered as he looked up at his drunken master.

"My husband, do not wake the boy so! He has toiled all day in the fields," Imani said calmly.

Kaemwaset raised his foot to climb into the carriage, but his foot missed the step. He fell forward, catching himself. "Help me into my carriage, you little scoundrels!"

Nakia grabbed Kaemwaset's arm as Nassar placed his foot on the step. The man pulled himself into the carriage with a hiccup and a groan.

Nassar climbed onto the back of the carriage and gripped onto the metal in front of him.

Imani boarded the carriage and sat beside her husband. "I believe you have celebrated enough, my husband."

Nakia sat in the front seat and grabbed the reigns with a tired yawn. "Hamza, Hadi, time to go home." Nakia fluttered the reigns as the two horses began to trot away.

Nakia lead the horses through the front gate of the palace, still guarded by heavily armored guards. At the feet of the soldiers, he saw three peasants laying dead in the road. "Take care tonight, my lord. The filth of the streets will be out in full force now that darkness has covered the land."

Kaemwaset bowed his head. "Thank you. Keep our new king safe. Praise be to Pharaoh Runihura and may his reign endure!"

Imani shifted closer to her husband as the carriage pulled away from the palace. "My lord, what shall we do if thieves attack us?"

Kaemwaset chuckled. "We'll just give Nassar to them. That will be his punishment for his disrespect of the great Pharaoh Runihura."

Nakia turned his head as he gripped the reigns of the horses tighter. "No, sir! Please don't separate Nassar from me! He's all I have!"

"Eyes front!" Kaemwaset bellowed as Nakia's head quickly turned forward.

"My husband, we cannot separate the twins," Imani said. "Pharaoh Atenhotep requested that we not tear them apart."

The man grinned. "We won't tear them apart, but I know the savages living on the streets will. They'll take Nassar and rip him in half. That is the barbarism of those people. The poor will cook him alive for their food. It matters not to me what they do to him."

Nassar swallowed nervously as he looked around the dark streets. Shadows crept along the ground as the carriage traveled through the night. A few drunken poor stumbled through the streets. A group of women were gathered outside one house. Candles burned in the windows. The moonlight illuminated a sign above a door reading 'Mbizi's Meeting House.'

Kaemwaset watched as two women lead a man through the entrance. "My son, you do not want to associate with rats such as these. They bring disease. They give disease."

The carriage continued as they heard cheers and singing. "A son has been born to us! Long live my son, Azizi!" The men and women in the home cheered.

Kaemwaset looked at the sleeping boy in his mother's arms. "I'm afraid they multiply the same way as rats, my son." Kaemwaset smiled as he put a loving hand on his son's cheek. "Make me proud, my only son."

V

## Mistresses of the Nile

Khepret bundled her newborn in a blanket. She bound the blanket around her shoulder and across her hip. The new mother placed her son against her breast and hoisted a bundle of material on her back. She left the home and began to walk through the streets of Heliopolis towards the River Nile. The streets were bustling with people selling possessions as well as pieces of pottery and jewelry. People were willing to part with treasured possessions for coin.

Khepret shook her head as she saw a woman pleading for a man to buy a child's toy she had made so she could provide milk for her children. She stopped as she heard the marching of soldiers approach. Her heart leaped into her throat as she saw a man in chains being lead through the streets towards the gallows in the middle of the quarter.

"He dared to approach a Nobleman and beg for a hot meal," she heard a man say behind her.

Khepret turned and saw a tall, obese man standing in front of her, blocking her path towards the Nile. "What crime is there in that?"

The man smiled, two teeth were missing from his smile. "No crime at all, except he should have taken what he wanted instead of asking politely."

Khepret took a step backward. "I am on an errand, sir. Please excuse me."

The man stepped in her way. "You carry a heavy burden and I see you have had a child."

Khepret smiled happily. "Yes, Osiris has blessed our family."

"You worship the God of the Dead? You are brave, celebrating death in a city where the Sun God is worshipped. However, seeing as Pharaoh Runihura has come to power, Heliopolis may soon become the City of the Dead. Pharaoh Atenhotep was not so bloodthirsty as his son."

"The pharaoh cannot live forever. The gods will judge him."

The obese man laughed, his belly jiggling. "How can the gods judge one of their own? Below here, our people suffer while those in higher places feast until their heart are content."

Khepret sighed as she looked down at her sleeping boy. "We will make things better for our children. Pharaoh Runihura's reign will end and this will all be a bad memory best left forgotten."

The man looked at the bundle tied to the front of her body. "Did you have a boy child or a girl child?"

Khepret looked down as the little boy opened his eyes slowly and yawned. "Osiris has blessed me with my first child, a son."

The man smiled. "I can believe that times are difficult for you now. Do you have any money?"

Khepret shook her head. "No, my husband and I struggle to feed ourselves. My child feeds from my breast, but I cannot feed him if I cannot afford bread."

The man smiled. "I can provide you work. My name is Mbizi. That is my establishment over there. Should you ever need money or employment, you are a very beautiful woman and I know I would find you no shortage of work."

Khepret looked at the building where women with bare breasts stood outside. They kissed the men as they exited. "I thank you, sir, but I do not believe I could do that."

Mbizi bowed his head. "My offer stands. Have a nice day."

Mbizi walked towards the entrance to his building as Khepret continued through the city gates. People with carts of fruits and spices called out their wares as she passed. The baby cradled against her breast began to suckle quietly as he snuggled against her.

"Is my little Azizi hungry?"

The baby looked up at her from inside its swaddled refuge. Khepret smiled down at her son as he fed quietly. She walked through the city gates, watching children play with their dolls and pulling toys on wheels.

"Make way!" Khepret heard as a chariot raced towards the palace. She looked up and saw the chariot in front of her. "I shall run you over, street-rat!"

Khepret screamed and jumped quickly to the side of the road, making her nipple separate from her son. Azizi let out a cry of protest as he balled his fists.

"That's the Captain of the Guard, Gahiji," Khepret said as she glared at the carriage pulling away. Khepret put down her laundry and wrapped her arms around her crying baby. "Don't cry, Azizi. You are not hurt."

Khepret offered her breast to the baby who began to suckle once more. "Good boy, Azizi."

Khepret replaced her burden on her back and continued to walk towards the Nile. In the distance, she saw the pyramid that Pharaoh Runihura commanded be erected for him. Ghazi was working there and would not return home until the sun began to set in the horizon. The heat of the day made her sweat and she wondered how her husband toiled in the oppressive heat of the mid-day sun.

"How your father can toil for such a tyrant is unknown to me, Azizi. Your father breaks his back for barely enough for us to eat. The new pharaoh keeps more than his share." Khepret looked down at her little boy as he stopped feeding. "I want you to be a good man, Azizi. I pray that Osiris gives you a good heart so that it may not speak against you when you join him in the Land of the Dead."

The baby boy looked up at her and yawned again. He placed his head against her and whimpered.

Khepret watched the laborers in the fields, singing and cutting grain. She sang to her son quietly as she approached the banks of the Nile. She kneeled beside the water and looked around for evidence of crocodiles and hippopotamus. Khepret placed her swaddled infant beside her as she unfolded her bag of linens to wash.

"Nakia! Be careful!" Khepret heard behind her as she turned her head.

A little boy was carrying an armful of linens towards her. The linens blocked his view as he ran over the banks and fell into the water.

"Nakia! Nakia!" a woman called as she carried a swaddled infant and laundry. "You can't swim, child!"

Khepret saw the fallen boy splash in the river. Khepret reached into the water quickly as the boy splashed. She lifted the child out of the water, who began to cough and sputter.

"You must be careful around the Nile," Khepret said, placing the boy on the land. Nakia coughed as Khepret pat his back. He nodded as he looked at her.

"Many thanks to you," a teenage girl said as she arrived beside the coughing boy. "Nakia, don't worry me like that!"

Khepret retrieved the boy's linens from the river. "He carried too many things."

"I thank you for helping my slave child," the woman carrying the baby said as she bowed her head.

Khepret stood up and looked at the Noble woman in front of her. Khepret reached down and gathered Azizi in her arms. She wore a long, white linen dress. Gold bracelets and a gold necklace adorned her body. Four golden rings circled around her fingers. A golden ankh hung around her neck as it dangled against her chest.

The woman smiled at the poor woman in front of her. "I remember you. I saw you while traveling to the palace for the coronation ceremony for Pharaoh Runihura."

Khepret nodded. "I remember seeing you, my lady."

"My name is Imani. This is my newborn son, Amsi. He was born two suns ago. This is my wet-nurse, Qamra. Nakia has never learned how to swim, so I thank you again for saving him. I see the gods have blessed you with your own child."

Khepret cradled the baby closer to her. "Yes. I have named him Azizi."

Imani took a small step closer and looked at the woman's child. The infant raised its arms to shield its eyes from the sun. The child kicked its legs as it tried to avoid the sun's light.

Khepret saw Amsi laying peacefully in his mother's arms. The baby did not flinch from the sun, but turned his head to view the other baby. She placed Azizi against her chest again as the baby began to relax.

Qamra kneeled beside Nakia and brought him into her arms. "I do not wish to bring your body to your brother. He would be heartbroken to hear of your death, Nakia."

Nakia lowered his head solemnly. "I am sorry, Qamra."

"You must be careful around the Nile banks," Imani said. "Many a child has been food for the hungry beasts of the waters. I do not wish you to be among them."

Qamra unrolled a cloth and placed it on the ground. Imani sat on the cloth and rocked her infant. She placed a bowl of fruit in front of her mistress. Nakia kneeled beside Imani and fed her a grape.

Khepret placed Azizi beside her and began to wash one of her linens beside Qamra. "I am amazed that you do not wash your clothes elsewhere."

"What do you mean?" Qamra asked as she removed a cloth for washing.

"You are a Noble family and you are washing your clothing beside mine. Do you not have a place to wash your linens in your home?"

Qamra shrugged. "I am doing the laundry for the servants. My lord does not allow my clothing to be washed with his linens."

"I see. Why has your mistress come?"

Qamra smiled. "My mistress needs to exercise. She cannot return into the home for twelve suns. She will be purified in the birth tent until then."

Imani looked into the clear sky. "Rā has blessed his children with a beautiful day, Qamra."

"Yes, my lady. The gods have smiled upon us today."

"Why couldn't Nassar come with us, Qamra?" Nakia asked.

Qamra took a deep breath as she thought of Kaemwaset's harsh command that Nassar remain behind as punishment for some indiscretion from the night before. "I do not know the reason, Nakia."

Nakia fed Imani another grape and began to fan her with a fan of elaborate feathers. Nakia looked at the baby on the ground beside Khepret. "He's funny!" the boy laughed as he saw Azizi shield his eyes and turn his head from the sun. "Maybe I should cover the sun from his eyes." Nakia turned the fan to shield the sun from the infant. Azizi lowered his arms and yawned. "He's tired!"

The infant closed his eyes and began to fall asleep. Nakia returned to fanning his mistress. The boy coughed as he gripped onto the pole tightly.

"Thank you for calming my Azizi, Nakia," Khepret said with a smile.

"You are welcome!" Nakia giggled.

Qamra looked over at Khepret as she wrung out a piece of material. "I am amazed you chose to save his life."

"He may serve the Nobility, but I bear him no ill will for the changes that have happened since the passing of Pharaoh Atenhotep."

"He does not serve willingly," Qamra said sadly. "Neither do I, my lady."

Khepret turned her head. "Why can you not leave?"

"It's not as simple as simply leaving," Imani said. "People have given themselves to servitude out of need or to pay a debt. Now people cannot escape such oppressive conditions. Wars, poverty, these things have created perpetual slaves, servants who cannot leave. They are bound to their masters out of desperation and necessity."

Khepret nodded. "My husband toiled on the pyramid of Pharaoh Atenhotep. The new boy pharaoh has commanded that work on his father's tomb cease and to begin construction on his own tomb."

"The new pharaoh has made his position clear that those who are in service to the Nobility are not worthy of the old ways of treatment. People work and they go nowhere. I believe that the gods have given us balance and to say that the Nobility is more blessed than the working poor upsets the stability of Ma'at."

"My master has always raised his voice as long as I can remember. Nassar makes him angry, but he doesn't mean to do so. He defends me a lot." Nakia added. "I hope my master does not separate us."

Khepret looked down at her sleeping son. "I will do everything I can to assure my son does not live the life that his father and I lead. I want him to have a better life in this one and the next."

Amsi began to cry as Qamra turned her head in response. Imani held up her hand. "I will feed him, Qamra. You continue with your laundry."

Qamra bowed her head. "Are you certain, my lady? I could feed the child."

Imani offered Amsi her breast as the boy began to suckle at her nipple. She caressed the baby boy's cheek. "There you go, Amsi. You're a good boy."

Qamra removed another piece of linen with a sigh. "My lady is very forgiving. She is a kind and patient mistress."

"I still believe in the old ways and I pray that my husband begins to understand. In ten years he has not changed and I do not foresee any changes in the future."

Nakia coughed as he turned his head from his mistress' sight. His body shuddered with his congested chest. Nakia coughed harder than usual as he began to lose his footing.

"Nakia, are you not feeling well?" Imani asked.

Nakia shook his head. "I'm fine, my lady." The boy turned and coughed harder.

"Kaemwaset never should have kept you in the cold air with the horses last night," Imani said sadly. "With those poor lungs of yours, I regretted leaving you outside. My protests would have landed on deaf ears."

"Nakia and his twin brother did not sleep when they returned to our quarters, my lady. They were cold and hungry. I warmed them and fed them."

Imani reached toward Nakia's forehead and touched it lightly. "You are warm, but the sun could have made you hotter."

Khepret smiled. "I am glad to see you care for your servants, my lady."

Qamra placed her linens on the ground and walked towards Nakia. She placed her hand on Nakia's forehead as the boy began to waver unsteadily on his feet. Nakia lowered the fan in his hands and dropped it on the ground. Imani watched as Nakia fell to the ground sitting and holding his chest. "You poor boy. When we return to the family land, I shall make you something to eat to help you feel better."

Nakia's nose wrinkled. "The last thing you gave me to make me feel better tasted bad."

Qamra chuckled. "You recovered, did you not?"

Nakia nodded. "Yes, Qamra."

Qamra brought the boy against her. She hugged him tightly. Nakia returned the embrace as he coughed. The teenaged girl kissed Nakia on the forehead, making the little boy whimper and snuggle into her.

"Finish your laundry so we can return Nakia to his bed," Imani said. "The boy looks ill. Nakia, sit down beside me."

Nakia sat on the blanket beside Imani and stared at the sand, his head lowered. Imani heard the boy cough and whimper. "Nakia," she whispered gently as she caressed the boy's side-lock. Nakia rested his head against her. Imani smiled and put her free arm around him. Nakia blinked silently as he snuggled against his owner.

"You're a good boy, Nakia," Imani said tenderly, making the little boy smile up at her.

"Nassar will have to feed the horses tonight," Qamra said, returning beside Khepret. "I've cared for the twins since they were brought to the Al-Sakhir family land. I have cared for the children since I was sixteen years old. I'm nineteen now and I have no children of my own, but I am learning how to be a mother from Imani."

Khepret nodded. "You are so young to be in service to such a wealthy family."

"My family needed money, so they sold me to the Al-Sakhir family. The children and the other slaves are my family. I bear my family no ill will. I just do not like to see the children have no time to enjoy their youth."

Nakia approached the women and kneeled between them. Khepret watched as the little boy scooped water into his mouth from the Nile. Khepret saw a tattoo on Nakia and Qamra's upper right arm. It bore the same image, the eye of Rā and a scarab.

Nakia splashed some water over his head and shivered. He sat between the two women and grabbed a piece of linen belonging to Khepret. "I will wash this for you."

"You should rest, child."

Nakia shrugged and dunked the cloth in the water. "It is no problem." Nakia rubbed the material together as he soaked his feet in the water.

Khepret watched the little boy wash the cloth with a smile. "You have my thanks, Nakia."

The little boy smiled and nodded quietly, coughing with his mouth closed.

## VI

### I *Own* You

Jinan sat outside of the servant quarters, sipping water from a clay cup. He saw his master standing on the balcony hovering over the fields. From his perch, the land owner could survey his lands, assuring his field workers were working to their full capacity. The old man looked up at the stars twinkling in the night sky.

Karida ran outside to Jinan and tugged on his white skirt. "Nassar is crying for Nakia. Where is he?"

Jinan looked down at the four-year-old girl. "I don't know. It is late. Qamra is never home this late."

Baruti, a young man of seventeen, stepped from the entrance. "Nassar is in no condition to tend the horses tonight with his brother."

"Nakia did not look well this morning. The boys were awake late last night and now Qamra has not returned with Nakia."

Baruti looked down at the old man. "Do you think Qamra knows?"

Jinan shook his head solemnly. "Nassar is quick to speak. He has the spirit of Seth inside him. Qamra loves those boys and I know the boy's punishment hurts her deeply."

"I saw the master today carrying Nassar under his arm. He passed the mistress' birth tent. He scolded me to continue harvesting."

"Our master has been possessed by Sekhmet. The war goddess has entered his heart and has filled it with disdain and hatred for all around him. Many years ago, his actions would have ostracized him from Heliopolis. He would have been reprimanded."

Baruti glared at the figure on the balcony and clutched his fists tightly. "He will pay for what he did to Nassar! That boy is only a child!"

The old man sipped from the cup again. "The gods will find a way to restore Ma'at, Baruti. Until then, this old man will be content to sit and wait."

"Nakia!" Karida exclaimed as she saw Qamra and Nakia approach the servant home. Karida ran to Nakia and hugged him tightly. "Nakia! Nassar need you! He cries for you!"

Nakia ran towards the house. "Hello, Jinan! Bye, Jinan!"

Nakia ran into the home and saw a group of slaves gathered around the corner of the single room. "Nassar! Nassar! I'm back!" The room was lit by a small fire in the center of the room.

Nakia pushed through the crowd to find his brother laying on his back, his body covered in bruises. Nakia gasped and kneeled beside his brother. "Brother! My brother, I'm here! Open your eyes! Who has done this to you?"

Nassar opened his eyes weakly as he turned his head towards his twin. Nakia gathered his brother into his arms as his twin whimpered in pain.

"Did the master do this to you?"

Nassar nodded slowly as he began to cry. He reached up and threw his arm around his twin, hugging him.

"I'm here, my brother," Nakia said as he began to cough. The child's body shuddered as he coughed against his twin. "Tell me who did this!"

Nassar shook his head emphatically as he pointed to his mouth. Nakia's eyes widened as he realized what had happened.

The group of slaves parted as Qamra stepped through the crowd.

"Nassar?"

Nassar turned his head and saw Qamra sitting beside him.

Qamra asked as she sat beside the boy. "Come here."

The boy released his twin and reached for the woman. Qamra gently picked up the boy and set him on her lap. She cradled the boy's body against her, rocking him gently.

Nakia looked up at the other slaves. "What happened to him?"

Baruti joined the group. "Kaemwaset took him to the palace. Kaemwaset left him here alone."

Nassar trembled as he held onto Qamra. The boy's cheeks flooded with tears.

"It's alright, Nassar. It's all over," Qamra whispered quietly as she kissed the boy's head. "You're a good boy, Nassar. Let me see."

Nassar opened his mouth slowly. Nakia's eyes watered as he saw the inside of his brother's charred mouth. His brother had his tongue removed and the injury cauterized to prevent him from bleeding to death. The pungent smell of burned flesh wafted from the boy's open mouth.

Nakia leaned over and hugged his twin. "I love you, brother." Nakia's thin body shuddered as he coughed.

"Nakia, I must tend to the horses for you. You are too ill and I think Nassar would want to stay with you. When I come back, I will make you some medicine."

Nassar nodded and gripped onto his twin tightly.

"I'll stay with him," Nakia said. "If the master comes back for him, I won't let him get near my brother!"

Baruti looked at Qamra. "I'll watch over the children while you are gone."

"Thank you, Baruti," Qamra said.

"Don't leave!" Karida pleaded, holding onto Qamra's white skirt.

Qamra smiled down at the little girl. "Nakia cannot look after the horses tonight, Karida. I will not be long." Qamra stepped out of the home as Jinan looked up at her.

"Where are you off to now, girl? You just returned home."

"I must feed and tend to the master's horses. The twins are in no shape. Nakia is ill and Nassar should remain where he lies."

Jinan sipped from his clay cup again. "Lovely night, isn't it?"

"Yes, it is."

Qamra took one of the torches and walked towards her master's stable. The Al-Sakhir family owned four horses. She had heard from Najam, the cook, their master was planning to purchase more horses, which would require a larger stable, which would require more labor or to build a completely new stable to accommodate the new horses. After the harvest, Kaemwaset wanted work to begin on the stable.

She heard rustling in the corn nearby and she stopped quickly. She turned and saw nobody behind her.

"Hello?"

Silence was her only answer.

Qamra turned and continued walking towards the stable. She thought of a coughing Nakia laying on his reed mat. She prayed that the boy would recover quickly from his ailment which had been aggravated by the cold air of the night. Nassar was always the faster healer. Qamra had hoped since Nassar had his twin returned to him, that the boys would sleep better and would be able to recover better together.

She opened the large wooden doors of the stable and placed the torch into the pedestal near the entrance.

"Hello, Hamza, Hadi, Naji, and Munir." The horses whinnied and snorted in return. Qamra reached out and pet Hamza's snout. The black horse snorted and watched her every move intently. "Nakia is not feeling very well tonight, so I'll be feeding you your meal." Qamra grabbed a pot of grain and gathered the baskets in front of the individual horses. She began scooping some grain into baskets to feed the horses. She filled Munir's basket first and placed it on the shelf beside his stable. The white horse began to munch hungrily.

Qamra smiled as she pet the horse's mane. "Good boy."

Qamra began to scoop grain into Naji's basket when she heard the door to the stable creak open. She stood and turned. Kaemwaset was shutting the door behind him.

Hamza reared in his stable, whinnying loudly in alarm. Hadi stomped his foot on the ground in protest on Kaemwaset's right side.

Qamra kneeled on the ground and bowed her head. "My lord, what brings you to the stable at this time of night?"

Kaemwaset remained by the torch and looked at Hamza clicking his teeth angrily and kicking the floor angrily. "I came to see you."

Qamra swallowed nervously. "My lord, Nassar and Nakia are in no shape to care for the horses tonight, so I have volunteered to care for them."

Kaemwaset chuckled. "You care too much for the sons of a defeated people."

"They are only children, my lord. The fact that their people were defeated should not reflect on them."

"But it does, nevertheless. Nassar was easily subdued, just like his mother and father."

Qamra's head raised quickly and she rose to her feet. "What did you do to that poor boy, my lord? He is only seven years old!"

"He is a child who could not control his tongue!" Kaemwaset screamed angrily. The horses whinnied again from the bite of their master's bark. "So the pharaoh and I removed it for him," he added calmly.

Qamra straightened her back. "He is such a sweet boy. Nassar has a good heart!"

"He is a child who needed to be put in his place," Kaemwaset walked towards her and smiled down at her. The torch light from behind him hid his face from view. Qamra took a step backwards. "Why do you appear frightened?"

"My lord, I must finish this before I return home. I must make Nakia medicine."

Kaemwaset chuckled as he raised his hand slowly. Qamra closed his eyes and grit her teeth tightly, preparing for a slap across the face. Instead, a gentle hand pressed against her cheek. She opened her eyes and found her master's face inches within her own.

Kaemwaset pressed his lips against hers and moved his hand to the back of her head. She pressed her hands against Kaemwaset's shoulders and attempted to push him away.

Hamza slammed himself against the reinforced stable. The black stallion protested loudly.

Kaemwaset broke the kiss and turned to Hamza. "Keep it down!"

Qamra pushed against Kaemwaset as she began to growl. "My lord, release me!"

Kaemwaset chuckled as he held the girl against him. "You are so beautiful, Qamra."

"My lord, I must finish feeding your horses! Nakia needs his medicine!"

Kaemwaset narrowed his eyes. "Are you denying me my right to your body?"

"You have a wife, my lord! Your wife has just given birth to your son! You do not need my body!"

Kaemwaset licked his lips. "My wife is still unclean from her birth," Kaemwaset pressed himself against his slave girl and caressed her hair lovingly. "She cannot return to my home for another twelve suns. My bed is lonely. Besides, I own you."

Qamra looked into the eyes of her master and she began to shake. "My lord, I cannot betray the Lady Imani. Your wife is in her birth tent! Go to her."

Kaemwaset's hand went to her breast and cupped it lovingly. "You will not need a birth tent, my beloved Qamra." His hands wandered to the front of her belly.

"No!" Qamra shouted defensively. "I will not let you! Not after harming Nassar! I know what you did to that child and you are a monster!" Qamra punched Kaemwaset in the shoulder angrily. Kaemwaset released her holding his shoulder. "It's your fault Nakia has taken ill!" She bellowed, balling her fists tightly, ready to fight.

Kaemwaset glared at her. "I will personally see to it that Nakia dies!"

Hadi and Munir whinnied loudly in fear.

"You leave that little boy alone!"

Hamza reared again in his stable, crying in alarm loudly and angrily. Naji stomped the ground.

Kaemwaset laughed. "He is easily replaceable, my dear. What do you say we begin the replacement process?"

Qamra grabbed the basket of grain and threw it at Kaemwaset. She ran towards the exit, but the master had grabbed her wrist. Qamra turned and to punch him again. "Baruti! Jinan!"

Kaemwaset slapped Qamra across the face and threw her into the pile of hay. Qamra turned and saw Kaemwaset on top of her.

He grabbed her wrists and turned her on her back. "Shall we begin?" Kaemwaset chuckled as he pressed his lips to hers roughly.

Hamza's furious vocalizations rose into the night, hiding Qamra's screams of protest. Jinan turned his head towards the stable and sipped from his cup. "There is an

awful lot of commotion coming from the stables. I bet
Hamza is refusing to eat from Qamra's hand."

Baruti looked towards the stables. "Hamza never makes
such a raucous when Nakia feeds him. Maybe Nakia can
calm his spirit so Qamra may feed him." Baruti stepped
into the dwelling of mud-brick and looked at Nakia
clutching onto his brother. "Hamza is unhappy and I
believe he needs you."

Nakia opened a weak eye and struggled to his feet. He
took an unsteady step forward and looked up at Baruti.
"I'm not well. Nassar needs me. He's hurt badly."

"Only you can calm Hamza, Nakia. He listens only to
you."

"Up?" Nakia asked, raising his arms to Baruti, wiggling
his fingers.

Baruti picked the child into his arms. "You need to eat
more. You weigh as much as the feather of Ma'at!"
Baruti tickled the little boy as he laughed.

The child smiled and yawned as he leaned against
Baruti's body. The child hugged Baruti as he was carried
towards the stable where Hamza's protests became
louder.

"Hamza is not happy at all, Father Baruti," Nakia said. "I
wonder if he doesn't like the way Qamra put the grain in
his basket. He's the fussiest creature I have ever tended."

Baruti's ears perked when he heard a scream as they
approached the stable. "Qamra?"

Nakia turned to the stable. "Baruti! Is that Qamra?"

Baruti ran towards a window into the stable. Baruti and Nakia looked inside and saw Kaemwaset and Qamra on the hay. Qamra was punching Kaemwaset angrily as he laid on top of her.

Nakia let out a scream. "Qamra! What's Kaemwaset doing to her, Baruti?"

"What should I do?" Baruti gasped and quickly turned his back to the window. He looked around in the night, shivering nervously. Qamra was being hurt and if he interceded, he could bear the force of his master's fury. Nakia looked up at Baruti with large, dark brown eyes. He tugged at Baruti's side-lock of youth.

"Help her! Let me down!" the boy exclaimed, shifting in the boy's arms.

Nakia fell from Baruti's arms and ran to the front door of the stable. Baruti followed Nakia to the front door of the stable. The boy opened the stable door and ran inside. Baruti ran into the stable behind the child watching with horror at the scene before him.

Hamza looked down at Nakia with fire in his eyes. The black stallion leaned down its head and bared angry teeth at the little boy. Baruti grabbed Kaemwaset and tugged at his master.

"Baruti! No! He can hurt you!" Qamra exclaimed.

Kaemwaset turned, seeing the young man and Nakia behind him. The obese man smiled as he looked at the little boy. "Nakia, my boy, come here."

"No, Nakia! Stay away! Go to Nassar!" Qamra cried.

Kaemwaset shoved Baruti back as he removed himself from Qamra. He stood up and looked down at the child with a grin. "Come here, little boy. Do not disobey your master."

Baruti looked down at the bleeding girl on the hay. He narrowed his eyes as he clenched his fists tightly. "You son of a jackal! How dare you violate Qamra!"

Kaemwaset glared at Baruti. "Return to your dwelling before I whip you! Leave the boy and Qamra."

Hamza nuzzled Nakia with his snout. The boy caressed Hamza as the horse's protests silenced. Nakia looked up at Kaemwaset in fear as he held onto Hamza.

Kaemwaset removed a silver dagger from his robes and stepped towards Nakia. "Come here, little boy. I'll make certain you do not speak of what you have seen here tonight."

Hamza turned his head angrily towards Kaemwaset and kicked the front door to the stable violently. Nakia whimpered as a tear fell down his face. "No, please, sir! I'll be a good boy!"

Baruti stepped in front of Nakia. "I won't let you murder that child!"

"Get out of my way, Baruti."

Qamra jumped on Kaemwaset from behind and grabbed the arm which held the dagger. "Baruti! Take Nakia and go!"

Hamza and Naji whinnied loudly. Hamza snapped his teeth at Kaemwaset as he approached the boy.

Baruti flew his fist at Kaemwaset and connected with the large man's jaw. The man staggered backwards. Baruti punched his master again as Qamra fell off him. Kaemwaset fell backwards on the hay, the silver dagger tumbling out of his hand. The man lost consciousness as he laid on the hay.

Nakia trembled as he caressed Hamza's snout. "It's okay, Hamza. Calm down. Nakia's here. You're a good horse."

The horse's protests silenced as he nuzzled Nakia. Nakia looked down at Qamra as Baruti kneeled beside her.

"Qamra, get to your feet! We must leave before he wakes!"

"Nakia?" The little boy looked up at Qamra, his body shaking and tears coming down his face. "Come here, child."

Nakia left Hamza and threw himself at Qamra. He wrapped his arms around her neck and kissed her cheek. "Mother Qamra…"

"I didn't want him to kill you. I love you, Nakia."

Baruti helped Qamra to her feet. The girl stood on quivering legs as she held the boy against her breasts. "Can you walk?"

Qamra caressed Nakia's back. "I have to get the boy away from the master."

Baruti looked down at Kaemwaset. "He's no better than a crocodile!"

Qamra carried Nakia towards the servant quarters. The boy shivered in the cold night as he was brought inside the small slave home.

Nassar heard his brother crying and opened a tired eye. Qamra sat beside the sleepy twin and placed Nakia beside his brother. "You rest with Nassar. I need to make your medicine."

Baruti kicked the side of the home angrily. "How dare the master violate you! We should use that dagger on him!"

"Don't be so impetuous," Jinan said. "The wrath you feel will return to us tenfold and we will all end up victims of your anger."

"But you are old, Jinan!" Baruti said. "All you do is sit on that step and drink from your cup! Don't you want better for these slave children?"

Jinan sipped from his cup again. "Soon I will enter the Hall of Osiris. I will be free soon, so it matters not to me."

"You are selfish!" Sabi protested. The young woman of twenty-one years glared at the old man. "You care not for the young! Why is Qamra bleeding, Baruti? What did he do to you, Qamra?"

Qamra grabbed a mouse that had crept near Nassar. "I wish to keep silent." The mouse squeaked in terror as Qamra grabbed a knife.

"Our master was bouncing on her!" Nakia exclaimed.

Baruti's lip curled in disgust. "When I pass the Rite-of-Passage ceremony, I shall never engage in such behavior! If Pharaoh Atenhotep were still alive, Kaemwaset would be severely punished."

"If Pharaoh Atenhotep were still alive, we wouldn't be here anymore," Tabari said as he leaned against the wall as he cradled a sleeping Karida in his arms. "We would be able to simply stand up and leave."

Qamra looked up at Baruti from the bowl of mouse blood. "You will become a fine man, Baruti. I know you will not become a man of hatred and unnecessary violence."

Nassar began to cry as he laid on his reed mat. The boy turned his head and began to arch his back. Issâm, a priest of Thoth, took the young child in his arms and rocked him. The middle-aged man's muscular arms dwarfed the tiny child against his body. Nassar placed his hand on Issâm's chest and whimpered.

"Baruti, we do not wish to bury you before you become an adult," Issâm said as he looked over at the teen.

"What do you propose we do?" Baruti asked angrily.

"Go to sleep so we can begin work at dawn?" Jinan asked as he laid on his mat, placing his cup on the ground beside him.

Issâm looked down at Nassar and caressed the boy's cheek. "Don't cry, child. You are here with people who care for you. Poor boy." The boy yawned as Issâm rocked him gently.

"You have my gratitude," Qamra said as she smiled at Issâm.

Issâm kissed the top of the orphan's head. "This child is a good boy. I cannot stand to see this child suffer."

Qamra placed the skin of the mouse in a separate bowl and sighed. "The master wanted to kill Nakia."

Issâm looked down at the sleeping boy on the mat. "Why would he want to kill him? Nakia is a good worker and he tends the livestock."

"He said I care for those two children more than I should."

Issâm rolled his eyes. "These children have no parents. Pharaoh Atenhotep's army slaughtered them. Somebody has to be there for them." Issâm's nose wrinkled at the smell of the cooking skinned mouse over a small fire. Issâm looked down to see Nassar's head limp against his chest and his arm dangling from Issâm's strong arms.

"May Isis bless this mouse and alleviate Nakia's ailment." Qamra placed a gentle hand on Nakia's shoulder. "Nakia, wake up. Your medicine is done."

Nakia opened a tired eye with a cough. "I'm very tired, Qamra."

"I have your medicine ready."

Nakia sat up slowly as he looked at the skinned mouse. "You want me to eat this?"

"It will help cure you. I have prayed over it and I will make an elixir with the blood for you in the morning."

Nakia groaned as he looked at the mouse. "No."

"Nakia, you will get more ill if you do not do this," Qamra said calmly.

Nakia sighed in resignation as he took a bite of the cooked mouse. "Yummy," the child said sarcastically.

Qamra caressed Nakia's back. "Good boy."

## VII

### Days of Darkness

Ghazi bowed before the statue of Osiris and folded his hands in prayer. His eyes were closed as he implored his god to deliver Heliopolis out of the hands of the pharaoh-god. Khepret cradled Azizi as she leaned against the wall of the mud-brick home. Her stomach growled as she looked at the sleeping baby.

"Great Osiris, protect my family from the wrath of the pharaoh-god. Please send us your bounty and grant us deliverance."

Khepret sighed as she looked at the empty basket in front of her. "Ghazi, we have no bread."

The man turned his head and looked at the empty basket. "Perhaps we can trade with Garai. He may have some bread that he has not sold today."

Khepret looked up at him from the small fire. "Mbizi offered me work today."

"Don't you go within an inch of that man, Khepret! I have seen how he treats his women and I do not wish to see you in the arms of another man for the price of a few coin."

"If we do not do something, my love, we shall starve and Azizi will have nobody."

Ghazi looked at the sleeping boy. "I would rather my son be alone than for you to have to sell your body."

Khepret gasped as she cradled Azizi closer to her. "My husband, you cannot be serious!"

Ghazi stood up and glared at his wife. "I will not have my wife throw herself into the arms of another man who would mistreat her, Khepret. I love you and I do not wish my son to see his mother sell her body."

Khepret stood, hugging the infant to her breast. "I love my son, Ghazi. I do not wish to see my son living on the dark streets of Heliopolis alone."

Azizi opened his eyes and looked at his father. The infant clenched his fists and cooed.

"My son would not be the first street orphan out there."

"There must be another way, Ghazi! Today I was washing our clothes by the Nile and I met a Noble woman who seemed very generous."

Ghazi narrowed his eyes at his wife. "I forbid you to talk to that woman again! How could you speak to the very people who are the cause of all of our misery?"

"She was not a cruel woman! She seemed to care for her slaves as it was in the old days."

Ghazi shook his head. "You will not speak to such snobbish people! If the Nobility believes we are rats, then maybe we should bite at their heels as rats do!"

"That will not change anything, my husband!" Khepret exclaimed.

Ghazi approached her and glared down at her angrily. "You will not speak to them. Do I make myself clear?"

Khepret looked down at Azizi and sighed. "I apologize for evoking your anger, my husband," Khepret said as she returned to her seat by the fire. "I will speak no more of this."

Ghazi's lip curled in disgust. "I cannot believe that you would interact with such people after all the changes they have implemented. They have disrupted Ma'at and that is why the people are suffering! We have nothing to eat because the Nobility has chosen to act as vultures and fly in for the kill. They are jackals snarling at our door, ready to eat us and our infant child alive and you speak to them."

Khepret trembled as she held Azizi against her protectively. "Things weren't always this way, my husband."

Ghazi took the empty basket and looked down at her. "It is the way things are now and I forbid you to speak of this again."

Ghazi left the home, pulling the material to the side. He stepped into the night and saw men staggering from Mbizi's Meeting House. They hiccupped and laughed in drunken stupors. Many were speaking in groups, exchanging food for wine.

Hetem stood outside his dwelling and chuckled. "Out of bread again, Ghazi?"

"I am afraid so."

Hetem looked towards the gallows. "It seems more of us have joined poor Keket as he dangles from his rope."

"How many more will there be?"

Hetem shrugged. "I will not be going quietly into the Land of Osiris. I will fight for the freedom enjoyed by our forefathers!"

Ghazi's eyes widened. "Be careful how loud you proclaim that name, Hetem! The guards could be near! Gahiji has ears everywhere."

"The goddess of destruction will protect me, Ghazi. She will protect her loyal followers who die in the name of a righteous war!"

Ghazi looked around nervously, hoping no guards were within ear-shot. He clutched the basket close to him. "I do not wish calamity to befall my family because you are shouting for revolt."

"Then we shall die as martyrs for the cause, my Ghazi! Our names shall be remembered as Pharaoh Runihura's name fades into obscurity! We shall be heroes in the faces of the gods!"

Ghazi looked at the bodies of the hanging poor. Keket's body was now missing a leg as the wild dogs chewed at him. The birds had already removed his eyes from their sockets. His abdomen was swollen as flies flew freely around him. Ghazi swallowed nervously.

"Their families are not permitted to remove their bodies," Hetem said.

Ghazi looked with pity at the body of the hanging teenager. "Keket was a very good musician. He showed promise in his profession."

"His spirit cries for revenge, Ghazi. I will fulfill that desire."

"Hetem, I do not wish my family to pay the price for your lust for revenge. I wish not for my son to die."

Hetem chuckled. "I am not afraid. Go to Garai. He sings songs of harmony and pacification."

Ghazi walked towards Garai's home. From inside the home, he could hear music coming from a flute. Ghazi called to him. "Garai, it is Ghazi!"

Garai pulled back the material covering the entrance to his house and smiled at his visitor. "Ghazi, my friend! How goes things with you?"

"Garai, do you have bread?"

Garai tapped his chin with his finger and turned to his basket. "I could spare half of a loaf and one fish. That is all I have to give."

"My wife will make you a loaf of bread and return two fish to you for what you offer."

Garai nodded. "That is acceptable." Garai placed the half-loaf and fish in Ghazi's basket. "You look flustered, my friend. Please come into my home."

Garai lead Ghazi into his one-room home. In one corner stood an altar to Ra where two candles burned in tribute to the Sun God. A small fire in the center of the room dimly lit the small confines of the home. Ghazi watched as shadows flickered on the walls from the small fire.

"My wife informed me that Mbizi offered her work and that she has spoken to a Noble woman by the Nile."

Garai sat on his reed mat. "This bothers you, my friend."

"How can she speak to those people? How can I allow my wife to work under Mbizi? I cannot allow strange men to touch her and have their way with her, Garai! I will not have it!"

Garai offered Ghazi a cup of water to drink, but Ghazi refused with a raised hand. "There are many women who have taken Mbizi's offer for employment. I do not trust the man's reputation from what I have heard from people around the city."

Ghazi gripped onto his basket tightly. "My wife has spoken to a Noble today while washing linens."

"Your wife is entitled to speak to whomever she desires and that includes those of the more...privileged classes."

"Privileged classes, indeed, Garai." Ghazi rolled his eyes sarcastically. "I will not have my wife speak to the very people who are responsible for our poverty! I will not permit my son to befriend someone who beats him like a dog all for the sake of class distinction!"

Garai looked up at his friend calmly. "You have an anger problem, Ghazi. I know you can control it before it controls your spirit."

Ghazi laughed. "I do not have a problem with my anger, Garai!"

Garai sipped from his cup quietly. He looked up at his friend. "I have seen you while you work. You have become quarrelsome and I saw you hit Chenzira over nothing more than stepping on your foot by accident."

"He did not look where he was going. Now he will watch his steps more closely."

Garai shook his head despondently. "You have changed, my friend. The Ghazi I knew even ten suns ago would not have struck a man needlessly."

"Would you permit your son to befriend someone of Noble Blood, Garai?"

"We are all Rā's children, regardless if we eat bread and water or lamb and fish. I bear no ill-will towards the pharaoh, but I pray to Ra daily that the gods remove the seeds of hatred from his heart."

Ghazi narrowed his eyes at Garai. "I would rather see my son dead before he befriends one of Noble Blood!"

Garai gasped and his eyes widened at Ghazi's furious proclamation. "Surely, my friend, you do not hate your son so much as to wish death upon him! Ghazi, the gods would be displeased, especially the god Osiris who has blessed your household with your first-born son! Do not anger the God of Death or he will smite you and your family with great misfortune and disease!"

Ghazi turned his back on Garai. "I treasure the gift the gods have brought Khepret and myself, Garai. However, I will not forgive those of Noble Blood for what they have done to our people. We are their beasts of burden not fit enough to be fed a morsel of bread during a long day's work. We cannot feed our families while they grow fat on lamb and beef. The new ways have replaced the old. We cannot survive under such conditions. My wife and I are starving under the pharaoh's fist as well as everyone who once served Pharaoh Atenhotep."

"What do you propose, my friend? Do you propose an uprising such as Hetem has demanded?"

"Something must be done, Garai," Ghazi said taking a deep, calming breath. "It's only a matter of time before Hetem's heresy is discovered. When it does, nobody will be safe in the streets of *Iunu*."

Garai lowered his head. "I know. I pray to Rā himself that peace may cover this land and Ma'at be restored. Balance in everything is a gift from the gods and lately that balance has been disrupted. May Rā bless you and your family, Ghazi, and may the Sun God keep you from danger."

"Thank you, Garai. All of us could use the blessing of Light in these days of Darkness. I shall have Khepret make you bread. Thank you again for the food, my friend."

"Ma'at will be restored someday, Ghazi. When that time comes, all of Rā's children will raise their hands in praise to the Great One and Aten's light will bathe us in the favor of the gods."

Ghazi nodded. "I hope you are right, Garai." Ghazi stepped into the street, carrying his fish and bread. He held his basket tightly as he fled home. Khepret looked up from her seat beside the fire. Ghazi watched as Azizi slept quietly on a pile of clean linen. The newborn boy's fingers twitched in his sleep. Ghazi placed the basket before his wife. "Garai has given us some food. I said you would bake him bread and give him two fish in return."

Khepret took the fish in her hands and grabbed a knife. She began to prepare the fish. "Very well," she said quietly.

Ghazi took a piece of bread and placed it on the altar to Osiris. He kneeled before the altar and lit the candle in front of the statue of Osiris. "Great God of Death, Osiris, accept what offerings I give. Protect my family from the ravages of Pharaoh Runihura. Make my son's body strong and his mind wise. Make him a great man and brave in the face of danger. Give him strength of mind and body."

# VIII

## Speechless

Kaemwaset looked down menacingly at the young man and woman kneeling before him. Baruti and Qamra looked at each other sideways, not turning their heads. Kaemwaset's lip curled in disgust. "Is this true, Qamra?" the Noble asked, his rings glimmering in the sun's light.

Qamra nodded her head slowly. "It is, my lord. I have spoken only the truth."

Kaemwaset slowly turned his back to the two kneeling slaves. He stepped gradually towards the mantle made of marble imported from Greece. Baruti raised an eye to see his master take a silver dagger in his hands, the same dagger he had used to threaten Qamra's life three months prior. Baruti reached out slowly and took Qamra's hand.

"This news is…unfortunate."

Qamra swallowed nervously as she held Baruti's hand. She closed her eyes, mouthing a prayer to Isis. She could feel Baruti's hand shaking nervously, his side-lock of youth hanging over his shoulder. Qamra did not mind that Baruti's hand was dirty from his work in the field. Kaemwaset had summoned him from his work without notice.

Kaemwaset paced slowly towards the kneeling couple and lightly touched the blade of the dagger. "Have you told my wife or anyone about that night in the stable, Qamra?"

Qamra shook her head. "No, my lord. I have spoken of this to no one."

Kaemwaset took the blade of the dagger and placed it under Baruti's chin. He tipped the teen's head to look him in the eyes. "Tell me you have kept silent about what you have seen."

Baruti swallowed nervously. "I have told no one, my master!"

"I have told you that should you speak of what happened, that you would find yourselves food for the jackals, have I not?"

Qamra and Baruti nodded vehemently. "Yes, my master," they said in unison.

"Nassar would not be the only one without a tongue and I would send you to the mines where your backs would be broken in a matter of days. I would see to it that you suffered greatly breaking rocks for the Great Pharaoh's pyramid!" Kaemwaset removed his dagger from Baruti's chin and stood in front of Qamra. "How could you do this to me, Qamra? How could you conceive a child and threaten the marriage with my wife that is already in jeopardy?"

Amsi cooed from the corner, his arms were waving and his feet were kicking happily. The baby boy played with a rattle as he laid on his back.

"My master, I had no choice in the matter," Qamra said quietly. "I tried to resist you."

"Now you carry my child, Qamra," Kaemwaset said. "Have you laid with any other man?"

Qamra shook her head. "No, my lord. You were the last man to lay with me."

Kaemwaset's eyes narrowed in anger. "I am disappointed in you, Qamra. Your womb has spoken against me and will surely betray me."

Qamra's hand slowly went to her stomach. "I did not conceive this child willingly, my lord."

"My wife is still furious that I have taken Nassar's tongue as his punishment for his vile words towards the pharaoh. How will she hear that I have fathered a child by you without her consent or knowledge? Qamra, you are a vile woman and your ill-begotten seed should be food for the jackals!"

Amsi let out a cry from the corner, startled by his father's anger. He dropped his rattle and arched his back with a startled cry.

Qamra buried her face in her hands and cried. Baruti put his arms around Qamra and held her close. Baruti looked up at his master, his face covered in dirt and sweat.

"Qamra did not choose her fate," Baruti said. "She is not a vile woman, my lord!"

"Careful, Baruti, or I shall take your tongue and beat you like I did Nassar!"

"Then beat me! I care not!" Baruti swallowed hard. "That child did not deserve the punishment he was dealt. Qamra is a good woman with a kind heart!"

Kaemwaset walked to Amsi and picked his son into his arms. He cradled Amsi and kissed his son on the cheek. "There, now, my son. Do not cry. There is only one person here who deserves her sorrow."

Baruti leaned into Qamra's ear. "Don't listen to him. You did nothing wrong," he whispered.

Kaemwaset rocked his son in his arms as he returned in front of the kneeling teenagers. "You have upset my son, Qamra. What say you?"

"I am sorry," Qamra whispered, keeping her head lowered.

Kaemwaset caressed the baby's cheek. "The child you carry in your womb shall not be a member of my family. It shall not bear the Al-Sakhir name." Amsi turned his head and looked at Baruti and Qamra kneeling in front of his father. Baruti saw the little baby reach out a hand towards them. The infant opened and closed his fists as if waving to them. "Before the birth of the baby, Qamra, I shall release you from my service. Another of my friends would be delighted to have you as a servant. He has offered good money for your services."

Qamra looked up at her glaring master. "I cannot leave the children behind, my master! I am the only mother Nakia and Nassar know. I am the only servant who knows about medicine. Nakia's illness knows no cure and only I can make him medicine! Should I leave, he could die!"

"He is an orphan, captured from the enemy. He is only fit to dodge the pharaoh's arrows as target practice for the young king."

Baruti held Qamra closer to him. "Qamra cares for your son. Would you send away the only woman who knows how to care for your infant son?"

"I risk my son becoming ill from the vile milk which flows through her breast. I shall find another wet nurse to suckle my son. Najam will work nicely." Kaemwaset stepped closer to Baruti. He reached down and grabbed the teen's side-lock. "You are the baby's father now, do you understand? It is you who put that child in Qamra's womb!"

Baruti swallowed nervously. "I would not touch Qamra in that manner! She is my friend!"

Kaemwaset pulled viciously on Baruti's hair, making the teen cry out in pain. "You are the baby's father, Baruti! If you say anything to the contrary, I will take your phallus, sever it, and feed it to the fish like Seth did to Osiris!"

Amsi let out a cry of alarm again, making Kaemwaset quickly try and pacify the child with gentle rocking. Baruti rubbed his head from Kaemwaset's harsh pull of his hair. Qamra looked Baruti in his dark eyes and returned his embrace.

"Do not forget my threat, Baruti. You are the father of the child in Qamra's womb. My child needs his mother and I will not lose my wife because you have spoken against me."

Amsi looked at Baruti and gave a worried look. The baby reached towards the teenage boy and waved at him again.

"Return to the fields, Baruti. Qamra, you will inform my wife of the child that Baruti and you have created."

The two teenagers bowed their heads and rose to their feet slowly.

The door to the room opened as Imani stepped inside. "I apologize, my husband, but the glorious Pharaoh Runihura is here for an audience."

Baruti and Qamra kneeled again as the pharaoh entered. Imani turned and calmly left. The boy looked down at Baruti and Qamra. "Kaemwaset, I do not like the stench of slave in here."

"Both of you leave and forget not what I have told you!"

Baruti and Qamra left the room. The pharaoh looked at his faithful servant kneeling before him. Janani stood behind Pharaoh Runihura as she looked at the Noble infant laying in his father's arms. The baby boy was moving his arms and kicking his legs sporadically. Tiny noises escaped from the infant watching the scene in front of him.

"Words of revolt are being spoken in the poorer districts of *Iunu*, the merchant quarter, Kaemwaset. The poor seek to undermine my power given to me by the gods themselves."

"They shall learn that they cannot challenge the embodiment of the gods in this mortal world."

Pharaoh Runihura glared past Kaemwaset. "These words of revolution had reached my ears after my father's…untimely demise. However, three moons have passed and the words have become louder and more powerful. These voices can no longer be ignored."

Kaemwaset raised his head. "Any attempt at revolution can be easily subdued with the right tactics, my lord."

"Removing their tongues from their heads will not suffice. I must assert my authority in a more demonstrative manner," the pharaoh said with a smile. "I need to know that you and the other Nobility will support me."

Kaemwaset bowed his head. "Name anything you wish, my lord, and if it is within my means, you shall have it."

"My words and my actions are not enough to instill fear into the hearts of my subordinates. I need that which will make my enemies cower in fear. I need power that will rival the strength of the gods' themselves, Kaemwaset."

"Is there such a power to be found in the realm of mortals, my pharaoh?"

"When I ascended to the throne, I had vowed to make Egypt the most powerful force of this world. I will be

more powerful than Rā himself if I can find such relics."
Pharaoh Runihura grinned and turned to Janani. "Leave.
Common slaves like you do not need to hear the great
words which come from my lips."

Janani bowed her head and calmly walked out of the
door. Janani leaned against the wall and sighed. She tried
to listen to the words being spoken through the door, but
the thickness of the wood refused to let her hear the plans
within.

"Baruti's manhood ceremony is coming up, Nassar,"
Nakia said as he walked beside his brother. Nassar shook
his head vehemently. Nakia looked over at his brother
and made a cutting motion with his hand across his arm.
"But that's a good thing! He'll be a man!"

Nassar shook his head and trembled. Nakia sighed sadly.
He knew why Nassar was afraid of attending the
ceremony.

Nakia looked towards Janani and ran to her, followed by
his silent twin brother. "Janani? Why are you here?"

"Pharaoh Runihura is inside with Kaemwaset and Amsi."

Nassar let out a guttural groan and jumped behind Nakia.
Janani looked around Nakia to see Nassar shaking. "I'll
protect you, Nassar."

"What happened to him?"

Nakia reached to his shoulder and covered Nassar's hand
tenderly. "Kaemwaset and Pharaoh Runihura removed
Nassar's tongue three moons ago."

"Nassar, I apologize," Janani said sadly. "Pharaoh Atenhotep never would have allowed that to happen."

Nassar shook his head quietly behind his twin.

Nakia's lip curled into a sneer. "Well, the pharaoh gave his permission to our master to remove his tongue! Now my brother will never speak to anyone again!" Nakia's body trembled with fury.

"I'm sorry," Janani said quietly as she folded her hands in front of her and bowed her head.

Nassar stepped from behind his twin and reached for Janani's hand. He took her hand and pat it, shaking his head. Nassar turned to his twin and shook his head. He pointed to Janani and curled his fingers like claws. He opened his mouth in a silent scream and made a sudden motion forward towards Nakia. Nakia wasn't certain whether to be afraid of Nassar's sudden motion or the fact that when his brother opened his mouth, no tongue could be seen. Nassar pulled back and shook his head.

"Angry?" Nakia asked as his twin nodded. "How can I not be angry at her?"

Nassar pointed to Janani and made a cutting motion by his mouth. He shook his head.

"What is he saying?"

"He's saying I shouldn't be angry at you because you didn't cut out his tongue." Nassar nodded in response as he turned to Janani.

Janani smiled at Nassar. "Thank you, Nassar."

The twin smiled as he reached out and hugged Janani tightly. Janani returned the hug as Nakia looked at the closed door to the master's room. "Getting Amsi isn't going to be easy. I'll get him. Nassar, you stay here."

Nassar gasped and turned to his twin quickly. He grabbed Nakia's arms tightly and shook his head violently. "But Imani wants her son and we have to clean the rugs and clean the Al-Sakhir shrine to Rā and we have to help make the bread and we have to help with the harvest and we have to bathe Amsi and-!"

The door to the room opened and Kaemwaset looked down at the three children angrily. "Nakia, what are you yelling about out here?" Kaemwaset bellowed.

Nassar jumped in surprise as Nakia bowed his head. "My Lady wishes to see her son, my lord!"

"If you keep screaming like that, I will give you something to scream about, boy! I am with the pharaoh now and we are making serious plans!"

Nakia bowed again. "My apologies, my lord! I will take the child to his mother with your leave, sir!"

Pharaoh Runihura stepped beside Kaemwaset and smiled at Nassar. "Hello, Nassar. Don't you have any good words for me?" Nassar glared at the boy-pharaoh. "Not even a hello? What a shame. You should learn to respond to those who ask you a simple question." The pharaoh chuckled. "You're speechless in my presence! That is a nice change of pace from what made you lose your tongue in the first place."

Kaemwaset brought his son into his arms and placed him in Nakia's arms. "Nassar is much more compliant now that he cannot speak. I prefer him quiet like his twin."

Nakia brought the baby to his chest and stepped back. "I'm sorry to bother you, sir! Thank you, sir! Let's go, brother." Nassar followed his twin down the hall and looked back at the pharaoh with contempt.

Nakia and Nassar turned the corner as Nakia breathed a sigh of relief. "That was close, Nassar! Keep looking at the pharaoh like that and he'll take your eyes as well!"

Nassar folded his arms rebelliously.

"Baruti!" the twins heard Imani exclaim. "Baruti? He is the father of your child, Qamra?"

Nakia held Amsi close to him as he stopped quickly. Nassar bumped into his twin and groaned in frustration. The twins slowly approached the room and looked inside.

Imani was sitting on a chair beside a window. Qamra was standing with her hands folded in front of her. The young woman's head was bowed in deference to her mistress. "Yes, my lady. Baruti has fathered the child."

Imani stood up slowly, her gold earrings dangling as she approached her servant girl. The woman's gold ankh hanging around her neck glimmered in the afternoon light. "Baruti has not completed his manhood ceremony. He still wears the side-lock of youth and yet he has given you a child? Why, Qamra?"

Qamra kept her head lowered, trying to hide her eyes from her mistress. "I respectfully wish not to answer, my lady."

Imani stepped up to Qamra and touched the servant's chin. She tilted her head up to look her slave in the eye. "Qamra, you are hiding something," Imani said calmly, looking into the other woman's dark brown eyes. "Why are you afraid?"

Nakia coughed as he stood in the doorway. The seven-year-old twins bowed as Imani turned her head towards them. Amsi began to cry in Nakia's arms.

"Little Master, do not cry," Nakia said. "Your mother is here."

"Come in, boys," Imani said with a smile.

Nakia and Nassar relaxed as they approached Imani. Their tiny feet patted on the imported marble floors as they walked to their mistress.

Imani took Amsi into her arms and snuggled him against her breast. "Amsi, do not cry, my child," Imani said, kissing the baby on the forehead.

Qamra watched the baby's face turn red as he cried. "Perhaps he is hungry, my lady."

Imani gave Amsi to Qamra. Qamra freed her breast and offered her nipple to the crying baby. Amsi rubbed his face against it until he found what he wanted. He fed hungrily from her as the twins looked up curiously.

"Qamra, I wish you could tell me what secret you hide. You have not been yourself as of late."

Qamra looked at Nakia. The little boy folded his hands behind him and looked down at the ground. "I have been thinking about the baby, Mistress Imani. It has me nervous."

Imani reached out to Amsi and caressed the boy's cheek. "Do you love Baruti?"

Qamra looked down at the nursing infant. "Baruti is a nice person. I do not dislike him."

"Baruti's manhood ceremony is approaching!" Nakia said. "I don't know why it's taken so long to do it."

Imani nodded. "Now that he has fathered a child, that ceremony must be done."

"The master has said that before the baby is born, I shall be sold to another Noble family. I must leave."

Nakia looked up at Imani. "Will Qamra have to leave, Mistress Imani?"

"Qamra, you shall not leave my service," Imani insisted.

"I don't want Qamra to leave!" Nakia whined, flying to Imani and tugging at her white robe. "Please don't let the master send her away! She is like the mother Nassar and I lost! I'll be a good boy! I promise!"

Imani placed a gentle hand on Nakia's head. "Qamra will not leave, Nakia. Nassar, why are you crying?"

Nassar rubbed his eyes as tears came down his face. A series of vocalizations attested to Nassar's attempt at speech. *I don't want Qamra to leave! I already lost my real mother! I don't want to lose anyone else who is special to me!* Nassar looked up at Imani with tears streaming down his face. *I want to tell you, to plead with you not to let Qamra leave, but you wouldn't understand me if I tried to say one word. Please, my merciful mistress, please don't take Mother Qamra from me.* Nassar looked up at his mistress with sparkling, sad eyes. *Please, have mercy!* The little boy's unintelligible moans mingled with sniffles.

"Boys, Kaemwaset will not sell Qamra. Kaemwaset will know my anger like none other since he has removed your tongue, Nassar."

Nassar looked up at Imani and joined his twin pulling on her robes and moaning. Imani reached down and pet Nassar's hair lightly. "I know it hurts, Nassar."

Qamra watched the twins cower against Imani. Qamra had heard furious screaming when Imani had discovered that Kaemwaset had mutilated the little slave boy. Imani had brought Kaemwaset to the slave quarters and showed her husband the effects of his actions. Nassar was terrified of his master and held tightly onto Nakia, who had developed a fever from remaining in the cold the night of the palace festivities. Qamra watched with surprise as Imani slapped Kaemwaset angrily across the face for his cruelty towards the child. She had also refused to share a bed with her husband as a result.

Imani had hardly spoken a word to her husband since that incident. Imani's angered voice could be heard across the field where the field slaves were working.

Qamra held much respect for her mistress who had refused to back down against her stronger, vicious husband. He did not retaliate, but put more of a distance between himself and his wife. Qamra wanted to tell the truth regarding the baby's conception, but knew if she did, Kaemwaset's wrath would be beyond measure. She did not want to see the twins suffer any more than they already had under their master's fist. Imani would not take lightly her husband threatening to kill the little boy.

Nakia looked up at her with wide, sad eyes. "Please, mistress! I will do anything for you, just please don't let Qamra leave us!"

"Nakia, Nassar, don't worry. Qamra will not leave and that is my order."

"What if the master wants to send Nassar and I away?"

Imani leaned down to the children. "That will not happen, Nakia."

The twins gave her a slow smile. "Thank you," Nakia said, hugging Imani.

"You should get to Najam and help her bake the bread. She's probably wondering where you are."

Nakia and Nassar bowed before Imani and scurried from the room.

Imani smiled as she watched the little boys run from the room. Amsi had calmed in Qamra's arms. "Qamra, you will make a wonderful mother."

Tears welled up in her eyes. "I don't know if that is true, mistress."

Imani reached for Amsi and cradled her son in her arms. She smiled at Qamra. "I know as much. Baruti will make a good mate for you, Qamra. Does he know you have begotten a child by him?"

Qamra nodded quietly, avoiding Imani's gaze. "I have informed him."

Imani smiled at her servant. "I pray to Rā that he blesses your child."

"Thank you, my lady. I must hurry to Najam and help her prepare your evening meal."

"Thank you for taking such good care of Amsi."

Qamra bowed her head and hurried from the room. How can I possibly tell her that Baruti is not the child's father, but a child conceived by the loins of her own husband?

## IX

### Prophecy

Kaemwaset has been a loyal friend of the royal family for many years. He offered money to help me in the suppression of the revolt by the poor. He does not have many horses, but he has offered to pay for thirty soldiers to help subdue those who would speak and act against me. I knew I could trust Kaemwaset to do his part in maintaining my absolute power over the people of Egypt.

I left the Kaemwaset lands, given to him by my father. I saw the boy whose tongue had been removed. He saw me leave and I couldn't help but give him a satisfied grin as I departed. My father would have shown mercy. My father was weak. I refuse to be a weakling pharaoh, allowing those who oppose me go unpunished. That child has learned a valuable lesson: Do not question his superiors, especially myself.

Weak nations fall because of weak leaders. I will build a people of strength and ferocity, one that the world has never known! In order to make my people strong, I must eliminate those who stand in my way. I must eliminate those who are weak, who are a festering disease on the body that is Egypt. My father bandaged the wound of the lower classes without eliminating the festering infection within the wound itself.

My father never understood how the weak are undermining the efforts of superior peoples. My father tried to teach me the old ways. The old ways involved cooperation, which means the weak could take a greater advantage of the rich. The Nobility offered what they had to those of unfortunate circumstances. Those days are over. Many people called my father a hero. My father was a delusional old man with out-dated ideas, unlike my mother.

My mother wielded power and strength. She was my pillar, my rock. My strong mother was not strong enough to fight the illness within her. Mother coughed a lot and she became ill and feverish. My mother intentionally allowed a scorpion to sting her so she would not suffer. Mother wanted to mold me into a strong man. I placed the scorpion in her hand as she had wished and I watched it sting her. I watched my mother die.

'*Runihura*,' she told me, '*I do not wish to appear weak and suffer as a dog, trembling and in pain. Release me from my pain, my son. You have the power over my death, which I willingly choose.*'

My mother gave me power. It felt like power unimaginable to take a life. I was helping my mother just as I helped my father and the glorious land of Egypt! I helped Keket, too. That power made me invincible. One taste of that power was not enough. I want more! I crave more power!

Power is what people fear and respect. I will use the power given to me by the gods themselves to destroy those who will resist me. The power of the gods may not be enough to silence those tongues which speak of revolution. I will need more power, glorious, absolute power that rivals the gods! I will find it, even if I must raid every tomb and village to obtain what I wish!

The answer must lie within the ancient scrolls, the ancient tomes written by my forefathers. Therein may lie the key to the power which I seek.

Who does not wish to control the elements? Who would not want to move mountains upon command with the snap of the fingers? Who would not want to be the master of life and death? These are the powers of the gods. These are the powers I crave. My father counseled me that only the gods should lay claim to these powers; Mere mortals did not deserve the power to decide the fate of other people.

My father was a fool; I am wise.

As pharaoh, I am the intermediary between these mortal imbeciles and the gods. They ask for the gods' blessings and the gods rain down their gifts upon the faithful. Very soon, people will be worshipping me as a god. The entire world will be bowing at my feet! History will not forget the name Pharaoh Runihura of Heliopolis! I will write history!

There must be some way to achieve immortality and not just through my glorious deeds! I mean true immortality where I shall live forever in this body! I could be unstoppable! With the power of the gods and the blessing of immortality, I shall reign supreme.

Who would dare try and stop me? Decapitate me and I shall live! That immortality is priceless beyond measure. I will achieve it. I will achieve god-like glory and my legacy will be one for eternity!

Janani's very quiet. She has learned her lesson not to speak unless I give her permission. My father loved her. She could do no wrong in his eyes. Janani was more of a daughter to my father than I was his son! I do not mourn my father's death. It is quite unfortunate that Keket had to die as a scapegoat, but his soul will join Osiris and he will be free of pain. He needed to die to take the blame of my father's murder. Hakim helped me slaughter him because he would have seen me pull my dagger. At least Kek fell to my level where I could send his soul to the Land of the Blessed Dead. I shall bestow that favor to all who oppose me. I'm sure Keket's family will celebrate now that their son has joined his ancestors in their eternal, blissful slumber.

My enemies will enjoy their slumber as I eliminate them in their beds. Like a scorpion, I will strike without notice. My stinger will be held high, waiting to deliver a lethal toxin into the blood of the peasantry. Like the scorpion's sting, I will be lethal. All that will remain will be those of the superior class, the Nobility.

As my chariot drives through the streets of Heliopolis, I see women crying and men begging. Some are peddling their useless wares for mere coin. The infection grows by the day here in Heliopolis. A woman is crossing the street in front of me, carrying one of her little vermin in her arms.

I gave my horse a good lick of the whip and it started to race ahead. Let's see if she can jump out of the way of my chariot in time! Let's see if I can time this just right.

"My Pharaoh! No!" Janani called from beside me.

"How dare you spoil my fun!" I yelled at her, shaking my fist angrily.

I'll teach her to ruin my fun!

"Khepret! Watch out!" I heard a man call out in alarm.

I look ahead of me and the woman is frozen with fear. She's clutching the baby closer to her. Good, my target is frozen with fear. Time to send you and your little vermin into the waiting arms of Osiris!

"Khepret! Jump out of the way!"

I saw a man run towards the woman. I whipped my horses again. I'm going to get to her before you do! Just try and stop me!

"Khepret! Azizi!" the man pushed the woman out of the way as I felt the chariot buck up and down, accompanied by the crunching of bone.

I turned my head as I saw the man laying in the street. His beautiful, anguished scream of the man and the infant rose as a trail of blood followed me down the road. The woman, baby, and man were laying on the ground. I missed my targets, but at least I hit one mark. I hit one of them, though. It could have been the man or the infant I ran over with the chariot. They were both screaming in pain.

Janani looked behind us, her face had turned pale. "My Pharaoh! You almost killed that mother and her baby!"

"They were in my way," I said calmly as I slowed the horses to a calm trot.

The next time, they will not be so lucky. They were in my way. Next time, maybe they will clear the streets for people who are better than them and I will not have to use them as target practice.

As we arrived at the palace, I descended my chariot and looked at the wheels. The blood had worn off and only a small coating could be seen on the gilded wheels.

"Janani, clean the vermin blood off of my chariot."

"My pharaoh, you could have hurt those people."

I laughed. I not just 'could have', Janani. I hit one of them at least! Now get my chariot cleaned or I will suspend you in the gallows by your arms for three suns!

You have to keep the young trained well or they will join the revolution. A cowering subject is less likely to hold a bow and arrow against you. Once I obtain the power I seek, then nobody would want to challenge me.

The gardens look exceptionally good today. Hamadi does a very good job keeping everything looking and smelling fresh and new. Of course, if he does not, he knows he will be disemboweled and thrown on the outskirts of Heliopolis to die alone. I reached down and took a flower between my fingers. I plucked it, breaking it from its green stem. The flower smells fragrant and beautiful, like my mother before she crossed into the Land of the Dead. This one flower, amongst hundreds of thousands, helpless between my fingers, made me smile.

"Glorious Pharaoh, you have returned!" my Captain and General of the Guard approached me. He kneeled before me and bowed his head. "It is good to have you back at the palace, my king."

"Gahiji, my loyal friend, have you begun the preparations which I have requested?"

Gahiji nodded his head. "Yes, my lord! The preparations are nearly complete."

"I have good news, Gahiji. There will be at least two people who will prove easy targets during your little invasion. A man and an infant were unfortunate enough to find their way under my chariot. See that you end their misery. Surely they will not be able to run from you."

Gahiji bowed his head with a smile. He had served my father well. Gahiji was the hunter that his name suggested. He pursued the enemy for miles and was a vicious fighter. My father admonished him about unnecessary cruelty, but I respect Gahiji. His soldiers are tough and he expects much from them. My father never had a standing army. Citizens were conscripted for battle. I do things differently.

"Notify me when the preparations are complete. I will be in my library."

"Yes, my pharaoh."

I walked along the garden path, turning right instead of entering the palace. Along the walls of the garden, chisel marks peppered the wall where I erased the name of my father from the hieroglyphs. My father's reign will not be remembered as much as my own. My reign will be glorious and unmatched. Once I find what I am looking for, I will be worshipped as a god! I will have the power over life and death, just like my power over the death of my parents.

Hamadi bowed to me as he saw me walk past. He was about my age. I didn't know exactly how old he was and since it made no matter to me, I kept on walking.

I turned the corner and looked around me cautiously. Nobody knows about this library. My mother hid this library from my father's knowledge. It is an ancient library, its location passed from pharaoh to pharaoh. It contains the knowledge and magic of the ancients. The spells within contain Noble Magic, written in a language only those with Noble Blood can read. The common street rat would be able to read it, but some words would prove illegible.

The magic of the commoners involved charms and potions. Noble Magic is blessed by the gods and it is our gift from them. I have heard that eating skinned rats was part of one Common Magic spell. You will never see one from the Nobility feast on one of their own.

Nobody is around. Perfect. There is a crack in the wall where my finger fits just nicely. It looks like an ordinary crack; nobody knows that it is the trigger for the secret entrance. I heard a click and I pressed a part of the wall. It opened for me and I lit a candle beside the opening. The little, delicate flame sprung to life as I closed the entrance behind me.

The room came into view, lined with ancient scrolls and magical books. Those common rats do not know the fire with which they play and how dangerous it could be.

Will these common rats stand against me? Will their revolt succeed? They cannot win. I cannot fail. It is that simple. They must be crushed. They must die. They ALL must die. If some survive, they will prove to be good target practice later. I will not have my absolute power questioned!

Lighting another candle, I opened a scroll nearby. This one is nothing more than the recipe for my father's murder. The recipe was nothing more than for a brilliant potion of exotic herbs which Gahiji tracked down for me. It was simple to slip them into my father's food. The potion was potent. I was going to feed Hamadi a piece of the poisoned fruit, but I could still have some use for him. Other scrolls offer special recipes of similar purposes, as well as medicinal cures and spells to bring one closer to the gods.

Why do I need such a scroll for that purpose when I know they favor me? They will protect me against my enemies who seek to dethrone me. I will show my appreciation for their favor with a sacrifice of flesh and blood. The gods will enjoy the blood of their precious servant, their beloved creation.

Many of these scrolls include prayers worshipping the great warrior goddess, Sekhmet. She must be pleased at my father's removal from the throne since she has not struck me down with illness or malady. Sekhmet will be on my side until I shall become as great as she. The goddess of revenge shall bless the destruction of those who oppose me. Her mighty roar shall echo in their ears before their heads are severed from their bodies. May Sekhmet bless and watch over me as I conquer my enemies! Her arrows of fire will join mine in my quest for greatness. If Sekhmet blesses my quest for power, I shall build a shrine to her greatness never seen before in this mortal realm!

Here is another magic scroll and its purpose is none other than to provoke malevolent gods to enter the dreams of my enemies. I could ask the goddess of revenge to enter the dreams of my rivals and fill their hearts with fear. Sekhmet will strike fear and terror into their hearts, weakening them so as to make their deaths come on swiftly from my arrows.

My mother spoke of prophecies made by ancient sages who had recorded visions given to them by the gods. The visions spoke of a great pharaoh who would ascend to the throne of Egypt through great struggle. My mother told me that the prophets foretold of my birth and glorious ascension to power. This must be the prophecy of which she spoke. My mother spent long hours in this library teaching me how to read the tongue of the ancient prophets. I will fulfill my destiny as foretold in the scriptures.

I reached to the top of a shelf of scrolls and grabbed one wrapped in black sheepskin. This is the Scroll of Thoth. Thoth had blessed the ancient prophets and bade them to write the prophecies which the gods dictated. The ancient ones complied and left their legacy, the sparkling gem of my library collection. I unraveled the scroll carefully, grinning as I did so. This scroll holds the key to my destiny. If I shall be known as the greatest pharaoh of all time, then this scroll must detail my heroic deeds.

> *From the ashes of Iunu, he rises as Aten's light to the dawn. The Agent of Sekhmet strikes at the heart of the Ram. The favor of the Sun God falls not upon his deeds as Sekhmet rides through the streets of blood, flooded by his lust for Death. Ra is blinded by his greatness. The Great Pharaoh's arms shall extend over the land and shower the people with his glorious light.*

This prophecy must detail my great ascension to power! My people will bathe in my glory and they will adore me!

I knew the goddess Sekhmet would bless my reign. I knew since I was a child that she favored me. From the moment I handed my mother that lethal scorpion, I knew I was in her favor. It pained me to see my mother die a painful death. I remember her body twitching from the poisonous venom. My mother knew I had the fire of Sekhmet in my heart when she watched me beat up Janani for spilling my drink. She was pleased that she had birthed a strong son.

I wonder what the Ram means in this prophecy. The Ram is the favored animal of Osiris. What have I to do with the God of Death? The majority of the people worship the Sun God. It seems as if the Scroll of Thoth deems me as Sekhmet. I will strike fear into my enemies as she. I will not relent.

> *The Blessed Servant of Osiris shall rise from the streets of Iunu and sever the head of the lion's servant. His blood shall bring peace to all of Egypt and restore the blessing of the gods upon Iunu and her people. Sekhmet's servant shall be defeated, but not without sacrifice of flesh and blood. The Blessed Servant will not be alone. The Blessed of Osiris and the Anointed Companion of Rā shall restore Ma'at and Rā will smile upon his children once more.*

No! I will not be defeated by followers of the Sun God and the Lord of the Dead! They will not succeed. I shall not be defeated as easily as believed. Heliopolis celebrates Ra, the Sun God's temples are everywhere. If the rats which scurry about the streets harbor my enemy, then the sooner I begin the destruction of my enemies, the better. If I can eliminate my enemy, no one will stand in my way. I must begin my campaign. I shall eliminate the so-called Blessed of Osiris and the Anointed One.

*The Book of Thoth shall one seek*

*To change the brave man into meek*

*To bring the defeated spoils of victory*

*To change the course of written history.*

*To give the Book of Thoth its sacred power*

*Seek ye out where life fails to flower.*

*Recite the spells within this tome*

*And The Book of Thoth will be yours to own.*

I blew out the candles and quickly exited from my secret library. I must go to my shrine to offer tribute to Sekhmet. Hamadi bowed to me again. When he bowed, I looked down at him. His side-lock curled over his right shoulder, revealing the back of his neck. Hamadi was my age, my father accepted him as an orphan from the streets. My father felt pity for him. The people my father pitied are the same ones who now plot against me! Down the garden path once laid my father's shrine. I erected my own shrine in its place. The guards posted outside bowed to me on bended knee as I approached.

I entered my shrine and closed the door behind me. I kneeled before the statue of Sekhmet and touched my forehead to the ground. My father's statue of Ra had been moved beside the Sekhmet statue. Rā's favor could help me achieve my ambitious goals. He will help me smite my enemies.

Almighty Lords of the Earth and Sky, Mighty Princess of Destruction, hear the cry of your faithful servant, Pharaoh Runihura! The people's hearts are filled with anger and hatred towards me. Their voices scream loudly for revolution and vengeance. They plead for deliverance. Amun-Ra, grant me the power to outshine my enemy. Help me to shine and make the people bow before me as they so do to you at the dawn of a new day! Glorious Sekhmet, may I strike fear into those who oppose me! May their vermin blood soak the ground and flow in crimson rivers. With this dagger in my hands, I slice my hand, shedding my blood as sacrifice for your favor, Lion-Goddess! Smite my enemies and guide my club so that I may quell the anger in the people's hearts. I offer this bowl of blood as offering to the Great One of Vengeance. May death reign supreme and rebellion crushed under our mighty fists! Grant me the strength and guide my soldier's swords, for I must slaughter the Blessed Servant of Osiris and the Anointed Companion of Rā. I will not stop until they are dead!

# X

## Rite of Passage

Qamra clapped her hands as she danced beside Baruti. She smiled brightly as she danced to the tune of Jinan's cistern and Sabi's flute. Baruti clapped his hands with her and took her hand. He spun around her, his body moving gracefully to the music. The teenage boy kicked his legs with the rhythm. Karida was using clappers as she watched the two teenagers dance.

Nassar was watching the adults dance and frolic to the music. He hummed with the music as he cradled Amsi in his arms. He looked down at Amsi, who was watching the little boy's face intently. Nassar opened his mouth, making unintelligible sounds towards the infant. Amsi looked up at him and reached out for Nassar's mouth.

The little boy pulled his head back as Amsi put his fingers in his mouth. Nassar kissed the baby's forehead and snuggled the baby against him. He tried speaking again, but only little groaning sounds could come from his mouth. Amsi touched Nassar's nose and tried to touch the little boy's eyes. Nassar chuckled as he shook his head.

Amsi looked up at Nassar and smiled. The little boy returned the smile. It was the first time the baby had smiled at him. Nassar brought the baby closer to his chest and sighed happily.

"Nassar? Do you want to dance?" Nassar heard as he raised his head. Karida was standing in front of him.

Issâm took the baby from Nassar. "You go dance, Nassar. Have fun, child."

Nassar stood and brought Karida beside the fire. He joined Qamra and Baruti in their dance. He mimicked their movements as he watched the adults.

Sabi smiled and quickened the pace of the dance as she watched the children join the festivities. Tonight was the night of Baruti's Rite of Passage. After tonight, he would be an adult in the eyes of the other slaves and in front of the gods. Baruti had bathed himself in oils in preparation for this night. Sabi had made a feast of duck, bread, salad, and beer. Qamra and Sabi had managed to take the food which their master did not finish for dinner. The children were happy for such bounty and quickly forgot about the penalty if the servants were caught stealing scraps from the master's table. The slaves sat around the fire and ate the duck with their fingers hungrily, their stomachs growling ravenously. Issâm and Tabari worked on the numbing ointment for the ritual circumcision. Issâm was a former priest of Thoth whose temple was destroyed by foreign invaders. Issâm sold himself into slavery and had labored on the Al-Sakhir family lands in exchange for food and shelter.

When the dancing and feasting had concluded, Tabari lead the slaves in a prayer for Baruti. The servants gathered around the fire as Issâm and Baruti stood facing each other.

"I must tend to the horses, Qamra," Nakia said looking up at the stars.

"Be careful, Nakia. Return when you are done."

The child lit a torch using the fire. Nakia ran from the group and towards the stable. He opened the door and placed the torch in the entry. Hamza neighed loudly as he saw the child enter. He lowered his head and bared his teeth at the child.

"Hello, Hamza! Are you a good boy?" Nakia asked, petting the horse's muzzle.

Naji shook his head and stomped his foot. Nakia walked over to him and pet his muzzle. He heard Baruti let out a scream as he grabbed a basket of feed. "Don't be afraid. Baruti is becoming a man now! One day when I become a big boy, I'll have to do that ritual, but I have a few years yet."

When he finished feeding and tending to the horses' needs, Nakia ran from the stables as fast as his little legs could carry him. The seven-year-old's hair flopped against his shoulder as he ran towards the slave home. A bright light emanated from the back of the small hut where a bonfire burned. He heard another painful scream from behind the home. When he arrived at the back of the house, Nassar was holding Amsi and sitting beside the fire. Qamra was sitting beside the fire as Issâm kneeled in front of a naked Baruti with a knife. Karida was playing with a doll made of corn husk. The little girl was rocking her toy as she smiled, oblivious to the importance of the ceremony taking place in front of the bonfire. Jinan shook a sistrum beside the fire praying to Rā loudly through song.

Issâm looked up at Baruti and stood before him, placing a bloody knife on a cloth. "Today, Baruti, you have become a man. No longer are you a child, but are crossing into a new life." Issâm stood up and smiled peacefully at the sweating teen. He put a gentle hand on the boy's forehead. "As Glorious Rā rises in the east, so shall you begin life anew. Baruti, may your Light shine bright in a world now shrouded in darkness."

Baruti leaned forward as Tabari supported him. Tabari planted his feet in the ground as Baruti trembled with pain.

"Will Baruti be alright?" Nakia asked as he stood beside Qamra.

Qamra nodded as Amsi began to cry in Nassar's arms. Nassar handed the baby to her and perked his ears up at a sound nearby.

"Amsi, my little lord, don't cry," Qamra said, rocking the baby boy. Amsi looked up at Qamra , focusing on her smiling face. Qamra caressed his cheek tenderly. "Do not cry, Amsi."

Amsi looked up at her and smiled. Nakia gasped as he held onto Qamra tightly. His face lit up with a smile as he jumped up and down excitedly. "The little master smiled, Qamra!"

"The little master is happy and content with us, Nakia."

"Amsi, smile for me! Smile for Nakia!" Nakia exclaimed.

The little baby looked at Nakia and smiled widely.

"Baruti swoons, Tabari!" Issâm gasped, grabbing Baruti from under the arms. Tabari and Issâm slowly lowered Baruti onto the ground beside the fire. Baruti leaned backwards against Tabari, sweat pouring down his naked body. The teen panted heavily as he looked up at Issâm.

"Good job, my boy. The numbing ointment will wear off soon," Issâm said, touching Baruti's cheek lightly. "Your father would be proud."

"Mighty Rā, bless Baruti's passage into manhood! Grant him wisdom, strength, and bravery!" Jinan cried into the night as he rang his sistern louder.

Nassar heard another sound emanating from the front of the slave home. He crept around the side of the hut and crouched low, careful not to let himself be seen. He heard Kaemwaset's voice speaking low with another deep male voice.

"The pharaoh is grateful for your donation, Kaemwaset Al-Sakhir."

"Lord Gahiji, nothing shall please me more than the deaths of those who oppose our glorious pharaoh."

Nassar gasped and hid behind the wheat, his body shaking. He watched Kaemwaset and heard the click of coin in the General's hand.

"The pharaoh begins his campaign tonight, so be not alarmed should you hear the screams of street rats as they flee from our swords and clubs."

Nassar covered his mouth with fear. He could sense bloodlust in the General's voice and he knew the cruelty of which his master was capable.

"What shall I do should some of them scurry here?"

Gahiji smiled. "Let them be. The remaining people, if any do survive, will be too terrified to join the rebellion against Runihura. The pharaoh will strike fear into their hearts and minds."

"I wish you luck in your crusade, my Lord Gahiji."

Gahiji's belly shook with laughter. "No luck will be needed, Kaemwaset. This will be as simple as killing a bound gazelle. There is no place to run and all it can do is watch and wait for the fatal blow. This campaign will be no challenge and the people will respect our pharaoh."

Nassar saw Gahiji's horse standing nearby and he smiled. He had to do something to set the General back on his plans. He crept silently, careful to test his step before he placed his foot down on the wheat. He looked back at his master and the General.

"What is that light behind your slave house?"

"Baruti is undergoing his Rite of Passage into manhood. I heard him scream when Issâm performed the circumcision."

Gahiji chuckled. "Now you can work him twice as hard."

Nassar reached for the belt under the horse's stomach. The belt held Gahiji's saddle in place. Nassar's dexterous hands loosened the belt. He grinned mischievously as he turned to creep towards the back of the home.

"Does the pharaoh intend on cleansing the servants of the Nobility?"

Nassar's eyes widened and he stopped. He perked up his ears as he heard the question. *What? They intend to kill the servants of the Nobility, too?*

"The pharaoh's prophecy has stated that a follower of Osiris and Ra will rise against him. My job is to see that does not happen."

Kaemwaset scratched his bearded chin. "My servants worship different gods. Jinan and Tabari favor the Sun God."

Gahiji narrowed his eyes. "Bring them to me."

Kaemwaset walked around the back of the home. Tabari looked up at Kaemwaset as he wrapped his arms around Baruti protectively. The servants kneeled before their master.

"Qamra, why do you have my son so late in this night air?"

"My lady said I could bring Amsi to Baruti's ceremony. I will not have him out here much longer, my lord."

Amsi looked up at Qamra with a smile. When he saw his father, the smile quickly faded.

"Tabari and Jinan, come with me."

Nakia looked around and found his twin absent. "Where is my brother?" Nakia walked around the group of slaves and found Nassar absent. "Nassar? Brother?" Nakia found Nassar hiding in the shadows watching the General intently. "Nassar, what are you-?"

Nassar grabbed Nakia's wrist and pressed his finger to his lip. He shook his head, a silent communication to his twin. Nakia's attention was taken by the two men being brought to the General.

Kaemwaset lead Tabari and Jinan in front of Gahiji. Kaemwaset gave Tabari a violent shove forward. "On your knees, you cur!" Tabari fell onto his hands and knees before General Gahiji. Tabari looked wide-eyed at Gahiji's sandals. Tabari swallowed nervously as he slowly raised his head to see two eyes glaring down at him. The shaking slave looked up with fear at the man standing before him. Jinan kneeled on the ground, bowing his head reverently.

"Tabari. Jinan. Kaemwaset has informed me that you worship Rā, the Sun God. Is this true?"

Jinan folded his hands reverently. "I do so, my lord, and have done so for many suns."

"I do worship the Great One, my lord," Tabari said, uncertainty clear in his voice.

"There are rumors that pharaoh's subjects are planning to remove him from power. You two wouldn't dare join a rebellion against the mighty pharaoh, would you?" Gahiji asked, placing the blade of his sword against Tabari's throat.

Tabari looked up at the General nervously, his blood racing through his veins. "Please do not kill me, my lord!"

"Tabari, no," Nakia whimpered, holding Nassar's hand.

"What about you, old man?" Gahiji asked, placing the blade against the old man's chest. "Do you seek to remove the pharaoh from power?"

Jinan shrugged. "I am an old man who already has both feet in the tomb. What care I for revolt? I am old, too old to raise a weapon against my king. Tabari is young. The young always lust for revenge and revolt."

"Is that so!" Gahiji growled, pointing the blade at Tabari's throat. Tabari's face glimmered with sweat as he breathed quickly. "Jinan! Hold your tongue! You will get me killed!"

"If you lust for blood, Tabari, I could satiate your thirst!" Gahiji grabbed Tabari's hair and pulled his head back. Tabari let out a scream of horror as he grabbed Gahiji's wrist.

"No! Tabari!" Sabi cried out as she ran to the screaming slave. "My Lord, don't kill him!" Sabi put her hands on Tabari's shoulders.

"I'm only a field slave! Please don't do this!" Tabari pleaded. "I'm not behind the revolt!"

"Please do not kill him, my lord!" Sabi pleaded.

"Sabi, run before he kills you, too!" Tabari exclaimed.

Nassar broke free of Nakia's grasp and ran in front of Tabari. He wrapped his arms around Tabari protectively.

"Nassar, what are you doing?" Sabi asked.

Nassar whimpered and made incomprehensible noises as he hugged Tabari.

"I do not actively seek battle, my lord. I work in the field and I toil for the palace food. Please do not kill us."

Gahiji released Tabari's hair and lowered his weapon. Tabari trembled with fear as he held the little boy against him. The little boy moaned as he hugged Tabari.

"You could have been killed," he whispered in the boy's ear.

"If I hear word that the Kaemwaset slaves are waging revolution, every one of you will have your throat cut and your hearts removed from your still-living bodies. Do you understand me?"

Tabari and Sabi nodded quickly as Baruti cried out for Tabari. Gahiji calmly walked around the side of the building followed by Kaemwaset. Gahiji and Kaemwaset saw a naked Baruti laying beside the fire. Gahiji looked down at the teenager and lifted his sword over Baruti's stomach. The twins followed the General and watched.

"Baruti! Roll!" Issâm exclaimed, turning Baruti out of the way as the sword stabbed the ground where the teenager lay.

Karida began to cry and hold onto Issâm as she watched Baruti evade the deadly strike.

Gahiji laughed with amusement as he stabbed towards Baruti again, but the teen rolled himself out of harm's way.

"My lord, he's still recovering!" Qamra yelled in alarm.

Kaemwaset stood beside the fire and glared at Qamra. She looked up at her master with his baby in her arms. "Please do not kill Baruti! He has just completed his Rite of Passage into adulthood!"

Tabari ran around the side of the building and arrived beside Baruti. He brought the teenager into his arms again.

"Now that Baruti has completed the manhood ritual, he can now learn to die like a man!" Gahiji exclaimed with a smile.

Baruti winced with pain as he looked up at the General. Baruti's lip curled into a snarl and he kicked Gahiji's knee angrily, making the heavy-set man stumble back. "Get away from me."

Tabari gasped as he saw Gahiji's face grow red with anger. "Baruti! What are you thinking?"

"You just signed your death warrant, boy!"

"Don't hurt Baruti!" Nakia exclaimed as he ran behind Qamra.

Nassar broke from Nakia's grip and stepped in front of Gahiji. The little boy looked up at the corpulent General and huffed defiantly.

Tabari and Baruti gasped as they saw the small child standing in striking distance of Gahiji's sword. "Nassar! Step aside!"

Gahiji laughed loudly. "Do you think you can stop me, child? The pharaoh and Kaemwaset have already ripped your tongue from your head. Now you stand in my way in your pathetic attempt to protect Baruti."

Baruti backed away as Nassar huffed defiantly again. Nakia ran towards his twin when Kaemwaset grabbed the child and held him by his collar.

"You can watch your brother die," Kaemwaset said.

"Nassar! NO!"

"Don't kill the boy, my lord!" Sabi cried out.

Amsi began to wail in Qamra's arms. The child flailed his arms wildly as he arched his back. Qamra held the infant close to her body as she watched Nassar nervously.

Gahiji laughed as he sheathed his sword. "Boy, you are no challenge for me. I will be sure to continue this little confrontation with you later. I must carry out my orders set forth by the Great Pharaoh." Gahiji leaned forward, glaring at the child. "We already took your tongue. Your eyes are the next to go."

Nassar returned the glare and released a little growl. Gahiji looked at Kaemwaset. "That child is violent. I suggest you do something about that."

Kaemwaset released Nakia, who ran to his brother hugging him tightly. "I will contend with the child, my lord."

"I must not be tardy for the pharaoh's campaign. Farewell, Kaemwaset Al-Sakhir."

Kaemwaset watched Gahiji walk around the building. He turned to Qamra and took Amsi in his arms. The baby fussed and continued to cry as he held his son.

Nassar took advantage of Kaemwaset's distraction and ran beside the house. General Gahiji mounted his black horse and shook the reigns. Nassar watched as the horse burst into a fast gallop. The General's saddle became unfastened and Gahiji fell off the horse with a loud cry of surprise. Nassar hid in the shadows covering his mouth as he burst into quiet laughter. *That is what happens when you are mean to my friends!*

"Nassar Al-Sakhir, get over here this instant!"

Nassar's laughing ceased as he watched General Gahiji run after his horse. Nassar walked slowly towards the back of the home to see Kaemwaset standing beside the fire with fury chiseled into his face.

Kaemwaset looked down at Nassar. "Even as a mute, you still cannot hold your tongue, I see. You are a rotten, disobedient little rodent."

Nassar opened his mouth and made a series of noises as he pointed to Baruti. He made a stabbing motion with his hand against his fist and shook his head side-to-side violently. He screamed as he jumped up, put his hands on his hips, and glared at Kaemwaset, his chest rising and falling as he huffed. *I will not let you kill Baruti! Don't look at me as if you don't know what I'm saying!*

Everyone looked at Nassar, confused as to his message. Nakia stood by his twin, understanding every silent word in a manner that only twins could comprehend.

"Shame on you. You are a very bad, unruly boy, Nassar," Kaemwaset said as he walked away with Amsi.

Nassar watched Kaemwaset walk away and his body relaxed. He looked down and put his finger to his lips.

Nakia leaned over to look his twin in the eye. "You weren't going to let Baruti be killed. Is that what you were trying to say?" Nassar nodded. "Do you realize you could have been killed instead?" Nassar looked up into his twin's eyes. A single tear fell down his cheek as he nodded. He put his fingers together, made a mouth motion, and shook his head. "You wish you could talk again?" Nassar sighed as he looked down.

"Nassar?" Baruti asked. Nassar lifted his head slowly as he looked at Baruti. The teenager opened his arms to him. "Come here." Nassar ran to Baruti and threw himself into the hug. Baruti could feel tears falling from Nassar's eyes. The teenager held the seven-year-old tightly against him. He kissed Nassar's ear and felt the boy trembling.

*Father Baruti, I didn't want to see you get hurt. You're my friend.*

Issâm carried Karida and stepped beside Sabi. "We should get the children inside."

Sabi nodded as she approached Nakia and brought him into her arms. "It is time for bed, Nakia." Nakia reached out for his brother as Sabi carried him.

Jinan looked up at the sky as he stepped beside Qamra. "The stars are quite beautiful tonight, but they look ominous tonight."

Qamra took a deep breath. "Death is in the air tonight. I can feel it. Let us get everyone inside."

Baruti caressed Nassar's head. "You are a very brave child, Nassar." Baruti took Nassar and stood him in front of his eyes. He looked at the child in the light of the fire. The flames rose into the air, casting dancing shadows on the boy's face. "I don't want you to die for me, Nassar. I don't want you to suffer because of me."

Nassar opened his mouth and tried to speak calmly, but all that emanated from his mouth was unintelligible groans. *Baruti doesn't know what I'm saying. I wish I could speak. Maybe Kaemwaset was right. Maybe I am a bad boy.* The child lowered his head and his shoulders sagged.

Baruti tipped Nassar's head upwards. "You are a strong protector, Nassar. Thank you. We love you and none of us wish to see you harmed." A little smile crossed Nassar's face.

Baruti and Nassar turned their heads as they heard a series of loud screams coming from the city nearby. The loud neighing of horses accompanied screams of pain.

"Tabari, Baruti, we all must get inside. Come here, Nassar." Qamra took the little boy into her arms and carried him. "Nassar, you are a good little boy."

Nassar snuggled against Qamra with a contented sigh. Tabari helped Baruti to his feet. Tabari took a bucket of water and doused the flames. He walked beside Qamra and Baruti towards the front of the slave quarters. They looked up and saw smoke bellowing from the city and the light of fire. Blood-curdling screams rose to the heavens with the smoke.

"Sweet, merciful Isis," Qamra sighed, covering her mouth.

"This cannot be happening!" Tabari gasped. "Is the pharaoh responsible for this?"

Baruti angrily narrowed his eyes. "Great Anubis and the Lord of Eternity will be busy this night."

Nassar's eyes widened as he heard people screaming in pain and fear. He tugged at Qamra's white robe desperately. Qamra brought Nassar's head close to her body and covered his ear. She kissed him on the forehead tenderly as the boy's body began to shake.

Jinan stepped out of the home with his cup calmly as he sat on the front step. "The stars are beautiful tonight."

## XI

### The Rise of Sekhmet

Khepret held Azizi in her arms as she sang a hymn to Osiris. The infant nursed as he looked up at her. The baby boy's hands waved at her slowly as he fed. Khepret caressed the baby's face. "You will grow up to be strong, my son. You will be the pride of the gods."

The infant pulled his head back and reached up to touch his mother's face. She kissed his tiny fingers as they neared her mouth. His face lit, sporting a happy smile as he looked up at his mother.

"What is it you want, Azizi?"

The baby opened his mouth and tried to speak, but only a happy squeal emanated from the baby boy.

Khepret lifted her head as she saw Ghazi enter the home. "How is Garai?"

Ghazi walked towards his wife and lightly touched his son's head. "The doctor had to remove his leg. How is Azizi?"

Khepret looked at the scratches on the baby's face. A little cut was healing on the infant's right cheek when he landed on the ground. When she was pushed to the ground out of the path of the pharaoh's chariot, she tried to fall so Azizi would not hit the ground. If she had not turned, the baby would have fallen under her. "He's smiling at me, Ghazi. Hold your son. Azizi, show your father your beautiful smile."

Ghazi lifted the boy into his arms. He held the infant in front of him. Azizi looked at his father with his brown eyes. Azizi reached out to touch his father's face. The infant kicked his legs as he smiled at his father.

"My son will please you much, Osiris. He is a beautiful boy," Ghazi said as he brought his son against his chest. He hugged the baby boy with a smile. Ghazi caressed Azizi's head as the baby yawned tiredly.

"This is it, men! Fight for your freedom and die with honor!" Ghazi heard Hetem call loudly.

Ghazi lifted his head in alarm. Khepret rose to her feet as she heard the sounds of screams echo down the street. She stepped beside her husband and put her hand on his shoulder.

"Did you hear that, my husband?"

"Take no prisoners! Kill all who oppose the Great Pharaoh!" Gahiji screamed loudly.

Ghazi heard a woman scream in pain as he looked at his altar to Osiris. "Take Azizi. Hetem's cry of revolt has reached the pharaoh's ears. We must leave, Khepret."

Khepret brought Azizi into her arms. She looked up at her husband nervously. "What if the soldiers pursue us?"

Ghazi grabbed a dagger from his altar to Osiris. "Great Osiris, protect my family and grant repose to the souls of the dead." Ghazi grabbed his wife's hand. "Do not release my hand, Khepret."

Khepret nodded as she looked down at her son, who was showing signs of alarm. "Don't worry, Azizi."

Ghazi led Khepret out of the house. He saw Gahiji on his horse, riding up the street and slicing through people with his sword. The smoke of fire began to creep through the streets, obscuring his vision. Women were running away with food and children in their arms. Men were scattering in confusion, unable to see through the thick smoke, their bodies crashed to the ground as soldiers speared them.

"Crush their heads! Slice open their bellies!" Ghazi heard as he saw Pharaoh Runihura on his black horse, surrounded by soldiers.

Khepret screamed as she saw soldiers advance through the streets, hacking their victims and bludgeoning others with clubs. Ghazi pulled Khepret away from the advancing soldiers towards Garai's home. They ran into

Garai's home where they found the wounded man laying on his mat.

"Garai, you must get to your feet! Pharaoh Runihura is riding through our quarter slaughtering everyone!"

"My friend, I cannot move," Garai said. "You must leave."

"I cannot leave you, my friend! Please, you must stand!"

The cries of a young child sounded nearby and were quickly silenced. Azizi began to cry in his mother's arms. He clutched onto her as tightly as possible and began to shake.

"Garai, you must get to your feet!" Khepret begged. "The pharaoh is approaching!"

Garai smiled up at Khepret. "Take Azizi somewhere safe. Don't let him fall to the pharaoh's fury."

Ghazi looked towards the door, his heart racing in fear for his family's safety. "Garai, may you see the face of the gods."

Garai took Ghazi's hand. "You are a good man, Ghazi. Go."

Ghazi looked at Khepret and took her hand again. He led her out of the home as a soldier ran towards them. Ghazi blocked the soldier's club with his dagger. The soldier pulled a dagger of his own and stabbed towards Ghazi. The father moved his hips out of the way as he kicked the soldier.

"Tear their bellies open!" Gahiji bellowed to his soldiers as he advanced closer.

"Show no mercy to these vermin!" the pharaoh called loudly as he was surrounded by his soldiers.

Azizi cried against his mother as she cradled him. Khepret watched as Ghazi punched the soldier, knocking him down. Ghazi grabbed her wrist and pulled her away from the advancing General Gahiji. Khepret turned her head as her husband pulled her from Garai's home.

Pharaoh Runihura raised his blood-covered sword. "Where are you, Blessed Servant of Osiris?"

Khepret held the crying baby in her arms closer to her chest. A tear fell down her face as she saw Gahiji enter their home. She began to cough as the bellowing smoke filled the streets.

Ghazi turned down a street and saw bodies lining the ground. He ran his wife and child down the street covered with blood. Men, women, and children lined the road with slit throats, crushed skulls from which brains had escaped, and multiple stab wounds.

"Ghazi, we have to leave the city!"

"Where are we going to go?"

Khepret saw an arrow bury itself in a wood support nearby.

"You missed, Gahiji!" the pharaoh laughed.

"I will not miss again! Anubis, charge!" Gahiji cried loudly as the horse's hooves echoed through the alley.

Khepret turned her head and saw the General's large, black horse thundering towards her and her husband. Khepret screamed as she faced forward. "Ghazi, General Gahiji is coming!"

Ghazi turned the corner sharply and ran down the next street. "We cannot outrun them all night, Khepret!"

"Give me that child so that I may cut him in half!" Pharaoh Runihura called as his horse's thunderous hooves advanced closer to the couple. "I will offer his blood to Sekhmet! Cut his throat when we get him, Gahiji!"

Gahiji laughed as his horse ran closer to the couple. "I get the female!"

Khepret's heart raced as thick smoke began to obscure her vision. The heat from the flames beside her and her husband made her face cover in sweat. She struggled for breath as she ran beside her husband.

The air was suffocating. It gripped her by the throat and squeezed. The streets seemed to move beneath her feet as she held her baby against her protectively. The baby's cries soon began to quiet. Khepret's heart jumped into her throat. What if Azizi had died from lack of oxygen? The air was becoming heavy and it was difficult to breathe.

Ghazi turned back to see his wife though it was difficult to see her. "We must run from the city! Hold onto me, Khepret!"

The air became thin as the flames licked at their clothing, edging closer. Khepret held Ghazi's hand as they neared the entrance to the city. She struggled to see in front of her.

"Die, you pathetic vermin!" she heard Pharaoh Runihura exclaim as she felt Ghazi's hand suddenly separate from her grasp in the dense smoke.

"Ghazi!" Khepret cried as she continued to run. Tears fell down her face as she held Azizi with both hands. Azizi needed air, but her heart sank at the thought of losing her husband. Maybe he had tripped over someone's corpse. If she turned back, the pharaoh and the General would certainly slaughter her and her baby boy.

"You're next, female!" Gahiji called from the thick blanket of smoke. "Where are you?"

Khepret could barely see the arch to the city as she continued to flee. Much to her relief, Azizi began to cry again. Behind her the sounds of fighting men rose with the smoke. Men screamed in anger, fury, and pain. Women were running and calling out for their husbands. Children were crying for their mothers from whom they had been separated.

Khepret turned back, unable to see through the thick smoke behind her. Ghazi was not behind her or trying to grab her.

"All will bow before me!" the pharaoh called out as a man screamed in pain behind her.

"Ghazi!" Khepret called again as she ran towards the arch, which had been littered with bodies of women and children.

The smell of death mingled with the smoke of the fires. Rivers of crimson formed beneath the pile of bodies, some gasping their last breath. Khepret trembled as she stepped over the bodies. She ran from the town as Pharaoh Runihura's laughter echoed.

Azizi began to wail loudly in her arms as she ran towards the Al-Sakhir plantation.

She screamed as she ran. Tears fell from her eyes as she approached the slave home. Khepret knew she had nowhere else to run. The woman to whom she had spoken at the Nile was a kindly woman. Her servants were also very friendly.

She approached the slave quarters, crying and shaking.

Standing on the porch, she saw the noble's servant to whom she had spoken at the Nile. She was holding a sleeping little boy in her arms.

"It's you!" Qamra exclaimed. "How did you ever escape from *Iunu*?"

Khepret stood in front of Qamra, her face barely illuminated from the torch beside the step. "My husband was separated from me."

Nakia stepped out of the house, yawning and rubbing his eye. "Do I hear a baby cry?"

Qamra looked in her arms and gently shook the little boy in her arms. "Nassar, go to bed with your brother." The little boy groaned as he was placed on his feet. "Nakia, go to bed. Take your twin with you."

"Alright," Nakia yawned tiredly, taking Nassar's hand and leading him inside the home.

Qamra hugged Khepret tightly. "How is your son? Is he hurt?"

Azizi cried as he held onto Khepret, his little body was trembling with fear. Khepret sobbed as she held onto her boy.

"I had no where else to go," Khepret cried.

Qamra touched Azizi's head lightly. "He doesn't appear to be injured. Thank you, Isis."

Khepret looked over at the flames reaching towards the stars. She held her son against her tightly. "Ghazi, may you be avenged."

## XII

### Lesson Learned

Sawaret inspected the young Noble's hieroglyphic writing meticulously. The five-year-old boy stood before his tutor as instructed, silent and still. Outside he could hear the workers in the field toiling and singing in the oppressive heat of the Egyptian sun. His father never permitted his slaves to sing, but Kaemwaset had made a journey to the Royal Palace for a conference with Pharaoh Runihura.

The little boy watched as his tutor corrected an improper strike of Amsi's reed. He lowered his head, his eyes going to the gold ankh and gold rings around his fingers.

*'It is important for you to be literate, my son. Thoth will not bless you if you do not learn the ways of script to worship him. This is an advantage those under our fist will never obtain,' he heard his father speak inside his mind. 'We are privileged and we must take advantage of that privilege or famine will come to our fields and we will lose our favored status.'*

Amsi's eyes looked at his right shoulder where his hair rested. Kaemwaset insisted that Amsi excel in his sacred script, but his mother reassured him that his father's demands were a testament to how much his father wanted him to succeed. Amsi was destined to control the Al-Sakhir family lands upon Kaemwaset's death.

*'When I die, my son, you shall inherit all of my lands, all of my property, and all of our servants. You will give offerings to my Ka at my tomb so that I may continue to prosper in the afterlife.' Kaemwaset smiled at him. 'When it is time for you to take a wife, my son, she will be a fertile field for you and you will know the pleasure of having your own son and enjoying a life of leisure. You will truly he blessed by Rā.'*

Issâm had helped him with some of his hieroglyphic exercises. As an educated priest of Thoth, he was eager to help the young boy learn the art of writing. Kaemwaset had urged Amsi never to seek aid from the servants because he claimed they were uneducated and were plotting to undermine him in his education. Amsi had found the opposite to be more truthful. Issâm was intelligent and a talented writer. Sawaret found no errors when he proofed Issâm's writing. '*You praise the gods through with every movement of your reed, Master Amsi,*' Issâm had told him. Amsi was careful not to be caught seeking help from Issâm. He knew the wrath of his father would know no boundaries should he be caught in the act.

"You are improving with your script," Sawaret said as he looked at his pupil. The tutor handed the boy his ostraca and his reed. "Your strikes must be precise, my boy. If a hieroglyph has been improperly formed, it could ruin a prayer, a blessing to Rā. Your mistake could be seen for eternity. Amsi, do you wish to disgrace your father with incorrect grammar?"

Amsi shook his head. "No, sir."

"Do you wish for him not to have the proper incantations to travel through the Underworld and honor Osiris in the Hall of Judgment?"

The boy shook his head again and focused on the tutor's gaze. "No, Sawaret."

"You should practice more. Have your father help you upon his return from the palace. Practice and show him what you have done. Make him proud, Amsi, so that you do not disgrace him before the gods."

Amsi bowed his head. "Yes, Sawaret. I will do so."

The tutor stood up and left the room. Amsi took a deep breath and sighed. He ran down the hall to his bedroom where he put his writing reeds and his ostraca. He grabbed his ball and his sword made of wood. The little boy ran down the hallway and into the garden. Najam was collecting carrots and onions for the family's dinner. He ran to her and smiled at her.

"Hello, Najam! I'm done my work for today!" he said happily.

Najam chuckled. "So what are you going to do now, little master? Are you going to play?"

Amsi nodded enthusiastically. "Is Nassar with you?"

"Your father takes the twins with him to the palace when he goes, Amsi. They will not be back until tonight."

"Can you play with me?"

Najam smiled at the boy and pet his arm. "I'm sorry, my boy, but I must cook dinner. Your father will be very angry if he finds that he has no dinner for tonight."

"My father gets angry at you and Qamra a lot."

"Don't you worry about your father, Amsi. You run along and play. If your father gets home in time, he may instruct you in your archery lesson."

Amsi nodded. "Alright. I should go. Goodbye, Najam!"

"Goodbye, my little master."

Amsi ran out of the gardens. He saw Issâm on his knees showing five-year-old Laila how to pull weeds. Amsi grinned as he crept quietly behind Issâm.

"You must be careful to grab the entire weed, my girl. If you leave some behind, it will grow again."

Laila looked up at Issâm. "Where is my mother?"

Issâm looked down at the little girl, the daughter of Qamra, fathered by Kaemwaset. She had Kaemwaset's eyes, but her mother's delicate features. Kaemwaset had ordered that Laila work in the field, and not be placed as a house servant. Kaemwaset wanted to keep his daughter far from the eyes of his wife, whom he feared would suspect a connection between himself and the child.

When the child had been born, Imani had requested Issâm's presence in her chamber. She questioned Issâm regarding the child's parentage. It was with a heavy heart that Issâm told a lie that Baruti had, indeed, fathered Laila upon orders from Kaemwaset. It was now Sabi's turn for that honor. Kaemwaset had ordered Tabari to make Sabi with child since more slaves were needed for the fields. Tabari had succeeded in his demand and Sabi was in the middle of her pregnancy.

Issâm felt disgusted with the command, arguing that is how one bred horses. Tabari alleviated Issâm's concerns when he said he had feelings for Sabi. Issâm insisted that is not how the gods intended for their children to bring other children into the world. Tabari had taken Sabi to the fields and laid with her. When she urinated on seeds and they began to sprout wheat, Tabari was pleased. Sabi was so happy she threw herself at Tabari with a tight embrace. The fact that their mating was demanded didn't eliminate their enthusiasm.

Issâm smiled at the little girl. As far as the slaves were concerned, this was Qamra's daughter no matter who fathered her or the circumstances of her conception. "Your mother is in the home, Laila. That is her place of work."

"Stop right there, Issâm!" Amsi exclaimed, pointing the wooden sword at Issâm's back. Issâm turned his head. "Well, if it isn't Master Amsi! Have you finished with your studies?"

"Yes!"

"What did your tutor say?"

"I'm better," Amsi said, pulling the sword away.

Issâm smiled at the child. "I am proud of you, Master Amsi."

"Really?"

Issâm bowed his head. "You are placing great effort into your studies. Your father should give you an archery lesson tonight should he return from the palace before nightfall."

"Can't you teach me my archery lessons?"

"The twins are better archers than myself. Their tribe was trained in the art of the bow and arrow. Ask Nassar to show you some of his skill. That boy could have been a prized archer for the Egyptian army."

Amsi reached behind his head nervously as he looked down at the ground. "Why does Nassar never speak,

Issâm? My father said that Nassar had a forked tongue like a serpent and he spoke of heresy before the pharaoh."

"Nakia had told me that Nassar was defending himself against the pharaoh. Nakia said the pharaoh was being very mean to Nassar. The pharaoh removed Nassar's tongue as punishment."

Amsi's jaw dropped and his eyes widened in surprise. "That must have hurt!"

"Nassar was stricken by a terrible fever and infection as a result." Issâm placed his hands on Amsi's shoulders. "My boy, you must watch your words before the pharaoh and your father. They are both very dangerous men. I know you love your father, Master Amsi. You will find your own path in life. I pray to Thoth that you follow the path of our ancestors."

Amsi looked into the dark eyes of Issâm and smiled at him. "I will do as you say, Issâm."

"Good boy. Run along and play, Master Amsi."

Amsi ran down the path, waving to the servants as he passed them. Those that seen him returned the wave and continued their toil. Amsi ran through the arch as he exited the Al-Sakhir lands. He took a deep breath as he looked around him. A path leading to Heliopolis crossed the front of the archway and disappeared, leading into the ominous desert nearby.

His father had warned him never to enter the desert. Bedouin tribes, Kaemwaset told him, were looking for Egyptian children to sacrifice to their evil war gods.

Bandits and thieves lived there looking to ransack caravans of the Nobility. The desert was a very dangerous place for everyone, especially a child of Noble Blood. The desert was the land of the god Seth and was filled with evil.

Amsi looked ahead of him where he could see the banks of the Nile. Tall reeds rose from the bank, providing a perfect hiding place or a place for adventure. The reeds could become a dense forest to make new discoveries, a home of one's own, or an oasis far from the noise of the city nearby. Amsi looked down the road for his father's chariot, but it had not emerged from the city.

The only ones emerging from between the gargantuan statues of Rā were women carrying baskets on their heads, some with children strapped to their chests. Some people sat outside the city, asking passers-by for food or medicine. Tired workers from the nearby pyramid sauntered through the gates looking weary, their backs bent from the heavy burdens they carried throughout the day. Some men stumbled out of the city, singing loudly and hiccupping.

Amsi ran towards the reeds of the Nile holding his ball and wooden sword. He smiled as he ran towards the vast jungle ahead of him. Kaemwaset had warned him of the dangerous crocodiles and hippopotamus which lurked in the Nile and its banks. The jungle ahead of him posed many dangers, but he wasn't afraid. He was going to explore the vast wilderness and laugh in the face of danger.

He arrived at the reeds and ran through them laughing. He pushed the leaves aside with the sword, watching out for a ferocious tiger that he heard Sabi speak of in one of her stories around the fire at night.

*Where are you, tiger? Beware of Amsi Al-Sakhir Ibn Kaemwaset!*

Amsi gasped as he heard something in the water splash lightly nearby. He stopped and crouched down low to prevent being heard. *I'm not afraid of you, tiger!* He heard something dip in the water again and he smiled. *I have you cornered, tiger! You can't escape me!*

Amsi jumped out of the reeds and held his sword in front of him. "Freeze, tiger!"

A little boy kneeling by the Nile jumped, startled by the sudden intruder to his privacy. Both boys looked at each other with surprise. Amsi watched the other little boy slowly stand up and look at the wooden sword quizzically. The other child looked into Amsi's eyes.

"I'm not a tiger," the child said calmly.

Amsi lowered his sword slowly. "Sorry. I was looking for a tiger."

The child standing before Amsi was very skinny. His ribs slightly poked from his sides. The boy had a scar on his right cheek that ran under his eye to the middle of his cheek. A white skirt was hanging on the child's bony hips. The bottom of the skirt was frayed and it was dirty. His eyes went to the ball and the wooden sword.

"What are you doing?"

"I'm playing with my toys."

The child held out a handful of pebbles to Amsi. "I'm playing with my toys."

"How do you play with them?"

The child took a pebble and giggled. "Watch this!" The boy tossed the small rock and threw it, watching it skip across the water. He turned his head to Amsi. "You want to try?"

Amsi put his ball and sword on the ground. He took a rock from the other boy's hand and looked confused at the rock and at the water. "How do I do it?"

The little boy took Amsi's hand and showed him how to hold it. He showed Amsi in slow motion how to toss it. The boy made another pebble skip across the surface of the water. "You try it."

Amsi tried throwing the pebble, making it sink to the bottom of the Nile. "It's not as easy as it looks."

The other child made another pebble skip. "Keep trying."

"Do you have a sword or a ball?"

The child shook his head. "No. I don't have money for that."

"Do you want to play with mine?"

The child looked over at the toys laying on the ground longingly. He had seen other children play with those toys. He had watched them play in the fields. The rich children decorated in gold jewelry carried swords and played mock battles outside of the city walls.

The boy dropped his handful of stones and approached the ball slowly. He looked down at it and nudged it with his bare foot. Amsi ran up to the ball and held it in his hands. "Catch!" Amsi threw the ball at the boy, who caught it as it flew into his arms quickly.

"I've seen other kids play with this, but I've never played with it before."

Amsi grabbed the wooden sword. "Ever play with one of these?"

"No."

Amsi looked at the boy dressed in the dirty white, tattered skirt. His appearance was one of the children who ran through the city streets in the northern quarter. When his father would ride with him in the chariot, he would tell his son that these children were dangerous. They were all little thieves who would steal his toys and would rob him of any money he would possess.

At dusk he would sometimes run behind the slave house and play with Karida and the twins. They never tried to steal his toys, despite what Kaemwaset had taught him. The little boy in front of him bounced the ball, but wasn't trying to steal it.

"Throw it to me!" Amsi called.

The child threw it to Amsi, who caught it in his hand. Amsi looked at the other boy, who had kneeled beside the

Nile and began to drink from the water. "What is your name?"

The boy turned his head as he scooped another handful of water into his hand. "Azizi Keket Ibn Ghazi."

"Do you live in the city?"

Azizi nodded. "What is your name?"

"Amsi Al-Sakhir Ibn Kaemwaset."

"Can I play with your ball more?"

Amsi dropped the ball and kicked it to Azizi. Azizi kicked the ball back to Amsi, who dropped his sword and kicked the ball back to Azizi. Azizi missed the ball as it flew into the reeds. The child ran for the ball, watching it emerge from the brush and run into the road. Azizi looked up as he saw a chariot racing down the path. He grabbed the ball and rolled out of the way before the horses could trample him.

"Out of my way, you foolish little child!" Kaemwaset bellowed as Azizi sat up.

Amsi ran out of the reeds and watched his father's chariot enter the family land. "My father has returned from the palace!"

"You father is mean," Azizi said, narrowing his eyes at his companion.

"I'm sorry, Azizi. Maybe he did not see you."

Azizi stood up and brushed the sand off his clothing. "He saw me." The boy's hand went to his stomach as he groaned. "I'm hungry. I should find something to eat."

"Najam is making a big dinner for tonight! Her food is very good."

Azizi looked at the ball and back at Amsi. "I need to go find my mother."

"Amsi Al-Sakhir Ibn Kaemwaset! Get over here!" Amsi heard his father call from the front of the arch.

"Bye, Azizi."

"Bye, Amsi."

Amsi ran towards his father carrying his toys. He arrived at his father's feet and bowed his head. "Father."

"Were you talking to that little runt I almost missed on the road?"

"Yes, sir."

Kaemwaset leaned down and glared at his son. "You are lucky to be alive, my boy. That child could have hurt you."

"We were just playing, father."

Kaemwaset put a hand on his son's shoulder. "My boy, those people are dangerous. I do not want to lose you to their barbarism."

"But, father-."

"No, Amsi. I am telling you this for your own safety. Stay away from their kind. Shun them. They are bad people."

Amsi looked his father in the eye. "You almost hurt Azizi with the chariot. That wasn't very nice."

Kaemwaset kneeled in front of Amsi. "Their kind is expendable, my son. Kill one today and another six will be born tomorrow. Let me ask you a question, Amsi. Do you believe it is acceptable to hurt someone very bad?"

Amsi shook his head. "No, sir."

"If you could stop someone before they hurt you, do you think that is acceptable?"

Amsi looked at the sand below his sandals. He bit his lip in thought. "I wouldn't want to be hurt, no."

"Then it is only right to stop someone from having a chance to hurt you, right?"

Amsi nodded. "I guess so."

"I don't want you to be hurt, my boy. I'm only looking after your best interests. Do you love your father?"

Amsi nodded. "Yes, father."

"Then I would have you heed my warning and never speak to that child again, my son."

Amsi turned his head and looked towards the city. He saw Azizi disappear between the large statues of Rā.

"Father, what about Qamra and Baruti and Issâm? Would they want to hurt me, too?"

Kaemwaset smiled at his son. "If they ever so much as raise a finger to you in anger, my boy, you tell me and I will see they are disciplined severely."

"But Issâm and Qamra and Baruti are nice to me."

Kaemwaset grinned. "That is because they know you are my son. They wish to remain in my good favor. Their kind is only good for toiling in our fields, Amsi. They know little else. We are favored by Rā so we are more intelligent than their kind. I would caution you about becoming too friendly with the slaves, Amsi. They will corrupt you against me."

Amsi nodded and bowed his head. "Yes, father."

"Now, return to the home and grab your bow and arrow, my son. It is time for your valuable archery lesson."

## XIII

### Survival

Azizi ran between the statues and into the bustling streets. People were calling out their wares to potential customers loudly, some approaching the pedestrians begging for their business. A group of young boys ran into an alley chasing another boy. Women were carrying babies in their arms as disagreements and arguments filled the marketplace.

Azizi stopped at a cart full of grapes and apples. The fruit was round and large. The harvest had been good that year, making the price of the food increase. His eyes grew wide as he looked longingly at the bushels of apples on the cart. Azizi stepped up to the cart as he put his hands on the edge, looking at the fruit with a lick of his lips.

"Step back, child. Do not touch my cart!" the man yelled at him, startling the boy.

Azizi stepped back slowly as he continued to look up at the fruit. He looked up at a corpulent man standing in front of the cart. He tugged lightly on the man's jacket. The man looked down at the skinny child.

"What do you want? I'm busy."

Azizi pointed to the apples. "Can I have one?"

"Do you have money to pay for it?"

Azizi shook his head. "No."

"Then you can't have one."

"But, I'm hungry!" the child exclaimed, rubbing his scrawny stomach.

The man waved his hand, batting the child's hand away from him. "Get out of here, you little mongrel!"

"Please?"

"Get away!" the man growled, shoving him roughly away.

"You're mean," the child pouted as he walked away slowly, turning his head back slowly to look at the large, juicy fruit on the cart.

He watched the man who had shooed him away slip an apple into his pocket as the shopkeeper turned his head to take payment from another customer. Azizi watched the man walk calmly away.

The little boy walked through the streets to a tall building the surface of which was charred black in some places. 'Mbizi's Meeting House' was freshly painted above the entrance.

Azizi walked through the entrance where the strong smell of spicy incense lingered in the air. The room was lit by candles and two openings on either side of the entrance. Men were sitting beside women on chairs lined with luxurious material. Kahla, a ten-year-old girl, was serving wine to guests as they negotiated payment and waited for the next available woman to emerge from the stairs to the second level.

"Hello, Azizi!" Kahla waved with a smile.

"Hello, Kahla. Where's my mother?"

Kahla pointed to the steps as she stepped in front of him. "She's upstairs. She should be back in a few minutes." Kahla leaned into Azizi's ear. "Mbizi is in a bad mood. Be careful."

"Azizi, you're late," Lakia said as she waved to him. "Where have you been?"

"I played with a boy by the lake! He let me play with his ball!"

Lakia chuckled as the man hugging her began kissing her neck, his large hands groping her breast. "Did you have fun?"

Azizi nodded happily as his smile quickly faded. "This mean man wouldn't buy me an apple and I even said please!"

"Ask your mother when she comes downstairs."

Azizi saw Mbizi emerge from another room. He was a bald man of middle age. His belly stood prominently in front of him. His clothes were made of the finest linen, imported from across distant lands. His chin was adorned with a beard which was beginning to grow sporadic patches of gray. His hands were large and when he walked there was a waddle to his step. His breathing was deep and heavy as he looked around the crowd in front of him.

Azizi smiled widely when he saw his mother come down the steps with a man in a white linen skirt. The man hiccupped as he smiled and kissed his mother on the cheek.

"How did you enjoy my Khepret?"

The man chuckled as he placed some coin in Mbizi's hand. "She wasn't bad. She is a good screamer."

Azizi ran to his mother and wrapped his arms around her leg, hugging her. "Mother, I missed you!"

Khepret looked down at her boy with wide eyes and a smile. She couldn't help but think of the price she paid daily to see that smile on her little boy's face. She kneeled down and brought Azizi into her arms. "I love you, my son."

Azizi sighed contentedly as he wrapped his arms around her neck. "Mother, can we buy apples? I'm hungry."

Khepret hugged Azizi tightly. She could feel the thin boy's skeletal frame as she hugged him. She worked long days every day and still did not have the money she needed to feed herself and her son. Khepret kissed Azizi's cheek lovingly. "We shall see, my boy."

Mbizi hovered above the mother and son. "This is all Maskini gave me for a tip? If you expect to keep your position, I need to be given more than this, girl!"

Khepret stood up slowly as she looked into her boss' green eyes. "I'm sorry, sir. If the clientele are poor, they won't be able to give much of a tip. I did the best I could."

"Your best isn't good enough!" Mbizi growled as he grabbed her throat. Khepret grabbed his wrist tightly as she struggled.

Azizi ran to Mbizi and kicked his leg. "Let go of my mother!"

Mbizi looked down at the little boy kicking his leg. "You insolent little child! Your father never beat you enough when he was alive!" Mbizi kicked his leg, sending the child flying backwards into a table. The little boy let out a loud cry as Oraida brought him into her arms.

"My lord, he is only a child!" Oraida exclaimed, cuddling the crying boy against her exposed breasts. Azizi held onto Oraida tightly, his body shaking.

"Azizi!" Khepret gasped as she struggled to pull away from Mbizi. The bordello owner released her as she ran to her son. She carefully took Azizi from Oraida and hugged her son. "It's alright, Azizi." Khepret kissed Azizi's cheek and rocked him, glaring at Mbizi.

"You need to teach your son some manners," Mbizi pointed an accusatory finger at the child.

Khepret held the whimpering boy against her. "You don't kick a little child."

"Get out of here, Khepret. Your son will not see you from sunrise to sunset tomorrow!"

Khepret turned her back slowly to Mbizi and left the bordello with her son in her arms. She looked down at Azizi and brushed his side-lock behind his shoulders. "Are you hurt, my child?"

Azizi looked up at her with wide-eyes. "I don't like him."

"I know, Azizi. I'm sorry."

Khepret put Azizi on the ground and held his hand as they walked to their home. Azizi walked close to his mother through the busy streets of the quarter.

Azizi watched a son greeting his father. The little boy ran into the open arms of his father and he looked up at his mother. Azizi watched the smile on the child's face as he was embraced.

"Mother, when will I have a father?"

Khepret stopped and looked down at Azizi. "Your father is sleeping, Azizi. Osiris has taken your father to live with him in the Underworld."

"If I ask for him to come home, will he?"

Khepret shook her head as she kneeled in front of her son. "No, my beloved. Osiris has taken your father home and he will not wake up from his sleep. I'm sorry, Azizi."

"Could I get a new father?"

"It's not as easy as you may think. Your father had no brothers. My family does not live in Heliopolis. It is only you and I. You are my world, my child. You are all that I have in this world." Khepret hugged her son tightly. Azizi saw the crowds walking around him and his mother. Some people looked down at him and his mother while others walked past apathetic.

Azizi looked down sadly as they returned to their home. Khepret kneeled to her basket and took a small loaf of bread. "Tomorrow, Azizi, you should go to the Nile and catch some fish by the banks."

Azizi grabbed a stick and began to draw in the sand. "I played with a boy at the Nile today, mother. He had such fun toys! He had a sword and a ball! He let me play with it!"

Khepret tore a piece of bread and handed it to her son. "Be careful around the Nile. Crocodiles and the hippopotamus can attack little children and drag them below the waters. Keep a sharp eye out for such dangers."

Azizi nodded as he took a bite of the crunchy bread. "Yes, mother. I am careful."

"Good child."

Azizi swallowed and scratched at his teeth, tasting sand within the bread. "His name is Amsi and I showed him how to skip rocks on the water!"

"Amsi?" Khepret's eyes widened in surprise. "Amsi Al-Sakhir?"

Azizi nodded quickly with a smile. "I hope I can play with his toys again! It was so much fun!"

Khepret lit a fire and looked at her son. "Azizi, you must be careful with whom you play. Amsi's father, Kaemwaset, does not like people like us."

"He tried hurting me with his big cart!" Azizi exclaimed.

"Don't let Kaemwaset catch you playing with his son. He could get very angry."

Azizi looked up at his mother. "Why?"

Khepret handed her son another piece of bread as he reached out to her for more.

"The goddess Isis and her brother and Great Lord of the Dead, Osiris, loved each other very much. One day,

Osiris' brother, Seth, was overcome with anger and jealousy at his brother. Seth, after many attempts, finally murdered Osiris. Seth cut Osiris' body into many pieces and scattered them across the land. Isis, very sad that her husband and brother was dead, struggled to gather his body parts. She finally succeeded and reanimated Osiris with the help of the jackal-god, Anubis. Osiris and Set fought each other endlessly and their differences were never resolved. My son, Kaemwaset is just as Seth. His heart is full of rage and anger. Beware of those who are consumed by their own rage so that it blinds their eyes to the world around them. Such people are dangerous."

Azizi continued to draw in the sand as he lifted his head. "Is Amsi like Seth, too?"

"I have spoken to Amsi's mother and his family's servants. Amsi does not appear to be filled with the spirit of his father. Be careful, still, my son. The scorpion is a creature of beauty, but it is very deadly." Khepret handed Azizi a piece of bread. "Offer that to Osiris, my son."

Azizi stood up and walked to the Osiris altar in the corner of the room. He placed the piece of bread in the offering bowl in front of the Osiris statue. "Osiris, take this offering of bread and give us protection from bad things in the night." Azizi bowed as he was taught and returned to his mother.

"Azizi, I am so blessed to have you. Osiris has blessed your father and I with your spirit. It is now time to sleep, my son."

Azizi laid beside the fire on his reed mat. Khepret covered him with a blanket and caressed the little boy's cheek. Azizi closed his eyes as Khepret caressed his back. She watched her son drift slowly into sleep.

Khepret looked at the empty basket of food and at her sleeping son. Her own stomach continued to express its displeasure at the lack of sufficient nutrition. As her child slept, she thought of Azizi's excitement of playing with a toy of a Noble child. Azizi's pleas for apples ran through her head. Her child was hungry and knew she could not afford an apple for her son. Mbizi allowed her to keep only a few dinars from her day's work. Khepret looked at the shadow of Osiris flickering against the wall. She knew the dangers of what she was contemplating. *What choice do I have? My little boy will starve if I cannot feed him. Ghazi, I pray to you every day to watch over our son. If I do not do something, he will join you in the Land of the Dead. Azizi is so young. I cannot allow him to become another child starved under the pharaoh's reign. Too many children I have seen fall on the streets from lack of food and perish in the arms of their parents or stepped over by casual passers-by. I must do this for him.*

"I love you, my precious Azizi," Khepret whispered as she leaned over to kiss her son's cheek. "Lord Osiris, protect my son in my absence."

Khepret stood and looked down at her sleeping boy. She took her cloak and slipped into the night.

## XIV

## <u>Moving Target</u>

Nakia held the bow steady as he looked at an invisible target. "Make certain you hold the bow straight towards your target, Amsi."

The little boy looked at his tutor and ahead of him as he focused into the desert. "This is hard."

"You're doing fine, little master," Nakia said with a grin. "Focus ahead of you on your target. Hold your breath. Make sure your hand doesn't shake. Release."

Amsi and Nakia released their arrows as they flew into the air and into the sand. Nakia smiled at Amsi's progression. His arrows were traveling farther and were flying straight ahead. Amsi's first attempts were flying to the side and he wasn't strong enough to fire the arrows.

Kaemwaset had chosen the twins to assist in tutoring his son in the art of archery. Kaemwaset knew the Nubians were expert archers and the pharaohs had employed them as such in the army during combat. Nassar and Nakia were expert archers and horsemen. Nakia, despite Kaemwaset's command, was happy to tutor the young child in his studies. Nassar would be a "pointless tutor," according to Kaemwaset since the boy could not speak. Nakia was brought along as the expert. The twin was more than elated to leave the confines of the family lands and run free.

Nakia dismounted Hamza and ran for the arrows. He grabbed the arrows and whistled to Hamza. The black stallion galloped towards Nakia and lowered his head. "Good boy, Hamza," Nakia smiled, petting the horse's shoulder. "Up!" Hamza kneeled on his front legs as Nakia pulled himself onto his back. The horse stood as Nakia pat Hamza's thick neck. "You're a good boy, Hamza."

Nakia handed Amsi his arrow. "Pull Naji close to me, Amsi."

Amsi tugged on the reigns, but Naji didn't move. Amsi moved the reigns up and down. "Naji, move!" Amsi called.

Nakia giggled and pulled Hamza's reigns to the right. Hamza moved right towards Naji. "Move the reigns in the direction you want him to go. I moved right. Which way would you need to move the reigns if you wanted to move Naji to the left?"

Amsi looked at Nakia and looked down. He put his finger to his lips as he thought. He tugged the reigns to the left and Nakia nodded.

"Good job, Amsi!" Hamza grunted and shook his head. Nakia laughed. "Good job to you, too, Hamza."

"Continue with the lesson, boy," Kaemwaset grumbled as Munir stood on the other side of Amsi.

Nakia handed Amsi his arrow. "Let me see you knock the arrow."

Amsi held the arrow as Nakia had instructed him earlier. Nakia's knees gripped onto Hamza as he leaned over to correct Amsi's grip. He stuck Amsi's pointer finger forward. "Use that as your focus. Where your finger points, that is where your arrow will fly. Can you see where your finger points?"

Amsi focused ahead of him. "Yes?"

"That is your target as long as you hold your arrow straight."

Amsi looked at Nakia. "You know much!"

Nakia smiled. "I had good teachers. I will teach you how to hit your mark. My people were excellent archers."

"If they were such excellent archers, why they were slaughtered in the hundreds by the great Egyptian army and defeated?" Kaemwaset asked calmly, turning his head to look into the desert. "It seems your father's skill with a bow didn't prevent your mother's throat from being cut."

Nakia's eyes narrowed as he gripped the reigns. "They were attacked without notice!"

Kaemwaset turned his head casually. "That is a poor excuse."

Nakia seethed angrily, his lip curling in anger at his master. "I still can hear their screams! I can still see the ground run red with blood! My tribe was slaughtered and your people worshipped Atenhotep for his cruelty! I begged them to stop! I can hear them still! I do not call that an excuse!"

"Nakia?" Amsi asked as he stared at Nakia with wide eyes. "Why are you angry?"

Nakia straightened his back as he looked at Amsi and ignored Kaemwaset's grin. "It isn't important, my little master. Let's begin again. Get your arrow ready." Amsi raised his bow and knocked his arrow backward. "Remember your finger. Point it forward. Pull back on the arrow as far as you can." Nakia reached out and held Amsi's hand steady. "Hold your bow and arrow still, Amsi." Amsi's arm began to shake as he pulled back the arrow. "Focus on your target and release." Amsi's arrow flew straight and impaled itself into the desert sands. Amsi raised his bow and his fist in the air. "I did it! I did it! Nakia, did you see it?"

Nakia clapped his hands. "That is a very good shot, my lord!"

"Father, did you see it? Did you see what I did?" Amsi asked excitedly as he pointed at the arrow and bounced in his saddle.

Kaemwaset nodded. "Very good shot, my boy."

Amsi bounced on Naji's back happily. Amsi began to waver, but Nakia put his hand on Amsi's shoulder to prevent him from falling.

"Be careful when on horseback, Amsi. If you fall, you can hurt yourself or you can die."

"Die? What does that mean?"

Kaemwaset and Nakia exchanged glances. "Tell my son what death is, Nakia. You have seen much of it."

Nakia swallowed hard and looked at the little boy beside him. *I still remember that day. The Egyptian army came from everywhere. They swarmed like locusts during the dry season. My mother looked at me with sad eyes. She pleaded for her life as my brother and I held onto each other and watched. 'Ulan,' she told my brother, 'Protect Kelile!' The soldier cut her throat and her blood sprayed on my face and chest. My brother and I were spared and given to Kaemwaset. We have been slaves since we were five years old. I'll never forget that day when our tribe was slaughtered. Since that day, Nassar and I do everything together. We do not like to be separated.*

"You don't move if you get hurt too much. Your heart stops. You don't live anymore."

"I don't wish that for you, my boy," Kaemwaset said, putting his hand on Amsi's back. "You are my pride and joy."

Amsi looked at his father. "You don't live anymore? You can't talk?"

"No, my son."

Amsi shook his head. "I don't want that."

"Then heed Nakia's warning and be careful on horseback."

Amsi nodded emphatically. "Yes, father!"

Nakia looked at Amsi. "Let's move on to our riding lesson."

Nakia held Hamza's reigns as he rode beside Amsi. Nakia's side-lock flowed behind him as he rode the fiery steed. The twelve-year-old smiled as he felt the wind flow through his hair. The hot, desert wind caressed his cheeks as Hamza's hooves stamped into the ground. The child's eyes lit up with joy as he pat the black horse's thick neck and ruffled his hair. The open desert lay before him, welcoming him and offering him liberty. The chains of slavery dissolved into the open desert, the warm wind, and the freedom of movement. Nakia let out a screech of happiness as he looked up into the bright sky. Only riding afforded the slave boy the freedom he had once known. The child turned his head to see Amsi gripping onto Naji's reigns tightly and nervously.

"Relax your grip, Master Amsi. You do not want to restrict Naji's movements. Let her run, but you control her speed."

Amsi looked over at Nakia nervously. "I don't know how."

"Use your knees to steer her and balance yourself," Nakia said patting his bare knees.

"Hamza, Ga'Ewe!" Nakia cried out with a smile.

Hamza neighed loudly and began to run faster.

"Nakia! Wait!" Amsi called.

Kaemwaset carefully watched the slave boy ride in front of him. He grabbed an arrow from his quiver and placed it in his bow. "Nakia! Get back here! Stop!"

Nakia turned his head and saw Kaemwaset pointing an arrow at his direction. His eyes widened as he pulled Hamza's reigns. The big, black horse voiced its fury, stamping its hooves on the sand and shaking his head.

Kaemwaset lowered his bow and rode to Nakia. The slave boy swallowed nervously as he saw his master approach. His knees tightened against Hamza. He held onto the reigns tightly. Amsi and Kaemwaset arrived beside Nakia.

The man grabbed Nakia's hair and tugged it roughly. "Remember what I told you back at the home?"

"Father, don't hurt Nakia!"

"Quiet, Amsi!" Kaemwaset barked, turning to his son. "I'm teaching you how to handle slaves who do not listen to your command." The man turned his narrowed eyes towards the twelve-year-old boy. Kaemwaset's tight grip trembled as he roughly tugged on the hair, making Nakia cry out loudly. "What did I tell you before we left?"

Amsi watched his father with wide eyes, his hands trembling at the sight of his father's fury.

"If I tried to escape, you would-." Nakia breathed heavily as sweat pooled on his face.

"What would I do to you if you try to escape your slavery, Nakia, son of a slaughtered people?"

Nakia grabbed Kaemwaset's wrists decorated with gold cuffs and bracelets. "You said you would kill me with your arrows."

"Don't make me show you how good of a shot I can be." Kaemwaset looked at him with a smile and back at Amsi. "Are you paying attention to this, boy?"

Amsi nodded quietly, a tear coming down his face. "Father, don't hurt Nakia! He's my friend."

Kaemwaset laughed. "He's your friend, Amsi?"

Amsi nodded. "He didn't mean to run away, father. We were having fun."

"Amsi, we are not playing a game. You are learning how to be a good citizen. You are learning the virtues of literacy and the fine arts of archery and horsemanship. Do you not want to make your father proud?"

Amsi nodded. "I want to make you proud, father!"

"Then you must do as you are told," Kaemwaset said, releasing Nakia's hair from his grip. "You must be ready to defend yourself and the great pharaoh, Amsi. You must also be ready to discipline your slaves should they try and make their escape." Nakia's eyes shifted from Amsi to Kaemwaset nervously. "Take your bow into your hands, my son."

Amsi slowly took his bow into his hands as his father handed him one of his arrows.

"Nakia, ride."

Nakia swallowed nervously. "What, my lord?"

Kaemwaset grinned. "Ride away."

Nakia swallowed nervously and began to ride away, riding low. He looked back as Kaemwaset and Amsi followed him. He leaned over on Hamza and closed his eyes. "Hamza, run! Please."

Kaemwaset took his own bow into his hands and placed an arrow there to fire. "Follow my example, son."

Amsi looked over at his father and watched as he knocked an arrow backward. With a grin, he released the arrow as it flew towards Nakia. Nakia moved his head to the other side of Hamza as he looked behind.

*Great gods, he wants to kill me! Nassar! I can't leave Nassar!* Nakia thought as tears fell from his eyes. *I can't let him kill me! Nassar will be alone!*

"Father, don't kill Nakia!" Amsi cried as he lowered his head. "Please! Do not hurt him!"

"He volunteered to be our target," Kaemwaset grinned as he removed another arrow. "Place the arrow in the bow like so, my son. Put your finger…no, make it look like this. Good boy. Now, pull back on the arrow. Now release it."

Nakia watched as Amsi's arrow fell into the sand nearby. "Hamza, return home! Hurry!"

Hamza turned right, exposing Nakia to Kaemwaset's view. Nakia closed his eyes and whimpered as he saw Kaemwaset release another arrow. The arrow whipped through Hamza's hair.

"Try again, my son!" Kaemwaset called.

"No!" Amsi yelled defiantly.

"If you do not try, you will no longer be welcome in my home and you will have disappointed myself and Rā! You will make him angry! Do you wish to see the sun god angry? He will fry you alive, boy!" Kaemwaset screamed at his son with a clenched fist.

Amsi rubbed his teary eye as he saw Nakia ride towards him. "I do not want to hurt him!"

Kaemwaset knocked back another arrow. "You will need to learn how to hit a moving target, my son."

Kaemwaset released the arrow. Amsi watched as Nakia screamed and fell from Hamza onto the desert sand. Hamza stopped running and ran back to Nakia laying on the desert sand facedown.

"NAKIA! NO!" Amsi exclaimed, racing Naji towards Nakia.

Kaemwaset rode beside his son and watched as the black stallion grunted. Hamza reared quickly on his hind legs beside the fallen Nakia. Kaemwaset dismounted Munir and walked towards the boy. Kaemwaset saw anger in the black stallion's eyes. Amsi looked down as Naji approached Nakia.

"Father, get me down! Father, get me down!" Amsi cried as he clenched his fists angrily.

Kaemwaset calmly walked to Amsi and lifted him from the horse's back. He placed Amsi gently on the ground, who ran over to Nakia laying on the sand with the arrow buried in his right shoulder.

"Nakia! Nakia!"

Kaemwaset reached down and pulled the arrow out of Nakia's shoulder, eliciting a cry of pain from the boy.

Kaemwaset's sandal dug under Nakia's body and flipped him over. Nakia arched his back and clenched his fists in pain. The boy threw his head back as he cried.

"These things cost money," Kaemwaset said holding the bloody arrow in his hand.

Amsi looked at Nakia, his bottom lip trembling. "Nakia, get back on Hamza."

Nakia's eyes slowly moved to Amsi as tears fell down his cheeks. "No."

Amsi took Nakia's wrist and began to pull on him. "We must go home, Nakia!"

Nakia took a painful breath. "No. Master Amsi, tell Nassar that I love him."

Kaemwaset kneeled beside Amsi and put his hands on Amsi's shoulders. "I love you, my son."

"You hurt Nakia, father. That's not nice. Is he going to die?"

Kaemwaset caressed Amsi's cheek. "I want you to grow up strong, my Amsi. I want you to make me proud. Today you have made me very proud."

Nakia held his shoulder as he began to whimper in pain. Tears flowed from his eyes as he rolled over on the sand, blood trickling from his open wound. *Nassar, please forgive me.*

Kaemwaset smiled at Amsi. "You are a fast learner. One day, when I pass into the Land of Osiris, I know that you will make me proud. You will watch over my house and you will be a strong man. That is all I want for you, my boy." Kaemwaset kissed his son on either cheek. "I love you, my child."

Nakia reached to Kaemwaset with a weak hand. His tiny hand touched Kaemwaset's wrist, his hand trembling as blood seeped from his open wound. "Please, my lord. Help me." Nakia's shoulder and his arm were covered in blood.

"You must be thirsty from your lessons today, my son. Let us return home for food and drink."

"Nassar will miss Nakia!"

"Nakia's good as dead, my son," Kaemwaset said looking down at the bleeding child. "Nobody will miss him. He is easily replaced."

Nakia's arm fell weakly onto the sand, closing his eyes. "My lord, please help me," the boy whimpered as he gasped for breath.

Kaemwaset picked Amsi into his arms and placed him on Naji. He reached for Hamza's reigns, but the horse reared angrily as it stood over Nakia. "Then you perish with him, Hamza."

Kaemwaset returned to Munir and mounted his steed. Nakia watched as Kaemwaset lead Amsi towards the Al-Sakhir home. Amsi turned his head to see the slave boy laying in the sand.

Nakia closed his eyes as he felt Hamza nuzzling him. "Hamza, go home. Get Nassar."

*Nassar, I'm sorry.*

Nakia felt the sand shift beside him. Hamza was sitting beside him. He could feel the warmth of the horse beside him, making him smile. The horse nudged Nakia with his nose. With a groan of pain, Nakia cuddled against Hamza's body. The gasping, trembling boy touched the horse, leaving a trail of faint blood on the black body. Nakia's breaths came in sharp gasps as the warmth of the horse comforted him. Hamza lowered his head. Nakia looked into the dark, hypnotic eyes of the wild beast. The horse gazed at him, making him feel a mixture of intimidation and devotion. "Why are you not leaving?"

The horse leaned its head down and nuzzled Nakia with his nose tenderly. Nakia grabbed the reigns and held it with a trembling hand. "Hamza, thank you." The boy looked at the horse with a weak smile.

*I'm not alone. Nassar, please forgive-.*

## XV

### The Blessed Servant of Osiris

Azizi opened his eyes and yawned, rubbing the sleep from his tired eyes. The blurry world came into focus as he reached behind him. The reed mat below him felt bumpy and vacant. *Mother?*

The five-year-old turned his head and saw his mother absent. He lifted his head and looked around the one room home he shared with his parent. The shrine to Osiris stood in the corner, an offering bowl and two candles flanked the sides of the wooden table. The basket beside the opening was empty. His mother had told him to go to the Nile for fish. The fire pit beside him was full with smoldering ashes from the night before, the smoke sending a thin wisp of bitter smoke into the air.

Azizi sat and looked at the sunlight on the dirt floor. "Mother?" he called, looking around. The little boy stood up and yawned, stretching his arms into the sun. "Mother, where are you?"

Azizi pushed aside the material covering the entrance to the home. He looked into the streets and saw them empty. At this time of morning, the streets were busy and loud with the sounds of blacksmith hammers and the calling of merchants.

"Mother? Hello? Where's my mother?" The child stepped into the streets as he heard sounds of shouting coming from nearby.

Azizi walked slowly towards the noise of people shouting. "Mother?"

Azizi approached a crowd and maneuvered through the forest of human legs. He screamed as he emerged from the crowd.

Khepret was kneeling with her arms tied behind her back. Gahiji was holding the hood of her cloak in his hand. He glared at the newcomer.

"There is her child, my lord!" a woman screamed as she pointed to the five-year-old boy.

"Run, Azizi!" Khepret called.

Azizi turned quickly to escape as Mbizi grabbed his arm. Azizi let out a scream as he tried to tug his arm away. The child continued to scream as the man pulled him from the crowd and brought him in front of his mother.

"Mbizi, please don't do this! Release my son!"

"He will be a nice addition to my staff upon your death, Khepret," Mbizi said with a grin.

Azizi and Khepret looked at each other. Azizi shivered in the grip of the older man with tears falling down his face. "Mother, help me!"

"This woman has been caught thieving!" Gahiji called to the crowd, who responded with angry, loud threats.

"Azizi, I'm so sorry," Khepret said as she lowered her head slowly.

Azizi looked around the crowd nervously. Azizi tried pulling his arm away from the man's grip. Mbizi put Azizi against his body facing forward, making his arms and legs dangle helplessly in front of him. "Let me go!" Azizi punched the man's obese stomach, only providing amusement for the brothel owner.

"Quiet, you little rat!" Gahiji growled at Azizi. "There will be no words from you or I will remove your tongue!"

"Don't hurt my son!" Khepret pleaded loudly.

Gahiji slapped Azizi's mother harshly, making the child cry and struggle with his captor. Khepret's head whipped to the side from the impact as the crowd began to murmur. "Behave yourself, boy. Your struggle will only make this harder on your mother. Your mother has already condemned you and her to a swift death."

"NO!" Khepret screamed. "Don't kill my son! He's only a baby!"

Gahiji laughed, his head flying backwards and his body jiggling. Azizi's eyes widened in fear as Gahiji removed his sword from its sheath. He had seen what those large metal sticks could do. The five-year-old's hands gripped the arm of the man holding him tightly. "The pharaoh will make a sport of your deaths. You will serve as a reminder of what happens to those who dare to steal from the people of Heliopolis!"

"My son did nothing!"

Gahiji grinned as he approached the man holding Azizi. Gahiji leaned down and looked the child in his teary eyes. "I consider this mercy killing. Your son will starve without you, so we will send him to Osiris along with you. You can both stand before him in judgment."

"The Great Pharaoh Runihura approaches! Make way!"

The crowd parted and increased their distance from the captives and soldiers.

"I'm so sorry, Azizi," Khepret lowered her head and sobbed. "What have I done?"

The teenaged pharaoh stepped from his gold chariot. The bull tail hanging by his belt swayed as he walked with a strut and a proud smile. "Well, what do we have here, General Gahiji?"

Gahiji held up Khepret's head. "We have ourselves a common thief and her little vermin, Great One!"

Pharaoh Runihura stepped in front of Khepret and looked down at her with a smile. He tilted his head to the side as he looked down at her. "You are a pretty common rat. What a shame it is that you must sacrifice your son's life as well as your own!"

Khepret looked up at the pharaoh with tears running down her face. "My lord, please do not kill my son. He is only a child and I only stole that apple so he may eat. I had to feed my son!"

"How does it feel to die for the sake of an apple?"

Khepret shook her head. "Please, my lord, have mercy!"

Pharaoh Runihura looked down at the woman, narrowing his eyes at her. *Mercy is for the weak, my son,* his mother had told him. *Those who are weak are quickly dethroned and their names are erased from history. You will be great, my son. I will see to it that you become a strong and great leader for your people. Power over patience is how a great leader shall rule his people.*

Runihura reached down and cupped her cheek tenderly in his hand. "If I release you, you will raise your son to be no better than a thief. I cannot allow my mercy to breed anarchy within my state."

Khepret shook her head. "My son will not become a thief, my lord! Please let him go!"

Pharaoh Runihura turned his head towards the man holding the child in his arms. "What is your name, filthy boy?"

Azizi watched as the pharaoh approached him with a lip curled with disgust and disdain. Azizi kicked his legs and he squirmed in the man's arms. Azizi curled his toes and held his breath nervously. Runihura put his hand under the child's chin and held his head upwards, exposing the boy's neck.

"Do not make me repeat myself, you little rat. What is your name?"

"A-Azizi," the child whimpered.

The pharaoh smiled. "I want you to know before you die, that you are to blame for your mother's death."

Azizi looked at his mother as a tear fell onto Runihura's hand. His bottom lip was trembling as his body shivered. His chest tightened as he felt his heart began to race. Sweat began to form on the child's forehead as he looked at the sword hovering over his mother's head.

"Please don't hurt my mother," Azizi cried. "I'll be a good boy, my pharaoh."

"It's alright, child," Runihura said calmly as he leaned towards the child's face. "It will all be over soon." Runihura looked the child in the eyes. "You are to blame for your mother's death, Azizi. Do not fret, child. You will die with her. You will not have to live with the guilt of her death for long."

Pharaoh Runihura stepped beside the man holding Azizi in his arms. "Gahiji, it's time to send her soul to Osiris."

"Azizi, your mother loves you," Khepret said as her body began to quake.

Gahiji raised his sword above his head.

"OSIRIS, WATCH OVER MY SON!" Khepret raised her head, screaming loudly into the sky.

"Mother!" Azizi screeched loudly, reaching his arms toward her.

Gahiji's sword swiftly sliced through the air, severing Khepret's head from her body. Azizi screamed loudly as her head fell to the ground with her body. Blood spilled on the ground beneath her body. He watched in terror as the body twitched on the ground. Azizi's heart raced quickly as he struggled in the arm of his captor. His shrill, ear-piercing scream rose over the crowd as he kicked his legs. He looked at his arm dotted with his mother's blood.

"Mother! Mother! Wake up!"

Pharaoh Runihura grabbed the woman's severed head and held it in the air to show the crowd. The disembodied head's eyes blinked twice and remained still. "This is what we do to criminals! I will show criminals no mercy! Lawlessness will not be tolerated in my kingdom!"

Azizi felt a drop of sweat fall from his face onto his hand as Gahiji turned his face to him. "Mother."

"You will join her soon, boy," Gahiji said.

Pharaoh Runihura threw the head beside the body where it bounced once and laid on the ground, its lifeless eyes looking at its living son. "Where did these rats live?"

Azizi lowered his head as he cried. He gripped Mbizi's arm tightly as he sobbed. "No, my mother."

Mbizi bowed his head. "I will show you, your Grace."

Mbizi held Azizi in his arms as the child continued to cry and struggle. He punched Mbizi's stomach, but the man continued to laugh at the child's attempt at freedom.

The pharaoh, Gahiji, and the crowd followed Mbizi to the Keket home.

"Burn it," Pharaoh Runihura said, removing his own golden dagger from its sheath.

Azizi let out a scream as the people set the home ablaze. Thick, black smoke rose from the home as red-orange flames licked through the openings in the home. "Osiris! Stop them!"

Pharaoh Runihura looked down at the child with a grin. "Why pray to Osiris? He will not save you." The pharaoh smiled as he stood in front of Mbizi. "Gahiji, take the child."

Azizi punched the General as Mbizi released him and Gahiji took him into his grip. Runihura's eyes widened as he remembered the prophecy. The child's mother beckoned to Osiris before she died. Could this child be his nemesis? *The Blessed Servant of Osiris shall rise*

*from the streets of Iunu and sever the head of the lion's*
*servant.*

"No, it can't be!" the pharaoh growled. "Do you
worship the God of the Dead, boy?"

Azizi nodded slowly. "Yes."

The pharaoh's eyes went to the scar on the child's face.
Pharaoh Runihura laughed in the light of the fire. He
glared at the boy and raised the dagger towards the boy's
throat. "I will kill you, Blesséd Servant, before you have
a chance to kill me!" Runihura leaned down and kissed
the boy's cheek. "I thought I killed you five years ago. I
will not fail this time. This will be a pleasure."

Azizi reached out and raked his nails down the teen's left
cheek quickly, making Pharaoh Runihura's head turn to
the side quickly and drop his golden dagger.

"My Lord!" Gahiji called, his grip momentarily
weakening.

Azizi's left hand curled into claws as he scratched down
the front of Gahiji's face. The child's finger sunk into
Gahiji's left eye as the sharp nails raked down his face.
Gahiji let out a scream and dropped the boy on the
ground.

Azizi grabbed the dagger and looked up at the two
holding their faces and rubbing their eyes free of tears.

"Get back here!" Pharaoh Runihura exclaimed as Azizi
began to run down the street away from the crowd. "Get
that child! Five hundred gold dînars to the man who
brings me that child's mangled corpse!"

Azizi looked over his shoulder as he saw several men from the crowd chasing him. Soldiers carrying spears pursued him; Some men on horseback charged towards him with their swords raised.

Azizi gasped as he held the dagger tightly in his hand. Sweat and tears slid down his cheeks as his assailants quickly closed the gap between them. His little legs carried him as fast as they could go. His bare feet patted against the hard ground as he turned the corner.

"Osiris, help me!" Azizi cried out as his eyes darted around for something to slow the advance of his pursuers. Azizi grabbed an apple from a merchant's basket and threw it towards the advancing men.

The apple hit a man in the forehead, making the man hold his head, but it didn't stop the man's advance.

Azizi turned down a narrow alley as he began to wheeze. His chest tightened further at his attempt to escape the crowd following him. One of the men raced to him and grabbed him by the back of the neck.

"I got him! Those five hundred dînars are mine!" the man exclaimed.

Another man grabbed Azizi's leg and began to tug on him. The child let out a cry as the two men tugged at him violently.

"We have to kill the child before we get the money!" the man holding Azizi's neck said. "And that money is mine!" Azizi watched as the man holding his ankle stabbed the other man with his dagger, spotting Azizi's white, tattered skirt in crimson.

The murderer grabbed Azizi's arm and held him into the air. "You're coming with me, boy!"

Azizi raised the golden dagger in his free hand and plunged it as hard as he could into his new captor. The man dropped him as he fell onto the hard ground. The child watched as the crowd filed down the narrow alley towards him. Azizi grabbed the golden dagger and continued his escape.

Azizi looked briefly as the crowd stepped over the two corpses on the ground. The child let out a scream as the men continued their pursuit. Azizi watched as arrows flew past him. They embedded themselves in wooden carts at the end of the alley. The child ran between the two carts and darted to the right.

The boy looked both ways down the road, his heart racing faster at the sound of approaching feet behind him and the sound of horses in front of him. Azizi saw the people beginning to emerge from the alley. He ran behind the carts and continued to run towards the entrance to the city.

"Where did he go?" one man asked.

"We'll find you, boy!" Another man said, running towards him through the street.

"Azizi, show yourself!" Mbizi called loudly. "We know you are here!"

Azizi held his breath and hid under a cart; his breathing was sharp as he heard a loud crash. Mbizi had taken his sword and sliced through a wooden table.

"We'll find you, boy, even if we have to destroy all of these carts!"

"That is my table you just damaged!" a man growled at Mbizi. "How am I going to sell my wares now?"

Mbizi narrowed his eyes at the man. "This child can be anywhere! Would you prefer to lose a few dînars to purchase a new table over five hundred new ones! You could buy yourself a new home, Talib!"

Azizi watched as the men began stabbing material and slicing through carts searching for him. Some men were throwing over carts as the mass hysteria approached him.

"Find that boy!"

"His corpse is worth financial security!"

Azizi ran behind the carts as the hysteria behind him focused on destroying the carts. Azizi grabbed an apple from a basket on the ground and turned the corner. The welcoming entrance loomed in front of him. The little boy dashed from the city gate into open land. His body shuddered as his breathing came in sharp gasps. The hairs on the back of his neck stood up, his heart raced, making the veins in his neck pulse quickly. Tears flowed down his cheeks as he continued to run. His eyes darted around him as people calmly were walking towards the city. Azizi quickly ran towards the banks of the Nile.

*Be careful around the Nile. Crocodiles and the hippopotamus can attack little children and drag them below the waters. Keep a sharp eye out for such dangers,* his mother had told him.

*Mother and Father, I'm coming.*

## XVI

## <u>The Blesséd Dead</u>

Amsi looked at the desert behind him. He held onto Naji's reigns tightly as he thought of Nakia's death. His father had told him that Nakia was dead and that meant that Nakia wasn't going to live anymore. Kaemwaset had told him not to worry himself over Nakia's absence. Sabi was expecting a new child and Nakia was a member of defeated people who were weaker than the Great Egyptian race. Nakia could be with his parents and sending him to be with them was an act of mercy. When asked about Nassar's reaction, Kaemwaset was quiet and without looking at him said that Nassar would join his brother soon.

Amsi saw the Al-Sakhir family lands coming into view. He looked down thinking of how Nassar would react to the death of his twin brother. *Nakia was a good friend. If he's not going to live anymore, I'm going to miss playing with him. Great Rā, maybe you can bring Nakia back to us. Could you talk to Osiris and have Nakia returned? I'll be a good boy and give offerings to you every day for a thousand years!*

"Do not worry yourself over Nakia's death, my son," Kaemwaset said as they approached their lands. "You have performed your duty well today. What is this ahead?"

Amsi looked up and saw smoke rising from the city. "Fire, Father!"

Kaemwaset nodded. "It's coming from the Merchant Quarter."

"Will it burn the whole city?"

"We are safe where we live, Amsi. We need not worry about the merchants," Kaemwaset said as he led Amsi through the gate to his family lands.

Amsi watched as the slaves were working the land with tools. Karida was pulling a basket of cucumbers across the soil, her face covered in sweat from the hot Egyptian sun. Tabari's fingers dug into the soil to loosen the ground nearby his pregnant girlfriend. Sabi was pruning the vegetables, her pregnant belly showing through her white linen robe.

Issâm raised his head to see Kaemwaset and Amsi return. *Where are Nakia and Hamza?*

Kaemwaset dismounted Munir and helped Amsi off Naji. "Issâm! Get over here!"

Issâm shook his hands free of dirt and quickly brushed the soil off his white skirt. He ran to Kaemwaset and bowed before his master. "Take Naji and Munir inside and feed them. They have had a long day."

"Where are Nakia and Hamza, your grace?"

Amsi watched as Kaemwaset kicked a foot into Issâm's face. The man grunted and fell to the side holding his nose.

"It is not your place to ask questions of me, Issâm. Do as I command!"

Issâm returned to his position, holding his face. "Yes, sir. Sorry, my lord."

Kaemwaset turned and walked towards the home. Amsi stepped up to Issâm and looked down at him.

"Are you hurt, Issâm?"

Issâm shook his head. "No, little master. Where are Nakia and Hamza?"

Amsi lowered his head. "My father said Nakia is dead."

Issâm gasped and covered his mouth. Tears were pooling in Issâm's eyes. "What happened?"

Amsi rubbed his eyes as he opened his mouth. He remembered watching Nakia's attempt at escape. The child was trying to hide behind Hamza. The horse struggled to keep distance between his rider and his assailant. He heard the cry of pain coming from Nakia as the child-slave fell onto the sand. On the sand, Nakia was bleeding and his breathing was becoming rugged. *'Please, my lord. Help me!'* echoed in Amsi's mind.

"Hamza did not want to leave Nakia on the sand."

"Did Nakia fall off of Hamza?"

Amsi looked up at Issâm as a tear came down his face. "My father killed Nakia."

Issâm held his breath as his tears finally broke free. *Nakia. He was only a boy. Nassar is going to be crushed. He's all alone now. He cannot even speak about his brother to keep his memory alive.*

"Nakia was my friend, Issâm! Why would my father do that to him?"
Issâm put his hands on Amsi's shoulders. "I know it hurts, Master Amsi. Nakia was a beautiful child. His memory lives on in the words you speak of him. A good man is not truly dead as long as people speak well of him after his death. Our memories of him will keep him alive, my boy." Issâm wiped Amsi's tear away gently. "Don't cry, Amsi. The Great Thoth will write his name in history and he will not be forgotten."

"Hamza was Nakia's friend. He stayed with him."

A small smile crossed Issâm's face. "That does not surprise me in the least. Hamza would only allow Nakia near him. It is only fitting that the horse stayed with his master until he perished."

Amsi reached out and hugged Issâm, wrapping his arms tightly around Issâm's neck. Issâm returned the embrace. "Don't cry, Master Amsi. It will be alright, child." Amsi cried into Issâm's shoulder as he held onto the man tightly.

"I must put Naji and Munir into the stable, Amsi. You should try and find Nassar before your father."

Kaemwaset entered the home, stepping into the reception hall. The walls were lined with murals detailing Rā defeating the serpent, Apep. He advanced into a hallway and looked both ways. "Qamra! Qamra, where are you?"

Qamra stepped out of Imani's quarters and ran towards her master. She bowed before him. "Yes, my lord."

"Where is Nassar?"

"I believe he is picking vegetables in the garden for Najam."

Kaemwaset grinned with satisfaction. "Stand up."

Qamra straightened and found herself suddenly in the arms of her master. Kaemwaset pulled Qamra into a kiss. Qamra pushed against her master. She tried pulling her head back, but Kaemwaset kept a firm hand on the back of her skull.

Kaemwaset moaned into the kiss as she growled angrily. When he severed the kiss with a smile, she glared at him wildly. Kaemwaset raised his hand and cupped her cheek in his hand. "Of all of my slaves, you are my most favored, my precious Qamra."

"I do not share your sentiment, my lord," Qamra said, still attempting to push him away from her.

Kaemwaset chuckled. "Laila is a beautiful child. She has been a wonderful addition to our little household, wouldn't you agree?"

"I love my daughter, but I despise you."

The master smiled. "Rā himself told me to bring her into this mortal plane through your body."

"I do not think Rā would agree, my lord."

"Rā has a purpose for his commands. Should he command me to bear a son by your womb, how could I reject his decree?"

Qamra glared at Kaemwaset. "You have a son by your wife. You do not need me."

Kaemwaset kissed Qamra's cheek. "That remains to be seen, my dearest Qamra. Return to my wife. I must find that mute child."

Kaemwaset released Qamra and walked down the hallway towards the gardens. He smiled proudly as he stepped into the rays of the Aten and looked around at the variety of flowers in large vases. Nassar was kneeling in the bed of vegetables, pulling weeds. The boy grunted as he pulled harshly.

"Nassar!"

The little boy jumped when he heard his name bellowed nearby. Kaemwaset stood at the entrance to the gardens, his arms crossed sternly over his chest. Nassar dropped the weed in his hand and ran to his master. He stopped abruptly in front of Kaemwaset and kneeled, placing his forehead on the ground before his owner.

"Nassar, your brother is dead."

Nassar gasped and his eyes widened. His chest tightened as he raised his head. His mouth opened, but he couldn't speak. *What? My twin brother is dead?* Nassar straightened and looked at Kaemwaset.

"Your brother was slain, hit by an arrow during Amsi's archery training. He lies dead in the desert." Kaemwaset calmly turned his back on the boy with tears coming down his cheeks. "Return to your work."

Nassar kneeled on the ground as he watched his master disappear. *My brother is dead. I watched my mother and father killed before my eyes. Nakia was my life. He was always beside me. He was my comforter and I was his protector. Now my brother is dead. Whom do I have now? I am alone. My entire family is dead. I can't live without Nakia.*

*How can I live without my brother? Great God Osiris, why did you take him from me? How could you do this to me? Why? Why? Why?* Nassar slammed his clenched fists on the ground angrily. He glared at the entrance to the garden where Kaemwaset had disappeared. *I hate you! I hate you! I hate you! Master Amsi would never shoot my brother! You did it, didn't you? You killed my brother! You wanted my brother dead! You are going to pay for this!*

Nassar stood on his feet and stamped his foot angrily on a bed of hyacinths. *How dare you kill my brother!* Nassar reached down and tore the flowers from their bed. His hands trembled as he grabbed the flowers and shredded them in his hands. He reached down and ripped the flowers from their bed, throwing them into the wind and scattering them. *You took everything away from me, Kaemwaset! I will never forgive you for this!*

Tears fell down Nassar's face, blinding him as he grabbed a head of lettuce and threw it on the ground angrily. He grabbed two cucumbers and slammed them on the ground, watching them shatter into tiny pieces. The boy screamed loudly and fell to his knees.

He watched as his arms trembled. His hands clenched into fists.

*I cannot live without Nakia. I just can't live without my brother. If Kaemwaset sees what I have done here in the garden, he will kill me anyway.* Tears fell from Nassar's eyes. *There's only one thing for me to do. I must join him.*

Nassar stood up and walked calmly out of the gardens and down the hall. He entered the reception hall, taking deep breaths with every step, knowing these breaths would be the last ones he would take.

He stepped out of the home and walked down the path towards the entrance. Laila saw him and waved to him.

"Hi, Nassar! Are you coming to help us?"

Nassar continued his solemn walk as he continued past Laila, his head bowed low.

"Nassar?" Laila asked as she ran to him. Laila ran in front of Nassar and looked up at him. She saw tears coming from his eyes. Although the boy could not speak, Laila could tell that Nassar was holding back. She saw the tears flowing down his face. "Nassar, are you crying?"

Laila watched as Nassar's mouth opened wide in a fierce scream. She gazed with horror at the tongue-less mouth opened wide to her. The back of his mouth had been charred black, the tiny remnant of the severed tongue twitched in the back of his throat.

*Get away!* "E-ay!" Nassar screamed loudly, pushing Laila on the ground harshly. Laila watched as Nassar's mouth was opened wide in a scream. She gazed with horror at the tongue-less mouth opened wide to her. Laila began to wail loudly as Issâm stuck his head out of the stables.

Issâm saw Nassar walking towards the entrance and Laila crying on the ground. Issâm ran out of the stables and towards the little girl laying on the ground sobbing.

"Nassar pushed me!" the little girl sobbed as she pointed to Nassar walking away calmly.

Issâm turned his head. "Nassar, did you push her?" Nassar continued to walk towards the entrance quietly. *Maybe he was told of his brother's death.* Where could that boy be going? "Laila, stay here, alright?"

"Nassar pushed me!" Laila cried.

"I will go speak to him, Laila. You stay here like a good little girl."

Issâm followed Nassar at a distance. The pre-teen boy walked out of the entrance. *Maybe he's going to the desert to find Nakia.* Nassar walked towards the nearby Nile. Issâm watched as people ran out of the city, their swords were raised high. They began to run into the open lands as smoke bellowed out of the city. Some men pointed at Nassar and Issâm felt his body tighten. *That mob is going to hurt Nassar!*

The mob of armed men raced towards Nassar. The boy turned his head and stopped. He watched the angry mob of men race towards him.

"Kill that boy!" the men called loudly.

"Five hundred dînars for his mangled corpse!"

Issâm's heart leapt into his throat as he saw Nassar stand calmly in the path of the furious mob. The men raised their swords and some men loaded bows with arrows to slay the boy. "No, don't kill this child!" Issâm called as he ran to Nassar's side. Issâm shielded Nassar with his kneeling body as the men hastily approached.

The mob approached and saw Issâm shaking as he kneeled in front of the boy to protect him. Issâm held his breath as the men stopped behind him. *Glorious Thoth, please protect me!*

"This child is too old! You! Have you seen a five-year-old boy run through here with a golden dagger?"

Issâm turned and shook his head. "No, I haven't!"

"If you find him, give him to us! The pharaoh will pay five hundred dînars to the one who brings the mangled corpse of the boy to him!"

"That boy must be here somewhere! Find him! Kill him!"

The men ran past Issâm and Nassar. Issâm sighed with relief. Thank you, my Lord Thoth!

Issâm looked into Nassar's eyes as he kneeled in front of him. Nassar's eyes were dull and red from the tears flowing down his cheek. Issâm touched the boy's cheek lightly. "Nassar, my boy, did Kaemwaset tell you about your brother?"

*I wanted to die, Issâm. Why did you stop them? I cannot live without my twin brother!*

Issâm watched as Nassar's face tightened. A flood of tears fell from Nassar's eyes as he fell forward on Issâm. Issâm held the boy against him tightly. Nassar rested his head against Issâm's shoulders as his body quaked.

"I am so sorry, Nassar," Issâm said, kissing the boy on the cheek. "It will be alright. I promise you."

*He's my brother and I won't ever see him again! Kaemwaset killed my brother! I cannot live without him! Why didn't you just let the mob slay me? I would be with my brother! I'm all alone! I loved my brother and now he is dead! Dead! If I would have been with him, I could have stopped Kaemwaset! Now my brother is dead!*

Nassar punched Issâm's back angrily. Issâm listened as Nassar tried to speak, but only incomprehensible mumblings came from him. "I know, Nassar." Issâm pulled his head away and looked at the child in the eyes. "We love you, Nassar. Myself, Baruti, Qamra, we all love you. We are your family. We can never take Nakia's place in your heart. Ever since you were brought to our home, I have always felt that you and your brother were the sons I never had."

*I know, Issâm. I remember our first night on the Al-Sakhir lands. My brother was crying and I was trying to be strong for him. Our warrior-father's courageous battle cries rang in my ears. Our parents had died that day in front of our eyes. That night, Qamra picked Nakia into her arms and she held him beside the fire. She rocked him in her arms, singing her songs of Isis. My poor brother cried all night. I fought you, but you held me in your arms. You hugged me tightly. I was afraid; I didn't know whom to trust. I was so tired; I couldn't fight anymore. You held me all night. Even though it looked like I didn't want you to hold me, it made me happy when you didn't give up on me.*

"Nassar, come back with me. You have had a difficult day."

*Issâm, I cannot return with you. I want to be with my brother and my parents again. I do not wish to live without Nakia!* Nassar pushed against Issâm, muttering unintelligibly.

"Nassar, I know this is difficult, but we must return back to the land before the master finds us absent!"

*Once the master sees what I did to his garden, he'll kill me anyway! If he finds you with me, Issâm, he'll kill you, too!*

"Nassar, it's time to go!" Issâm said as he stood up and took Nassar's hand.

*This is for your own good, Issâm. I'm sorry.*

Nassar clenched his free hand and pulled back. With a sharp motion, he harshly punched Issâm between the legs. Issâm quickly released Nassar and fell onto the ground holding his aching genitals. Issâm coughed deeply as Nassar walked away. The man reached out for the boy as Nassar left him on the sand.

Nassar walked calmly towards the Nile banks. He stepped into the reeds and searched for the edge of the water. Nassar stepped to the edge of the water after pushing through the reeds. He stepped into the water and smiled at its warmth. The water seemed warm and welcoming. He waded into the water and looked around him. When he would accompany Imani and Qamra to the water, he had seen the beasts of the waters and was warned of the dangers.

*Qamra has been a wonderful mother to me. I know she will miss my brother and I, but I know she will understand that I can't live without Nakia. I will ask the gods to smile on her and set her free from Kaemwaset's tyranny.*

He spread his arms in the water as he began to swim. *Soon I will be opening my arms to greet my mother and father in the land of Uala. They will be happy to see me. I will be able to speak to them and my spirit will be free from hunger and beatings from Kaemwaset. I will be happy to see my brother again. My brother and I will be reunited and we will be happy for eternity together.* Nassar looked towards the land as he heard Issâm's screams echoing through the air. Nassar dove under the water and held his breath. He clenched his fists, but soon swam to the surface gasping for breath and splashing.

*I must do this! Maybe there's something I can catch my foot on so I'm not tempted to swim to the surface.*

Nassar swam to the bottom of the Nile bed and searched for roots or a rock to trap his foot. The boy's lungs, deprived of oxygen, began to burn. He grit his teeth tightly to keep himself from surfacing. His chest tightened as he found a fisherman's net and a rock at the bottom. Nassar grabbed the net and placed the rock on top of the net. Nassar surfaced, tying the net around his right ankle, tears coming down his face. When he swam to the bottom of the Nile, he would only need to roll the rock beside his foot and he would be trapped.

*Nakia, welcome me home.*

Nassar dove below the surface and rolled the rock beside his foot. He released his grip on the rock and his arms rose above his head. Nassar looked above him and saw the sun sparkling over the surface of the water. The glittering surface above him made him smile in its beauty.

Nassar stopped holding his breath and opened his mouth. Water seeped in from his nose and his mouth. He floated in the water, looking upwards at the shimmering surface above him. *It's so beautiful.* He struggled for air which would not come. The rock had him successfully bound to the floor of the river.

His chest tightened from lack of oxygen. His arms, raised above him, waved with the motion of the water.

Bubbles raised from his nose as his body instinctually tried to breathe in its environment.

The twelve-year-old felt the water around him ripple as he felt himself slowly suffocate. Tears from his eyes merged with the water as he felt a set of hands on him. The child breathed deeply, bringing only more water into his lungs. Nassar's eyes rolled into the back of his head.

*Mother? Father? Is that you?*

The hands tugged on him harshly as the water waved around him. Nassar felt his body go numb and he smiled. *My brother is coming for me. I have no fear. I will join my mother and father.*

The hands tugged on his ankle as he felt his body move to the surface. A body knocked into him as he felt his pulse begin to stall. His head began to feel pressure.

His eyes watched as he began to approach the glittering surface.

*Mother and Father, welcome me home into your arms.*

Nassar felt himself break the surface as another person coughed and gasped for air. He felt an arm wrap under his arms and drag him across the water.

"He's not breathing!" the one holding him exclaimed.

"Nassar! Breathe!"

Nassar's head fell against the body as he felt his body weaken. His heart gave a last tired beat.

"Tabari! Watch out!"

Tabari looked behind him and saw a crocodile glaring at him. The reptile opened its jaws and snapped as he approached Tabari with his burden. "Seth!"

Tabari swam quickly towards the shore, keeping his eye on the approaching animal. Baruti threw rocks at the crocodile as he kneeled on the banks. The crocodile growled angrily and broke off its pursuit. "Be gone, creature of Seth!"

Tabari looked down at Nassar in his arms. The boy was not breathing. Tabari tensed as he felt the limp boy in his arms.

Tabari brought Nassar to the shore. Baruti pulled Nassar onto the ground and put his fingers to the boy's neck. Tabari panted heavily and coughed as he looked at Baruti.

"The boy is dead," Baruti said, shaking his head.

"We lost both of the twins in one day," Tabari said with a sad sigh.

Baruti pressed his lips to Nassar's and blew into the boy's mouth. He straddled the boy's hips and pressed upwards on the boy's chest.

"What are you doing, Baruti?"

"We must get the water out of the child's lungs! Maybe he will be able to breathe."

Baruti breathed into the boy's mouth again and pressed on his chest. "Come on, Nassar. Come back to us."

Issâm staggered to the two men and fell to his knees beside Nassar. "Poor child. Is he alive?"

Tabari shook his head. "He has no heartbeat."

"Baruti, do something!"

"I'm trying to, Issâm!" Baruti growled angrily.

Baruti breathed into Nassar's mouth and gave the boy's chest a light punch. "Nassar! Come back!"

Baruti breathed into the boy's mouth again as the child began to gag and cough. Nassar turned his head as water flowed from the child's throat. The child wheezed as air filled his lungs and his body quivered.

Baruti pulled the boy into his arms. "Glorious Anubis, praise you for returning this boy!"

Nassar trembled as he gripped onto Baruti tightly. The child began to cry in Baruti's arms.

Tabari caressed Nassar's back as Issâm planted a kiss on Nassar's forehead.

*I failed. I wanted to die. Why won't you all just let me die?*

Baruti cupped Nassar's face in his hands. "Why did you do such a foolish thing, Nassar? You could have died!"

*It's what I wanted!*

"We love you, Nassar! Do you really think we want to see you dead?" Baruti sobbed as he brought the boy into his arms and hugged him.

Issâm put a calm hand on Baruti's shoulder. "Nassar, Tabari could have died. He risked his life to save you."

Nassar turned his head to see Tabari coughing. His body was dripping from the Nile waters as he laid on the ground panting heavily. Nassar reached out and touched Tabari's hand.

"Nassar, I don't want to see you dead," Tabari said.

*I'm sorry I scared you. I didn't want anyone hurt because of me. Why couldn't you just leave me alone? I would have joined my family!*

The three men listened to Nassar's incomprehensible speech.

"Nassar, we don't want to see anything happen to you. Why did you give us such a fright?" Issâm said.

Baruti nodded. "We look after each other as a family. I will fight anyone who attacks a member of my family!"

"Baruti and I won't let anyone hurt you, Nassar," Tabari said. "I will be here to listen to you, even if you cannot speak. I know you speak through your actions." Tabari looked at Issâm. "May I say that punching Issâm in the genitals was not a very honorable action."

Nassar looked at Issâm and murmured something quietly. Issâm caressed Nassar's cheek. "I forgive you, but I know I won't be walking right for a day or so."

"Issâm was looking after your welfare," Baruti said. "That was not very nice, Nassar."

Nassar reached out to Issâm. Baruti released Nassar and stood. Issâm gathered Nassar into his arms and hugged him tightly. The former priest kissed Nassar on the cheek.

"I don't want you to die, Nassar," Issâm cried. "Please don't leave us." Issâm stood and picked the boy into his arms. Nassar held onto Issâm trembling. Issâm held Nassar in his arms and caressed the boy's back. "You are getting to be difficult to carry." Issâm placed Nassar on his feet.

"We should return to work before our absence is noticed!" Tabari said.

Baruti lead the group through the reeds as Gahiji rode down the path. The General turned his head and saw the three men with a child.

"You, there! Let me see that boy!"

Issâm stepped in front of Nassar. "A group of men came through here looking for a young child earlier. We haven't seen him."

Gahiji rode towards the group. Baruti and Tabari stood in front of Issâm. "You are slaves on the Al-Sakhir family land. Why are you outside of the walls?"

"We had to find Nassar," Tabari answered.

"Did you find him? Let me see him."
Issâm shook his head. "My lord, he is not the child you are searching for."

"Come from behind that man, Azizi!"

Nassar peeked his head from behind Issâm timidly.

"Have you seen a five-year-old boy with a golden dagger around here? His name is Azizi."

The men shook their heads. "No, sir."

"What has the boy done?" Baruti asked.

The General narrowed his eyes at his subordinate. "He is wanted by the pharaoh."

"So you are chasing after a young child with a mob of armed men? How can a young child defend himself?" Issâm asked.

Gahiji drew his sword and pointed it at Issâm. "You do not ask me questions."

"What crime has this child committed that you have the entire city armed and searching for him?"
"You speak too much for your own good, filth."

Baruti narrowed his eyes as Tabari held onto him. "Let go of me, Tabari!"

"No, Baruti! You can't do this!"

"It looks like I found myself a few slaves bent on escape from their master."

## XVII

### <u>Kaemwaset's Fury</u>

Amsi pulled the mobile horse behind him by its rope.
The painted wooden toy made by Tabari squeaked behind

him. He laughed as the horse bobbed up and down on its wheels. He ran down the hallway, watching it move as he heard his father's voice booming from the garden.

"Maybe animals tore at the beds," Imani said calmly.

Kaemwaset raised his fists in the entrance. "Nonsense! This is Nassar's doing! When I get my hands on that boy's neck, he will join his brother sooner than he thinks!"

Amsi dropped the rope of his toy and ran towards his furious father. The flowerbeds were ripped from their foundations. Vegetables were smashed against the ground into tiny pieces. Najam was kneeling in front of her master trembling.

"My husband, we cannot blame the child without speaking to him about this."

"Kaemwaset Al-Sakhir!" Amsi heard the pharaoh's General calling from the other side of the garden walls. "I have recovered your escaping servants!"

Imani and Amsi looked up at Kaemwaset whose face had turned red with fury.

"Kaemwaset! Wait!" Imani called to him as he stomped down the hallway angrily.

"Father!" Amsi followed after him. "Wait!"

Kaemwaset burst from the gates and saw Baruti, Tabari, Issâm, and Nassar on their knees in front of Gahiji. "What is the meaning of this?"

Gahiji pushed Baruti forward. "Your servant does not know how to hold his tongue."

Kaemwaset glared at Nassar and stood before him. "Did you rip up my garden, you little mongrel?" Nassar swallowed hard and lowered his head. Kaemwaset slapped Nassar across the face. "Did you tear up my flowerbed, you rotten, evil child?"

Imani ran to Nassar's side and gathered him into her arms. "My husband, hold your hand still!"

Kaemwaset turned to the three men. "Were you attempting to flee from my estate?"

"I followed Nassar to the Nile, my lord," Issâm said calmly.

"He tried drowning himself," Tabari said. "Baruti breathed life into his body again."

Kaemwaset glared at Baruti. "How dare you save this child's life!"

"I was not going to let him die, sir!" Baruti said loudly. "I did not want the child dead!"

Tabari looked into his master's wild eyes. "I swam into the Nile and saved him. I am the one who pulled him from the water before a crocodile could eat him."

The man glared at the three men kneeling before him. "I am disappointed in all three of you. Nassar, if you want to die, I certainly can do the honors!"

Imani wrapped her arms around Nassar and held him close. The boy panted heavily in the arms of the woman.

"Father, don't kill Nassar like Nakia!"

Imani glared at her husband as she slowly approached her husband. "Kaemwaset Al-Sakhir! Did you slay the boy Nakia?"

Amsi watched as the slaves stopped their work in the fields. Qamra had emerged from the house at the sound of her mistress' angry voice. Amsi stepped behind Qamra for protection.

"Tell me, Kaemwaset. Did you kill that poor child?" Imani asked as a tear fell from her eye.

Kaemwaset narrowed his eyes at his wife. "That child was going to escape! Can I be blamed for him running into the path of my arrow?"

"I asked him not to fire!" Amsi called out.

Kaemwaset turned to his son. "Amsi, return to the home."

"You hurt Nakia and you left him to die! He was still moving when we left!"

Nassar's eyes widened. *Maybe my brother isn't dead! Maybe he still lies in the desert!*

"That child was beyond repair! No doctor could have saved his life! Nakia is easily replaceable."

"So you left that poor child to die alone in the desert?" Imani whispered sadly. "I cannot believe you, my husband! I cannot believe you would kill that child in cold blood!"

Gahiji stood beside Kaemwaset. "It was just a slave child, my lady. They are easily replaceable."

"You hold your tongue! This is between my husband and myself!" Imani snarled.

Issâm grabbed Baruti's arm nervously. Nobody commanded the General of the Egyptian army to be silent! Tabari shuddered nervously as he remembered Gahiji threatening to slay him five years before.

"You cannot command me, woman!" Gahiji retorted.

"I cannot believe that you would treat your slaves so poorly! That you would make a sport of their deaths is appalling, Kaemwaset."

Kaemwaset pointed at the kneeling men. "What do you suppose we do with these three, my wife? They tried to escape!"

"We tried to save Nassar!" Issâm exclaimed.

"Silence!" Kaemwaset growled at Issâm, raising his hand to the priest. Imani grabbed her husband's wrist before it could connect with Issâm's face.

Imani stepped to Gahiji. "Thank you for returning them, General Gahiji. You may leave."

"I can ensure that they never run again," Gahiji said, gripping the hilt of his sword.

"No. You may leave."

Amsi felt Qamra's hand on his shoulder as General Gahiji sheathed his sword. He mounted his large, black horse and glared at the woman.

"Should any of them escape again, I will execute them for abandonment."

Amsi watched as Gahiji rode down the path. He watched his mother approach his father.

"You will let them go."

Kaemwaset glared at his wife. "Nassar destroyed my garden. He needs to repair it!"

"The child has lost his brother to your hatred today. He has suffered enough at your hand. Let him go."

Kaemwaset glared at the men. "Get out of my sight." Kaemwaset glared at his son as he stood on the top step. Amsi gripped onto Qamra's skirt as he trembled at the sight of his furious father. "Get out of my sight, my traitorous son."

Amsi watched as Kaemwaset burst through the doors to his home. He trembled as he watched his mother stand in front of Tabari. Imani reached down and cupped Tabari's cheek in her hand. "Tabari?"

Tabari tensed as he startled. Tabari bowed his head to her. "My lady."

"Thank you for saving Nassar's life."

Tabari raised his head, his skin still dripping from swimming in the Nile. "I couldn't let the boy die."

Qamra walked to Baruti, who bowed before his mistress. Amsi ran to his mother and tugged on her skirt. Imani brought her son into her arms. Imani and Amsi watched Qamra approach Baruti. Qamra tilted Baruti's face upwards gently. "You are very brave, my love." Qamra pressed her lips to Baruti's, cupping his face tenderly in her hands.

Baruti raised his hands and put them delicately on her hips. Baruti returned her tender kiss, closing his eyes and moaning between them.

Imani snuggled Amsi against him and looked down at Issâm. "Take Nassar home, Issâm. Take care of him."

Issâm bowed his head and stood slowly. "Thank you, my mistress." Nassar walked to Imani and hugged her around her waist. Imani caressed Nassar's head.

"I'm sorry for your loss, Nassar. I will pray for his Ka."

Issâm put his hand on Nassar's shoulders and lead him towards the slave home. "I will care for the boy, my lady. May the gods protect you."

Tabari stood and bowed his head to Imani. "Thank you, my lady. If you were not here, our master would have beaten us."

"You were not trying to escape. You were trying to save Nassar. I believe you."

"Baruti, let us go." Tabari looked down and saw Baruti and Qamra continue their kissing. Baruti's hands had pulled Qamra closer. "Baruti, are you trying to breathe life into Qamra?" Qamra whimpered into the kiss as she turned breathless. The two breathed quickly as their embrace became more heated. Baruti rubbed her back and began to caress her hip.

"I think Baruti is trying to do more than breathe life into her," Imani said with a chuckle.

"Remember, Amsi, that makes babies," Tabari said as he watched Baruti and Qamra.

Amsi watched wide-eyed. "Mother, is that right?"

Imani caressed her son's head. "That can be the beginning of it, yes, my son."

"I must get to Sabi. It is almost time to eat."

"How is Sabi's pregnancy progressing?"

Tabari smiled proudly. "Our child is active. I pray to Rā that our child is healthy."

"You have my blessings, Tabari. Go find Sabi."

Tabari bowed his head. "Thank you again, my lady."

Imani watched Tabari walk towards the grain. Sabi put her tool on the ground and embraced him. Imani looked at Qamra, who had pulled back from her kiss with Baruti and was caressing his face lovingly. "Qamra, perhaps you should return to your home. Nassar may need your presence." Baruti and Qamra continued to look into each other's eyes as they caressed each other. "Qamra, dear?"

Qamra gasped and turned her head. "My lady? My apologies!"

Imani chuckled. "You should return home. Nassar will need you tonight and your daughter will want her dinner."

Qamra bowed her head as Baruti stood beside her. "Yes, my lady!"

Amsi waved to Qamra as she and Baruti walked towards the slave home. Imani carried Amsi into the home and put him on the ground.

"Amsi, could you please tell Najam to return to the servant home? I will speak to your father."

Amsi nodded as he ran for the toy he abandoned in the hallway. He grabbed the little toy horse and ran to the garden where Najam was replanting the flowers she could salvage.

"Najam, mother said you may go home now."

"Is your father still angry?"

Amsi nodded. "My father is very angry."

"Stay away from him until he calms himself," Najam said.

Amsi nodded and returned into the hallway. He heard his father's voice raised in anger. *If my father hits my mother*

*as if he hit Issâm today, he could hurt her! I don't want
him to hurt my mother!*

Amsi crept towards his mother's bedchamber holding his
toy horse against him. He walked against the wall,
holding his breath as he heard his father yell angrily.
Amsi peeked inside the slightly open door.

"You cannot question my authority in front of my slaves!
They are our slaves, Imani! They are not our child! They
must be treated as the property that they are!"

Imani stood in front of her husband. "They are human
beings, Kaemwaset! They are children of Rā just as
ourselves! They are not beasts of burden!"

Kaemwaset stood in front of his wife and beat his chest
angrily. "I earned them! They are gifts given to me for
valor and serving my pharaoh!"

"Just because a few of them sold themselves into
servitude does not mean that they can be treated like
dogs!"

The man pointed an angry finger at his wife. "You cannot
tell me how to treat my slaves!"

"I see how you treat Qamra! You treat Issâm like horse
dung under your feet! You beat Baruti mercilessly on
your whim! They do not deserve such harsh treatment
from you!"

Kaemwaset rolled his eyes sarcastically. "I do not beat
Baruti! I simply discipline him."

"I watched you, Kaemwaset." Imani said, crossing her arms defiantly. "You beat him until he was bleeding. I don't know what he did to warrant such cruelty. What did he do?"

"That is none of your affair, woman!"

Imani glared at her husband. "You had Qamra and Baruti in your office and you were beating that boy for some purpose! What was it?"

"He had impregnated Qamra without my consent," Kaemwaset grinned.

"Our slaves need not your approval to live their own personal lives, my husband! That is no reason to smile! You should be ashamed of yourself for beating Baruti!"

Kaemwaset raised his fist angrily. "If he repeats that action again, I will beat him harder!"

"Why do you care if Baruti and Qamra have a child? Would you have beaten me had I not bore you a son?"

Kaemwaset lowered his fists. "No, my wife."

"The birth of a child is something to be celebrated. You don't beat the boy for having desires for a woman as beautiful as Qamra."

Imani stepped up to her husband. "Why do you hate the servants with such a deep loathing?"

"Kalila's blood was spilled by their kind. She was violated and slain. She believed those people were kind-hearted such as yourself. Look at how her life ended!"

Imani put her hand on her husband's shoulders. "Their hands did not spill your sister's blood. They did not violate her."

"My sister's life was taken by mongrels with morals such as theirs!"

Imani shook her head. "Did Issâm kill her? Issâm wouldn't hurt a fly. What about Tabari? My husband, these men did nothing. I know none of them would harm me."

"I do not trust them. I will not have my son see his mother killed by a savage! My son will learn not to trust their kind! They are dangerous! They only seek to destroy! I will not have my son influenced by the evil in their hearts!"

Imani stepped beside the fireplace. "You should know about evil in the heart, my husband."

"What is that supposed to mean?"

"How could you slay Nakia? Kaemwaset, he was only a boy."

Kaemwaset narrowed his eyes. "He was a boy who could grow up and rise against me and slaughter my wife."

"Nassar is alone and it is because of your hatred, Kaemwaset. I guarantee you that boy has pain in his heart because of your actions."

Kaemwaset turned his back on his wife. "His heart knows no pain. His type knows only violence."

"How could you say such nonsense? When those boys first arrived, they were so terrified! They were sweet boys, Kaemwaset. I am going to miss their laughter."

Kaemwaset's lip curled in disgust. "Nassar still laughs."

"Since you took his tongue, he has changed. You took that child's laughter away," Imani said, tears coming down her face. "You hurt that child and I will never forgive you, Kaemwaset, for causing such pain on that little boy."

Kaemwaset turned to his wife. "That child belongs to me! Had Pharaoh Atenhotep not favored me, his army would have killed that boy along with his mother and father! That boy owes me his life and now look at what he has done to our garden!"

"That boy is angry at you for slaying his brother!"

"If you feel so strongly about the boy, Imani, maybe I should go and cut his throat now! If that child belongs to me and he is my property, then I have every right to do it! It will be no different than killing a lamb!"

Imani looked at her husband with pity. "I'm sorry you feel such malice towards a helpless child."

Kaemwaset took his golden dagger in his hand. "I'll do it right now!"

Imani ran in front of her husband, blocking his path. "You will not lay a finger on that boy!"

"Step aside!"

"You will not harm that boy!"

Kaemwaset seethed angrily. "I will not have my boy grow up to think that he can be made a fool by his servants! He will grow into a strong man who will not be afraid to discipline his slaves, his property!"

"Amsi does not share your hatred for the slaves, my husband."

Kaemwaset glared at his wife. "He should learn the evil which dwells in their hearts. He needs to grow tougher skin. My son will learn how to be a strong property owner. When it is his time to take a mate, I will choose from a family that I know will be a perfect match. I will make certain his wife does not share your mercy."

Kaemwaset pushed past Imani and opened the door quickly. Amsi watched his father walk down the hallway angrily.

## XVIII

### Reunion

Qamra placed a blanket over Nassar as he laid on his reed mat. Qamra's eyes went to Baruti who was tucking Laila under her blanket. Baruti looked up at her and smiled. Qamra returned the smile and looked down at Nassar.

"Nassar, I'm glad you're still here with us. You worried me." Nassar looked up at Qamra and blinked silently. "I really would have missed you, my little warrior." Nassar reached for Qamra's hand and gripped it tightly. Qamra smiled at the boy. "I pray that Isis welcomes Nakia home. I pray that she protects you in your dreams, Nassar."

Nassar opened his mouth and muttered unintelligible sounds. "You are a loving boy, Nassar," she said caressing his cheek lightly. "Dream pleasant dreams."

Nassar's eyes slowly began to close, but snapped open suddenly.

"Don't be afraid to sleep, Nassar. Tabari and Sabi are outside the home. Issâm is sitting beside the fire here. He won't let anything bad happen to you." Qamra saw Issâm writing on papyrus. His inkwell sat beside his feet as he muttered quietly. "Issâm? What are you doing?"

Issâm looked up at Qamra. "Thoth has inspired me to tell Nakia's story. He is speaking through me. I will show you what I have written when we are finished."

Qamra looked down at Nassar. "Issâm won't leave you alone, alright?"

Nassar nodded and yawned. He turned on his side and looked into the fire. Issâm was murmuring quietly as he dipped his reed into the inkwell again. Baruti kissed Laila on the cheek and sat beside the little girl.

Qamra watched Nassar's eyes close and his body relax. "We almost lost him today, Baruti." Qamra kissed Nassar on the cheek, making the drowsy boy smile and sigh with contentment.

"I know. When I saw him lifeless beside the Nile, I was afraid. I didn't want to lose him."

Qamra caressed Nassar's head. "I feel badly for him."

"I know how he must feel. He was an orphan and now he has lost his only brother."

Qamra watched as Laila slipped into slumber. "Baruti, let us go for a walk."

"Do you think we can really leave Nassar alone? What if he needs you?"

Qamra stood and walked beside Baruti. She reached down and caressed his cheek. "What if I need you?"

Baruti grinned as he felt Qamra's soft hand caress his cheek. He stood up and looked down at Issâm. "Could you watch the children?"

"Consider it done," Issâm said as he continued to write tirelessly.

Baruti took Qamra's hand and lead her outside. Sabi was straddling Tabari's lap and kissing his neck tenderly. Tabari kissed her shoulder, rubbing her back.

"We will be back shortly," Qamra said. "The children are sleeping and Issâm is writing."

"Very well," Tabari giggled as Sabi nibbled at his neck.

Tabari's hand glided up Sabi's body towards her breasts, making the woman moan.

Baruti lead Qamra down the path. "Do you think they heard a word you said?"

"I don't believe they did," Qamra said as she held Baruti's hand. She looked up at the sky which was filled with twinkling stars. Baruti held her hand tightly as they walked down the path. "Praise Isis that Imani was with you and the others today."

Baruti shook his head. "I was almost certain that Kaemwaset would have whipped us. We were just trying to rescue Nassar."

Qamra stopped and pulled on Baruti's arm lightly. Baruti turned his head and saw Qamra's head lowered in the moonlight.

"Qamra?"

"Nakia," Qamra whimpered as she began to cry. "My poor little Nakia. I'm going to miss that boy."

Baruti wrapped his arms around her slowly as he looked into the sky. "He is in no more pain, Qamra. He is no longer subject to Kaemwaset's anger."

"Nakia was such a loving boy, Baruti! He had such a beautiful smile!" Qamra sniffled as Baruti brushed a tear from her cheek. "I couldn't cry in front of Nassar. I have to be strong for him."

Baruti nodded. "Nakia was a peaceful soul. He never fought with anyone. He was always obedient and I've never seen anyone be able to communicate with the animals as well as he."

Qamra looked into Baruti's eyes. "I was afraid that Kaemwaset would order the General to kill you."

Baruti raised his hand and caressed Qamra's cheek. He leaned down and kissed her gently on the lips. He wrapped his arms around her and held her close. They both moaned into the kiss as Baruti felt her right leg hook around him and hold him close to her. Baruti's hand drifted down to her buttocks and rubbed them lightly.

Qamra whimpered into the kiss as she felt Baruti reach down and pick her into his arms. He carried her into the field of corn. He laid her on the ground and rested beside her. He continued to caress her thighs softly as she whimpered into the kiss. Qamra moaned under Baruti's light touch.

Baruti kissed down Qamra's neck as she kissed his ear. "Qamra, there is something I must ask you."

Qamra turned her head and cupped Baruti's cheek in her own. "Yes, Baruti?"

Baruti took Qamra's hand and kissed it. "Would you do me the honor of becoming my wife?"

Qamra's eyes widened and she gasped. "Baruti?"

"I would want for you to be my mate, Qamra. I love you. I would like to take none other as my wife for eternity."

Qamra sat up and looked down at Baruti. "How can we, Baruti? The master would forbid our union!"

Baruti sat beside her. "I care not for what Kaemwaset wishes! If he forbids our union, I would fight him!"

Qamra looked down as a tear fell from her eyes. "Baruti, the master took me into his arms and kissed me today."

Baruti narrowed his eyes angrily. "That son of a jackal! If he touches you, I will rip his hands off myself!"

"Baruti, he could have you killed!" Qamra exclaimed. "I don't want that to happen."

"I love you, Qamra, and I will not tolerate that snake putting his slimy scales on you!"

Qamra sniffled as she took his hand. "Baruti, I believe he intends on taking me again without my consent."

"Did he say anything to you?"

Qamra looked at Baruti. "He claimed that Rā commanded him to father a daughter by me." Baruti glared at the house. "Kaemwaset then said that should Rā demand that he father a son by my womb, that he would obey Rā's command."

Baruti turned to Qamra. "I will not allow him to hurt you, Qamra," Baruti said kissing her hand.

"I fear the master's anger, Baruti. What if he makes me with child again?"

Baruti kissed her hand and pressed his lips to hers again. Qamra wrapped her arm around Baruti as the man kissed her to the ground. Baruti kissed Qamra's jaw and caressed her cheek. "The master will not succeed. If I must challenge him and should I die in the process, even death will not stop me from loving you."

Qamra whimpered as she felt Baruti rubbing against her. Qamra looked into the sparkling pools of Baruti's eyes. "Baruti, I adore you."

Baruti leaned down to her and kissed her forehead. "Will you do me the honor of becoming my wife, Qamra? I vow to protect you and to always love you."

Qamra smiled at Baruti. "I will be your wife, Baruti," she said as she kissed his ear.

Baruti smiled and kissed her forehead. "You have made me the happiest man in Egypt, Qamra."

Qamra moaned as she felt Baruti caress her. She closed her eyes as she felt Baruti kiss down her neck. She whimpered as she felt Baruti grind himself against her.

Qamra turned her head to the side as she felt Baruti kiss her neck. She whimpered as she felt Baruti's hand wander between her legs. "Baruti, I love you," she whispered.

Qamra heard the neighing of horses and opened her eyes. She tilted her head back as she felt Baruti touching her intimately. "Baruti, I think the horses in the stable are uneasy." Qamra heard a familiar neighing of a horse. "That sounds like Hamza!"

"They probably miss Nakia," Baruti moaned as he cupped Qamra's breast in his hand.

Qamra shook her head. "No, it's coming from the entrance! Baruti, remove yourself from me! Five horses just entered through the gate!"

Baruti raised his head and saw five elaborately decorated horses gallop quickly through the entrance. They both heard the barking of several dogs. *The jackal-god Anubis beckons!* The horses ran towards the slave home. "I hope that is not the mob from this morning! Issâm said that a mob of men almost killed Nassar!"

Qamra gasped as she felt something tighten around her throat. Sabi and Tabari screamed in fear. "Baruti, remove yourself! We have to get to the home!"

Baruti reluctantly removed himself from Qamra as the woman stood on her feet. "I'll be there in a moment!"

Qamra ran to the horses and saw five men dismounting. "Stop right there!" Qamra called loudly.

Qamra saw Tabari and Sabi backed against the wall of the slave home. The torch burning outside cast light on their terrified faces.

"Don't kill us!" Tabari exclaimed. "My girlfriend is with child!"

Qamra breathed quickly as she arrived beside the couple. "What is it that you want here?" Qamra asked as she heard Baruti's footsteps nearby.

Issâm stepped from the entrance of the home and looked wide-eyed at the men dressed in long, black cloaks. Their heads were covered by cloth, revealing only their eyes. One of the men held an object covered in a black cloth. The jackals which accompanied them sat at their masters' feet, panting and yipping.

Issâm stepped beside Sabi. "You are the Bedu of the desert! I have heard of your kind."

Baruti arrived beside Qamra and glared at the five Bedouin men standing before the other slaves. "Why are you here? If you are here to slay my friends, then you are sadly mistaken."

"Let them speak," Issâm said, holding out a hand to the fiery Baruti.

The man approached Qamra and held the object towards her. "We have been instructed to give this to you."

Qamra looked at the long object covered by the black cloak. "What is it?"

Issâm looked towards the edge of the cloth and saw two little motionless fingers sticking from the bottom. "Sweet, Blessed Thoth! Nakia!"

Qamra reached out and took the long, light object in her hands. She felt her heart leap into her throat as she looked down at the body covered in the black cloth. She could feel bones and dried blood against her skin. Her eyes swelled with tears as she looked up at the men.

"Where did you find him?"

"We travel the desert. We travel to Heliopolis to sell our wares."

Issâm put his hand on the cloth as he lowered his head and bit his lip. "Poor Nakia." Issâm felt his hand rise against the cloth. "Could it be true? Nakia?" Issâm pulled back the cloth covering the child.

Qamra and the others watched as Nakia's breathing was shallow. The child's fingers twitched, his shoulder had been bandaged. "You have saved him!"

"The child was found on his back and instructed us to bring him here. We know not what power kept him alive," the leader spoke. "Our jackals lead us to him. We thought they had found another corpse in the desert."

Another man stepped beside the leader. "His steed would not allow us near his body. We tried chasing him, but he resisted leaving the child's side."

"The wound was packed with sand when we found him in the desert," a woman said. She added with a smile, "He did not enjoy the medicine I gave him."

Qamra chuckled as tears fell down her cheeks. She sniffled with a nod. "He doesn't enjoy my medicines either, my lady. Thank you very much for returning our little Nakia to our family."

Issâm returned inside the home and emerged a few moments later with a handful of coin. He approached the leader with a smile. "I would like to offer you this as a token of our gratitude."

The man raised a cloaked hand. "I cannot accept."

"Then we shall purchase some of your wares as a token of our appreciation," Issâm said.

Issâm bought a gold necklace with the Ibis of Thoth. Baruti had bought himself and Qamra matching rings as a symbol of their new commitment to each other.

"You may want to give the child water. Anubis may yet call him back to the Land of the Blessed Dead," another man said as he mounted his horse.

The men mounted their horses and looked at the group of adults hovering over Nakia. Qamra kissed Nakia's forehead as Tabari took the boy's hand lightly. Sabi caressed Nakia's cheek tenderly as Issâm prayed.

"May the gods keep you safe," the Bedouin leader said, bowing his head. "Imshi!"

The jackals howled as they followed their fleeing masters.

Tabari took Hamza's reigns and lead him towards the stables. The tall stallion reared reluctantly. "Hamza, Nakia will be alright! You cannot stay out here! Follow me! I'll feed you and treat you!" Upon hearing 'treat,' the horse quickly complied and followed Tabari towards the stables.

Qamra carried Nakia inside the home and laid him beside the fire. "Sweet Mother Isis, please tell me what I need to do for this child!"

Baruti took a cup of water from a bucket. Issâm supported the boy's upper body as Baruti pressed the rim of the cup to Nakia's lips lightly. "Drink, boy. Come on."

Nakia's lips opened slightly as Baruti gently tilted the cup. Baruti smiled as the boy sipped.

"Be careful not to give him too much," Issâm said. "We cannot have him choke on his vomit."

Sabi ran to Nassar and took the boy's arm, shaking it lightly. "Nassar! Nassar! Wake!"

The boy clenched his fists and tried to punch Sabi in his sleep. "Nassar, boy! Look who is here! Nakia is back!"

Nassar's eyes opened slowly as he looked up at Sabi. The smiling woman looked down at him. "Nassar, your brother has been returned to us alive."

Nassar turned his head and saw his brother's arm laying beside the fire. Issâm was caressing Nakia's forehead lovingly as Baruti was slowly offering his brother water from a spouted drinking cup. "Good boy, Nakia," Issâm said quietly. "Drink."

Qamra was kneeling beside his brother, praying to Isis and holding Nakia's hand.

Nassar slowly stood on his feet and held his breath as he approached his brother's side. He watched as Nakia laid limp against Issâm, his chest rising quickly and sharply. His shoulder had been bandaged and written on the bandages were hieroglyphics. Dried blood was caked on Nakia's arm.

*Nakia? Nakia. My brother, I never thought I would see you again! What did that beast do to you?* "Ah-e-ah?" Nassar whimpered as he stood beside Baruti. Baruti looked over at Nassar and moved aside beside Qamra. *When I heard you were dead, there was nothing left for me to live for. Now, you are here with me again. Brother, open your eyes.* Nassar kneeled beside his brother and touched his shoulder gently. *Brother, please open your eyes! I'm here, my brother. I thought you were dead. A piece of me had died, but I found it resurrected again in your return! Please say something to me! I love you, my brother. Welcome home.*

"Ah-e-ah?" Nassar whimpered again. The twin hugged his brother tightly, his body wracked with heavy sobbing. Nassar buried his face in Nakia's neck and wept, his fingers digging into Nakia's skin. He felt his chest tighten and his heart race. Issâm reached over and touched Nassar's back as a long, loud, sorrowful wail came from the boy.

*I'm never going to leave you again, Nakia,* Nassar thought as he laid beside his brother.

Issâm continued to hold Nakia against him. "Baruti and Qamra, I will care for the twins tonight."

Qamra looked down at Nakia and caressed the boy's cheek. "He needs his rest. I trust that you will care for him, Issâm. Baruti and I shall return to the fields."

Tabari returned to the home, yawning. "Hamza put up a good fight, but when I gave him a carrot, he was quickly placated."

Sabi looked at Tabari. "How are we going to explain Hamza and Nakia's return to the master?"

"The master rarely enters the stables," Qamra said. "By the time he notices Hamza's return, Nakia should be recovered."

"If he survives the night," Issâm said, looking down at the boy with shallow breathing and sweat beading on his forehead.

"What about little Master Amsi?" Sabi asked. "He comes and listens to Issâm's stories."

"Master Amsi was very upset at the loss of Nakia. Knowing Nakia is safe will help him feel better."

Qamra sighed as she looked down at the boy. "I will look for medicine for him. Perhaps I can find some sweet-tasting leaves to put in there so he cannot taste the bitterness."

Qamra and Baruti left the home and walked down the path. As Qamra held Baruti's hand, she turned to him. "I cannot believe that Nakia has returned! It is the blessing of the gods that he has returned to us."

"Is it?" Baruti asked, looking away from her. "Nakia could have been free! Nakia could have been away from this place!" Baruti turned to her, his body tensing. "Why in the name of Anubis would he wish to return to his place of tyranny and unnecessary cruelty?"

Qamra reached up and put her hand on Baruti's shoulder. "Nassar. The twins have never been apart."

Baruti sighed. "I guess what you say is the truth."

"When Kaemwaset takes one of them, they immediately seek each other out upon their return. Nakia would rather suffer here than be without his brother."

Baruti lead Qamra to the field where they had been before the Bedu had arrived.

"I cannot believe that Nakia is alive," Qamra whispered as she sat on the ground.

Baruti reached to Qamra's cheek and caressed it lovingly. "It is a sign from the gods. It is a blessing onto our home."

Qamra smiled. "Yes, perhaps it is an omen of good things to come."

Baruti returned the smile and leaned over to kiss his new wife. Qamra laid on her back, pulling Baruti on top of her. Baruti looked down at her with a grin. "Where were we?"

## XIX

### <u>Forbidden Friendship</u>

Amsi's eyes switched from his mother to his father anxiously. Qamra and Nassar held pitchers of wine and water for their masters to drink. Amsi watched as his father glared at his mother. He ate a piece of apple slowly as his eyes looked at his mother, sitting beside him and eating calmly.

"Qamra! Wine!" Kaemwaset bellowed as he slammed his golden goblet on the table, making it shake from the impact. Amsi and Nassar gasped as they jumped.

"Husband, do not frighten the children. They are not to blame."

"My son was not afraid. He is an Al-Sakhir! We are afraid of nothing!" Kaemwaset growled.

Amsi swallowed hard as Qamra poured a cup of wine for his father. Kaemwaset brought the golden goblet to his lips and drank quickly, slamming it on the table again.

"My son, what are my expectations for you?" Kaemwaset asked as he faced his son.

Amsi stared wide-eyed at his father, who stared at him intently. Kaemwaset's body was tight, his shoulders were leaned forward. His falcon-like eyes pierced through Amsi, as if staring into his soul. Kaemwaset's fists were clenched tightly as they rested against the table. His lips were stiffened, ready to open wide and flood with room with a bellowing voice should his answer not be the correct one.

Nassar saw the monster of rage trying to break forth from Kaemwaset and he backed behind Imani. Imani could hear the jug rattling in Nassar's nervous hands.

"Kaemwaset, let us not ruin a wonderful meal," Imani said calmly.

"Hold your tongue, woman!" Kaemwaset growled. "I am speaking to my son, my future heir! He shall be the one to make offerings to my tomb upon my departure to the Underworld! My son, what do I expect of you?"

Amsi looked at Nassar, who was looking at him from behind Imani.

"Do not look to that silent vermin for your answer, boy! What do I expect of you?"

Amsi looked at his father. "You wish for me to be lord of the land and give offerings to you?"

"Yes, my son," Kaemwaset smiled. "In fact, I have arranged a marriage for you. Her father is a wonderful, rich, and powerful man!  She will be a woman of great virtue for you!"

Imani put down her piece of bread. "My husband, I thought we were not going to arrange a marriage for our son."

Kaemwaset beat his chest. "I am the father and my word is law! My son is going to be as strong as I! He will follow in my footsteps and he will continue the great legacy which I have started!"

"I want him to love a girl whom he wishes to marry, Kaemwaset!" Imani said, holding out her hands. "This is not right."

"When we have a girl, you may do with her as you wish. This is my son and we will do things the way I believe they should be done! He will learn how to be strong and manage my slaves well."

Imani stood and looked at Qamra. "I am finished eating, Qamra. Come with me, please."

Qamra placed the wine jug on the table beside her furious master.  She followed Imani to her bedchamber and watched as Imani sat beside the window.

"I wish I could quell the anger in your master's heart, Qamra," Imani said sadly. "I love him and yet I find his demeanor becoming more overbearing with every passing day."

Imani looked below at the working field slaves.  Laila was carrying vegetables, skipping as she carried them to baskets lined beside the road.  Baruti was using a bronze hoe to till the soil. His body was covered in sweat as he worked in the hot field. Issâm was bending over, pulling dead plants from their foundation and weeding the soil. Karida was carrying cups of water to the toiling men.

"I worry what will become of all of you should Kaemwaset have his way," Imani said with a sigh.

Qamra kneeled before Imani and bowed her head. "You are a merciful mistress. It is my hope that Master Amsi learns from you the old ways, the ways things used to be before Pharaoh Runihura assumed the throne."

"There is venom in that boy's voice. His heart is so full of disdain. Kaemwaset is completely loyal to him. Rest assured, Qamra, my hand will never be raised to you in anger."

Qamra smiled at her mistress. "Thank you, my lady. I have some wonderful news. Baruti has asked for my hand in marriage." Qamra showed Imani the Bedouin ring that Baruti had purchased.

"Where did you get a ring?"

Qamra smiled as she put a hand on Imani's leg. "My mistress, Nakia has been returned to us."

Imani gasped and covered her mouth. "Nakia! How is the boy?"

"Do not tell your husband, my lady! Nakia is resting in our home. It was hard dragging Nassar away from his brother. Issâm is returning every hour to water the boy and Sabi is feeding him. The boy has not moved since he was returned after nightfall."

Imani sighed. "What are his injuries?"

"His right shoulder was bandaged and he may have some internal injuries from falling off of Hamza. He must have lost a great deal of blood when Kaemwaset removed the arrow. I believe that is our biggest obstacle is to his recovery."

"I want to see him," Imani said. "I do not want my husband to see me enter during the daylight hours. I will visit him tonight."

"I think he would like that, my lady."

Amsi and Nassar ran into Imani's bedchamber. "Mother, Nassar is trying to tell me something, but I don't know what he wants!"

Nassar tugged on Imani's long, white skirt. He let out unintelligible mumbles as he jumped up and down with a smile on his face.

"Nassar, what is it?" Imani asked.

Nassar pointed to himself and to an empty space beside him. He jumped up and down and tugged on her skirt again.

"I just told her that Nakia is back," Qamra explained.

Amsi gasped. "Nakia!"

Imani pressed her finger to her lip. "Amsi, do not tell your father that Nakia is back. He could become angry."

Amsi smiled and jumped. "I have to see him!"

Nassar nodded and took Amsi's hand. The two boys dashed from the room. Nassar's white skirt whipped behind him as he ran. Amsi's gold necklace and bracelets jingled as he ran, struggling to keep up with the other boy.

Nassar lead Amsi down the hall and out of the door leading to the outside. He ran Amsi down the path towards the slave home.

Sabi was rocking Nakia against her breast as the two boys ran into the house. "Good boy, Nakia. Oh! Hello, Little Master Amsi!"

"Ah-E-ah!" Nassar exclaimed.

"Nakia!" Amsi ran to Nakia. "Is he awake?"

Sabi smiled as Nakia laid limp in her arms. "He's asleep right now," Sabi said, rocking Nakia's upper body. "He's a good boy," Sabi whispered quietly, caressing Nakia's cheek.

"I thought my father made him die," Amsi said, reaching out cautiously and touching Nakia's limp arm.

"He may still cross into the Land of the Dead, Master Amsi. We must see if the gods wish to take him."

Amsi hugged Nakia lightly. "I don't want him to go!"

"Do not tell your father he is here, Amsi. Your father could come here and hurt Nakia. We don't want that."

Amsi shook his head. "No, I don't want him hurt. I'm happy he's back."

Nakia gasped for breath as his fingers twitched and his head fell back. His lungs wheezed as his eyes opened. Nakia's eyes rolled into the back of his head as he struggled for air. Sabi listened as Nakia's chest rattled. She could hear the congestion in the child's lungs as he breathed deep.

"Nakia?" Sabi asked, holding Nakia closer. "Nakia, breathe, little one." *Nassar told us that he was born with weak breathing. His parents didn't expect the weaker second twin to survive. Poor child.*

Amsi waved his hand towards Nakia, hoping to give the boy more air. Nassar watched with a worried face as his twin gasped for air.

Sabi took Nakia's hand and held his head upwards. "Breathe, little one. Watch me." Sabi took a deep breath and exhaled slowly. "Do it with me." Nakia squeezed her hand as he hacked the familiar cough. Nakia turned his head and coughed blood onto Sabi's breast. The child took in deep breaths, wheezing and trembling.

"Good boy," Sabi said as she felt the boy's body shake with coughing. "Good boy," she said, kissing the boy's ear.

Nakia whimpered as he held onto her weakly.

"Is Nakia sick?" Amsi asked.

Sabi caressed Nakia's cheek as the boy's body relaxed against her. "Since Nakia arrived here, Amsi, he has had difficulties with breathing. He coughs often because his lungs have difficulty holding air. When he was a baby in his mother's belly, his lungs did not become strong like yours or Nassar's."

Amsi pointed to Sabi's stomach. "Will your baby have good lungs?"

Sabi smiled. "I pray to Bes and Tawaret that she does."

"Nassar, you should return to the home before the master comes looking for you."

Nassar hugged Nakia and ran from the home. Amsi looked at Nakia and watched him fall asleep against Sabi. The boy's fingers twitched in his sleep as Sabi laid him on the ground. She covered him with a blanket and caressed his head.

"I must return to my work. Please try not to wake him, little master." Sabi turned to the entrance.

Amsi looked up at Sabi with a smile. "I won't."

Sabi stopped at the entrance and turned her head. "If you plan to play by the Nile today, little master, proceed with caution. There is a crocodile there that almost made a meal of Nassar yesterday."

Amsi gasped. "Wow! I'll be careful."

Amsi looked down at Nakia and put a timid hand on him. *I'm glad my father didn't kill you, Nakia. I was scared when I thought you would die. I'm glad you're back and I promise not to tell him that you are here.* Amsi thought of Sabi's warning and Nassar.

*A crocodile almost ate Nassar by the Nile? I wonder if it's still there. What if it tries eating Nassar again? Amsi's eyes widened. What if it tries to eat Qamra or my mother? I can't let that happen!*

Amsi ran out of the slave house and towards the stables. He slipped inside the open door and saw Hamza glaring at him. Amsi kept a vigilant eye on the large, black stallion, who was returning the vigilant gaze. Amsi grabbed his bow and arrow.

*I can't stick it with my dagger. I have to hit it from far away so I don't get bitten. That is what Tabari told me once. I can't hurt Nakia with my bow and arrow. I promise not to hurt anyone I care about with this.*

Hamza stamped his foot and bellowed air from deep in his powerful lungs.

"I'm sorry about Nakia, Hamza. He's getting better." Hamza's stamping quieted in response to Amsi's words of encouragement.

Amsi ran out of the door with his quiver and bow. His little sandals pat against the dirt as he ran towards the entrance to the land beyond. Ahead of him, he saw the reeds of the Nile.

*Here I come, big crocodile! Beware of Amsi Al-Sakhir!*

The child grabbed an arrow from his quiver and placed it in his bow. He held onto the back of the arrow and the string as he cautiously entered the reeds.

*Here I come, big crocodile. It's time to be afraid of big, strong Amsi!*

Amsi crept through the brush, moving as silently as possible through the thick underbrush. *Amsi, the hunter-warrior, is coming for you, Sobek! Be very afraid and cry like an infant!*

Amsi's lips curled into a smile as he took a deep breath, stalking his prey. His heart raced as he enjoyed his stalking game. His sandals trampled the leaves and crunched them as he walked.

The five-year-old stopped as he heard a noise nearby. "Hope you like your last yummy meal, Sir Sobek!" Amsi pulled back on the arrow and jumped out of the reeds pointing the arrow at the target.

Azizi turned his head quietly, his eyes full of tears. "Hello, Amsi."

"Azizi, what are you doing here?" Amsi asked, looking at the object of Azizi's attention:a floating corpse in the Nile.

Azizi took a reed in his hand and poked a headless body floating in the water in front of him. "My mother will not wake." The reed snapped as Azizi buried his face in his hands and cried. The boy leaned over, touching the ground with his forehead, sobbing into the soil.

Amsi placed his bow and arrow on the ground and walked beside the body. He kneeled on the bank of the river and put his hand lightly on the body. The cold, headless corpse bobbed in the water as Amsi pressed on it.

"Mother, why did you have to sleep? Why did Osiris take you and father?"

Amsi turned to the boy crying on the ground. "Why are you here, Azizi? There are big crocodiles here who tried to eat my friend, Nassar. You should go home."

Azizi sniffled as he raised his head. "The pharaoh put fire to my home!"

"You can't stay here or a crocodile will eat you!"

Azizi straightened his back and nodded, rubbing his eyes. "Let it come. I won't run," Azizi said as his eyes focused on the floating body in front of him.

Amsi sat beside Azizi and put his arm around him. He looked at the other boy beside him. Azizi's eyes were blood-shot red, his hair was dirty, and the child's skin was covered in mud and dried blood. Amsi breathed deep and wrinkled his nose at a slight odor coming from the boy. "You don't have anywhere to go?"

Azizi shook his head slowly. "I'm not going until Sobek comes."

Amsi looked down at Azizi's blood-stained skirt. "I can get my ball! Do you want to play with that?"

"No." Azizi held his stomach as it began to sting again from lack of food. "I'm so hungry."

Amsi looked around nervously, hoping that the crocodile was not waiting for the perfect moment to strike. *I don't know what to say to him. Playing helped me feel better when I thought Nakia was dead. Maybe if I get him to play maybe he'll feel better.* "Stay here! I'll be right back!"

Azizi grabbed onto Amsi's arm. "Tell nobody that I'm here, Amsi!"

"Ow! You're hurting my arm, Azizi!" Amsi screamed.

Azizi released Amsi's arm quickly. "Sorry." Amsi turned as Azizi looked up at the boy decorated in gold. "Amsi?" Amsi turned, his gold glittering in the mid-day sun. "Hurry back," the dirty, starving boy said sadly.

Amsi nodded. "I will! Stay here!"

Amsi ran towards his home and ran through the door leading to the gardens. His sandals patted against the ground as he ran into the kitchen.

Najam was removing fresh bread from the clay oven when she saw Amsi grabbing a small basket. "Are you hungry, Amsi?"

"Yes! I'm very hungry, Najam! Do you have some bread and some fish?"

Najam chuckled as she saw the child rummaging through some jars and placing oranges and raisins in a small basket. "Are you going to eat all that food, little Master Amsi?"

Amsi nodded as he shoved a handful of raisins into his mouth. "Rathins yunny!" he smiled with a full mouth.

"One would think you have not eaten in three days, child!" Najam said as she placed some fish and some duck into the basket. "Why do you need all this food? If your father sees you feeding the other servants, you know how angry he will become."

Amsi swallowed and took the basket in his hands. "I'll be back in a moment! Don't take this food, Najam!" Amsi ran out of the kitchen and returned with his toy ball in his hands.

Amsi picked the basket into his hands and kicked the ball across the ground as he hurried out of the garden gate. Amsi grunted as he carried the heavy basket in his hands and put it on the ground, panting.

"Amsi, do you need help with that?" Baruti asked.

"It's heavy," Amsi said.

Baruti dropped his work and picked up the basket. "Where do you want this, Amsi?"

"Follow me!" Amsi called, bouncing the ball on the ground. Baruti watched as they walked outside the boundary. Amsi skipped, playing with his toy one last time.

"Master Amsi, where are we going?"

"Follow me, Baruti!" Amsi called, running towards the reeds. He bounced on his feet as he saw Baruti approach the reeds. "STOP!" Baruti stopped walking and raised a curious eyebrow at his master. "Drop it!" Amsi said, pointing to the ground. Baruti slowly lowered the basket of food on the ground. "Go away!" Baruti's eyes widened at the sudden, harsh command. Amsi watched as Baruti stood his ground. He crossed his arms sternly.

"Master Amsi?"

"Go! Leave!" Amsi waved at Baruti with his open hands. "This is a secret, Baruti, and you can't know about it!"

*He sounded just like his father*, Baruti thought as he turned his back on Amsi and began walking away. When he turned his head to watch the boy, he was dragging the basket of food into the reeds. Amsi grunted as he pulled the heavy basket of food into the reeds towards Azizi. He dragged the basket towards the body and turned his back.

Azizi was absent.

"Azizi? Azizi, where are you?"

Azizi peeked his head out from the reeds. "I heard an adult coming."

"That was Baruti. He carried this for me."

Azizi stepped out of the reeds and watched wide-eyed as Amsi dragged a basket of fruit, bread, fish, and duck towards him. Amsi smiled as he stood beside the basket.

"This is for you."

Azizi's eyes stared at the basket of food, his mouth beginning to salivate at the sight of the bounty before him. He took a step towards the food and wiped his mouth as he felt himself begin to drool. Azizi's eyes slowly raised to look Amsi directly in the eyes. "Why?"

Amsi looked down at the food and shrugged. "I never get hungry. We have lots of food and my mother feeds the slaves when my father is not watching."

Azizi remembered the well-dressed man at the apple cart who shooed him away and refused to buy him an apple. He took a step back. "Are you going to hit me?"

"Why would I hit you? Here! Try it! Najam made it this morning!" Amsi took the loaf of bread and tossed it to Azizi.

Azizi caught it in his hand and looked at it longingly. His fingers touched the warm crust, his nostrils breathed deep the sweet aroma. Amsi could hear the other boy's stomach begging for the nourishment. He watched as a drop of drool coursed down the starving boy's chin.

Azizi fell to his knees and sunk his teeth into the warm, soft bread. He quickly took a couple of big bites and chewed quickly. He no sooner swallowed and his mouth was ravenously tearing at the bread for the next bite. Amsi watched as the boy grunted hungrily and growled as his canines dug into the feast in his hand.

"Be careful or you will hurt yourself," Amsi said.

Azizi's fingers dug into the bread, clawing into it greedily. Amsi watched as Azizi's eyes turned wild and fierce. He stepped backwards and watched as crumbs dropped from the sides of the starving child's mouth. Azizi began to cough as he scurried to the water with his bread clutched close to his chest. Azizi scooped water into his mouth before clamping onto it again with voracious teeth.

Amsi watched as the other five-year-old boy ravished the bread, leaving a little piece uneaten. Azizi laid on the ground, wincing as his stomach struggled to hold the first meal he had eaten in days. Azizi rubbed his stomach with a groan. "I think I ate too much."

Amsi shook his head. "I told you not to eat so fast."

Azizi glared at Amsi. "I'm hungry! You wouldn't know about that because you have a rich mother and father who feeds you!"

"I was trying to help you!" Amsi growled.

Azizi hiccupped and sat up looking at the floating body in the river. "I'm sorry, Amsi. Thank you for the food. Nobody else would give me food when I was hungry."

Amsi sat beside Azizi and leaned back on his hands. Azizi watched beside him as the boy's gold jewelry sparkled. His feet were well manicured and he smelled of fragrant oils. Around Amsi's neck hung a protective golden ankh.

"What else did you bring?"

Amsi pulled the basket towards him and showed Azizi the contents. "Look underneath the food."

Azizi's eyes widened at the sight of the apples, raisins, dates, duck and fish. He pulled a clean white linen skirt from the bottom of the basket. "New clothing!" Azizi held up the white skirt embroidered in gold trim and turquoise beading.

"You don't want dirty clothing with blood on it."

His hands began to tremble as he held up the new clothing. He lowered it slowly and let out a quiet cry.

"Azizi? Don't cry. You should be happy! You have food and a new skirt!"

Azizi buried his face in the skirt and leaned forward sobbing. Amsi wrapped his arms around Azizi and held him tightly. "Why do you shed tears?"

Azizi pulled back his head. "Nobody has ever been this nice to me. My mother didn't have money for anything new."

Amsi smiled. "Now you have food and something new to wear! People will think you are one of my people!"

Azizi shook his head slowly. "I will never be one of your people, Amsi. I will never have money or food like you. I don't like your people."

"Why not?"

Azizi sniffled as he turned his head slowly towards Amsi. "Your people killed my mother and father," the boy said quietly with a tear coursing down his cheek.

Amsi sighed as he looked at the body in the river. "I would not have wanted to kill them, Azizi."

"What if you were a big person?"

Amsi shook his head. "No. I don't think making people die or get hurt is right. When I thought my father killed Nakia, I was sad. It made me feel bad for Nassar."

Azizi sighed. "I had to hurt someone to run from the mean pharaoh. I don't feel bad."

Amsi smiled at the other boy. "Try that new skirt!"

Azizi smiled and stood up. "Don't take that food away!"

"I won't."

Azizi scampered into the reeds and untied the skirt around his waist. He dropped the bloody, dirt-covered, and mud-caked skirt on the ground. He tied the clean white skirt around his hips. The skirt was longer in the back, dropping to the back of his knees. The front of the skirt was hanging half-way up his thigh. He stepped out of the reeds and Amsi clapped.

Amsi crossed his arms as he stood in front of Azizi. "Do you like it?"

"Thank you, Amsi."

Amsi reached to the ground and handed Azizi his toy ball. "I want you to have this."

Azizi's eyes widened as he reached for the toy with trembling hands. He slowly took the ball in his hands. He looked up at Amsi. "Your favorite toy?"

Amsi nodded. "Now you won't be sad. You can play with it. I have other toys."

Azizi held the ball gingerly in his hands. He looked at it, his hands treating it as a holy relic. His fingers rubbed the surface of the hide ball reverently. *Good Osiris, is he honest? Really? Why is he being so nice?*

"Why are you doing this? You like this ball very much."

Amsi looked at the other boy. "You're sad. If you play with it, you won't be sad."

"Really?"

Amsi nodded. "You can have it, Azizi."

"Thank you! Thank you!" Azizi smiled as he hugged Amsi tightly.

Amsi returned the hug happily. The boy in gold raised his head to look at the position of the sun in the sky. He squeaked in surprise. "You enjoy your gifts. I must return home before Sawaret wonders where I am!"

"Who is that?"

"My tutor! I learn how to read and write! I must study well to please my father."

Azizi stood on his feet, a smile on his face. Azizi looked at the ball in his hands. "I think I will play with my new toy."

"Enjoy your food, Azizi! May Rā bless you!"

Azizi bowed his head. "May Osiris give you happiness and blessings."

Amsi watched Azizi turn his back. "Azizi?" The poor boy turned his head. "Do you want to be my friend?"

Azizi's eyes wandered to his mother's floating decapitated body. *'What is your name, filthy boy?' The pharaoh asked me. That big, mean man refused to give me food. Amsi gave me food and a toy! I've only dreamed of having both. He's being nice to me. Nobody has ever been this nice to me before.*

"I'm your friend, Amsi," Azizi said with a nod and a smile.

Amsi and Azizi held their breaths as they heard footsteps nearby. "Hide, Azizi!" Amsi whispered as he ran out of the reeds. Azizi dragged the basket of food beside him as he hid in the reeds.

Amsi ran from the reeds and saw a young fisherman carrying a fishing rod and a net. "Do not go in there!" Amsi called loudly, pointing at the river bank. "It's a bad place!"

"What are you talking about, child? The waters are calm and I need to fish!"

Amsi jumped up and down frantically. "There's a big crocodile! It's huge like the sun itself! It almost eaten me!"

The fisherman looked at the calm water. "I see nothing, boy! Out of my way."

Amsi looked around frantically. "It's got big claws! There's a nest in there and it will eat you if you go to its babies!"

The fisherman stopped. "There's a nest in the reeds?"

Amsi nodded quickly, unaware that Azizi was watching the performance. Azizi swiped at the man's ankles with his open hand. The man jumped back and looked down at the ground.

"What was that?"

"It's the tail of Sobek! Quickly! You must fish downstream!"

Azizi covered his mouth as he laughed, struggling to keep down the volume. Amsi ran behind the fisherman and began pushing the backs of his legs. "Fish downstream! It's a bad place to be here! Go! Imshi! Imshi!"

Azizi swiped again at the back of the man's ankles with a smile and mischievous giggle. *Does Sawaret teach him how to play pretend? He's good at it.*

Amsi watched as the fisherman walked away quickly. The Noble boy laughed when the man was out of range. He doubled over laughing, holding his stomach. *That was fun!*

Amsi turned to the reeds and winked before running towards the Al-Sakhir land.

Azizi hid himself in the reeds rolling the ball in his hands. *When Rā settles and the moon rises, I will play with my new toy! Maybe I shouldn't have eaten so much bread. My stomach hurts. I'm tired. Goodnight, mother.*

Azizi closed his eyes and leaned forward, falling asleep on his new toy.

## XX

### Bird of Prey

Pharaoh Runihura looked down from his balcony onto the city below. His arms were crossed angrily in front of him as he scowled into the distance. He had failed five years ago to destroy his nemesis. He had the perfect plan to rid himself of any resistance to his reign. His teeth grinded in anger and a low growl emanated in his throat. *I know you are out there Blessed Servant of Osiris. Who could be the Anointed Companion of Rā? The entire city worships the Sun God. I cannot carry out the slaughter of the Nobility. They will not tolerate any retribution from me. I would rather slay a dog than slay a more valuable ally. The vermin in the streets are not as skilled with weaponry.*

*Enjoy your freedom while you have it, followers of Osiris and Rā. I will find you both and when I do, I will show neither of you mercy. I shall drink your blood and feast on your flesh.*

"You wanted to see me, my Great One?"

Pharaoh Runihura turned to Gahiji and glared up at the tall General. He clenched his fists angrily and glared daggers into the man's dark brown eyes. Runihura's top lip curled in disgust as he stopped inches within Gahiji's body. Runihura whipped the back of his hand across Gahiji's face angrily.

"You failed me, Gahiji. You missed your target." Runihura glared at the General. "Why should I tolerate such incompetence?"

Gahiji rubbed his cheek and stood upright in front of his king. "I have no excuse for my failure, my Great Pharaoh."

"I told you to kill him! He was supposed to die and now he is out there! He is plotting against me for certain now and it is all because you couldn't kill a simple child!" Runihura's bellowing, furious voice carried through the wind and echoed above the gardens. "I can show you how easy it is to kill a child! Just send one of my body slaves here and I will show you!"

"My lord, I was sent to kill a follower of Osiris! I did not know my intended target! If you kill one of your body slaves, you have them in front of your glorious person!"

Runihura's eyes narrowed in contempt. "That is a poor excuse for someone of your position. I don't want to hear excuses. I want to see results, Gahiji. Do you hear me, you incompetent baboon? RESULTS!"

Gahiji bowed his head to his pharaoh. "It will not happen again, my lord."

Runihura glared at his General. Pharaoh Runihura's body quivered with suppressed rage. "My nemesis has escaped from my grasp. He has slipped through my fingers and now he runs free! He is probably planning his attack on me as we speak!"

"Your Holiness, do you think this particular child is the one spoken of in the sacred texts? There are other people who worship the God of the Dead."

"I can feel it. He came from the streets of *Iunu*, the merchant quarter of Heliopolis. His own lips told me he worshiped Un-Nefer! Osiris has favored him, Gahiji."

Gahiji's fist pounded against his chest. "My Great Pharaoh, undoubtedly your great strength has scared him into hiding. He would not think of challenging your greatness!"

"What makes you so certain, Lord Gahiji? That child is destined to conquer me!"

Gahiji grinned with a predatory smile. "The child is yet young. Without his mother, he will surely have no way to survive. If he wandered into the desert, he will die of starvation and the rays of the Aten. Only the jackals will mourn him before they feast upon his bones."

Runihura turned his back on Gahiji and rubbed his chin pensively. "The desert, you say?" Runihura smiled. "Send for the *Nuu*. I wish to speak to them."

Gahiji bowed his head. "I shall send for Heh at once."

Runihura stepped towards the edge of the balcony and clenched his fists tightly. His fists slammed against the stone balcony. *I will not let you survive. If the heat and lack of water do not kill you, boy, then my hunters will. You shall not know rest. You shall not know sleep. You shall not know peace until you feel my blade slice across your flesh. You shall beg for the end, boy. I shall see to it, Praise Sekhmet!*

Runihura felt something rub across his ankles, a soft purr escaping it. Runihura looked down and saw his Egyptian Mau purring and rubbing its head affectionately across the top of his sandaled foot.

"Nusair, you have come to greet me in all of my splendor, my little pet," Runihura said as he walked to a golden chair. The brown striped and spotted cat quickly jumped into his lap and purred, rubbing its head against Runihura's chest. Runihura reached out and stroked the cat's soft fur. "Tell me, my little bird of prey, did you find a little mouse today?"

The cat meowed, opening its mouth wide and showing its fangs. Its owner smiled proudly.

"You are a good boy, Nusair." Runihura scratched behind the cat's ear. "You are such a pretty, deadly creature, so graceful, so hypnotizing, and yet, so incredibly dangerous."

Runihura raised his head when he saw a man of middle-age sporting a beard walk inside. His white skirt hung around his thin hips as animal pelts decorated around his shoulders. He carried a spear in his hands as he bowed his head and body before his pharaoh. "My lord, embodiment of the great Sun God, Rā, Ordained Minister of the Gods, what do you command of me?"

Runihura smiled down at his cat as it settled and rested its head on his knee. "Heh, you are to take a band of *Nuu* and go into the desert. You are to find a child and see to it that you slaughter him."

Heh lifted his head. "A child, your Greatness? What child would be foolish enough to wander into the Land of Seth?"

"You are to find a young child. The boy is around five years of age with bloody clothing. He carries with him a golden dagger which he has been taken from me. He has a scar on his right cheek that wanders from the bottom of his eye to his cheek below. He still retains the side-lock of youth. This child is a dangerous animal, Heh. I command you to show him no mercy when you find him."

Heh bowed his head. "Whatever I do, my lord, I do to please you. Health and Long Life to you, Great Pharaoh Runihura! What shall I do with the boy when I find him?"

Pharaoh Runihura glared at Heh. "I want you to drape the boy's corpse over your steed and bring him to me. My precious pet could use a new bed and his skin was so soft when I touched it." Runihura grinned. "Besides, my Heh, the wild dogs could use a few more bones to gnaw upon. You are dismissed, Heh. Summon Gahiji to me."

Heh stood on his feet. "I shall do what you command of me, your Greatness! Long Life to you, our Beloved Pharaoh!" Heh bowed and walked from the balcony. "I will kill the boy of whom you speak."

Nusair purred and dug his claws into his master with a kneading motion. Runihura grinned as he continued to stroke his cat's soft fur. The cat rubbed its head against Runihura's leg, making the pharaoh chuckle. "My beloved Nusair, my beloved animal of Bastet, you are loyal to me, which is more than what I can say about the Anointed Companion of Rā. Who could this person be?" Runihura's head turned to look over the city. "Perhaps I have felled the follower of Rā in my campaign five years ago. It is possible that he is already dead. The ancient texts did not tell me of the birth of the follower of Rā.

Should he be of Common Blood, it is possible that he has already been killed. What if he is of Noble Blood, Nusair? What shall I do? I cannot begin slaughtering the Nobility. I have already poisoned them against the commoners. I cannot poison them against me or my reign will end in disgrace and the monuments to my greatness will never be built! I will never achieve immortality if my name is not carved in the stones of ages."

Gahiji stepped onto the balcony and bowed his head. "My Lord, I know I have disappointed you. It will not happen again."

"Gahiji, have your ears heard of rebellion from those of Noble Blood?"

"No, my Lord. Your Nobility is faithful to you. I have heard no words of dissention from them."

Runihura glared down at the city. "The Blessed Servant of Osiris shall be silenced by the *Nuu*. Nobody knows the depths of the desert better than they. They will find the child and bring him back." Runihura smiled as he cuddled his cat against his chest. He pet the cat and kissed its head. "If they retrieve him alive, it will be all the more fun to listen to his screams."

Gahiji stepped to the edge of the balcony and looked down at the city. "The city speaks well of you, my pharaoh, for they are afraid of your greatness. They see your strength. They cower at your feet."

"Soon the gods themselves shall do the same, Gahiji," Runihura smiled as he pet the cat's fur, feeling every hair glide gracefully under his fingertips. "There is a follower of Rā below who would see me dethroned, Gahiji. I do not know of whence he comes, but he shall be our next obstacle to overcome should he have survived that attack of five years ago."

"My Great Pharaoh, what do you wish of me?"

Runihura felt the cat abandon his lap. He stood on his feet and looked over the lands. "Keep your eyes sharp and your ears sharper. Should you hear words of revolt from those of Common Blood, bring them to me. If you hear of words from Nobility, bring them to me and their lands shall be confiscated. Their slaves shall become my own." Runihura smiled. "I need a new body slave. Janani is fit enough to clean my palace." Runihura licked his lips. "The last body slave of mine had an unfortunate accident," he added with a smile.

"Did Icess displease you?"

Runihura chuckled. "On the contrary, my Lord Gahiji, she didn't please me fast enough."

Gahiji nodded. "That explains why Hamadi was not battle training as well as he should that morning. He told me that he had been awake early that morning to bury her body."

"She took a little tumble from my balcony. I certainly hope she did not fall on my beloved flowerbed."

Gahiji looked at his pharaoh. "Her legs did crush some flowers. I do not know if Hamadi was able to save them."

"He had better save them! My garden must look perfect! It must be worthy of my greatness!" Runihura growled.

"I shall speak to Hamadi about the flowers, my lord."

Runihura's lip curled in disgust. "Hamadi will pay if my flowers are not perfect!"

"Yes, Your Grace. I will speak to Hamadi immediately."

"You are dismissed, Gahiji."

*The gardens look beautiful from above. Different colored hyacinths speckled around the garden, offering pinks and purples in the mix of flowers with delicate scents. Bright yellow, fragrant poppy flowers lined the mud-brick path and swayed in the gentle wind. Delicate iris flowers were grouped together on tiny mounds. The larkspurs reached up towards me like my people to Rā himself. Their leaves reach up like the arms of the people, glorifying me! The fragrant flowers from below offer me their sweet aroma, which is greatly welcomed after my journey to the rat nest filled with Common Blood.*

*Separated from my precious flowers to the east lies the vegetable garden. Large green melons spread across the grass and were trying to push the lettuce away from them. A rectangular pool below my balcony was my own private wading area. Near the pool was a well that provided water for the garden. When the rays of the Aten were hot, I retreat to my purifying pool and become rejuvenated. The herbal garden smells the most wonderful. Thyme, dill, and parsley scatter across the garden.*

*What is that sound? I hear singing. Who is singing? That voice is-. Hypnotizing.*

Runihura looked at the well and heard Hamadi's voice rise in song. The teen picked a bucket of water into his hands. He carried it towards the flowerbed as he continued singing.

*Hamadi is singing! I cannot hear the words of his song, only the sweet melody. Who would have known that a little rat like him would have such a peaceful voice? His melody sounds like a hymn. It is quiet, reverent, and beautiful. What is that do I hear? A touch of solemn emotion lingers in every note? He's looking up to the sky! Is he worshiping Rā with his song? I will crush him like an insect if I hear he is singing to the Sun God. But if I crush him, he cannot sing for me. I want to hear what he is singing.*

Hamadi kneeled on the ground and scooped water from the bucket onto the irises. He smiled as his fingers dug into the dry earth. "Drink, my bounty, for your growth gives me pleasure in a world of pain." Hamadi took a bud into his thin hand with a smile. "You are beauty incarnate, my white doves," he said with a smile. "Your sweet smell gives me pleasure and brings a smile to my face." Hamadi stared at the plant in his hand, smiling as it looked up at him with its petals spread. Its green leaves brushed against his hand as they swayed in the wind. Hamadi breathed deeply, inhaling their perfume.

*The gods smile down upon me*

*Toiling in the soil*

*Giving beauty to a world*

*In a state of so much turmoil*

*I dig into the ground, the light of Rā upon my hand*

*Giving warmth to a world of cold*

*Until I rest my bones in sand.*

Hamadi reached into the bucket again and scooped more water onto the next flowerbed. His fingers curled and dug into the soil. He tore some weeds from their foundation and loosened the soil. Hamadi stopped as a swallow landed nearby. He looked at it with a smile. The bird pecked at the ground where he had laid some seeds for the birds to feed. The small bird took a nibble of seed and flew away into the sky. The teen watched longingly as it flew over the palace walls into the freedom of the sky. "That must be a wonderful feeling, to fly into the open wind. No walls and no cages would be set around me."

Hamadi felt something soft and fluffy brush across his arm. Hamadi looked at his arm and saw a white, long-haired Persian cat rubbing against Hamadi's arm. Zaki's gold and turquoise-studded collar glittered in the mid-day sun. The slave dipped his hands in the water and dried them on his skirt. He reached down and pet the pharaoh's cat with a smile. "Hello, Zaki. Have you come here to join me today?" The fluffy, white cat purred its content response and it laid on its back and exposed its belly to Hamadi. The teen giggled, enjoying the momentary break in his labor. Hamadi's callused, red hands caressed the cat's belly as it purred and swayed its tail. "You do not want to get dirty, Zaki. The pharaoh will become angry."

"Hamadi!" the teen heard bellow from above him. "Get back to your garden! You shall not touch what belongs to me!"

Hamadi's hand quickly flew from the cat and continued his work. Within a moment, he found himself falling forward as the cat scurried away, hissing. Hamadi turned his head upwards and saw Gahiji's large form in the sunlight. The rays of the sun shone behind the tall General as a sandal connected with his leg.
"The pharaoh has heard of your negligence of his flowerbed, Hamadi."

Hamadi put his arm in front of his face. "My lord, I have tended the flowerbed faithfully!"

"Were the flowers which broke Icess' fall from the balcony able to be saved?"

Hamadi swallowed hard, his body trembling. "N-No, my General! I could not save them."

"You will explain to the pharaoh why you could not save his beloved flowers!" Gahiji exclaimed, grabbing Hamadi's wrist and pulling him to his feet. "To the pharaoh with you!"

Hamadi screamed loudly, shrieking as he tried to pull his arm away from the iron-clad grip of the General. "No, please, my lord! I shall plant new ones! Please, my lord, compassion!"

Gahiji pulled the shrill-screaming teen into the palace. Janani lifted her head as she scrubbed the floor of the entrance hall. "Out of my way, Janani!"

"Janani! Help me!"

Janani watched Hamadi shudder as he passed her. She watched sadly as he was pulled, his feeble attempt at escape from the strong General made her heart sink. There was only one fate for people dragged to the foot of the pharaoh. Janani lowered her head sadly as he passed and continued scrubbing the floor.

"Janani! Please, my lord, release me!"

"The pharaoh will release you if chooses to do so, you worthless boy!"

Hamadi closed his eyes tightly and whimpered as he was pulled up the golden staircase.

Gahiji stopped at the top of the steps and turned to the teen. He grabbed his throat and looked his prey in the eyes. "Soldiers do not cry and scream like a woman, boy! I see you must learn this lesson tied to the post in the cold night air."

"My lord, I will fix the flowerbed. I promise I will make it to the pharaoh's liking!"

"I should throw you down these stairs and hope that your neck breaks!" Gahiji smiled as he looked into the wide-eyes of Hamadi. "Soldiers do not show fear, boy."

Hamadi's eyes closed tightly as he held onto Gahiji's wrists. "I don't...want...to die," Hamadi gagged through his constricted windpipe. "Please, my lord."

"The Glorious Pharaoh will decide your fate," Gahiji said releasing Hamadi's throat.

Hamadi trembled as Gahiji pulled him into the throne room and onto the balcony. Gahiji whipped Hamadi towards the pharaoh, throwing him at the pharaoh's feet.

Hamadi looked at Pharaoh Runihura's golden sandals, decorated with red and green stones. Hamadi swallowed nervously as he awaited those shoes to kick him in his face. His body trembled as he felt his chest tighten in fear.

"Hamadi, why do you touch what belongs to me?"

Hamadi lowered his head and covered the back of his head with his arms. "I'm sorry, my king! I should not have touched Zaki! A thousand pardons, my most merciful pharaoh!"

"The boy could not save your flowers, my king."

Pharaoh Runihura glared down at the other trembling teen. "Why not?"

Gahiji nudged Hamadi with his foot, making the boy squeak in fear. "Explain your clumsiness, you worthless swine!"

"I will plant new ones, my lord! I promise!"

Runihura leaned over and grabbed Hamadi's ear. He pulled the teen to his knees and looked him in the eye. Runihura could see Hamadi's neck pulsing with his rapid heartbeat. The teen's face as covered in sweat as his eyes showed nothing but fear and terror. Hamadi's breathing was quick and sharp as he looked into the dark eyes of his pharaoh.

Runihura released Hamadi's ear and leaned close to Hamadi's throat. Hamadi swallowed hard as he watched the pharaoh inspect his flesh closely. The pharaoh raised his free hand and glided his fingertips across the front of Hamadi's neck.

*He's going to cut it! He's going to cut it! I'm going to die! Isis, Divine Mother, please do not let him!*

"You touched his neck did you not, Gahiji?"

"This child was cowering in fear of your greatness!"

Pharaoh Runihura felt Hamadi's flesh quiver under his touch. A bead of sweat fell from Hamadi's temple and coursed down his cheek, jaw, and dribbled down the side of his neck, the veins thumping wildly. His lungs were so tense that he could hardly breathe. His body quivered as the pharaoh inspected the front of his throat, watching every vein tremble beneath his fingers.

Runihura leaned into the front of Hamadi's neck and brushed it with his fingers tenderly.

*His fear is so incredible. I can feel it in every pore, I can feel it in every vibration of his being. His body is in a complete state of terror. There's so much power in this hand of mine. With a single motion, I can spare him and send him back to his daily labor. I can strike him, injuring him quite severely.*

*These fingers....these strong fingers...can squeeze the life from him and I can watch as his lungs fail him from lack of air. What a beautiful sight that would be! Those melodious lungs screaming and gasping for air as I robbed them of their life! I could slice that beautiful, warm quivering windpipe, silencing him forever.*

*His skin feels so warm, his flesh is tender, his fear delightful. That beautiful throat just whimpered in fear. My little victim is terrified. I should like to see his heart burst from his chest. I wish to see him frozen in fear, my domination over him complete.*

*I leaned into him slowly and softly kissed the front of his warm, beautiful, quivering neck, hearing him whimper with fear and release a little helpless sob.*

*His fear is intoxicating!*

"Do not harm this throat, Gahiji. His singing entertains me," Runihura said as he pulled back slowly. He looked Hamadi in the eyes with a smile. "Sing for me and I will spare your life."

Hamadi gasped as he watched the pharaoh sit on his golden chair, his own gold jewelry sparkling like the sun. Gahiji stood beside the pharaoh with his arms crossed sternly, glaring down at Hamadi.

Hamadi wrung his hands nervously as he bowed his head. "Yes, Great One," Hamadi said nervously.

*Wonderful is his mercy*

*He who challenges the glory of Rā*

*Mighty is his fist with which he crushes his enemies!*

*Long may he reign!*

*Long may his name endure!*

*None in the heavens or on Earth is more glorious than he, Pharaoh Runihura!*

*Blessed be his name for all eternity.*

"It seems as if he is just as skilled with his tongue as his hands, Lord Gahiji," the pharaoh grinned. Gahiji continued to glare at the teen. "Why do you sing?"

Hamadi swallowed nervously at the pharaoh. "It gives me pleasure, my lord."

"You are aware that I can silence your beautiful song at my whim, correct? I can silence that beautiful voice of yours forever."

Hamadi lowered his head. "Yes, my lord."

"I shall not cut that beautiful neck of yours now."

Hamadi's eyes closed tightly as he prostrated himself before the pharaoh. "Thank you, my lord!"

"That does not mean that in the future, I will not have a change of heart."

Hamadi clenched his fists as he stared at the stone beneath him. "Yes, my lord."

"Return to your labor."

"Yes, my lord! Praise you!" Hamadi said, standing on his feet and bowing. He walked quickly from the balcony, his heart racing and his face covered in sweat.

*The pharaoh spared my life. That was close. The fact that he liked my singing is perhaps the only reason why I continue to breathe. I must return to the garden! Quickly, Hamadi, run! I don't want to die! I'm too young to die!*

"Hamadi! You return from the pharaoh's throne room with your head still attached!" Janani exclaimed, hugging Hamadi as he approached.

Hamadi hugged her back, his fingers digging into her bare back. "Janani, he almost killed me!" Hamadi quivered as he held onto the slave girl. "I thought he was going to do it this time."

Janani pulled back and held Hamadi's shoulders. "Praise Rā that you are alive, Hamadi!"

Hamadi nodded. "I want to leave, Janani. I want to leave, but there is no way out except as food for the jackals."

Janani nodded and hugged Hamadi tightly again. "If only Pharaoh Atenhotep had not left us. He was a kindly old man."

Hamadi looked outside of the archway into the garden. "One day, Janani, a new pharaoh shall sit on the throne. Sweet words will flow from his tongue like honey and the old order will once again be established. His hand will once again shower bread and milk upon his people. Fear will be abolished. One day, we shall all be free of despair, hunger, and pain. You must *believe*, Janani." Hamadi pulled back from the hug and looked into the eyes of the tired thirteen-year-old girl slave. "Do you believe, Janani?"

Janani looked into Hamadi's eyes. The gardener-
soldier's hands were rough and dry. They clutched onto
her desperately as they held onto her. His eyes were wide
and blood-shot. His body was tense as it stood before her.
"I believe, Hamadi. I have to believe that to keep living
within these palace halls."

"I must return to work before the pharaoh finds me
absent. I love you, Janani," Hamadi said, kissing the
girl's forehead tenderly. "Goodbye."

Hamadi walked towards the gardens with a sigh. Janani
and I have been slaves of the royal family for a long time.
*We were brought here within days of each other. We
were friends as children and played in the garden when
our chores were finished. I always had a way with
flowers and I was also instructed in the art of war. By
morning, I train in the pharaoh's army. By afternoon and
night, I work the gardens. By night, I sleep in dirt or in
the cold should General Gahiji bind me to the post in the
arena.*

*It sickens me that I should sing praises to a pharaoh such
as Runihura. How could I not when I knew he was ready
to slaughter me? I don't know which was more
disturbing: the fact that he was ready to cut my throat or
the fact that he leaned over and kissed my neck. Why did
he do such a thing? Pharaoh Atenhotep prized me for my
singing, but he never made contact with my body.*

*I returned to my work in the garden and I kneeled by the
poppies. I looked at their beautiful colors and smelled
their sweet fragrances. Pharaoh Runihura cannot remain
in power, but what can be done about him? Lord Rā,
great god of all, there must be something that can be*

*done. I fold my hands and pray my own supplication to the great Sun God. Please hear my prayer, Amun-Rā!*

*Little mercy does his person show*

*The Rise of Sekhmet beckons as she thirsts for human blood*

*Who defy his word to Tuat swiftly go.*

*Tears and sorrow sweeping the land in a great, overwhelming flood*

*May his reign die with haste*

*or to this land shall his hate make terrible waste.*

*Amun-Rā, your children need you!*

## XXI

### Betrothed

Issâm raised his arms to the shining rays of dawn. Thin veils of reds and purples swept above as his eyes raised into the open skies. Behind him, Baruti and Qamra were holding hands and looking towards the dawn of a new day and the new beginning of their new life together. No marriage ceremony existed in the Egyptian culture, but both of them wanted something special to remember the day they began a commitment to one another.

"Blessed One, who shines in the skies, who gives us warmth and bounty by day, show your rays of blessings upon Qamra and Baruti. May their commitment to each other remain steadfast and true. May their union be blessed with happiness, love, and many children." Tabari turned and placed his hands upon the married couple. "May Rā bless your union and keep you prosperous and content."

Issâm stepped forward and took Baruti and Qamra's hands in his own. "May the Mighty Speaker place words of love in your hearts. With his blessing shall you speak only the truth to one another. Great Thoth, grant Baruti and Qamra your blessing and may their union be chronicled in your sacred parchment of eternity."

Baruti leaned into Qamra and kissed her as the sun began to rise over the horizon. Tabari stood beside Issâm and crossed his arms proudly.

"I think we did well, Issâm."

The man nodded and put his hand on Tabari's shoulder. "Well done, Tabari."

Tabari heard Nakia's coughing and gagging from inside the home. "What are we to do with that boy, Issâm?"

Issâm sighed sadly. "I don't know what else we can do for him, Tabari. Qamra has tried every medicine she knows."

Nassar ran around to the back of the house and grabbed Qamra's skirt. "Ah-E-ah! Ah-E-ah!"

"Come quickly! Qamra! Baruti! Tabari!"

The adults followed Nassar into the home and crowded around Sabi holding Nakia in her arms. Nakia was looking up at Qamra and blinked slowly. Nakia reached out to Qamra with weak arms.

"Mother," Nakia whimpered as he wiggled his fingers.

Qamra kneeled before Sabi and brought the conscious child to her chest. "Oh, Nakia, praise the gods you are awake! You have made me so happy! Praise be to the gods! Our Sweet Nakia has returned to us!"

Nakia's weak fingers brushed lightly across Qamra's skin. "Water."

Nassar grabbed a cup from the bucket in the corner and ran to Nakia. He put the cup to his brother's lips and tipped it slowly just as Issâm had showed him.

"Drink up, Nakia. Be careful, not so fast."

Nakia pulled his head back and relaxed his body against Qamra. "Hamza?"

"Hamza stayed with you," Baruti said. "You should give him a treat when you feel better."

"I will. I was afraid. I didn't want to die without Nassar," Nakia said quietly as he snuggled into Qamra.

Tabari reached down and caressed the child's head. "You are back with us, Nakia, and we won't let anything happen to you."

"My arm hurts," Nakia moaned.

"Qamra and I applied some honey onto your shoulder to prevent any infection," Issâm said. "With a little rest, you will be back on your feet and riding Hamza again."

Nakia shivered. "No."

"We know, Nakia," Qamra said calmly. "We want you to relax here while we work. Do not let the master see you while we are gone. We don't want him to hurt you."

Issâm looked through the opening to see the sun rising completely in the horizon. "We should return to work before Kaemwaset comes here."

Qamra placed Nakia slowly on the reed mat. She covered him with a blanket and set a folded blanket under his head to help his breathing. Nassar watched as the adults stood and slowly walked out of the home. Karida and Laila followed the adults, but stopped at the door. "Nassar?" Karida saw the twins looking at each other quietly.

Nassar was kneeling beside his twin and looking towards the door. Nassar was holding Nakia's hand and rubbed the back of it slowly and gently. Nassar sniffled as he looked at his twin and lowered his head in a quiet sob.

"Nassar, you should go," Nakia whispered. "I don't want you to get in trouble."

"Ah-e-ah," Nassar said sadly. *I thought you were dead, Nakia. I didn't think you were alive. I wanted to die. How can I leave you now when you need me the most?*

Nakia listened to Nassar's attempt at speech. "Nassar, I don't understand you."

Nassar released Nakia's hand and clenched his fists angrily. *Why don't you understand me? I thought you were dead! Nassar punched the floor angrily and screamed loudly. I thought you were dead! I don't want to leave you, Nakia! Listen to me!*

"Nassar! You have to get to the master's home before he comes here!" Karida exclaimed.

*Damn Kaemwaset Al-Sakhir's to Ammut!* Nassar growled, making Laila run away screaming. *The pharaoh and Kaemwaset removed my tongue and it is their fault Nakia can't understand me! I hate them all! I hate them.*

"Nassar?" Nakia reached to Nassar's hand as his twin fell forward crying. "Nassar, look at me." Nassar raised his tear-stained face to look at his twin. "I'm sorry. Please don't be angry. I can tell what you're feeling. I know you're sad. I don't want you to be."

*Nakia, I'm trying to make words. I'm not angry at you. I'm sorry.* Nassar took Nakia's hand and pressed his forehead against it gently. "Ah-E-ah…"

"I will be alright here, Nassar. Go take care of the horses for me. Give Hamza an extra special treat from me, alright?" Nassar nodded, making Nakia smile. "I'm tired, brother. I need to go to sleep."

Nassar replaced Nakia's hand on his brother's stomach and covered him with the blanket. He leaned over and kissed Nakia on the cheek. *I love you, brother.*

Nakia watched Nassar run out of the house with a sigh. "I love you, too, brother."

Nassar ran out of the home and towards the Al-Sakhir home. He ran through the door and found Qamra waiting for him in the reception hall.

"Nassar, what took you?"

"Ah-e-ah," Nassar said, pointing towards the slave home.

Kaemwaset stood at the entrance to the reception hall. "Nassar, go to my son's quarters. Bring him to my office immediately."

Nassar bowed and ran towards Amsi's room. Nassar ran quickly down the hallway, painted with murals of Kaemwaset's ancestors. Much to Nassar's surprise, all of his family members were depicted as having passed the 'Weighing of the Heart' test of Anubis. Nassar had often wondered how Kaemwaset would pass that particular test in his afterlife.

Nassar knocked on Amsi's room. The boy opened the door slowly and saw Nassar standing there. Nassar pointed down the hallway and Amsi scratched his head. "Good morning, Nassar. Is Sawaret here for my lesson this early? I'm still tired."

Nassar took a deep breath and pointed to Amsi and then down the hallway. Amsi yawned and Nassar took the boy's hand. Amsi followed the slave boy who led him to his father's office.

Amsi and Nassar arrived in Kaemwaset's office where he was standing with another man and a little girl. Amsi looked at the girl dressed with flowers in her hair and a long, white robe. Around her neck was a golden amulet of Isis and around her wrists were bracelets of turquoise and gold. Gold rings decorated each of her fingers.

"Is this your son, Kaemwaset? He looks like a fine young man."

Kaemwaset laughed as he took his son's hand. "This is my son, my pride, Amsi Al-Sakhir. Nassar, get wine and food for our guests and be quick about it, boy!"

Nassar bowed and quickly fled the room.

Kaemwaset offered seats for his guests and placed his son on a golden chair beside him. "I am honored that you and your daughter have decided to journey to my home, Mahoma. Your decision to unite our families pleases me."

Amsi looked at the girl sitting beside her father. Her sandals were white and her robe draped over the sides of the chair as she sat. She smiled at him, making him swallow nervously.

"Where is the boy's mother? Should she not be involved in our affairs?"

Kaemwaset shook his head and waved his hand in the air dismissively. "I am the boy's father. It is my responsibility to assure the continuity of my household and I am responsible to see that my child acquires a wife appropriate to his greatness. Amsi, say hello to Ife." Amsi looked at his father timidly and shook his head. "My son, do not embarrass me. Say hello to Ife."

"Hello, Ife," Amsi said quietly.

"Hello, Amsi," the girl responded with a smile.

Nassar walked into the room carrying cups on a golden tray and a jug of wine. He poured the wine and handed each person a cup with a bow. Qamra entered the room carrying a tray of apples, dates, raisins, and grapes. She placed the fruit on a table in the center of the four chairs.

"Qamra, I want you to feed me a grape," Kaemwaset said with a grin. "Nassar, feed the children."

Qamra swallowed hard and took a grape between her fingers. Kaemwaset opened his mouth wide and she slowly slipped the grape between his lips. She watched as Kaemwaset's teeth dug into the skin of the grape and finally severed it in two with his teeth. He chewed with a grin as he turned his attention back to Mahoma.

"I wish to find a good husband for my darling Ife. She will make a suitable wife for any boy's hand," Mahoma said. "She is learning to play music and she is excelling in her studies."
Nassar fed an apple slice to Amsi. Amsi took the slice in his hand and smiled at his slave. "Thank you, Nassar," Amsi said with a smile.

"Your child is polite to his servants," Mahoma said. "That is a rare sight."

Kaemwaset watched as Nassar fed a slice of apple to Ife. Ife crossed her arms sternly.

"I don't want an apple. I want a raisin." Nassar put the apple slice on the tray and grabbed a raisin. He offered it to Ife. The little girl turned her head away from Nassar's hand and raised her nose in the air.

"Apples are good," Amsi said. "You don't like apples?"

"No, I don't want that raisin. I want it on a plate."

Nassar looked at Qamra with a frustrated glare. Qamra stepped to Nassar and put a calming hand on his shoulder. "I'll get you a plate, little lady."

Nassar handed Amsi the raisin he had handed to Ife. Amsi took the raisin with a smile.

"What do you offer as a dowry, Kaemwaset?" Mahoma asked as he took a date into his hand. "My Ife is a wonderful girl with a strong body. She will produce many sons for your family and bring pride to both of our houses."

Kaemwaset took a grape and popped it into his mouth. "I offer one thousand dînars for the marriage price and I will offer you Nassar here on the day of their union."

Nassar's head snapped up and looked at Kaemwaset. *No! I can't be sent away! I'll never see Nakia again!*

Mahoma looked at the boy. "You are offering this boy here as part of the dowry? Is he only a house slave?"

"Nassar works in the field when his house work has been completed for the day. Nassar, go to him."

Amsi looked over at his father and took his arm. "Father, you can't give Nassar to him! He's my friend!"

"He is property, boy. He cannot be your friend."

Amsi nodded his head emphatically. "He is my friend! Did you not tell him to take care of me?"

Kaemwaset nodded. "He is your body slave for now, Amsi. When you get older, you will be assigned a new body slave."

"But Nassar combs my hair good and he is nice to me!"

Kaemwaset leaned down to his son. "Amsi Al-Sakhir, I don't want to hear another word from you. Don't make Nassar feel special by giving him human qualities. He is property. He is no more human than the chair you sit on, boy! Nassar is our property like this chair or that desk. He can be broken and thrown away just as easily as a shattered vase."

Kaemwaset looked down at Nassar. "Go to him, child!"

Nassar walked slowly to the man as Qamra walked into the room. Qamra handed the plate to the little girl and saw Mahoma looking into Nassar's eyes.

Mahoma chuckled. "This is a wild one, isn't he?"

Kaemwaset nodded. "He has a fiery spirit in him. His uncivilized beginnings are to blame for that. He was a member of the Enzi tribe that was defeated by Pharaoh Atenhotep."

Mahoma reached for the boy's mouth and Nassar pulled away angrily. "Stay still, boy!"

Nassar took another step back as Mahoma reached for his mouth again. Kaemwaset leaned over and shoved Nassar into Mahoma's grasp. He opened the boy's mouth and saw the back of Nassar's mouth scarred and his tongue missing. The remnant of Nassar's severed tongue partly emerged from the back of the throat. What remained of the tongue had been cauterized and appeared as black scar tissue. "This child cannot speak. Why do you offer me such worthless goods like this boy for my daughter's hand?"

Qamra looked down at Nassar and saw the boy's eyes fall to the floor sadly. She saw Nassar's shoulders sag and his back slouch forward. *Poor boy. He's so sensitive about his lack of ability to communicate. Now that man is examining him like one examines a beast of burden.*

"Nassar is a very sweet child," Qamra said. "He is not worthless."

"That boy works hard," Kaemwaset said. "What better of a servant than one who cannot speak against you? A servant who cannot speak at all is more valuable than one who argues or complains."

Mahoma's hand traced Nassar's jaw and touched the boy's arms. Mahoma put his hand on Nassar's chest. "Breathe deep." Nassar took a deep breath and exhaled hard. "His breathing is good. How old is he?"

"He is aged about twelve-years, sir. Without a record of his birth, we do not know for certain."

Mahoma reached under Nassar's white skirt and the boy jumped back with a surprised squeal. "I'm ready to chain you to the ground, boy! Get over here!"

Nassar jumped at Qamra and clutched onto her white skirt, breathing heavily. He shook his head emphatically. His eyes were wide with fear as he looked at the stranger.

"Kaemwaset, control your slave boy and tell him to get over here!"

Kaemwaset glared at Nassar. "Boy, you will get over there or I will hold you down myself!"

Qamra felt the boy shaking against her as he clutched onto her. He looked up at her with large, pleading eyes. Her hand caressed his head as he buried his face in the material of her skirt.

"Get over here, child!" Mahoma exclaimed with fury.

Qamra heard a whimper come from Nassar. "Nassar, I'm right here. I won't let him hurt you."

Kaemwaset grabbed Nassar's arm and pulled him away from Qamra. Amsi watched as Nassar was brought before Mahoma. Mahoma reached under the boy's skirt, making the child scream. *I don't want him to touch me! Get your hands off of me!* Nassar punched Kaemwaset's arm angrily as he tried pulling his arm away.

"Father, release Nassar!" Amsi pleaded.

Nassar felt Mahoma's hands touch his thighs and his body shivered with revulsion. *This is wrong. Stop touching me!* Mahoma's hands rubbed Nassar's thigh, pinching the skin and examining the taut muscles of the boy.

Mahoma chuckled. "His noises are very peculiar."

Qamra watched as Nassar turned his head to her as the man examined the other leg. "He doesn't want you to touch him, my lord!"

"Qam-ah! Qam-ah!"

Qamra saw Nassar's body tense and tremble at the poking and pinching. "My lord, don't startle the boy!" Qamra pleaded.

"His muscles are strong. His people were excellent archers. Were they exceptional runners, as well?"

Kaemwaset chuckled. "Well, they could have been good runners, but they could not outrun the great Egyptian army."

"He appears to be a strong athlete. I can see why you place him to work in the fields. He would have a good back for work. Has he reached the age of manhood yet?"

Nassar's fist flew and quickly connected to Mahoma's face, making the man's head snap back. Amsi and Ife watched as Mahoma screamed into his hand, blood coming from between his fingers.

"Nassar!" Qamra exclaimed.

Kaemwaset glared angrily at the boy and punched the slave in the face with his free hand. Qamra watched as

Nassar's head flew backwards with a snap and the Kaemwaset throw the boy to the floor angrily.

"Nassar! Nassar!" Qamra exclaimed as she kneeled beside the boy's body. She gathered Nassar against her body and looked up at Kaemwaset angrily. "How could you punch a helpless child?" Nassar's jaw hung loose as blood crept from the side of the boy's mouth.

Kaemwaset ignored Qamra and put his hand on Mahoma's shoulder. "I deeply apologize for the actions of my slave boy, Mahoma!"

"That child is a menace, Kaemwaset!" Mahoma growled, holding his face in pain. "He is like a rabid dog!"

Ife climbed off of her seat and stood before her father. "Father, that boy is mean!"

"He is not mean!" Amsi demanded. "Nassar didn't want to be touched! You were scaring him!"

Kaemwaset turned to Amsi. "He was examining Nassar to make certain he was worthy of a good dowry! He was examining his new property!"

"I don't want that-that-beast, Kaemwaset!" Mahoma growled. "You should eliminate him! He is dangerous!"

"It's not nice to touch Nassar if he tells you no!" Amsi protested.

Kaemwaset turned to Amsi. "Go play, my son. This no longer concerns you."

Amsi slid off the chair and walked to Nassar. Qamra was cradling Nassar against her body as his breathing became shallow. "Qamra, will Nassar be alright?"

"Go outside and play, Master Amsi. Nassar will be fine."

Amsi turned to walk to the door. He looked up at his father. "It's not nice to hit. Mother said so."

Kaemwaset clenched his fists angrily as he watched his son leave the room. "His mother is a bad influence on him. He won't be the strong leader I wish for him to be with his mother teaching him lessons I do not wish for him to learn."

Mahoma took a cloth and held it to his bleeding lip. "I do not want that boy as part of the dowry for my daughter. Which other slave can you offer?"

"I have Sabi available. Sabi came to me from the north. I acquired her through Pharaoh Atenhotep's predecessor. She was the lone survivor of a conquered village in the north. In two moons, she will birth her child."

"Who is the sire?"

"Tabari is the father of her child. I required another slave for the fields and her pregnancy was commanded by me."

Qamra glared at Kaemwaset behind his back. Her eyes stabbed daggers into him and she regretted that he could not feel each piercing sting stabbing his skin.

"When she births her child, I can take her. She would make a good addition to my servants. She is mild-mannered, I hope."

Kaemwaset nodded. "Yes. She is polite and is good-natured. Not once have I had a problem with her speaking against me or raising a hand to myself or my family. I will need her to remain with her child for three years to breastfeed her. Then I shall send Sabi to you."

Qamra caressed Nassar's cheek. "My lord, what of Tabari? Tabari loves Sabi."

"Tabari will have nothing to say, Qamra. This is my decision."

Qamra sighed as she looked down at Nassar. *Tabari has feelings for Sabi. They are like Baruti and I. While they have decided not to have a formal ceremony for their union, Tabari and Sabi behave as a married couple. When Tabari discovered Sabi was pregnant with a girl, Tabari was elated. Throughout her pregnancy, Tabari has been there to rub ointment on her belly. He has been there to rub her back and show her affection. His arms are around her when they are not working. Tabari will be upset when he hears of this news.*

"That is wonderful news! I will accept your offer, Kaemwaset Al-Sakhir!"

"Upon my son's eighteenth birthday, my son will take your daughter as his wife! May they have a long life together and many sons!"

Ife smiled up at Kaemwaset. "Do I have to kiss that boy?"

Kaemwaset chuckled. "Yes, you will, my girl."

Ife's nose wrinkled. "That's disgusting."

Kaemwaset and Mahoma laughed and shook hands in agreement. "You may think so now, Ife, but when you become older, your mind will change."

"I hope not," Ife said.

"Ife and I must journey home with the good news of my daughter's betrothal, Kaemwaset! May our houses unite and be prosperous in Rā's name!"

"Health and happiness to you, my friend," Kaemwaset said as he turned to Qamra. "Show them to their carriage."

Qamra stood on her feet slowly, holding Nassar.

"Leave him here. Return here when you are finished."

Qamra looked at her master, a furious look in his eyes as he glared at the unconscious boy. Qamra lead the father and daughter from the room, praying to Isis that Nassar would not be dead when she returned.

Kaemwaset glared at the boy on the ground and saw his fingers twitching. Nassar groaned on the ground as he held his cheek. "I suppose it was not enough for you that we took your tongue. Must I take your hands from you as well?" Kaemwaset kneeled, his ample frame wobbling as he kneeled on the ground beside the boy. He grabbed the boy's side-lock and tugged roughly. "I could have rid myself of you once and for all! How dare you disrespect me in front of my guests! How dare you, you little runt!" Kaemwaset growled low and quietly, shaking the boy's head. "You will learn some manners if I have to pound them into you!" Kaemwaset punched his unconscious victim again, making his head whip to the side.

Nassar's body jerked violently as Kaemwaset pulled back his fist. The man saw a puddle of blood forming under Nassar's head.

"Wake up, Nassar," Kaemwaset growled as he picked the boy up by the hair and threw him on the ground again with a slam.

Nassar's body began to tremor, his fingers twitching uncontrollably. The boy whimpered as he laid unconscious, his throat gurgling.

Kaemwaset heard footsteps rapidly approaching. Qamra ran into the room and gasped.

"My lord, please! Stop this!"

Kaemwaset turned back to Nassar and grinned. "Stop this?" Kaemwaset's fist connected hard into the thin stomach of the slave boy. Nassar rolled over towards Qamra, his jaw hanging open and loose, his head bleeding from his mouth and ear.

"Please, my lord, don't hurt him anymore," Qamra begged, falling to her knees and folding her hands.

Kaemwaset grinned and gained his footing slowly. His large frame stood above her and loomed over her. Qamra watched as Nassar's body twitched and spasmed, blood trickling from Nassar's ear and his mouth. Kaemwaset walked casually towards the door with a mischievous grin.

Qamra scurried over to Nassar and put her hand on his arm. "My poor child, what has he done to you in my absence?" Qamra leaned over and kissed Nassar's cheek. "I love you, Nassar. You're such a good boy."

"A good boy? Nassar is far from being a well-behaved child."

Qamra looked up at her master angrily. "That man was grabbing Nassar like some type of animal!"

"Mahoma had to examine Nassar's body!"

"I saw how that man was handling Nassar and I must confess, my lord, I would have punched him, too, if he touched me where I did not wish to be touched."

Kaemwaset crossed his arms defiantly. "Mahoma had every right to touch that boy!"

"Nassar had no way to say no! He cannot speak and it is all because of you and the pharaoh!" Qamra growled, pointing an accusing finger at her master. "You want to talk of beasts? The only beast in this room is standing before me!"

Kaemwaset's face tensed and reddened with anger. "Silence your tongue, female!"

"You took that child to the palace and you cut out his tongue! You sealed the back of his throat with a hot poker to keep him from bleeding to death! How can you do that to a seven-year-old boy? I catch you punching the same unconscious child! You are a monster!" Qamra stood up, her fists clenched, and her lip curled in disgust.

"You are a terrible monster! You are a cruel, vicious, despicable person to do this to a child."

Kaemwaset stepped up to Qamra. "You are both my property and I will do with you what I wish!"

Kaemwaset pushed Qamra back and onto the desk. Kaemwaset leaned over on top of her, kissing her neck. Qamra punched Kaemwaset and pushed against him.

"Release me!"

Kaemwaset took her wrists and pinned them to the desk. "There is only one way I can release you," he smiled at her.

"Stop this!" Qamra exclaimed as she kicked her legs on either side of Kaemwaset's hips.

"Perhaps I need to examine you like Mahoma examined Nassar." Kaemwaset grinned, touching between Qamra's legs.

Tears filled Qamra's eyes as she growled, pushing against Kaemwaset.

"Why do you fight? Rā has commanded a son be born from your womb. Nassar here will not tell anyone about this. Who can he tell? He cannot write or speak."

"You are too late, my lord," Qamra said quickly.

Kaemwaset chuckled. "What do you mean?"

Qamra smiled at Kaemwaset. "I have already laid with another man."

"You lie!" Kaemwaset growled as he stood upright.

Qamra grinned as she sat on the desk. "I lie not, my lord."

Kaemwaset growled as he grabbed Qamra's wrists. "Harlot!"

Qamra tried to pull her hands free from Kaemwaset's grip. "I am bound to him in the eyes of the gods as of today, my lord. I have accepted him into my body and I love none other than him."

Kaemwaset threw Qamra to the ground as he stood over her. "How dare you allow another man to touch you! I alone reserve that right!"

Nassar's eyes opened slowly. The blurry vision before him showed Kaemwaset standing over Qamra. He could barely hear them. He reached out slowly, but his arm fell to the ground in the attempt to move. A trickle of blood fell into his right eye, making him whimper.

He saw the blurry vision of Qamra on the ground and saw a large object fall on her. He heard screaming as if from a distance. He saw Qamra kicking and heard her crying.

*Qamra? Is she in trouble?* Nassar thought as he laid on his stomach.

"Who has laid with you? Tell me who it is, Qamra?" Kaemwaset growled as he pinned her wrists to the ground. "Who have you accepted into your body when I alone have that right?"

Nassar dug his fingers into the ground and pulled himself towards the two blurry figures. As he crawled on his belly, they slowly came into focus.

Qamra grinned. "You need not know, my lord. You may try to give me a child, but I tell you that you will fail."

Kaemwaset felt a hand on his ankle and turned his head. Nassar was weakly pulling at his ankle. Kaemwaset shoved Nassar back with his foot, making the boy roll over onto his back.

"Your body belongs to me, Qamra! Do you hear me?" Kaemwaset growled as he gripped her throat. "You belong to me! Your body! Your mind! Everything!"

Nassar heard quiet screaming and saw Qamra's legs kicking. He heard her crying and Kaemwaset's angry growling. *I have to find help. Help Qamra. Must help mother. Help mother. Help. Help.*

Kaemwaset grinned as he leaned his face close to Qamra. "You are so beautiful. You shall not bear the child of another man. I will not allow it."

Kaemwaset raised his fist as Nassar gripped his arm and pulled. "Nassar! Get away!"

"Nassar, run!" Qamra cried loudly.

Nassar ducked under Kaemwaset's fist and draped his body across her stomach. Nassar blocked the punch, Kaemwaset's fist crashing into his spine making the boy wail loudly.

Qamra gasped. "Nassar! Go!"

Kaemwaset shoved the child off Qamra. Nassar laid beside Qamra, his body twitching and shaking from the bone-crunching punch. Kaemwaset leaned down and kissed Qamra on the lips hungrily. She tried pushing him off, but his girth made it impossible.

Qamra turned her head and saw Nassar watching, his body spasming. "My lord, I have to help him!"

"He cannot speak of what he witnesses," Kaemwaset moaned as his hand cupped Qamra's breast in his hand with a moan of pleasure.

Nassar reached for Qamra's hand, his fingers trembling, his eyes watching the scene before him. Qamra reached for the boy's hand as she began to cry.

"Nassar, go, please! I do not want you to see this!"

Nassar's body gave a weak jerk as he rolled onto his stomach. Qamra watched as Nassar stood on trembling legs. The boy took a step and fell forward onto the ground.

"Nassar? My lord, what did you do to him?"

Kaemwaset moaned with pleasure as he licked her collarbone. "It is amusing watching him try to walk, isn't it?"

"Nassar, are you alright?"

Nassar clenched his fists as he laid on the ground. Qamra's cries of protest sounded from far in the distance. The ground was soft below his cheeks. His back and his head felt as if they were on fire. His ears blazed with the

searing pain of the hot poker from years before. He stood
on his feet again, struggling to maintain balance. He
staggered towards the door. He opened it and fell again as
the door opened. The world around him spun out of
control.

"Nassar!" Qamra exclaimed loudly.

Nassar opened his eyes as he looked down the hallway. *I
have to help Qamra. I have to get somebody.* Nassar
pushed himself to his feet and wavered. He fell sideways
against the wall, holding onto it as he walked beside it.
The hallway twisted and turned as his head spun with
dizziness. He felt a drop of liquid fall onto his shoulder.
As he looked down, the red liquid tricked down his chest.
*I must get help. Don't give up on Qamra, Nassar. Keep
on your feet. Don't stop.*

Amsi ran from Laila, his hair flying behind him as he
giggled. Amsi ran behind Tabari and peeked behind his
skirt. Tabari saw Laila trying to circle around him and
grab the Noble boy. Amsi squealed with happiness as
Laila ran around Tabari.

"Children, be careful," Tabari said, holding his trowel
steady until the children were not circling around him.
"Go play with Issâm!"

Amsi ran towards Issâm, who was bent over, weeding
some of the garden. Amsi tried to jump over Issâm, but
the boy knocked into the man. Issâm fell to the side and
saw the little master laying beside him. "Master Amsi,
what are you doing?"

"Laila is chasing me!" Amsi exclaimed.

"Be careful in the fields, my little lord."

Laila reached out for Amsi as she gained ground. "I'll catch you!"

Amsi rolled to his feet and raced down the path. He saw Baruti pulling a cart with his hands. Sweat was rolling down his body as he breathed heavily. On the back of the cart, large piles of bound grain laid. The man stopped on the path and bent over breathing heavily.

"Laila, water?" Baruti panted.

"I'm playing now, Father Baruti!" Laila exclaimed as she chased Amsi around the cart.

Baruti sighed, wiping his wet face with his hands. He looked into the sky and down at the ground. "Hapi, God of the Nile, send me water!"

Baruti heard a cry coming from the house. He raised his head and saw Nassar staggering out of the front doors. The boy fell on his hands and knees and gave a loud, guttural scream. "Ba-oo-ee! Ba-oo-ee! E-am!"

Amsi stopped and turned his head. He saw Nassar stand on his feet and sway. "What does Nassar want, Baruti?"

"I cannot say, little master."

Amsi followed Baruti towards Issâm. Issâm looked up from his vegetables and brushed dirt off his clothing. Issâm saw the boy wavering on his feet and gasped. The boy's left shoulder, face, and chest was spotted with blood.

"I have no idea, my lord," Issâm said.

Nassar raised his head to the sky, calling with alarm. "Ba-oo-ee! Ba-oo-ee! E-am!"

Issâm and Baruti ran towards Nassar followed by Amsi. Nassar fell forward into Issâm's arms. Issâm held the boy against him protectively as Baruti looked down at the child.

"Nassar? What happened?"

"Qa-m-a! Qa-m-a! He-p! Kaemwa-et!"

Baruti narrowed his eyes and growled. Baruti pulled the doors opened quickly as Issâm gasped. "Baruti! Our feet are dirty!"

Baruti heard cries coming from down the hall. *Kaemwaset, that jackal! You are not going to get away with this again, you monster!* Baruti ran down the hallway and looked into the room where the screams were loudly tearing through the air.

"Get your hands off of her, you snake!"

Kaemwaset lifted his head from Qamra's body and glared at Baruti. "You get back to work!"

Baruti growled, his lip curling in disgust as he charged for Kaemwaset. He grabbed Kaemwaset and violently pulled at him. Baruti kicked Kaemwaset in the ribs, making the Nobleman cry out in pain and roll on his side.

Qamra gasped for breath and shifted away from her master.

"Father?" Amsi called from outside the door.

Qamra stood on her feet and stepped outside the room. She gathered Amsi into her arms and held him. "Amsi, there is nothing for you to see inside."

"My father is calling out," Amsi said. "Is he hurt?"

Qamra turned her head to look inside the room. Baruti and Kaemwaset were facing each other. Baruti's fists were clenched tightly, his teeth were grinding and his body was tense. Kaemwaset glared at the hostile slave before him. "Amsi, I thought you were outside playing."

"I was playing! I was playing with Laila. She caught me as I was running."

Qamra kissed Amsi on the forehead. "Go play, Little Master."

Amsi nodded as she set him on his feet. "Maybe we can play later, Qamra. You can try and catch me. I'm fast like the wind!"

Qamra smiled. "Then I will have a hard time catching you, my little lord. Go practice for our game tonight." Qamra watched as Amsi ran down the hallway, his arms extended like bird's wings.

Qamra ran into the room behind Baruti. Baruti glared at Kaemwaset. "What did you do to Qamra?"

"You go back to the field, you insolent, disrespectful swine!"

"You have no right to touch Qamra!"

Kaemwaset pointed to Qamra. "She belongs to me! Her body and her mind belong to me!"

"I belong to Baruti!" Qamra exclaimed, standing beside Baruti and wrapping his arms around his waist. The slave put his arm around his new mate with a mischievous smile. "She belongs to me, Kaemwaset. Her mind and her body are mine and I refuse to let her fall into your slimy hands."

Kaemwaset crossed his arms defiantly. "You belong to me, Qamra! I am your master!"

Qamra glared at her master. "I despise you. I loathe you. You will never have my love and I will never submit to you willingly!"

"You will never father a child from her again, Kaemwaset."

Kaemwaset growled. "You are interfering with the wish of the gods themselves, Baruti!"

Kaemwaset's eyes shifted between Baruti and Qamra. "Qamra, did you lay with Baruti without my consent?"

Qamra held tighter onto Baruti. "I need not your consent to lay with the one whom I love."

Kaemwaset stepped closer to Baruti and Qamra. "If I discover the two of you in the act of intercourse, I will tie you to the post and castrate you, Baruti! I forbid you to love him, Qamra! I forbid this rebellious union you have established for yourselves."

Baruti kissed Qamra's forehead. "She belongs to me, Kaemwaset. Not even the gods could tear us apart. You will not touch her again nor will you father a child by her womb! You are too late."

"You will spend the night tied to the post, Baruti, for mating with her without my consent!" Kaemwaset growled low in his throat. "I have every right to touch her as I please! I am her master! If I wish to use her body for my pleasure, it is my right and my duty!"

Issâm stepped into the doorway holding the unconscious Nassar in his arms. Imani stood beside the slave. "What did you do to this boy, Kaemwaset?" Imani asked.

"That child became unruly, so I disciplined him."

Imani looked at the bruise on Kaemwaset's face. Baruti held Qamra close to him tightly. "My husband, did you touch my body slave? Did you touch my Qamra?"

"Baruti and Qamra have entered into a union without my consent."

Imani looked at the two slaves. Qamra's body was quivering as she clutched onto Baruti.

"Issâm, Qamra, Baruti, follow me. My husband, I am most disappointed in you."

Baruti and Issâm's eyes went to the floor in front of Kaemwaset's office where a puddle of blood was laying.

Baruti looked over at Issâm and saw the other man much intimidated by this mysterious summoning. Baruti cautiously took Nassar in his arms. The slaves followed Imani to her bed chamber.

Imani sat on a gold chair and crossed her legs. "Issâm, kneel before me. Baruti, you may put Nassar on that chair over there."

Baruti placed Nassar on a reclining chair by the window. A whimper came from the boy as Baruti caressed Nassar's cheek. Qamra sat beside the boy and examined his ear. "Holy Isis, what has the master done, Baruti?" The boy's jaw was swollen and bruises covered the boy's cheeks.

Issâm swallowed nervously as he looked at his mistress. Never had she made a demand that sounded much like her husband's when he was about to strike him.

Imani looked at Issâm. "Kneel before me," she demanded again.

Issâm slowly approached Imani and bent on his knees before her. He prostrated himself, his forehead touching the floor in front of her feet. "Yes, my lady mistress. What is it you wish of me?"

"Is Laila Qamra's daughter?"

Baruti looked at Issâm nervously. Issâm looked at his mistress. Baruti watched as Imani looked at him. The woman's eyes were red, tears were falling down her cheek. "Baruti, kneel before me."

Baruti and Qamra exchanged uncomfortable glances. He slowly advanced beside Issâm and slowly kneeled before her. "Yes, my lady."

"Issâm, is Laila Qamra's daughter?"

Issâm nodded, his head placed on the floor at her feet. "Yes, my lady."

"Who is Laila's father?"

Issâm clenched his fists as sweat formed on his face again. "Baruti is Laila's father, my lady."

"Baruti, did you father Qamra's daughter? Is she the child of your body?"

Baruti looked at Qamra. The woman sitting beside the unconscious boy shook her head slowly. The slave looked his mistress in the eye. "No, my lady. Laila did not come from my body."

Imani looked down at Issâm. "Why did you lie to me, Issâm?"

Issâm swallowed hard and raised his head. He folded his hands in front of him. "I was told to keep silent, my lady. All of us were instructed to keep our tongues silent or they would be removed just as Nassar's."

"I am deeply saddened that you have lied to me, Issâm. I had thought that as a man of holy beginnings that you would not speak falsehood."

"We did so to protect you," Baruti said quickly. The woman looked at Baruti who lowered his head. "I lied to you, as well, my lady mistress. It was not the right thing to do, but we could not tell you the truth. Please understand. Do not be angry at Issâm."

Imani looked at Qamra. "Which of these men fathered Laila, Qamra?"

Qamra sniffled and rubbed a tear from her eye. Nassar's eyes opened as he began to paw at the air blindly. "Neither, my lady."

Imani sighed and looked down at her son. "So it is true. My husband fathered that child without my knowledge."

"I tried to fight him off, my lady!" Qamra said. "Nakia saw it happen. Kaemwaset wanted to kill the boy, but Baruti stopped him."

Baruti lowered his head. "Nakia is still recovering from the injuries he sustained from Kaemwaset. He is laying in the slave house."

"Issâm, bring the child here."

Issâm gasped. "If we bring him here, the master will know where he is! He is not healed yet!"

"Bring him here, Issâm."

Issâm bowed his head and stood on his feet. He walked from the room. Imani kept her eyes focused on Baruti, making the man's toes quiver out of his mistress' sight.

"Issâm has been praying very hard for Nakia's recovery. He has fasted and prayed since the boy was returned."

"Baruti, what does my husband do to those who lie?"

Baruti closed his eyes and braced himself for a strike. He clenched his teeth and his fists, waiting for a harsh punch from the mistress.

"Their Ka is food for Ammut!" Amsi smiled from the entrance.

The occupants of the room turned their heads to see the little boy standing in the entrance. Amsi smiled as he ran to his mother. Imani put her arms around Amsi in an embrace. "I love you, mother."

Imani smiled as she kissed his cheek. "I love you as well, my child. Lying is something I do not respect, Baruti. I expect all of you to set a good example for my little boy."

Amsi walked up to Baruti and gave the slave's shoulder a tap. "Lying is naughty, Baruti!"

Baruti opened a single eye. "I apologize, my lady. You are correct. I should not have spoken falsely."

"I want you to teach my son proper behavior, Baruti. I do not want for him to lie. I don't want him to learn that lesson from you, do you understand?"

Baruti bowed his head. "Yes, my lady. You must understand, my lady, that we were afraid for our lives. Issâm and I must protect the others."

Imani looked down at Baruti with a smile. "I trust you, Baruti. Thank you for sparing my feelings, but I'm afraid your silence has complicated matters."

"How so, my lady?"

Imani looked down at Amsi. "Go play, my son. I wanted you to see how to handle servants who do wrong. Do not raise a hand to them."

Amsi hugged his mother. "Laila and I were playing! Qamra said I can play with her tonight! Right, Qamra?"

Qamra nodded. "Yes, my little master."

"Go play, my son."

Imani watched as Amsi ran from the room happily. She looked down at Baruti. "You may stand."

Baruti stood before her. Imani's eyes scanned Baruti. The young man stood before her, sweat dripping down his bare chest and stomach. His muscular physique was tight with his daily labor. The woman smiled up at him. "I hear that you have entered into a union with Qamra. Is this true, Baruti?"

Baruti bowed his head. "Yes, my lady."

"She has told me that you and she have laid together as man and wife. Is that true?"

Baruti looked over at Qamra, who was smiling at him. "Yes, my lady."

"Do you love her, Baruti?"

Baruti swallowed nervously and looked at Qamra. "Yes, my lady. I love her for her beauty, her mind, and her soul.

I worship her at her feet by day and by night. My entire being belongs to her and I would lay with none other."

"You hope to have a child by her, Baruti?"

"Yes, my lady," Baruti smiled. "I do hope so indeed."

Qamra released Nassar's hand and stood beside Baruti. "Baruti has fathered my child, my lady," Qamra said, her hand going to her stomach.

"I wish you both blessings and happiness." Imani looked down slowly. "I cannot say the same for my own marriage."

Issâm carried Nakia cradled in his arms. Issâm set the child on the ground. Nakia opened his eyes and looked up at Imani with a smile.

"Hello, Mother Imani."

"Ah-e-ah," Nassar groaned from the reclining chair.

Nakia turned his head and gasped at the sight of his injured brother. "Nassar!" Nakia rocked himself to get to his knees. He tried standing, but fell into Issâm's arms.

"You're not well enough to move on your own, Nakia."

"I have to get to Nassar!"

Imani leaned over and put her hand on Nakia's shoulder. "Your brother will be fine, Nakia. I need to speak to you and I need you to answer me truthfully."

Nakia looked up at Imani and nodded. "What do you want, Mother Imani?"

"Kaemwaset said he and Amsi were attacked in the desert and that is what happened. Were you attacked?"

Nakia shook his head. "No, my lady. Kaemwaset shot me with an arrow and he rode away with Master Amsi. I begged him for help, but he didn't listen to me."

Imani shook her head sadly. "What cruelty."

"I pleaded with him. I was in pain. He pulled the arrow from my shoulder and it hurt."

Imani leaned back in her chair. "Did you see my husband hurting Qamra in the stable, Nakia? Can you tell me about that?"

Nakia took a deep breath. He scratched his head. "All I remember is that Kaemwaset was hurting Qamra."

"Qamra and I were brought into his office and I was forced to claim that child to be my own," Baruti said. The slave bowed his head to his mistress solemnly. "My lady, I deeply regret the falsehoods which have rolled from my tongue. Would you not lie to protect the one you love?" Baruti took Qamra's hand. "Had I not done so, my lady, the master would have killed her or myself. May Anubis strike me down for my lies, Imani. Please offer me your forgiveness."

Issâm bowed his head before Imani. "May Merciful Thoth forgive me for speaking unjustly."

Qamra looked over at Baruti, a small smile creeping onto her face. "Nassar protected me from the master's wrath, my lady. The master had already beaten him."

Imani looked down at Nakia, whose attention was now completely focused on his brother in the reclining chair. "Tell me why Kaemwaset assaulted that boy, Qamra."

"Ah-e-ah," Nassar groaned again as he opened his eyes.

"The master was arranging a marriage and the father of the intended bride was groping Nassar. He did not particularly take that too well. Nassar became afraid and punched the bride's father, cutting his lip."

"Issâm, take Nakia back to the home. Baruti, carry Nassar back to the home, as well. Qamra, I need your counsel."

Qamra watched as Baruti walked slowly over to Nassar. Nassar looked up at the tall, muscular man above him. Baruti looked over towards Qamra and shrugged his shoulders. His large hands toiled in the fields, pulling heavy carts and tearing plants from their foundations. How was he to handle something so fragile? Nassar lifted his arms to Baruti.

"Be careful with him, Baruti."

Issâm carried Nakia over to Nassar. "Support his upper body in one arm and his legs in the other. Lift gently."

Baruti slowly slipped his arm under Nassar's arms. The boy rested his head against Baruti's chest. The two children seemed to disappear in the muscular arms of the field slaves. Qamra watched as the twins were carried out by the men.

Imani lowered her head and buried her face in her hand, crying. "Qamra, how could Kaemwaset do this to Amsi and I? I love my husband and he has betrayed me."

Qamra kneeled in front of Imani and put her hand on Imani's knee. "My lady, do you blame me for what has happened?"

"No," Imani sniffled. "How could he do this? I have given him a son! His son is learning how to be his father and that frightens me. I do not want his soul to be devoured by Ammut."

"Master Amsi has learned from you, my lady. I have seen him show compassion on the slave children. Just now you heard that he was playing with Laila."

Imani sighed and rubbed her teary eyes. "He is young. Just like Pharaoh Runihura, he will grow older. Do you see how the pharaoh rules his kingdom now? He is more dangerous now than ever. He will continue to become deadlier as he matures. I have told my husband that I wish for our son to choose his own wife."

Qamra looked Imani in the eyes. "He gave Sabi to the father of the bride. She is to go with him in three years time when her child is finished feeding from her breast."

Imani clenched her fists. "Sabi is not going anywhere! She is staying here where she belongs! I shall not allow it!"

Qamra breathed a sigh of relief. "The man was offered Nassar in the beginning, but Nassar became unruly when he asked if Nassar had reached manhood. He was reaching between Nassar's legs when Nassar punched him."

"That poor child has suffered so much. I would send Nassar away, but I have no place of safety where he could go. I cannot throw him away to starve in the streets. Here he has food and shelter. I cannot part him from his brother." Imani reached up to touch Qamra's face lightly. She smiled at her body slave. "And Nassar has you, Qamra. I couldn't tear him from you. My husband has been unfaithful to me and the children should not suffer because of him."

Qamra covered Imani's hand with her own. "Why do you not leave, Imani? You do not need to stay here. You can be free of him."

"I cannot leave my son with him. He will learn from his father the ways of hatred and bigotry. I cannot leave you and the other slaves. Should I decide to leave, I have no place to go. My son needs me here. I could not provide him the education that my husband can afford."

Qamra smiled at her mistress. "Kaemwaset's betrayal was not your fault, my lady. You are a beautiful woman. Your heart is larger than the pharaoh's palace. The children adore you."

"You are very kind to speak such lies, Qamra," Imani said with a smile. "What have I told Baruti about lying?"

"My tongue speaks the truth of Ma'at, my lady."

Imani smiled and caressed Qamra's cheek. "Baruti is a lucky man to have chosen you as his mate."

"I have been blessed with that honor, my mistress."

"Qamra, I wish for you to return to the slave home. I want you to care for the twins today. I wish for time alone to think about my husband and what I shall do."

## XXII

### <u>Storm Front</u>

Azizi walked through the streets with his head lowered. The young boy's eyes lifted to see the food on the carts. The vendors were calling their wares loudly as the boy stopped to look at the produce. He had hidden his basket of food carefully among the reeds to prevent its discovery. The night in the open air was cold and he searched for a place to warm himself for the night.

He saw a man standing in the shadows, chewing on a piece of grain. He walked down the alley, his stomach beginning to rumble. The man watched as Azizi passed and tripped the boy with his staff. Azizi fell to the ground and felt the man's foot press onto his back.

"Give me your gold, rich boy."

"I don't have any gold!" Azizi protested. "Let me up!"

The man chuckled. "Do you think that I am a fool, boy? What is your name, little boy?"

"Azizi Keket!"

The man narrowed his eyes and reached down for the boy's arm. He pulled the boy to his feet and kneeled before him. "You lie!" The man's eyes looked at the scar under the boy's right eye. His hand reached to touch the scar, making the boy flinch with fear.

"You come with me, boy."

Darwishi held the boy under his arm. Azizi swallowed nervously as his arms and legs dangled in the man's grip. The man pulled a brown hood over his face and wrapped his cloak around him, covering the boy. "Let go of me! Let go! Help!"

*Where is this man taking me? I'm no rich boy! I'm Azizi! Osiris, please watch over me!*

Azizi's eyes fixed on the ground. The man was keeping to the shadows. He recognized the path towards the quarter where his mother had been murdered. *He's taking me to the pharaoh! Oh no! Stop! Let me go!* Azizi punched his captor and tried to reach for the dagger buried under his skirt. The man stopped suddenly and kneeled on the ground. He removed the cloak concealing the child and looked down at his captive.

"Do not reach for your weapon. I am much faster with mine. I have been trained to be so. You are not in danger. Keep silent and neither one of us will lose his head."

Azizi watched as the cloak covered him again. His heart raced quickly as he was carried through more streets. He heard a door open and the door close behind him.

"I have found him, my lady. I have found the boy."

"Let me see him."

Azizi watched as the cloak was pulled from over him and he was set on a dirt floor. The boy looked around him terrified. Candles lit the room decorated with reed mats and chests. Baskets of food decorated the corners of the room and scrolls lined pots. Azizi looked at the young woman standing above him.

"Are you Azizi?"

Azizi swallowed nervously as he turned to run to the door. His captor blocked the exit, standing in front of it with crossed arms. "Answer Aneksi."

"I want to leave," Azizi whimpered looking up at Darwishi.

"Azizi, it has been a long time," the woman said with a smile as she kneeled beside the fire.

The boy turned to her, his bottom lip trembling. "Are you going to hurt me?"

"Of course not," Aneksi said with a smile. "I have brought you into this world, my child. I have done the world a wonderful service through your birth."

"I'm hungry. I want to go."

Aneksi smiled and handed the boy a piece of bread. "Eat, child. You look thin and weary."

Azizi grabbed the bread and chewed it hungrily. When he finished, he licked his fingers clean and looked at the woman. "Don't hurt me like those bad people, please."

Darwishi chuckled in front of the door. "I believe I have startled him more than intended."

"You are dressed as a Noble child, Azizi. Where did you get that beaded skirt?"

"My friend Amsi gave it to me."

Aneksi looked up at Darwishi. "He has met the companion."

"Praise Rā in his glory," the man said reverently.

Aneksi smiled as she reached for the boy. Azizi jumped back and pulled the dagger from a sheath on his hip. He held it in front of him defensively. "Don't hurt me!"

Aneksi put up a calming hand. "Azizi, I do not mean to hurt you. I was a friend of your mother who delivered you into this mortal world. You are a very special little boy, Azizi. Do you know that?"

The boy narrowed his eyes at the woman. "Don't touch me!"

"My boy, put the weapon down. We are unarmed and we do not mean to hurt you. We mean to help you."

Azizi glared at the woman and his body slowly began to relax. "Mean people try to hurt me. They want to take me to the pharaoh! I cannot sleep in the streets because they wake me and chase me!"

"They will not be the first, Azizi. I will promise you. I have heard of your mother's death. I offer my condolences to you."

Azizi gripped the hilt of the dagger tightly. "My father is dead, too. Mother said he was slain by the pharaoh."

"Azizi, you are a very special, precious child. Your birth has been foretold. It has been ordained by the gods."

Azizi cocked his head to the side. "What does that mean?"

Aneksi chuckled. "You are The One, Azizi. You are the one to defeat the pharaoh and bring glory and peace to Egypt."

Azizi shuddered as he remembered the pharaoh glaring at him. The pharaoh blamed him for his mother's murder. The warm breath of the pharaoh's cheek brushed against his skin. Azizi looked down. "He is a scary boy."

Aneksi smiled as she put a hand on his shoulder and kneeled before the boy. "Be afraid of him, Azizi. He is one who has great power and yet who is powerless."

"Can he bring my mother and father to life again?"

Aneksi looked sadly at the boy, her smile fading quickly. "Azizi, I am truly sorry. Your mother and father cannot return to the land of the living. They are dead."

"Can you try?" Azizi asked, his eyes looking sadly at the woman. "Please?"

"My child, the dead deserve eternal rest. They are gone forever."

Azizi looked down sadly, his shoulders sagging, his bottom lip trembling. His eyes filled with tears as he rubbed them with his hands. "I miss my mother."

"I know you do, Azizi," Aneksi said calmly. "You are meant for so much, Azizi. You will do great things. You must learn to survive without the aid of your mother and father."

Azizi sniffled. "Amsi gave me food. He is nice to me."

Aneksi looked at her companion and back down at the boy. "Amsi Al-Sakhir?"

Azizi nodded as he rubbed his eye. "Yes."

"It has happened, Darwishi. The Annointed Companion of Rā lives! He must survive. If he does not, all is lost."

"Are you my new mother?"

Aneksi shook her head. "You are wanted by the pharaoh. He has placed money on your head, my child. If the guards see you, you will be killed. It is fortunate that you have a skirt of beads and fine linen. They are looking for a child who is covered in blood with a golden dagger. Be sure to hide that blade. We will teach you the fine art of thievery."

Azizi nodded and pointed to Darwishi. "That man scared me!"

"If I was a guard now, child, you would be dead and I would be exceedingly rich. I would not forget that."

"Darwishi is right, Azizi. You must always be on your guard. Everyone unknown to you is an enemy." Aneksi smiled at him. "The Common Texts have told of one child born who would end the tyranny of Sekhmet."

"I'm not special. I'm Azizi."

"You will learn the truth in time. You are a very precious boy, Azizi. Praise the gods for sending you to us, my king."

Azizi stepped back away from the woman. "I'm not a king! I'm only me! I want to go play with my new toy."

"Azizi, do not run away so quickly!"

"No! I want to play now!" Azizi pouted, stomping his foot on the ground in protest.

Aneksi smiled and stood. "Very well, child." Aneksi watched the child walk away.

"Are you certain that is the child the gods have sent to us? Can he defeat the beast sent by the Lion Goddess?"

"I do not know, Darwishi," Aneksi sighed. "The scrolls of Common Magic have told me of his coming. He is so young to have suffered so much tragedy, but had he not done so, he would not grow into the strong adult he shall become. Goodbye, our king."


Baruti tugged at the rope holding his bound wrists to the post. He looked up at the home in front of him, watching as dark clouds were looming overhead. He pulled at the rope again violently. The rope binding his wrists rubbed and dug into the skin as the naked Baruti struggled to free himself.

The slave glared at his sweating and panting master hovering above him. Kaemwaset dabbed his forehead with a white linen cloth, the struggle to subdue the slave causing his heart to race wildly. Kaemwaset's face turned red as he breathed heavily and glared at the bound slave before him.

"You will obey my orders, Baruti. Qamra belongs to me and you are forbidden to engage in relations with her without my consent."

Baruti spit at Kaemwaset's feet. "You have no right to do this!"

Kaemwaset grabbed Baruti's jaw roughly and held his face upwards. "I have every right!"

"Father, don't hurt Baruti!" Amsi exclaimed as he watched Baruti struggle again.

"My boy, when servants disobey you, they must be punished. Baruti here will enjoy a night in the open air to cool off from his hot temper."

"Why did you tie Baruti naked?" Amsi asked.

Baruti looked at Amsi. "Do not worry, Amsi. I obey only one power in this world. I obey the jackal-god Anubis, the Opener of the Ways. Your father wields no true power over me."

Amsi watched as Kaemwaset kicked Baruti in the chest. The boy walked to Baruti, but Kaemwaset grabbed the boy's hand. "You only watch. Do not help him."

"But you hurt him!"

"It's for his own good, Amsi."

Baruti glared at Kaemwaset standing behind his son. "May Great Anubis watch as your soul is fed to Ammut."

"I will break you one day, Baruti. You will be reverent before me and you will respect my son."

Baruti looked at the ground below him and then to Amsi. "You must be proud, teaching your son how to feel your hatred."

"I am teaching my son the proper way of behavior."

"You are a lying, filthy, adulterous son of a jackal and I would rather be dismembered and fed to wild dogs before I bow to you." Baruti struggled with his restraints. "I would rather die than see the filth of your bones impregnate Qamra once more."

Kaemwaset raised his hand and punched Baruti in the face. Baruti grit his teeth in pain as he felt a trickle of blood come down his chin.

"What a wonderful teacher you are," Baruti said with a grin. "I bear you no ill-will, Master Amsi. Learn your lesson well from your great and wonderful teacher, my child."

Kaemwaset's lip curled in disgust. "If I see you feeding Baruti tonight, Amsi, you will not see the light of day for seven suns."

Amsi swallowed nervously. "Yes, father."

Baruti lowered his head as he leaned against the post. His arms began to ache as they were raised above his head. Kaemwaset spit upon Baruti's face and calmly walked away. Amsi stepped close to Baruti and put his tiny hand on his shoulder.

"Does it hurt, Baruti?"

Baruti shook his head. "One day you will be a great man." The wind around Baruti began to gain speed. Above the walls of the garden, he saw sand whipping through the air.  He watched Issâm stand on his feet and look into the sky.  The sky darkened with sand as thicker clouds began to sweep closer to the Al-Sakhir family lands.

"Sandstorm! Everyone get inside the home!" Issâm called in alarm.

"Amsi, get inside the home! I don't want you hurt out here!" Baruti pleaded.

Amsi looked calmly around him. "Sand can't hurt you."

"You can become unable to breathe, little master. Get inside."

Amsi looked at Baruti and grabbed the ropes. He began to tug on them as hard as he could. "You need to get free!"

Baruti stomped his foot defiantly. "Amsi, listen to Baruti. Please go inside before the storm becomes worse."

"But-!"

"No, Amsi. Go. Please."

Amsi stepped back and looked towards the wall. The skies became black in the distance. Wild winds whipped over the walls, sending plants swaying. Amsi saw Sabi point to Baruti. Tabari was holding her in his arms protectively as the wind threatened to send the couple off of their feet.

"Get inside the house! Forget me!" Baruti yelled to Tabari.

Amsi ran towards the house and tried to hide his head behind his arms. He gripped onto the post as the wind began to push him. He felt a pair of hands on his shoulders as he held his breath. Baruti looked up and saw Issâm tugging at the rope binding him to the post.

"Issâm! Get to the house! Don't worry about me!"

"You'll suffocate! By Thoth, I will get you free! Even if I die, I will set you free!"

Baruti pulled violently, trying to dislodge the post from its base. Issâm began to cough and his eyes stung from the sand. Baruti gagged as he tugged violently on the ropes. With the tugging and pulling, he became winded. He breathed deeply and coughed harder as the sand in the air was forced into his lungs.

"Issâm, get to the house!" Baruti screamed. *Issâm's always willing to lend a hand, but doesn't he realize the danger he is facing? He could die for me and I won't have it!*

"Issâm, don't make me repeat myself!"

Issâm coughed as he wrapped his arms around Baruti. "I can't do anything! The ropes are too tight!"

"Go home, Issâm! Help Qamra with the twins!"

The wind blew hard, sending Issâm flying into Baruti. Issâm grabbed onto his friend when he heard a scream come from the field. Issâm lifted his head and barely saw Laila moving along the ground, propelled by the strength of the wind.

"Help her, Issâm!" Baruti coughed.

Issâm pushed himself away from Baruti and held his hand in front of his mouth and nose. The grains of sand whipped into his eyes as he struggled to remain on his feet. The wind stopped him and pushed him back as he strained to see the little girl through the blowing sand. He could barely hear the girl coughing as he struggled through the wind.

*I have to save that child! Qamra would never forgive me if I failed her! It's hard to breathe.* Issâm opened his eye and saw Laila clutching onto Tabari's tool which he had staked into the ground. Issâm grabbed her and held her face to his chest. "Hold your breath, baby girl."

Laila coughed hard and clutched onto Issâm. Tears fell from her eyes as sand crept under her eyelids.

"Laila! Issâm! Baruti! Where are you?" Qamra called from the slave home.

"Keep yelling, Qamra! I can't see!" Issâm's chest tightened as the wind pushed against him. The sand blocked his vision as the little girl began to cry. The dark clouds arrived over the Al-Sakhir lands, blinding Issâm to his path to the home. The horses' voices rose into the air, the only indication of where he was walking.

*Keep going, Issâm. Don't give up. The child will die if I can't get her home. Thoth, please guide my steps in the right direction!*

"Issâm! Baruti! Laila!" Qamra called again in alarm. "Are you out there?"

Issâm walked through the storm following the sound of Qamra's voice. He kept his eyes closed as he began to stumble. *So hard to breathe with the sand in the air…*

"Come this way, Issâm! I can barely see you!"

Issâm clutched tighter onto the girl in his arms. His foot banged against the first step and he gave a yelp of pain. Qamra put her hand on Issâm's shoulder and helped him inside. Issâm put Laila in Qamra's arms and leaned against the wall panting heavily. He coughed as he watched Laila hug her mother tightly.

"Thank you, Issâm. Have you seen Baruti outside?"

Issâm lowered his head. "The master has him already tied to the post. I tried to free him, but I failed."

Qamra looked outside, her face full of worry. "Baruti is out there in that storm?"

Issâm took a series of deep breaths and rubbed his eyes. "I tried to pull him. The rope was tied too securely."

"Will Baruti be alright?" Nakia asked.

"Baruti is a survivor. I know he will be alright, Nakia, but I'm still concerned. I don't want him hurt."

Issâm shook his head. "Don't go out there, Qamra. The children need you here."

*Baruti is out there*, Qamra thought. *How could I not go out there?*

A piece of material quickly flew in front of her face as Tabari and Sabi tried to cover the entrance. They coughed as they tried to keep the sand from flying into the house.

Nakia sat by the fire beside his brother. Nassar was looking into the fire sadly, his eyes fixed on the flames dancing before his eyes. Nassar's hand went to the tattoo on his right arm. Nakia rubbed his left shoulder.

"Do you think Baruti will be alright out there, brother?" Nakia asked as he looked left at his twin sitting beside him. Nassar continued looking into the fire silently. "Nassar! I'm speaking to you!"

Qamra turned her head and looked at the twins sitting beside each other. "Nassar, answer your brother." Nassar's head did not rise from the fire. *Maybe he's involved in his own thoughts. The master did beat him quite severely.* "Nassar?" Qamra asked as she kneeled opposite of Nakia. "Nassar? Can you hear me?" Nassar turned his head towards Qamra.

"Nassar? Can you hear me at all?" Nakia asked.

Nassar didn't turn his head towards his brother. Nakia took Nassar's hand and held it quietly.

Azizi shuddered as the wind whipped around him. He sat in the reeds of the Nile bank. The water was slowly creeping onto the land by the force of the wind. The surface of the water rippled violently as sand blew around. The basket that Amsi had given him was empty when he returned. He was being flooded out of his sanctuary, much to his dismay.

*This is bad*, Azizi thought. *I need a place to get out of the storm. It's hard to breathe. Maybe Amsi can give me some place to stay. I just have to stay out of his father's sight.*

Amsi covered his mouth and nose with his hand as he ran from the thrashing reeds. He ran towards the Al-Sakhir land and heard a voice pierce through the wind and sand. "Long live Anubis! May he smite my enemy and feed his soul to the Devourer!"

The wind knocked him to the ground and blew his side-lock of youth wildly. His vision went dark as the skies went black. Sand crept into his nose and into his eyes. He breathed and the sand was vacuumed into his lungs.

"Amsi! Where are you?" Azizi called as he struggled to his feet. He ran under the arch as he heard a cry of pain come from near the home. The scream rose into the air, making Azizi's heart leap into his chest.

*Somebody is outside? Why would somebody be outside in this storm?*

"Baruti!" a woman's voice called from nearby.

"Amsi! Where are you?"

Azizi staggered as the wind pushed him harshly. He heard the woman's voice become more clear.

"Amsi! Amsi!"

Azizi approached a structure and banged his toe on the step and fell forward. "Ow! That hurt!"

Azizi crawled up the step as the wind and sand slapped his face. "Amsi!" Azizi screamed as he felt a pair of hands reach for his wrists. They dragged him inside and pulled him to his feet.

"Master Amsi, what-?" Tabari released the child's wrists. "You are not Master Amsi. Who are you?"

Qamra looked at the little boy and stood beside the twins. "What brings you here, child?"

Azizi's eyes scanned the room around him. Tabari and Sabi stood beside him. Twin boys were sitting beside the fire, one of them looking directly at him. Issâm sat against the wall of the home watching him closely. Karida and Laila were sitting beside Issâm. Blankets covered the openings to the home to keep out the wind and sand.

"I thought Amsi was here."

"Are you looking for Master Amsi?" asked Issâm sitting beside the wall. "Master Amsi lives in the main home. This is the slave quarters."

Tabari and Sabi finished covering the entrance to the home and went to the corner. They grabbed two loaves of bread and broke them in pieces, handing them to the others. Sabi kneeled before Azizi and handed him the bread.

"You look hungry, you poor little thing."

"Thank you," Azizi said as he sat beside the fire.

Nakia watched Azizi closely as he chewed at his bread. "Do I know you from somewhere?"

Azizi shook his head as he looked at the boy. Azizi saw the tattoo of Rā and a scarab on the boy's upper right arm. All of the slaves had the same mark on their right arms. "I have seen you clean clothing in the river with her," Azizi said as he pointed to Qamra. "I hide so nobody sees me."

"Why do you hide?" Qamra asked.

"The pharaoh's men want to hurt me. The pharaoh killed my mother."

The slaves stopped eating and looked at the boy quietly. They exchanged uneasy glances and returned to their bread.

"I'm sorry to hear that," Issâm said from the corner.

Qamra heard Nassar whimpering as he ate his bread. She took a cup of water and handed it to the boy. "Soak your bread. It will make it easy for you to chew." Nassar took a bite of his bread and he whimpered in pain again. "No, Nassar. Listen to me. Put your bread in the water and let it get soft. You can eat it when it gets soft." *Why won't he listen to me?*

"Nassar, listen to Qamra," Nakia said.

Nassar scratched his left ear and threw his bread angrily on the ground with a guttural protest. Nakia took the bread and placed it in the water. He handed the bread to his brother and made a motion for him to eat it. Nassar was able to eat the bread without any protest.

"Why were you in this storm, Azizi? You should be home."

Azizi sighed as he put his bread on the ground. "I have no home. It was put on fire."

Issâm whistled to Qamra and motioned for her to approach him. Qamra left the twins and walked to Issâm.

"Qamra, we can't let that child into the storm."

Qamra nodded. "We can't let him stay here. The master would be furious. If he catches him here, Kaemwaset would hand the child to the pharaoh. We cannot allow that, either."

Issâm sighed. "He can stay here through the storm. He can leave in the morning when the winds cease."

Qamra nodded. "I want to go to Baruti tonight. Hopefully this storm does not last." The woman looked at Azizi sitting beside the fire. "I know him. My mistress and I would see the boy and his mother beside the river while I washed our clothing. Amsi and him would play together. Then there came a day when him and his mother ceased coming to the river. When I saw that scar under his eye, I knew it was him."

Azizi watched as Qamra and Issâm spoke in the corner. The woman had turned her head to see him then turned back to her companion. Azizi looked at the twins sitting beside the fire.

"My brother and I haven't seen you at the river in a long time," Nakia said.

Azizi looked at the twins looking at him. "I don't know you."

Nakia laughed. "You do know us, but you don't remember. That's all. I'm Nakia. This is my twin brother, Nassar."

"You look the same."

Nakia nodded. "We're identical twins."

"You know Amsi? He's my friend."

"Amsi is very nice. His father is-." Nassar punched Nakia's leg, making the twin wince in pain. "Don't hit me, Nassar! The master is not a nice man." Nassar's head shook wildly as he sucked on his wet bread.

Azizi finished his bread and walked to Nakia. He touched the tattoo on the boy's arm and looked at it closely. "What is that?"

"That tells everyone we are property of Kaemwaset. It's his family crest."

Amsi looked closely at a faded tattoo on the boy's chest. Three red lines with three red dots above them stood faintly against the boy's right chest. "What is that?"

"Those are tattoos of my tribe. Nassar has the same tattoo on his left chest."

Azizi looked down sadly. "I don't have a brother."

Nakia put his hand on Azizi's shoulder. "You can be my brother, too, if you want! We're all brothers of the Creator god. That is what my mother and father taught me."

Azizi smiled and giggled. "Amsi is my friend. You can be my brother!"

Nakia yawned as he rubbed his shoulder. "I need to sleep, Azizi. I worked hard today and my shoulder hurts."

Nakia laid beside the fire and put his head on Nassar's lap. Azizi watched as Nassar put a protective arm around his twin and turned his glaring eyes towards him. Nassar's other hand laid gently on Nakia's head and began to caress his twin lovingly.

"Are you mad at me?"

*I'm protective of my brother. He is all I have. He's hurt and I won't let anyone hurt him while I'm still breathing. I trust no one anymore. Had I been there when Nakia was shot, I would have thrown myself in its way. I would have gladly and willingly sacrificed myself for him.*

"Goodnight, Nassar," Nakia yawned. "Please get some rest."

*What did you say, brother? I know he said something. His lips moved, but I cannot hear him. Why can't I hear anybody? Qamra talked to me, but I could barely hear her. My ear hurts and it itches.*

Azizi watched as Nassar stopped glaring at him and scratched his ear. The boy moved his leg and carefully set Nakia's head on the ground. Nassar shifted behind his twin and slept with his arm draped his arm around his brother. Nassar pulled Nakia against him and closed his eyes with a yawn.

Qamra approached Azizi. "You may lay beside the fire tonight, child. Our master must not discover you, though we will tell Master Amsi that you were here looking for him."

Azizi nodded. "Thank you. The river bank was becoming flooded."

"Could the season of Akhet be upon us so soon, Issâm?"

Issâm closed his eyes as he leaned against the wall. "It is possible," he said slowly and tiredly. "We need new-." Issâm's voice trailed into a quiet snore. Laila and Karida curled beside Issâm's hips and fell asleep beside him.

Qamra looked at the material covering the entrance. Tabari and Sabi had fallen asleep beside the fire together. Qamra pulled back a corner of the material and looked into the night. The wind was not whipping so wildly. She could see candles burning in the windows of the home. Qamra lit the torch by the fire and walked into the night towards the house.

The screaming and the howling winds had ceased as a gentle wind caressed her face. "Baruti? Are you out there?" Qamra held her breath awaiting a response from her lover. "Baruti? It's Qamra! Are you out there?"

Qamra ran down the path towards the house. The post was placed near the steps to the home. She kept her eyes to the ground where some of the workers' tools had been broken or tossed into the road by the heavy winds. *Isis, please let Baruti call to me if he is alive!*

Qamra's heart raced and her hands trembled as she held onto the torch. She approached the post and stopped when she saw Baruti tied to the post. His arms were suspended above him. His body was leaning against the post, his head hung low.

"Baruti? It's me, Qamra."

Baruti didn't respond, his body remained still. *Is Baruti dead?* A tear crept down Qamra's cheek as she slowly walked to Baruti. The slave's eyes were closed as his head hung low. Qamra put the torch in a metal ring nearby. Qamra straddled Baruti's hips and reached for his face, her fingers quaking from her fear.

"Baruti, please be alive," she whispered as she tilted Baruti's head upward. She caressed his cheek tenderly and found his skin warm. "Baruti, open your eyes."

"I can't," Baruti said. "There's sand in them."

Qamra let a joyful cry escape her as she wrapped her arms around Baruti. She hugged him tightly and kissed his cheeks and lips repeatedly. "You frightened me!"

"Can you get the sand out of my eyes?" Baruti asked, shaking his head and making sand fly off of his skin.

Qamra carefully ran her fingers over his eyes to rid them of the sand particles. Baruti's eyes slowly opened as they became clear of sand. "I was afraid you were dead."

Baruti smiled at her. "Kaemwaset will have to try harder to kill me, my beloved."

Qamra caressed Baruti's cheek tenderly and leaned in to kiss his lips. They pressed their lips together in the night, the woman's hands drifting down to worship his chest with gentle massaging. Baruti's bound fingers twitched, itching to touch her and embrace her.

Qamra shifted closer to him and smiled. "Let the master find us and may he bind me with you."

Baruti moaned as his lover leaned to his neck, kissing his throat lightly. "If he binds you on the other side of the pole, I cannot enjoy myself as much as I am at this moment."

Qamra's hands caressed his belly as she pressed her chest against his body. "I shall suffer with you, my darling.

We can kiss on the pole all night until the rays of the Aten awaken us."

Baruti kissed Qamra's shoulder and her throat. "I cannot stop the master from beating you if I am still restrained, Qamra." Baruti's eyes closed with pleasure as Qamra's hands touched him. His breathing became sharp as his body tensed with her rocking against him.

Qamra pulled back from his neck and pressed her forehead to his lightly. She traced his lips with her thumb with a pleasant smile. "My body aches for you, Baruti," she moaned, touching her lover gently, caressing him and massaging him.

Baruti shifted under Qamra, his face covered in a thin veil of sweat. He tugged at the ropes again, his back arching in agony and ecstasy. "I can't touch you. Great Anubis, I want to touch you."

Qamra smiled as she kissed his lips tenderly. Baruti moaned into the kiss as his body began to shiver and rise against her. Qamra chuckled seductively into the kiss, her body quivering with pleasure. Baruti whimpered into the kiss as his body rocked against her, his body straining with the ropes that bound him.

"May our union bless us with a strong, healthy son," Baruti moaned as he felt Qamra's lips upon her.

Qamra looked at him with a smile and caressed his cheek delicately. "It is too early to tell if the barley or wheat will grow. I pray the barley sprouts and the gods grant us a beautiful boy with a courageous heart like his father."

"You are the only lord I worship," Qamra said, her hands touching between Baruti's hips. "My body and my soul belong only to you." Qamra kissed down his chin and down his neck. "Tonight, I will be your body slave," she whispered as she kissed down Baruti's chest and stomach slowly.

## XXIII

### Family

Baruti felt a gentle hand on him as the sun rose in the distance. The warm, gentle wind caressed his skin, heating it from the chilly desert night. The slave groaned and shifted his hips, noticing nothing holding him down. "Qamra, where are you?"

A little giggle beside him attested to the absence of Qamra. He opened his eyes slowly and saw Amsi standing there. "I'm not Qamra. I'm Amsi, Baruti! You're funny!"

Baruti's eyes looked around. "Where is Qamra?"

Amsi shrugged. "I don't know."

"Amsi, get away from him!" Kaemwaset bellowed. The man walked to Baruti glaring at him. "Tell me the lesson you have learned."

Baruti coughed and spit. "Sand tastes very bad. It doesn't make good food."

Amsi nodded. "It doesn't taste too good, no."

Kaemwaset grabbed a dagger and held it to Baruti's throat. "Do you know it's only a fine of thirty dînars if I cut your throat? I consider that petty money in comparison to the joy I will have of ridding me of your presence."

Amsi watched wide-eyed as his father grinned with pleasure. Baruti returned the challenging glare of his master.

"You would only be doing me the favor of watching your soul be consumed by the Devourer as I stand beside the great Anubis."

Amsi watched as Kaemwaset grabbed Baruti's neck and held him against the pole. Kaemwaset cut the rope around Baruti's wrists and pulled back slowly. "Get to the house and tell everyone to get to work before I lose my temper."

Baruti rubbed his wrists as he watched Kaemwaset walk away calmly. Baruti stood on his feet slowly and rubbed his stomach. "Master Amsi, you should return to the home."

Amsi watched Kaemwaset walk into the house. Amsi ran to Baruti and took his hand. Baruti stopped and looked down at the little boy. "What are you doing?"

"I'm going with you."

The slave smiled slightly at the boy. *It's not his fault that his father is a miserable old dung pile. I have seen his mother teach him the old ways. His father is teaching him the new ways. My heart goes out to this poor boy. My only hope is that he becomes more like his mother.*

As Baruti and Amsi approached the home, they saw Qamra running out and towards the back of the house. Amsi watched her holding her mouth as she ran into the field.

"Qamra?" Baruti released Amsi's hand and ran towards her. Amsi followed close behind the naked Baruti as he ran around the house and saw Qamra kneeling nearby and vomiting.

Baruti slowly approached her as he saw her body tense and vomit. Amsi's nose wrinkled as he saw the sight before him.

"I hope Qamra is not sick, Baruti."

Baruti kneeled beside her and put his gentle hand on her back. "Qamra? Are you still ill?"

Qamra's fists clenched tightly as she kneeled. She coughed and spit, her body gasping for air. "Baruti, you're here." Qamra turned and hugged him tightly. Baruti wrapped his arms around her and felt her body shivering. He caressed her hair and kissed her cheek.

"You have been sick for many suns. You worry me," Baruti said as he hugged her.

"Amsi?"

Amsi gasped and turned to see Azizi standing behind him. "Azizi! What are you doing here?"

"The wind was bad and I came looking for you," the boy said.

Amsi walked up to Azizi and pointed at the house. "I live there! This is the slave home."

Azizi's eyes widened at the big home. The home had two stories and eight windows on the front of the home. A walled garden protruded near the stables. "Your house is big! Great Osiris!"

Amsi chuckled. "It's the biggest home in all of Egypt, I bet!"

Azizi nodded. "It's the biggest I've ever seen!"

"If my father finds you here, Azizi, he's going to be very angry! If you need to stay with my servants, I don't mind, but don't get caught or my father will be very, very angry."

Azizi heard footsteps approaching the house and he gasped. He hid behind the house as he heard a scream from inside the house.

"What are you doing here, boy?!" Kaemwaset growled.

Amsi swallowed hard and grabbed onto Azizi. "Run! Run!"

Azizi nodded and ran down the path. Amsi followed Baruti and Qamra into the home where they found the twins backed into a corner behind Issâm. Kaemwaset was standing in front of Issâm, his body trembling with rage.

"Father! What are you doing?"

"You little rat! I thought I killed you in the desert!" Kaemwaset growled as he glared at Nakia.

Nakia swallowed nervously as he hid behind Nassar. Nassar returned the challenging glare at Kaemwaset and held his fists in tight balls. "I-The Bedu found me, sir!" Nakia said nervously as he clutched onto Nassar. His body trembled as he looked up at his master with fear.

"Issâm, step aside!" Kaemwaset growled.

"You leave these children alone!" the slave protested.

Kaemwaset stepped face-to-face with Issâm and glared at the slave furiously. "I gave you an order, Issâm. Obey me."

Issâm took a deep breath and swallowed nervously. He planted his bare feet on the ground. "No."

Tabari and Sabi watched anxiously from the opposite side of the room. Baruti stepped beside Issâm. Laila and Karida ran to Qamra and clutched onto her.

"I won't let you hurt my friends," Baruti said angrily.

Kaemwaset backed away from Issâm. "You just made a huge mistake, Issâm."

Kacmwaset raised his hand to Issâm when Amsi ran beside him. "I will tell mother!"

Kaemwaset looked down at his son angrily. "Since when do you defend these rats? When do you tell me what to do, Amsi? I am your father! You listen to me!"

"You can beat me all day, my lord. I won't let you put a finger on these children," Issâm said calmly.

The master glared at his slave. "I will hold you to that promise at a later date, Issâm," he said as he lowered his hand. Kaemwaset turned to Sabi and Tabari. "Sabi, I have sold you to Mahoma as part of the dowry for his daughter's hand."

Tabari put his arms around Sabi. "My lord? Sabi will be leaving?"

"I will allow Sabi to remain here for three years until the child is free from her breast. Then she will join Mahoma on his lands."

"My lord, please do not send her away!" Tabari pleaded.

"You do not have a choice, Tabari. You belong to me as much as she. You are my property and I have exchanged her as such."

Amsi ran beside his father. "I do not want to marry Ife!"

"You will do as I say, Amsi Al-Sakhir!"

"I don't want to kiss her! I don't want to do that!"

Kaemwaset leaned towards his son. "You do want it. I know what is best for you, Amsi. Do you love your father?"

Amsi nodded. "Yes."

"Then trust me when I say that I know what is best for you." Kaemwaset looked up at Tabari. "All of you get to work." Kaemwaset turned to the twins hiding behind Issâm and Baruti. "You get to work, too, Nakia. You have much to do."

Amsi watched his father walk out of the house slowly. He watched as Tabari wrapped his arms around Sabi and hold her. Issâm's body relaxed with a relieved sigh.

"That was close. I thought he was going to beat me."

Qamra walked up to Issâm and hugged him tightly. "You are a good man, Issâm."

Issâm returned the embrace. "You are a good woman, Qamra." Issâm looked at Qamra's complexion. "Are you ill, Qamra? You don't look very well."

Qamra's eyes widened as Issâm leaned closer to look into her eyes. "What are you doing?"

Issâm took Qamra's wrist and put his fingers to her thumping vein. He closed his eyes as he counted. "It has quickened, my Qamra." Qamra watched Issâm closely as he touched her stomach lightly. "Have you checked your barley and wheat?"

"It is too early to tell, Issâm, is it not?"

"I will keep an eye on you, Qamra," Issâm said with a wink. "We should return to work before the master returns."


Azizi looked both ways as he stepped from the reeds holding Amsi's ball tightly in his hands. His eyes looked at the Al-Sakhir residence towering above the Nile nearby. *Amsi must enjoy great comfort with a nice mat to sleep on and people to do whatever he wants.* Azizi looked down at the water creeping over the banks and touching the back of his bare feet. The ripples of the water began to lick at his toes as he watched the water's edge. The bank where he had hid from the guards became foul with the smell of his mother's rotting body. The flies bit him as he slept near her body, so he had no choice but to move up the bank at a distance from the scent of decay.

He crept out of the reeds carefully and ran behind the walls of the Al-Sakhir lands. He kept his eyes moving cautiously as he shifted his eyes nervously. When he was out of sight from any passers-by, he looked at his ball with a smile. His belly was full of bread and he had the first good sleep in many nights under a roof and beside a fire. Issâm had showed him how to build a fire to keep himself warm.

Azizi's head picked up as he heard the sounds of singing emanating from inside the walls. The Al-Sakhir slaves were singing songs of merriment, lead by one talented distinctive male singer.

*The gods are glad when they see Rā in his rising;*

*His beams flood the world with light.*

*He maketh bright the earth at his birth each day;*

*O mayest thou be a peace with me; may I behold your beauties!*

Azizi bounced the ball on the ground. *They were very nice to me. I'll have to see what I can do for them so I can be good to them.* Azizi laughed as he threw the ball against the wall and caught it in his hands. He threw the ball again and jumped to catch it, but the ball flew between his arms. He ran to the ball and threw it at the wall again. The little boy chuckled as he caught it.

Azizi threw the ball against the wall again and saw another child turn the corner and watch him. Azizi stopped playing with the ball and looked at the child. The other child looked him in the eye as he approached. The boy was dressed in a common white skirt. Azizi recognized the boy immediately as Kaphiri, the leader of the rival gang of street orphans who worshiped the god Seth.

"What do you have there?" the other little boy asked.

Azizi held his toy close to his body. "It's a ball."

"Give it to me! I want that!" the other little boy demanded angrily.

Azizi had seen him in the city taking the toys away from younger children that he coveted. "My friend gave me this."

The boy narrowed his eyes. "Give me that toy!"

Azizi glared at the boy. "You are always taking toys that are not yours! You break toys and make the other children cry!" Azizi narrowed his eyes. "No! This is my ball!"

"I am Kaphiri and I can take anything I want! That's mine!"

Kaphiri grabbed Azizi's ball and tried to pull it away. Tears welled in Azizi's eyes as he clutched the ball close to his body. He let out a scream of alarm as his fingers dug into the hide. Azizi's face became red as he struggled to hold onto the ball and hold back his tears. Kaphiri shoved Azizi to the ground and put his foot on Azizi's side. The child tugged at the ball angrily.

"Give me that!"

"No!"

Kaphiri kicked Azizi's hand, trying to make the boy release his toy. "That's my toy now!"

Azizi grabbed Kaphiri's leg as the boy kicked. Azizi tugged and the other five-year-old fell on his back. Kaphiri held his head as Azizi crawled on top of him.

"That is my toy! Not yours! You are bad always stealing toys and not returning them!" Azizi growled.

Kaphiri's left fist connected with Azizi's shoulder. Azizi gave a cry of pain as Kaphiri bucked his rival off him. Kaphiri straddled Azizi's hips and punched him in the stomach.

"Where is Kaphiri?" an older child asked nearby.

"Here he is!" another child called.

Azizi watched as four children turned the corner and pointed towards them.

"That ball is mine! Take that ball!" Kaphiri growled.

"No! That is mine!" Azizi screamed.

Azizi grabbed Kaphiri's side-lock of youth and tugged roughly. Kaphiri fell to the side as Azizi tugged. Azizi punched Kaphiri in the face, making the other children stop their advance on the couple. Kaphiri let out a cry of pain as his nose began to bleed from Azizi's assault.

Azizi stood in front of his toy and pulled the golden dagger from under his white beaded skirt. "Anyone tries to take my toy and they will get hurt bad! That is my toy!"

"What should we do?" one girl asked.

"We can just knock him down and take it. There are five of us and one of him," the one boy said.

Azizi tightened the grip on the hilt of the dagger. *Great Osiris, please protect me and my ball. Help me not to be afraid of these other children.*

Khephiri stood on his feet and stamped his foot on the sand. "I'm going to tell on you!"

"You're mean and you can't have my toy!"

"Give me that toy!" Kaphiri lunged for the toy again before giving a cry of pain. Azizi had used the dagger to cut Kaphiri's hand. Azizi watched as the blade dripped crimson onto the sand.

Kaphiri's shrill scream echoed into the air as he held his hands. "I'm telling on you now! You hurt me!"

"Stay away from my toy!" Azizi growled.

"May Seth punish you!" Kaphiri exclaimed as he ran away, the other children following behind him.

Azizi narrowed his eyes. *May Osiris send you to eternal rest without supper.*

Azizi replaced the knife under his skirt and threw the ball against the wall of the garden, continuing his play.

Qamra entered the home with Baruti and saw Tabari and Sabi carrying a bundle on their backs. Sabi looked at Tabari cautiously. The man put his arm around his pregnant girlfriend and held her close.

"Qamra, we are leaving," Tabari said.

Qamra's eyes shifted between the two. "What? You cannot leave, Tabari!"

"I'm not going to be separated from Sabi! I'm not going to allow Sabi to fall into anyone else's arms! I'm not losing Sabi and my child, Qamra!" Tabari looked with worry and sadness at Qamra. "You know as well as I do that if she leaves I'll never see her again. I want to see the birth of my baby. Qamra, you of all people have to understand."

Qamra nodded. "I understand, but do you understand what will happen when the master discovers you have ran? If you get caught, you will be sent to the mines. We will be punished in your place!"

"We can burn off our tattoos," Sabi said. "I'm willing to do it to be with Tabari."

Issâm approached Tabari and put his hands on Tabari's shoulders. "Of all people, Tabari, I would have least expected this from you. The Mighty Speaker may not be in agreement with your decision."

"Issâm, I respect you as a man of holy inspiration, but please understand. I cannot bear to see Sabi taken from me. I will never see my child again if I do not leave with her. Would you be able to bear seeing your child born into a live of slavery?"

Baruti crossed his arms sternly. "Do you know what the master will do when he discovers your absence? Do you know what could befall our little family? Kaemwaset's fury will know no boundaries. Not only will that happen, my friend. One of us will be sent in his place. What if he picks me?" Tabari and Sabi looked down at the ground sadly. "What if it's Issâm? What about Qamra? What if they separate the twins?"

Nassar and Nakia looked up at Sabi and Tabari from beside the fire. Tabari looked as the two pairs of sad eyes looked up at him and Sabi. The thin bodies sat huddled beside each other as they held each other's hands.

"He cannot send Qamra away. Qamra is Imani's body slave and cares for Amsi."

"Tabari," Qamra said quietly. "This is a very bad idea. I don't want to see you go. If you get caught, you could stand before the pharaoh. Imani will not allow Sabi to leave!"

Issâm gripped onto Tabari's shoulders. "Tabari, the pharaoh will hang you by your necks or you will be sacrificed to Rā!"

Tabari's head raised and looked at Issâm. "I would rather be sacrificed to my god than slave for that serpent!"

"You don't know what you are saying!" Issâm gasped.

Karida gripped onto Sabi's skirt and tugged desperately. "Don't go, Sabi! Please! I'll miss you!"

"You can come with us, Issâm," Sabi said.

Issâm released Tabari's shoulders and stepped backward to stand beside Baruti and Qamra. "I can't, Sabi. I miss my freedom, but I cannot leave with a clear conscience knowing the others will suffer Kaemwaset's wrath."

"You can all come with us!" Tabari said with a smile. "We don't have to live under Kaemwaset! We can run! We can be free from his hand!"

"Do you think I haven't thought about leaving?" Baruti asked. "I would love to stick a knife in the back of that crocodile and run. I know that if I am caught running, the pharaoh will have me rot and starve in his dungeon. Where would Qamra be then? Why would I risk her life to save my own? Why would I do that to the woman I love?"

Qamra folded her hands pleadingly. "Please reconsider, Tabari. You are a part of this family. We may not be related by blood and bone, but it is our closeness which binds us."

Laila looked up at Tabari with tears in her eyes. "Please don't leave us, Tabari."

Tabari took Sabi's hand tightly. "I have made my decision. I'm sorry."

Issâm narrowed his eyes. "You have just condemned yourself and Sabi to death, Tabari."

"If you wish to risk both of your lives, be my guest." Baruti walked over to the basket and took a loaf of bread. He broke it into pieces and split it among the children. He sat beside the twins and began chewing on his insignificant piece.

Qamra put her hands on Sabi and Tabari's shoulders. "I give you my blessing. May Isis watch over you and protect you."

"Thank you, Qamra," Tabari said. "Let's go, Sabi."

Tabari and Sabi walked into the night. Issâm watched the couple's departure with a sign of resignation. "May Thoth protect you both," he said folding his hands in prayer.

## XXIV

### <u>Noble Precepts</u>

What's that? Who's that? Oh, it's you. Nassar, what are you doing here? I want to go back to sleep. No. Don't wake me. Stop pulling on my arm, Nassar. I want to go back to sleep! My dream was wonderful! I was the head of an army facing hundreds of enemies and I defeated them all with one strike of my sword! I was brave in battle! Why'd you have to wake me up?

"Am-i! Awa-et!" Nassar exclaimed to me.

It's too early to understand what he is trying to say. What was that? Sawaret is here?

"Boy, your tutor is here! Do not keep him waiting!" My father yelled at me through the door to my room.

I'd rather go back to sleep. Nassar, give me back my blanket! That's my pillow you're taking! What the--? You're hitting me with my own pillow to wake me up? It sounds like he's laughing at me.

When I open my eyes and I look up at him, he's looking down at me with a large smile on his face and he hit my arm again with the pillow. Oh, he did not just hit me again! You're going down, Nassar!

Nassar laughed as I grabbed a pillow and hit him back. He hit me again on top of the head with a pillow and I smacked him again with a pillow. Nassar laughed in his very odd manner, but I guess I would laugh strangely, too, if my tongue had been removed. I can't imagine what it would be like to have no tongue, but Nassar's been a good friend to me for my entire thirteen years of life.

Next year, I will be celebrating my Rite of Passage ceremony. I will no longer have my side-lock of youth and I will be an adult in the eyes of the gods and high society. Issâm told me that he would prepare me for the ritual. Issâm knows much about rituals and religious ceremonies. He's very wise and he is a kind man towards everyone.

"Amsi Al-Sakhir Ibn Kaemwaset, are you awake?" My father asked angrily as he threw open the door.

Nassar dropped the pillow and fell to his knees on the ground. He leaned over and placed his forehead on the ground, shaking. My father looked angrily at Nassar. "Nassar, get my son bathed and prepared for his tutor! Don't make me repeat myself or I will deafen you in the other ear completely!"

Nassar shook his head quickly as my father left the room. Nassar quickly stood on his feet and looked down at me. He put his hand on his chest and bowed his head. Nakia told me that meant that he was sorry. Nassar had no hearing at all in his left ear. In his right ear, you had to scream at him for him to hear.

I remember that day. I was frightened to see Nassar receive a punch in the face. He did nothing wrong. Nassar was afraid and he didn't like Mahoma. He came to claim Sabi as promised, but she and Tabari disappeared seven years ago. Sometimes, I wish I had a chance to say goodbye to them. My thoughts wander to them on occasion. We never heard of them or from them since they had left.

"Don't worry, Nassar," I say calmly. I know he can't hear me, but I hope he can read my lips.

I climbed out of my comfortable bed stuffed with feathers and towards a basin that had been filled with water. Nakia must have helped him bring warm water from the kitchen. I stood in the basin and watched Nassar as he grabbed a cloth. He must feel very awkward doing this. He's been bathing me for as long as I can remember. The twins are my body slaves, but I don't mistreat them as my father.

Mother told me when I was an infant that they would help me walk down the hallway when I was learning how to do so. Nassar would hold my hand and Nakia would be calling to me. They worked in the garden; They cleaned our home and our bodies. They cleaned our linens and they helped to bake our daily bread.

The warm water feels so good this morning! It feels more hot and dry than normal in this season of *Shemu*. Nassar is sweating badly as he pours the water over me. He may just want to jump in this basin when I am finished and he may not care that the water is dirty. He took the towel and began to wash my body. He rubbed my arms and my legs clean with the water. He dampened my side-lock and washed my face. Nakia had a more gentle rub than his brother. If Nassar saw some dirt that would not come off, he would rub and rub until it was removed. I looked down at Nassar as he washed my legs, his side-lock of youth had been gone a long time ago.

His ribs were prominently poking through his dark Nubian skin. His twin brother looked just as frail I saw every bone in his spine as he bent over. Nassar gave much of his small rations of food to his sickly brother.

Scars from my father's whip crossed his back. Five deep cuts were scarred across his back from my father's wrath seven years before. When Tabari and Sabi were discovered missing, I remember how angry my father had become. My father grabbed and whipped Issâm in the field. Issâm prayed as my father beat him. Nassar heard his screams and ran to his aid. He punched my father intentionally so he would receive the punishment. I remember that night vividly. It was cold and everyone was made to stand around the bonfire. Nassar was tied to the post and whipped harshly. Nakia, his poor brother, could only watch. He tried wrestling the whip from my father. My father pulled and pulled, trying very hard to get the whip back from Nakia. Issâm threw himself in the path of the whip after he staggered to the bonfire. That was a difficult night. My father tried to justify his cruelty, but what fairness is there in beating someone who cannot defend themselves?

Nevertheless, Nassar continued to be pleasant towards my mother and I, despite his muteness, his deafness, and his scars. I know it takes its toll on him. Nassar gets frustrated when you can't figure out what he's saying. Usually, Nakia can figure it out.

I reached over and put my hand on Nassar's back and I feel him shudder.

"There's no need to be scared, Nassar. I think I'm clean now," I said loudly. You have to almost for him to acknowledge that you are speaking to him.

Nassar raised his head and smiled slightly. Maybe he was lost in his thoughts as much as me. I held onto his back as I stepped out of the basin. He dried me off with a clean towel and wrapped me in it tightly. He kneeled before me and smiled.

"Thank you, Nassar," I said.

He bowed his head and smiled pointing to three different perfume bottles. I get to choose, as I always do. He can't say the names, so he points to them individually.

"Nassar, Sawaret sent me to get Master Amsi! Are you ready yet?" Nakia called loudly.

Nassar tried to speak as he always does, but nothing understandable comes from him. It's a series of guttural grunts. Nakia can click with his tongue and talk in his native tongue. Nasser's body language speaks volumes.

"I will be there in a moment, Nakia!" I call to him.

"Sawaret is becoming impatient, Little Master!"

Nassar grabbed a random bottle from the shelf and began spreading it on my skin. He rubbed it on my arms, my neck, my chest, my back, and my legs. Nassar placed some on my palms so I could rub the oil onto my buttocks. Nassar will not touch me between my legs or my buttocks, except to clean my body. He does so quickly and I can tell he tries to avoid it. There have been times where he will hand me the towel so I could do it myself.

Nassar tied my white linen skirt around my hip and he placed my white tunic over my head and clasped my gold bracelets around my wrist. He fastened a golden chain around my ankle. Lastly, he placed my golden ankh around my neck. Nassar smiled down at me when he finished fixing my hair.

Nakia opened the door and quickly hurried me down the hall. "Good job, Nassar! Hurry, Lord Amsi! Go! Go! Go!"

Stop pushing, Nakia! I'm going! I'm going!

Nakia practically pushed me down the hallway towards the room where my tutor always waited. The twins stood behind me as I walked into the room where Sawaret waited. The twins bowed behind me as my tutor rose on his feet. They stood behind me at the door, ready to attend to my every need as usual.

"Master Amsi, you are not thinking of becoming delinquent in your studies, are you?"

"No, Lord Sawaret! My sincerest apologies!" I just wanted to get more sleep.

Sawaret nodded as I took my seat before him. "My boy, you must learn the virtue of punctuality. You must be attentive and you must learn that your behavior could insult those who rely on punctual attendance. Do I make myself clear as glass?"

"Yes, Lord Sawaret!"

Sawaret sat before his pupil with his writing reeds and his scroll. "You have your proper place in society, Amsi. You are born of Noble Blood. Writing is a sign of prestige and it is a privilege. People of lesser blood, for example let's say your slaves, do not have the privilege and they do not have the mind for writing ability."

I'm sure the twins behind me were exchanging looks. I've seen them do that when my father is belittling them for their incompetence and he turns his back.

"My lord, Issâm writes."

"Amsi, I guarantee you what he writes is wrong. You shall write perfect. Writing is the perfect profession, Amsi. The smith has fingers like Sobek. His skin is dry with scales. The mason aches from every limb. You need not worry about any of those pains. Nakia, come here."

I watched Nakia cautiously approach my tutor. I'm sure Nassar was keeping a sharp eye on his brother. I could feel his gaze from behind me, piercing right through me.

"You work in the house and in the field, correct?"

Nakia nodded. The twins didn't work much out in the field, but they have helped when needed.

"Let me see your hands."

Nakia held out his hands to my tutor. Sawaret grabbed his wrist and almost pulled him off of his feet when he showed me Nakia's palm.

"His hand is dry with years of toil. This has dug into dirt and notice the dirt under his fingernails. This has washed your clothing. You should be ashamed of your appearance, Nakia. His back is burned with hours of toil under the sun. These arms lift heavy bushels of grain and hay. His job as a slave will end only with his body burned by the sun and broken from heavy labor." Sawaret released Nakia's wrist. "Return to your twin. You will never need to lift a finger, Amsi. You instruct other

people to do their duty while you sit under a canopy and
be fed dates and fruit. When the gods fashioned you in
your mother's womb, Amsi, they had a purpose for you.
Your purpose was to enjoy your life of privilege and
luxury. Your duty is to teach those of a more…barbaric
birth like Nassar and Nakia over there…how to behave in
a civilized manner."

Sometimes I don't see my father as civilized. I've seen
him strike the slaves in anger over trivial mistakes.
Depriving the slaves of food and an adequate roof over
their heads doesn't seem very civilized.

"You will serve the Great Pharaoh Runihura, Amsi, with
your deeds and your words. The pharaoh is Rā's gift to
his people and Runihura is truly a blessing unto all of us.
He has brought order from chaos. Life and Health be unto
him, Amsi! One day you will join him in his court and
see the glorious radiance that is Pharaoh Runihura. How
will you behave in the face of a god, Amsi?"

I have seen how the pharaoh behaves and he's not much
different from my father. Issâm told me about the old
days and he has taught me the old precepts from the time
I could learn to walk and talk.

"Sawaret, the pharaoh mistreats his house slaves and I
have heard that he slaughtered people for his own
entertainment. If the Great Rā is kind and merciful, how
is it that the Pharaoh Runihura behaves with such
cruelty?"

Sawaret didn't look too fondly on my question. In fact, I
believe I have caused him great anger. "Do not speak so
ill of your pharaoh! He is a great man and the pharaoh

would never slaughter his flock needlessly! Words of revolt had reached his ears and he was suppressing a rebellion of those who dared oppose him! You must believe in the greatness of the pharaoh, long may he reign, Amsi. What you speak is heresy."

"Is it not cruel to mistreat those who are defenseless? Is it not cruel to strike with a club a man who is unarmed and bound?"

Sawaret's anger seemed to have faded slightly. "If they have taken something from you, if they have struck you first, if they need to learn an important lesson and they fail to learn it, then it is not cruel. You must be in a position of power at all times. Domination is a concept that the lesser people understand. They were born weak-minded and weak of body." Sawaret looked at the twins behind me. "They are like asses that need to be directed because they cannot think for themselves and you must teach them."

"Ah-ma-amawal!" Nassar exclaimed behind me. He doesn't sound very thrilled with my lesson today. I turned my head around, knowing that Sawaret would scold him. I didn't want him to get hurt.

"Nassar, silence!" I exclaimed.

"Nassar, don't say anything," Nakia said quickly. "Keep silent."

I don't think Nassar heard his brother. Nassar pointed to his open mouth where his tongue should have been and protested to Nakia. I had better do something before Sawaret gets to him.

"Nassar, be quiet right now!" I exclaimed, standing on my feet and pointed to him angrily. I walked towards Nassar and glared at him. "This is my lesson and you are interrupting it! Be quiet!" My fist punched Nassar in the stomach.

Nassar held onto his stomach as he moaned. The twins looked at me wide-eyed. I looked at my fist clenched tightly. Did I just sound like father? I looked at Nassar rubbing his stomach. Nakia wrapped his arms around his brother who began to cough. Did I just hit Nassar? Did I actually hit him? I can't believe I just did that. Nassar, I'm sorry!

"Good job, my boy," Sawaret said behind me. "Now Nassar will learn his lesson to hold his tongue. One would think that you would become more obedient once you had your tongue removed, Nassar. I see that you have yet to learn your lesson. Pity."

I saw Sawaret approach me and glare at Nassar. "What will it take, Nassar? Should we remove your eyes next? Should we cut off your nose or your ears? What will it take to subdue you?"

I saw Nakia began to shake as he held onto Nassar tightly. Nassar straightened his back as Sawaret stepped toe-to-toe with him.

"Nassar, I'm sorry," I said apologetically.

"Do not apologize, Master Amsi. You have learned your lesson well. You should never apologize to the son of a defeated people. They are weak. They understand only violence, especially the one who is deaf and mute and quite useless."

Nakia kept his arm around Nassar as my tutor looked at him as if he were looking at a dung beetle. Nakia glared at my tutor. "My brother is not useless."

Sawaret backed away from him and returned to his seat. "Sit down, Amsi, and we shall continue our mathematics lesson."

Sawaret taught me my writing, literature, and mathematics lessons, but I couldn't concentrate. I kept thinking about Nassar and what possessed me to strike him. I didn't mean to hit him. My mother would scold me not to hit them or anyone. My lesson from her was to use my words instead of my fists. It would seem I have failed that lesson for today.

When the sun reached its highest point in the sky, my lessons were completed. I bowed to Sawaret as he walked calmly from the room. I approached Nassar slowly and I lowered my head. "I'm sorry, Nassar." I hope he heard me.

Nassar turned and walked away silently. Nakia sighed tiredly as he watched his brother leave the room.

"Nakia, I didn't mean to hit him," I said. "I know I would be angry if Sawaret was saying those things about me."

"I think he knows that, Master Amsi. Nassar will be alright. He doesn't want you to be like your father, Amsi. I know he fears that. You are too nice of a person to become your father."

"Thank you." I looked at Nakia. "Please tell him I am sorry again. Can you do that for me?"

Nakia pat me on the head with a smile. "Nakia will handle his twin. Leave it up to me."

Nakia left the room and I followed him. Nassar was walking through the archway to the gardens. It was time for the twins to help prepare dinner for tonight. They had to pick the fresh vegetables from the garden and help Najam make her delicious bread.

That reminds me. I set aside some of the bread for my friend. I kept it in my bedroom wrapped in a white cloth. When my father asked why I was taking food from the table, I told him that if I was hungry later, I would have some bread. Father kept a close eye on the servants and had become angry when he discovered I was giving them food.

*They work for their food. If they don't work up to my expectations, they don't get fed!* My father scolded me harshly. That hasn't stopped me. My mother said that I was making the gods happy, especially Ma'at, if I showed kindness and respect to my slaves and to the poor.

My friend, Azizi, has told me of the pharaoh's soldiers in the city and what they had been doing to the poor of Heliopolis. He had no mother and father and I know that the pharaoh wants him dead. How can a person live that way, hunted day and night by anyone looking for coin? He was grateful for my generosity when I brought him food for the first time and since then, I have never known exactly where to find him. I've found him in the desert at night. I have found him in the city alleys during the day. I have found him in the reeds beside the Nile. I even found him disguised one time sitting outside the palace walls. It's difficult not knowing where to find him. Whenever I can't find him, it frightens me because that means he could be in the pharaoh's dungeon.

I grab the bread and run quickly out of the house. The jewelry that I wear had to be removed. It's important that I blend into the crowd as much as possible. If I look like a child of Nobility, the other children or adults looking for coin will rob me.

The slaves watch me as I hurriedly run down the path. Baruti looks upward and stands beside his children, Meskhenet and Khentimentiu. Meskhenet was older. She was eight years old. Khentimentiu was born two years after Meskhenet. Qamra had lost a baby last year and Baruti was very sad, especially since it was a boy. He loves Qamra very much and when they are not working, they are always together. Baruti is extremely protective of his son and daughter.

I run away from my family's lands and searched the reeds, calling for Azizi. I searched everywhere and I couldn't find him. It's the dry season, so he should be around here somewhere. Azizi, answer me! Where are you?

He can't be here. When he is here, he greets me. He must be in the city. I walked to the city gates and watched as a group of men raced away on horses. They were dressed as the *Nuu*, explorers of the desert who lead the Nobility into the desert wilderness. They were employed as scouts during hunting expeditions and nobody knew the desert

terrain better than them. My father took Nakia with us
when we went hunting. Nakia knew how to track the
animals and how to read the desert sands to stalk prey.
He impresses me with his knowledge and his courage
knows no boundaries.

The streets were busy as I walked through the quarter.
Pretty ladies in front of the bordello smile at me as I walk
by. Do I look that obvious that my family is wealthy? I
have no jewelry and yet they giggle and wink at me. I
looked down the first alley and saw nobody sitting or
walking. I continued to walk through the street to the
next alley.

A group of children run past me as they chased a younger
child with a toy. Ahead of me, I see the public gallows. I
have seen people killed there. Their eyes can pop from
their heads as their tongues slip from their mouths when
they hang. Sometimes their neck does not break and they
hang suspended as they slowly suffocate. The pharaoh
delights in watching the spectacle from the balcony of his
palace.

*How long do you think will it take for him to die, Amsi?*
The pharaoh asked me once when my father took me to a
public hanging. When I asked about his crime, the
pharaoh simply said that he wanted entertainment. A
man and his wife died for his entertainment that day. I
couldn't sleep that night. I ran to the slave house that
night and woke Qamra. Qamra calmed me and put me
back to bed.

What was that? I looked down and saw a ball that had hit
my ankle. I took the ball in my hands and looked beside
me at an alley. A body shrouded in black had laid on the

ground. Abandoned carts were lining the sides of the alley.

"Hello?" I asked as I slowly walked down the alley. My eyes shifted side-to-side and my body tensed as I crept down the alley. My heart raced quickly as my sandals touched the hard ground.

Azizi warned me of a gang of thieves, the Seth Clan, roaming the city lead by his rival named Kaphiri. They wouldn't care if I was a young child. They would steal from anyone young or old. They would butcher anyone and leave them at the front gate of the pharaoh's palace. When I had to find Azizi in the city, I made certain that I kept my guard up.

I passed a cart, my arms clutching the bread against my chest.

"AMSI!" I heard a scream and clawed fingers on my back.

I screamed and turned suddenly, jumping backward, and almost lost my footing when I saw Azizi bent in half laughing at me. Azizi laughed loudly, tears coming from his eyes as he laughed at my expense.

"You horse's ass!" I exclaimed as I shoved him backward. "You scared me!"

Azizi leaned against the wall of the alley and slid down, laughing on the ground. "I couldn't resist!"

"I brought you food!" I growled, throwing the food at his head. The bread bounced off of his head and landed on the ground beside him.

"Your reaction was worth all the gold in the pharaoh's coffers, Amsi!" Azizi said as he rubbed his eyes free of tears and took the bread into his hands.

I crossed my arms and sighed. "This is the gratitude I get for bringing you food?"

"Thank you, my friend," Azizi said, bowing his head to me. "Thank you."

My eyes perused the alley as I heard him unwrap and begin to chew on the bread. "Why are you here?"

Azizi shrugged. "I needed a place to sleep. When the night falls, I will leave to look for food. There are too many people around now."

My nose caught a scent of something foul. "How can you stay here? It smells like horse dung."

"I can't simply just walk out of here, Amsi. The pharaoh's guards search for me. The streets are my own little kingdom."

I walked to the body covered in a black shroud. Flies were buzzing around it and I could smell decay emanating from it. The ground was covered in dirt and I could see some fruit decaying in some of the carts. Flies and maggots were covering the rotten food.

Azizi slapped a fly that had landed on his knee. He continued eating passively until he wrapped the remainder of the bread in the white cloth. "Do you want your cloth back, Amsi?"

"You can keep it to hold your bread. I don't want the bugs getting to it and eating it on you."

My friend stood up and rubbed his stomach. He licked his lips and his fingers with satisfaction as he smiled at me. "I appreciate your generosity, my friend. That bread still tastes delightful."

"I don't see how you can stay here when there is rotting fruit and a rotting body. The ground is dirty and I smell horse dung!"

Azizi looked around at the alley. The objects in this alley were forgotten, abandoned. Everything was rotten and dirty. It was if this was a place to dispose of unwanted objects. I looked Azizi in the eyes. Was this place meant to dispose of human beings as well?

"Nobody would want to come down this alley, Amsi. I'm surprised you decided to come down this way."

I handed Azizi the ball that hit my ankle. "You threw this at me. I'm surprised you still have it."

Azizi chuckled as he took the toy ball into his arm that I have given him so many years ago. "I couldn't exactly yell towards you knowing that pharaoh's soldiers are wandering this place looking for me."

"I wouldn't want you to get caught because of me."

Azizi reached into a tiny cloth bag underneath a black cloak. He pulled out a few coins and handed them to me. "That is for the bread."

What? He actually intends on paying me for it? "Azizi, no, I don't want your money. Use that for buying your own food."

"But you gave me food and I am paying for it! Take it. I will steal bread from the baker, but I won't steal from you. Take my coin."

I shook my head emphatically. "I'm not taking it, Azizi."

Azizi narrowed his eyes at me. "Take it, Amsi!"

"No, Azizi! You can't make me take that money!"

Azizi tackled me to the ground and grabbed my money purse. "You're going to take this even if I have to shove it in your money purse myself!"

I grabbed his wrist and turned over quickly, pinning him to the ground. "Azizi, no!"

Azizi laughed and rolled over, straddling my hips. I grabbed his fist which held the money and slammed it on the ground. "Try to stop me, Rich Boy!" This is a game to him! I have to admit, it's fun!

The money scattered on the ground and I grabbed a handful of the money. Azizi grabbed my fist and pulled it closer to him. We rolled over each other before we knocked into a cart. The cart fell over on top of us. We crawled from under the empty cart and panted heavily.

Azizi and I looked at each other as we were panting. With matching grins, we jumped towards each other again. There's no way he is going to win! I grabbed his wrist and slammed them on the ground.

"You will not win, Azizi!"

Azizi bucked his hips upward and he pulled his arms free from my grip. He looked into my eyes and he stopped struggling. He started laughing at me. "Alright, Amsi, I surrender."

"Good! Because you are going to keep your money, Azizi."

I let Azizi stand up and before I knew it, he had tackled me to the ground. He took my arm and twisted it around my back. That hurts! Alright, I give up! I'll take your money! I'll take it!

"See? That wasn't so hard, was it?" Azizi asked as he stood up.

I rubbed my arm as I stood up. He stood in front of me and put the money into my hand. "You are a good friend, Amsi. I know that you are risking yourself by doing this for me."

I saw someone approaching from the end of the alley. Azizi turned his head and upper body to look behind him before I even noticed it.

"What do we have here?" General Gahiji asked as he walked towards me and Azizi.

"I must go," Azizi said as he turned to me quickly. I saw him run down the alley.

"Stop! Get back here, boy!" Gahiji called loudly as Azizi fled. "Catch that boy!" he called to his soldiers, who began to chase after him.

Run, Azizi! Don't let them catch you! Four soldiers ran down the alley, armed with spears and swords.

Gahiji looked down at me when he approached me. "Amsi Al-Sakhir Ibn Kaemwaset, what are you doing in this place of garbage and death?"

I couldn't say that boy robbed me. That would make Azizi in more trouble. "He called me down the alley and I wanted to know what he wanted."

"That boy is a criminal, Amsi. Once I catch him, he will be put to his death."

I don't want Azizi to die! He is my friend! He may not be able to afford gifts for me as ones I get for him, but he's my friend.

"Don't kill him, General Gahiji!"

Gahiji glared down at me. He looks really angry. "I believe you require an audience with the pharaoh, my young Al-Sakhir."

## XXV

### The Scribe of the Gods

The pharaoh sat at his golden table and looked at the Scroll of Thoth before him. The *Nuu* had returned with no information. They were not able to find a child in the desert with the description they were given. There were no children among the reeds. They had returned empty-handed to a furious pharaoh.

***The Scroll of Horus, protector of all***

*The Living Horus shall see*

*his reign come to fall.*

*The Eye of Horus shall the seeker obtain*

*For Uniting one's enemies and godly strength to gain*

*To harness the power of the almighty Heru*

*Search for the Scroll of Horus in his Glorious city of Edfû*

*The falcon's eye shall be found*

*Where King Nebseni's riches soaring high abound.*

*As Horus when his eye was lost to Seth*

*Immortality shall be one step closer yet.*

Pharaoh Runihura grinned as he read the Scroll of Thoth. He had found the answer he had been looking for. He had been assured that Osiris' servant had been killed. *However, there had been recent reports of one particular child-thief who had been seen throughout the city. That must be the child that had evaded me so long ago. It is impressive that you have been able to survive on your own, my little nemesis. When I catch you, like Seth and Osiris, I will scatter your body parts all over Egypt. Nobody will mourn your death but the rats which will miss biting your flesh.*

"My Great Pharaoh!" Runihura raised his head from his table and pounded his open hand on the table. "Gahiji, I am reading! You are interrupting me!" Pharaoh Runihura looked at the child.

Gahiji bowed his head as he held onto Amsi's wrist tightly. "A million apologies, my lord, but there is a situation with which you must become aware."

"You are the young Al-Sakhir!" Pharaoh Runihura stood as he looked down at the thirteen-year-old boy. "You have become a fine young man. Your father tells me of your marriage."

Amsi bowed his head and looked up at the pharaoh. "I do not wish to marry, my pharaoh."

Pharaoh Runihura smiled as he slowly walked towards Amsi, a calm demeanor made Amsi even more on-edge. He had seen the pharaoh in his fits of rage. He had seen the pharaoh revel in the pain and suffering of others. When calm, he was to be the most feared as he was unpredictable.

The pharaoh chuckled. "You have nothing to fear from marriage. Marriage allows you to continue the great Al-Sakhir family blood line. You will father strong sons and will know the pleasure of ruling your own little kingdom populated by your wife, children, and your slaves."

Amsi looked towards the open door when Zaki and Nusair walked in the room. "I do not care for the girl, my lord."

"You will learn to love her, Amsi. You are young and I don't expect you to fully understand the pleasures that a woman can give you."

"What do you mean, my lord?"

Gahiji and the pharaoh laughed. "When she kneels before you and gives you fruit and dates, when she serves your body and rubs you with beautifully scented oils, when you dominate her body like you do your servants, you will feel pleasure." Pharaoh Runihura kneeled as Nusair began to rub against Runihura. He put his hand on Amsi's shoulder. "When she belongs to you and you possess her, there is nothing greater. It's all about possession and domination of mind, body, and soul, my dear Al-Sakhir."

"My father dominates our slaves harshly. Is that what one does when they love another?"

Pharaoh Runihura grinned. "They enjoy it. It reminds them that you, my Al-Sakhir, are powerful. It's all about power, my boy. *Power.* Have you ever tasted true power? Have you ever held someone's life in your hands, my dear boy? "

Amsi looked at the pharaoh and tried to step back, but Gahiji had trapped him in front of the pharaoh with his belly. "I am responsible for my body slaves."

"Have you ever reminded them of your superior position?"

*Yes. I punched Nassar this morning. I didn't mean to do it. I didn't want him to get hurt and I know if Sawaret told my father about Nassar's outburst that he would be beaten again. I have to talk to Nassar tonight and tell him how sorry I am for hitting him. I hope he's not too angry at me.*

"I punched Nassar in the stomach this morning."

The pharaoh grinned at the teenager. "Why did you punch him?"

"He interrupted my studies," the teen responded looking down sadly.

Runihura reached for the boy's chin and tilted it upwards to look him in the face. The pharaoh leaned into the boy and looked him directly in the eyes with a soul-piercing gaze. "How did that make you feel? Strong? Powerful? *God-like*?"

*Nassar has always been good to me. He's never hit me out of anger. He's never exhibited any rage against me. I didn't want him to get hurt. Who wants to see a friend get beaten? Nassar behaved himself after I punched him. It made me feel relieved. It made me feel good that Nassar was not in danger after I hit him. I felt better. I did feel powerful, yes. Is that what my father feels when he beats the twins? Is that why he beats Issâm?*

"Nassar behaved himself after I hit him, my pharaoh. I feel bad that I had to hit him."

"When an animal misbehaves, do you not see the owner beat it?"

Amsi nodded. "I have seen it happen, my lord. Our slaves do not beat our livestock. Baruti raises his voice at them when the cattle do not move quickly during the plowing season."

"Your slaves are like cattle, Amsi. They only understand beating and scolding. Kaemwaset has told me that

Nassar punched Mahoma during the arrangement for your marriage."

Amsi nodded. "Nassar was not pleased with being touched under his skirt."

The pharaoh nodded. "That is how one buys cattle and horses. They do not accept their proper place, Amsi. You must teach them their proper place. When you take a wife, you will need to teach her the same lesson."

Amsi looked down and saw Zaki purring and meowing. Nusair hissed at Zaki and swiped an angry paw at the fluffy cat. Zaki returned the hiss and flicked the tip of his tail.

"They must learn to accept their position, Amsi. You must teach that to them. You are doing them a favor by correcting them. You did Nassar a favor and you showed him mercy."

Amsi looked up at the pharaoh. "My mother said that mercy is tenderness and showing compassion."

"When a child is reaching for a flame and you hit his hand, is that not protecting the child from being burned? Is that not showing compassion?"

Amsi nodded in response.

"You are showing that child love, correct?"

Amsi nodded again.

"You love the child, yet you must scold him. Kaemwaset loves his slaves, so he must show them their submissive position."

"But my father beats them until they bleed or lose consciousness! How is that mercy?"

Pharaoh Runihura chuckled light-heartedly. "That is the ultimate display of affection towards your slaves, my boy. Show Nassar your love and you will be doing him a great honor."

"It appears that our little Al-Sakhir has his affections corrupted, my king."

"What do you mean, Gahiji?"

Gahiji bowed his head. "I found Amsi talking to the little thief-boy we have been unable to capture. I have sent my soldiers to the Al-Sakhir family lands. Kaemwaset will be here to retrieve his son."

Pharaoh Runihura slowly pulled back from Amsi and stood on his feet. "Tell me this is not true, Amsi Al-Sakhir," the pharaoh glared down at the teenager. The pharaoh's fists clenched tightly.

*This could be bad*, Amsi thought as his knees began to shake.

"Why are you talking to street-rats, Amsi?"

"I wasn't talking to him, my pharaoh!" Amsi exclaimed.

The pharaoh crossed his arms over his chest. "Do you enjoy talking to my enemy? Do you wish to undermine my authority as the Living Horus?"

Amsi shook his head as he tried to back away, but Gahiji remained behind him, preventing retreat. "No, my pharaoh!"

"Amsi, you will not speak to him again! If my soldiers catch him, he will be brought here as my personal toy before I kill him! I will make him feel pain beyond his comprehension! I will enjoy his screams of agony! That child is a menace, Amsi, and I will not have you consorting with my enemy!"

"My apologies, my great pharaoh!" Amsi exclaimed, bowing his head.

The pharaoh grabbed Amsi's side-lock of youth and pulled hard, making the boy scream. "You need to be taught a lesson in mercy!"

Pharaoh Runihura pulled back his hand and slapped Amsi across the face. The teenager screamed and fell to the ground holding his cheek. Tears came from Amsi's eyes as he began to shake. His fists clenched on the floor as he rubbed his cheek.

"You will not defy me, do you understand?" Runihura growled angrily as he grabbed the teenager's wrist. "That child will kill you, Amsi! He is vermin running through our streets! He needs to die! I wish to save you before it is too late."

Zaki rubbed against Amsi, purring quietly and laying down beside him.

"Zaki! Go away!" Runihura exclaimed, making the cat hiss and run away through the doors. The pharaoh reached down and grabbed Amsi's side-lock again. He grabbed Gahiji's silver dagger. He placed the blade against Amsi's throat. "Do you seek to end my reign, Amsi Al-Sakhir Ibn Kaemwaset?"

Amsi's body quivered from the hostile glare of the God-King. His palms became sweaty and a thin veil of sweat covered his face. His bottom lip trembled and his breathing quickened.

The pharaoh pressed the tip of the blade against Amsi's flesh, making the boy's skin sting. "Do you wish to remove me from power? Do you know what I will do to you should you challenge me?"

"Please don't kill me, my king! Please!"

"I will remove your intestines slowly." Pharaoh Runihura leaned into Amsi, pressing his forehead against the teenager's. "I will mummify you alive."

A tear fell down Amsi's cheek as his body trembled with terror. "Please, my pharaoh, don't do that!"

"Do not challenge me, Anointed One," Pharaoh Runihura grinned. "I will show you no mercy. Do not disgrace your family. Should you defy my command, I will hang your family and your servants. You will watch them die one by one until I mummify you alive." The pharaoh grinned, licking his lips in a predatory manner. "I hear from Kaemwaset that Qamra is a very good body slave. I will enjoy her body first before I suspend her by her neck."

"Please don't hurt my slaves, my lord!"

Runihura's lip curled in disgust. "Do not challenge my authority, Amsi. When I obtain ultimate power, when I become immortal, you do not wish to be on my bad side. You want to be favored by the god to obtain anything your heart desires. If you are faithful to me and follow my precepts, my law, then you will have my blessing, my favor, and I will shower you and your family with gifts."

"Amsi Al-Sakhir! What have I told you about talking to that boy?" Kaemwaset bellowed, followed by Nakia.

Amsi swallowed nervously. "I didn't talk to that boy, father! It-It was a different boy!"

Kaemwaset walked up to Amsi and pulled the teenager's ear roughly, making the boy scream and stand on his feet. "You are disgracing me before the glorious pharaoh, my son! How could you do this to me?"

Pharaoh Runihura glared at Kaemwaset. "He has been corrupted by the boy. The child must have put some spell on him."

Kaemwaset's body trembled with fury. "Sawaret told me of your lesson today, my boy. How dare you speak of heresy? The pharaoh is not a cruel being! He is powerful and someone I expect for you to admire!"

"You must have Sawaret teach him the dangers of consorting with less civilized people. I hear the Bedouin have migrated near the Nile once again, for example."

Kaemwaset nodded and sighed with resignation. "I have tried to expel them from my land, but they have set their camp outside my wall by the banks."

"Amsi, it seems as if you have been corrupted by your slaves," Pharaoh Runihura said, glaring at Nakia. He slowly approached Nakia and quickly snatched the slave's throat. "What spell have you placed on him?"

Nakia swallowed nervously as he grabbed the pharaoh's wrist. "There's no spell on him, my king!"

The pharaoh slapped Nakia across the face harshly. "You do not touch me! You don't touch a god with your filthy, rotten, vile flesh!" The pharaoh threw Nakia to the ground beside Amsi's feet. "You break the spell with which you are corrupting Amsi! You hail from the Nubian Enzi tribe. Your father must have taught you the spells to turn Amsi's mind against me!"

Nakia shook his head as he covered his head with his hands. "My father was not a medicine man, my lord! He was a warrior!"

Runihura laughed. "Your sire was a warrior and you are so weak? There is no doubt why your father lost the battle against my father!"

Nakia closed his eyes tightly. *My father, I miss him. My father fought valiantly. I watched him slay an Egyptian soldier. His body was covered in sweat and blood. He gripped his club so tightly; I thought his fingers would break. His face was painted white with war paint. His face looked like a skull to instill fear into the enemy. Two white dots appeared above on his forehead, one for me and my twin brother. My father died in battle. I'll never forget when he turned his head to us. 'Kelile, Ulan, run!' he screamed to us. I watched my father die. His scream remains in my ears. He will not be silenced. My brother and I watched helplessly as his blood pooled beneath his body. Why did my father have to die? Why couldn't Pharaoh Atenhotep allow me to die with my father? Why?*

"Nakia did not put any spells on me!"

Kaemwaset growled. "It must have been Issâm! Issâm is a priest of Thoth and would know the secret incantations! He has poisoned you against us! I should have known that worm would do such a thing!"

Pharaoh Runihura raised a curious eyebrow. "Issâm is a worshipper of Thoth?"

Kaemwaset bowed his head. "Yes, my lord. He worships the Scribe of the Gods, my great pharaoh."

Pharaoh Runihura looked at the scroll on the table. *If Thoth has the power to grant life for millions of years to the dead, perhaps he can grant immortality to the living. He is the Great Lord of Time and perhaps if I make a sacrifice to him, he will grant me immortality.* Runihura tapped his finger against his chin. *I must have more information! If I must find the Book of Thoth, who else would know about it better than a scribe of the Lord of Writing?*

"Kaemwaset, I wish to speak to him. Gahiji, send two of your men for him. I will return him when I am finished with him."

Kaemwaset bowed reverently. "Issâm is an obedient servant."

"Kaemwaset, your son's affinity for the underprivileged upsets me. His mind is soft where it should be strong. I can see he has his mother's tender heart."

"She has poisoned his mind, my king. My fear is that her damage is beyond repair."

Pharaoh Runihura smiled. "No damage is beyond repair, Kaemwaset." Runihura looked at Amsi. "Does Issâm obey you?"

Amsi nodded. "Issâm does what I request of him, my lord."

"Perhaps you can help me, Amsi. You have many lessons to learn and this may be a good one for you to learn."

Kaemwaset bowed his head. "You may have my son if you will teach him lessons, but I will need my old farmer back, my king. If you kill him, my fields will have one less body to tend to it. In this season of harvest, I need as many slaves as possible."

"If Issâm is killed, I will obtain a new slave for you, Kaemwaset."

"Please don't kill Issâm," Nakia pleaded on his knees in front of the pharaoh. "Issâm is a good man and has no evil in his heart." Nakia kept his head lowered to hide his tears coming from his eyes. "My king, take me in his place!"

Runihura looked down at the trembling teen. "You have no information I could use. You come from Nubian blood. You do not worship Thoth. Kaemwaset, is there a slave of yours that worships Horus?"

"No, my pharaoh."

Runihura growled as his fist punched the table, making Nakia startle on his knees. "Issâm had better give me everything he knows. Your servant had better be cooperative."

"Issâm is very cooperative, my lord. He is submissive."

Runihura grinned. "Perfect. Gahiji, bring him to me immediately."

"Yes, my king," Gahiji bowed and walked from the room.

Amsi looked up at his father. "I don't want him to hurt Issâm, father! He's going to hurt him!"

"It is a gift to be brought before the pharaoh and it is time that Issâm make himself useful."

"But Issâm toils in the fields from sunrise to sunset! He works hard all day and often without food or water all day! He is not lazy!"

Kaemwaset crossed his arms in front of him. "He had better be cooperative or he will have much to answer for upon his return."

## XXVI

## <u>Thoth Is My Strength!</u>

Baruti watched as six-year-old Khenimentiu stood on the stalks of grain. He jumped on them as his sister tied them with string. Baruti chuckled as he held the grain steady for his son. "Be careful, Khenti. You don't want to jump on your sister's fingers."

The little boy looked up at his father. "There's much grain here to flatten, father!"

Meskhenet wiped the sweat from her forehead. "Father, I can't tie it anymore!"

Baruti dropped his scythe and picked up the tied grain stalks. "Tonight you can help Najam separate the grain, Meskhenet."

The little girl sighed. "I did that last night and we worked almost until dawn, father."

Baruti smiled at his daughter. "You do such a wonderful job, Meskhenet! I hear Najam is jealous of your skill."

Meskhenet smiled widely at her father. "Truly, father? She said she is jealous of me?"

Baruti smiled and nodded. "You are the best little husker in the entire land of Egypt! You can teach her much."

Issâm carried a bundle of stalks to the wagon and put them beside Baruti's. Issâm wiped his forehead and looked up at the sun. "Rā has given us a beautiful day, but I would love a little break from the heat."

Baruti watched as an elderly Issâm began to lean on his tool. Issâm's wrinkled hands held onto the handle of the tool; His face covered in sweat as he breathed heavily. Baruti walked to a bucket of water and scooped a small clay cup of water. He walked over to Issâm and put the cup in his hands. Baruti smiled at Issâm. "Drink, my friend. You are thirsty."

Issâm smiled at Baruti and lifted the cup to his lips. "Many thanks, Baruti." Baruti watched as Issâm drank from the cup slowly.

"We may have to ask Karida to fetch more water for us."

Issâm nodded as he looked at the children playing at Baruti's feet. "Meskhenet, Khenti, are you behaving for your father?"

The two children looked up at Issâm and smiled. "Yes, we are helping to tie the bundles of grain!"

"You are both good children."

Issâm and Baruti raised their heads as they saw five horses run through the archway. Khenti and Meskhenet ran quickly behind their father. Baruti narrowed his eyes at the sight of the General and his armed soldiers.

"Issâm, get behind me."

Issâm stepped behind Baruti. "What is it they want? Master Kaemwaset is gone."

General Gahiji and his men stopped in front of Baruti and pointed at Issâm. "Old Man, you will come with us. The pharaoh wishes to see you."

Baruti's lip curled in disgust. "What does the pharaoh want with him?"

"That is no concern of yours!" Gahiji exclaimed, removing his sword from its sheath.

"It is my concern when you come here threatening my friend with a sword!"

Meskhenet held onto her father's legs nervously. Khenti clutched onto his father's hand and wrist, shaking.

"We are taking Issâm even if we have to take him by force!" Four soldiers dismounted their horses and drew their swords.
Baruti growled. "It takes four armed guards to capture a frail old man?"

"Baruti, I don't want danger to come to your children. I will go with them willingly."

Baruti turned to Issâm and put his hands on Issâm's shoulders. He looked into the old eyes of his friend. Issâm's face had become wrinkled as crow's feet crept from his eyes. Baruti saw exhaustion in the old man's face. Issâm's wrinkled hands touched Baruti's shoulders. Those hands had worked the fields for almost twenty years. His nails were dirty and his hands bore calluses and cuts from working.

"Take care of your children, Baruti," Issâm said quietly, kissing Baruti on either cheek as a sign of friendship.

Issâm stepped from behind Baruti. The two soldiers grabbed onto Issâm's arms roughly and pulled him. The old man stumbled forward as they held him firm.

Gahiji stepped from the horse and grabbed a metal collar. Baruti watched helplessly as the metal collar was placed around Issâm's neck. Another soldier tied Issâm's wrists together. Gahiji grabbed the chain connected to the collar and mounted his horse.

"You should say something to your friend," Gahiji said with a grin. "It may be the last time you see him alive."

Baruti stepped up to Issâm, who was looking at the ground. "Issâm?"

Issâm's dark eyes rose to Baruti as he looked at his friend pleadingly. Baruti felt his heartbeat rising. There was nothing he could do to save his friend. He couldn't plead for him for his pleas would fall on deaf ears. He couldn't break the metal collar. Baruti raised his hand slowly and placed it on Issâm's chest. "May Anubis welcome you home, Issâm."

Issâm lowered his head as a lone tear dropped onto Baruti's hand. "I don't want to die, Baruti," Issâm whimpered as he trembled. "But if Thoth opens the gates for me, I will have no choice. May Thoth bless you and your family, Baruti."

"Time to go see the pharaoh, slave!"


Kaemwaset turned his head as the double doors to the throne room opened quickly. Nakia turned and watched Issâm be pulled into the room. The two soldiers holding his arms pulled and tugged at him roughly. They shoved

Issâm onto the ground beside Nakia. Nakia put a gentle hand on Issâm. "Issâm, are you hurt?"

Issâm grumbled as he rolled over on his back and held his head. "I'll live, Nakia."

Pharaoh Runihura grinned as he looked at the old man on the ground. "Issâm, I am delighted that you are here."

Issâm looked at the pharaoh above him and swallowed nervously. "My pharaoh?"

Kaemwaset kicked Issâm in the side. "Show some respect to your pharaoh and get on your knees!"

Issâm winced in pain as he rolled onto his knees in front of the pharaoh. "Yes, my lord."

Pharaoh Runihura chuckled. "He'd make a good dog, wouldn't he?"

"Issâm is not a dog! He's a person!" Amsi protested.

Nakia held onto Issâm tightly. Issâm shook his head as he held Nakia's hand. "Don't watch, my boy."

"Let's make Issâm a little more comfortable, shall we, men?"

The two soldiers grabbed onto Issâm again. Nakia held onto him tightly, his eyes flooding with tears and his body shaking. Amsi jumped towards Issâm and grabbed his upper arm.

One soldier pulled the metal collar around Issâm's neck roughly, making the old man fall forward in the grasp of the two young teenagers.

Kaemwaset grabbed Amsi's white tunic and pulled him back. "You will watch and learn, my boy."

Two soldiers grabbed Nakia's arms and held him back. Nakia clenched his fists and struggled to free himself from the soldiers' tight grasp. "Don't hurt him! Please!"

Amsi pulled his arm away and ran to Issâm as they pulled him to his feet. Amsi wrapped his arms around Issâm's chest, hugging him tightly.

"You will not harm him!" Amsi growled as he turned his head towards the pharaoh.

"Amsi, don't do this," Issâm said calmly.

Amsi looked up into Issâm's eyes. Despite the situation, he saw a tranquility come from the chained old man. "Issâm, say whatever they want you to say so you can come home."

The pharaoh grinned. "This is a very touching moment."

The guards pulled Amsi back and pulled Issâm to a pillar. They raised Issâm's struggling arms and brought the bound wrists above his head and placed it over a hook. Nakia's eyes filled with tears as he looked upon Issâm bound and nearly suspended against the pillar covered with protective hieroglyphs. "Issâm, no…"

Amsi watched as the pharaoh smiled. The torches burning beside Issâm illuminated his face. Issâm watched the pharaoh approach him, the torches lighting his grin.

"Issâm, you will obey the pharaoh's command. You are going to be a good lesson for my son to learn. Nakia, come!" Kaemwaset said calmly as he turned his back.

Nakia turned to Kaemwaset, his eyes narrowed with fury. His teeth were gritting with wrath. His lip curled with contempt. "No."

Kaemwaset stopped.

Nakia's deep breathing resounded through the hall, stealing attention away from the hanging old man.

"What did you just say?" Kaemwaset said slowly without turning his back.

Nakia's arms were trembling. *What are you doing, Nakia? Kaemwaset will surely beat you for certain now!* Nakia swallowed nervously. *Issâm has been like a father to me. He's protected me. When I was sick, he was the first one to hold me in his arms. He'd caress my cheek and kiss me on the forehead. It's my turn to protect you now, Issâm.*

"Nakia, stop it now!" Amsi growled at his servant.

"Nakia, go with Kaemwaset!" Issâm yelled from the pillar.

"This rebelliousness is more customary of your twin than yourself," the pharaoh said calmly.

Nakia took a deep breath as he looked at Kaemwaset nervously. "No. I will not leave Issâm!"

Pharaoh Runihura stepped up to Nakia. He put a calm hand on the teen's cheek. "You know I removed your brother's tongue. Would you like for me to train your little master how to remove a human tongue, Nakia? You and Nassar can grunt together."

"Nakia! By Thoth, stop this!" Issâm angrily called from the pillar.

Nakia's eyes went to Issâm. Two tears fell from his eyes and down his cheeks. *I can't leave you, Issâm. Don't make me leave you.*

"Nakia, come here," Issâm said calmly.

The pharaoh released Nakia and watched him walk to Nakia. Nakia walked over to Issâm and sniffled sadly.

"Issâm, if I leave and you die, I'll never see you again."

Issâm smiled at the boy. "You have a good heart, Nakia. You are a very special boy. I am an old man now. The last thing I want for my aged eyes to see are your tears."

Nakia closed his eyes and stepped close to Issâm. The boy wrapped his arms around Issâm's body and began to cry. "I love you like a father, Issâm."

The bound man smiled. "You should leave, Nakia. I want you to be brave like your brother. Take care of him, Nakia."

Nakia sniffled as he looked up at Issâm. "I always will care for him."

"Good boy. Go home, Kelile."

"Nakia, come now!" Kaemwaset bellowed.

Nakia hesitantly released Issâm and walked away slowly. Nakia turned around to see the pharaoh approaching Issâm. Nakia looked down at the floor sadly, fearing he would never again see the man whom he called had 'father' for fourteen years.

Amsi watched his father leave with Nakia. Pharaoh Runihura chuckled as he approached his prey. Issâm watched the dark eyes of the pharaoh sparkle in the torchlight.

"So you worship the God Thoth?"

Issâm nodded. "Yes, I worship the Lord of Law, my pharaoh."

Runihura grinned. "What do you know of the Scroll of Thoth?"

Issâm looked at the pharaoh. "I thought it was just a legend."

The pharaoh chuckled. "No, it is very much real." The pharaoh walked calmly to the table and held the scroll in his hand as he walked. "What do you know about the Scroll of Horus and the Eye of Horus?"

Issâm shook his head. "The holy scrolls were, as I believed, a legend."

The pharaoh pointed at the scroll in his hand. "I have the Scroll of Thoth right here, old man! Where is The Scroll of Horus? Where is the Eye of Horus? Where is the Book of Thoth? Do not lie to me or I will remove your head from your body! What do you know about these supposed legends?"

"They were thought to contain the location of certain items that could bring immortality to the bearer. The scrolls identify the location of everything that is needed. The ancient relics are useless without the scrolls to give them power."

Amsi watched as the pharaoh chuckled. The king approached the old man.

"What are these items, exactly, and where can I find them?"

Issâm shook his head. "I do not know, my lord. Until you have showed me just now, I believed these scrolls to be myth and nothing more."

"What power does the Book of Thoth hold? What can it give to me? What do you know of the Book of Thoth, old man?"

Issâm's eyes widened in surprise. *How does he know about the Holy Book of Thoth?*

*I cannot allow the Holy Book of Thoth to fall into the pharaoh's hands! The magic contained therein would make him an unstoppable menace.* Issâm winced as his shoulders began to burn. "I do not know, my pharaoh."

"Liar!" Runihura exclaimed as he slapped Issâm's face. "You are a former priest of the Ibis god and you have certain privileged information that the laity was never told! The priests of Thoth wrote this scroll and as a emissary of Thoth, you should know what I need to know! Tell me, old man!"

Issâm shook his head. "I don't know, my pharaoh!"

"What of the Eye of Horus? Where is the Book of Thoth and the Eye of Horus? Tell me or you will suffer, old man!" Runihura growled.

Amsi ran beside the pharaoh. "If Issâm says he does not know, he does not know!"

"Horus avenged his father's death, but lost his eye in the process to Seth. Out of myth comes the power of the scrolls. Find holy ground and you will obtain what you seek."

Pharaoh Runihura smiled. "Where are these items that I need? What are they?"

Issâm shook his head. "I do not know, my lord."

Pharaoh Runihura punched Issâm in the stomach violently, making the old man cough. "Where are they? Tell me!"

Amsi turned to Issâm. "Tell him!"

Issâm took a strangled breath as he coughed and whimpered from the pain in his shoulders. He looked at Amsi and closed his eyes. "My master, I do not know!"

Runihura walked calmly to the wall decorated with axes, swords, and clubs. The pharaoh took a blood-stained club calmly in his hands. "What are the items I need to achieve god-hood? I grow weary of your riddles."

Issâm closed his eyes. "I am strong upon earth before Rā. May my arrival be happy before Osiris."

Pharaoh Runihura growled as he stepped to Issâm. "Tell me what I need to know!"

"Hail Thoth, making victorious Osiris against his enemies!"

Runihura stepped back and struck the club harshly against Issâm's stomach, making the old man expel air quickly and painfully. Amsi gasped and tugged at the soldiers holding him back.

"My lord, you will hurt him!"

Pharaoh Runihura watched the old man gasp for breath and lower his head. "What do you have to say now, old man?"

"May I be stablished upon my stand like Neb-ānkh, may I be joined with Isis the divine lady, may they make me strong against the doer of injury to me."

"Reciting prayers from the Book of the Dead will not help you, old man!" Pharaoh Runihura growled and slammed the bloody club into Issâm's side, making the old man gasp for breath. "Bring him down!"

Two soldiers removed Issâm from the hook and dropped him on the ground. The old man arched his back as he gasped for breath. "I am, in very truth I am a shining being, and a dweller in light who hath been created and hath come into existence from the limbs of the god."

Pharaoh Runihura slammed the club against Issâm's hip. Amsi gasped as he heard the snapping of bone and Issâm's painful scream. Amsi kneeled in front of Issâm and looked into the old man's eyes.

"Issâm, please tell him what he needs to know so he does not kill you!" Amsi pleaded.

Issâm's breathing came in sharp gasps. "Great is Thoth! May he welcome me into the Underworld where there is no pain." The pharaoh placed the club in Amsi's hands. "It's your turn, Amsi Al-Sakhir."

Amsi looked at the club in his hands. He stood up slowly and looked down at the trembling old man. Issâm's body was trembling as he laid with his knees drawn to his chest.

"Thoth is my strength!" Issâm screamed as his body trembled.

*How can I hit him? He's bound and defenseless! Issâm is a good man! He would never hurt anyone and yet the pharaoh is treating him like an old mule!* Amsi looked with pity at the old man. Amsi held the handle of the club as Issâm opened his eyes slowly. The old man looked with fear at the sight of his little master with the bloody club.

"Beat him, Amsi," the pharaoh said calmly, putting a tender hand on Amsi's shoulder. "Give him a good strike with the club. Show Issâm what his friendship means to you."

Issâm always implored me not to be like my father. *I'm no better than him now. How can I do this to Issâm? He was always a patient, loving man and now he's being beaten for no reason by the pharaoh.* Amsi looked up at the pharaoh. "I can't beat him, my king."

Pharaoh Runihura took the club into his hands slowly. "I understand, Amsi." Amsi took a breath of relief. The club quickly found its way to Issâm's leg, snapping the bone through the skin. The bound victim wailed and screamed in pain as blood began to trickle from the open wound.

"My pharaoh, stop this!" Amsi screamed as he kneeled down to look at the injury. Issâm's leg had been broken, the tip of the bone protruding from the skin.

"Only you can stop this, Amsi. You have a choice," the pharaoh said handing Amsi the club once more. "You can end his pain. You have the power over his life and death. Feel the power, my boy. Feel the pleasure of deciding if he lives or if he dies."

Amsi looked at Issâm's face. The old man's face began to change color. He looked pale as his eyes were rising into his head. His face was covered in sweat. *How can Issâm survive these injuries? If he lives, he could be crippled and my father would sell him or hang him from his balcony like he did to Jinan. Jinan had become too old to work, so my father tossed him over the balcony and hung him. Jinan accepted his fate and willingly allowed my father to tie the rope around his neck. I don't want my father to hang Issâm. Issâm may not be able to walk if his hip has been broken by the club, either. My father will kill Issâm for certain. Why should Issâm linger and suffer if my father will kill him anyway? Issâm, how could I do this to you? I want Rā to decide your fate.*

"Strike him, Amsi."

"I cannot, my king! Issâm is a kind old man!"

Pharaoh Runihura leaned down to Amsi. "If you do not do so, I will beat you and hang you beside your friend for my amusement!"

*I hate the pharaoh. I hate that my father is forcing me to do this! I hate him! I hate him! I wish I could beat him instead for what he did to Nassar! I wish I could strike him for hanging Jinan!* Amsi closed his eyes and gripped the club. He brought it down harshly against Issâm's side.

Amsi opened his eyes and saw the club resting against Issâm's ribs. *What have I done?* His eyes widened and he dropped the club. "I'm sorry, Issâm! Forgive me!"

The old man trembled as blood trickled from the corner of his mouth. His breathing came sharp and quick.

"Gahiji, take Issâm and Amsi back to the Al-Sakhir family lands. I am done with Amsi's lesson."


Qamra and Baruti waited outside nervously for Issâm's return. Qamra held onto Baruti's hand tightly as they kept their eyes towards the entrance. Baruti swallowed nervously as his bare foot tapped against the wood plank of the step. Baruti shook his head slowly.

"I don't like the air tonight. I worry about Issâm."

"Issâm could have stood twenty years ago before the pharaoh and I would be just as concerned."

Qamra sighed as Khentimentiu walked out of the home. The little boy hugged his mother and father. "Has Issâm returned?"

"No, son. Get some sleep for tomorrow. We have another long day of reaping."

Qamra and Baruti watched as the twins ran down the path from the entrance. Nakia was waving his hands. "Horses! Horses!" Nakia screamed loudly.

Qamra and Baruti stood as two horses ran down the path. The twins stood on either side of Baruti and Qamra.

The four's eyes widened and they gasped as Issâm was removed from a cart pulled by one horse and thrown upon the ground. Amsi crawled off the back of the cart and looked sadly up at Qamra and the others.

"Have a pleasant night, Master Amsi," Gahiji grinned as he looked at the boy.

Amsi glared at the General as he ran away. *May Apep strike you!* Baruti ran to Issâm's side and turned him onto his back. The old man's congested scream echoed through the field. "Nassar, go get Issâm's knife. Master Amsi, what happened?"

*How can I answer that, Baruti?*

Qamra kneeled by Issâm's leg and shook her head. She reached to touch it when Issâm's pain-filled cry pleaded with her not to touch it.

"Amsi, what happened to him?" Nakia asked, touching Issâm's cheek.

"The pharaoh beat him."

Nassar ran from the home with the knife. Baruti leaned over Issâm and cut the ropes binding his ankles and wrists. Baruti touched Issâm's cheeks and looked the old man in the lightless eyes.

"Issâm, can you hear me?"

Nakia watched as Issâm gasped for breath, blood seeping from the corners of his mouth. "If only I could have been there for him," Nakia whimpered. Nassar put his hand on Nakia's shoulders, feeling his brother's heartbreak.

Issâm weakly reached for Baruti's shoulders. "Take me to the field, Baruti."

Baruti cradled Issâm's upper body in his arms. The older man buried his face in Baruti's shoulder as his broken leg dragged and the skin tore. The old man's screams bellowed into Baruti's skin, making the other man hold back tears.

*His hip has been beaten flat, his leg almost severed, his ribs are broken, and his lungs sound filled with fluid. There is nothing I can do for him*, Qamra thought grimly as she followed her husband to the field.

Amsi, Nassar, and Nakia followed Qamra, listening to Issâm's moans of pain and his gurgling chest. Baruti gently placed Issâm on the soil. Baruti kneeled beside Issâm and held the old man's hand.

"I'm not going to leave you, old friend," Baruti said, his fingertips lightly brushing against Issâm's cheek.

Issâm's breathing had become shallow as blood seeped down his neck. "You were always a good friend, Baruti."

Baruti closed his eyes and pressed Issâm's hand to his forehead. "May Anubis judge you fondly and may he guide you into the hall of Osiris."

Amsi stood beside Issâm and looked down at him sadly. "I'm sorry, Issâm. I didn't mean to-."

"No, Master Amsi. I ask of you-." Issâm gasped for breath. "Don't become your father. That is my last wish for you. Do not share his hate. Be merciful. Be kind."

Amsi rubbed his eyes to wipe the tears away. "I will not become my father, Issâm."

Qamra sniffled as she looked at Issâm with pity. "You will be alright, Issâm. You will live."

Issâm gasped for breath as he smiled at her. "We both know that is impossible, Qamra."

Qamra lowered her head and rubbed her teary eyes. "May Isis welcome you."

Issâm's body gave a violent spasm as he looked up into the starry night. "Praise Thoth, the Lord of Writing, the

Scribe of the Gods, the Lord of Law, Most Beautiful.
May he bestow his blessings upon all of you."

Nassar leaned over and placed his head on Issâm's chest,
his body quaking with the force of his cry.

"Nakia, Nassar, come here," Issâm gasped sharply,
opening each of his arms to the twins.

A smile crossed Issâm's lips as he looked at the sniffling
twins. Each twin took one of Issâm's hands. "You are
both beautiful boys. Your father says he is very proud of
both of you."

"E-am," Nassar sobbed.

"If only I could have been there, Issâm," Nakia
whimpered.

"Don't blame yourself, Nakia. You're a good boy with
such a beautiful soul," Issâm said, caressing Nakia's
cheek. "You're young and so full of promise. Do not
blame yourself. Make me proud, Nakia." Issâm said with
a smile.

Nakia nodded as he kissed the palm of Issâm's hand. "I
will, Issâm," Nakia whispered. "I promise."

Issâm smiled at Nakia as he caressed Nassar's cheek
lightly. "Beautiful Thoth, your faithful servant returns
into your waiting arms."

Nakia watched as Issâm's hand slowly fell onto the
ground beside him. The old man's eyes remained half-
open; The smile remained still on his face.

Nakia looked into the life-less, smiling face and felt his heart stop. Baruti reached for Issâm's neck and touched the side. He leaned down and put his ear against the smiling corpse's chest. Baruti closed his eyes and put his hand lightly on Issâm's forehead. Qamra heard Baruti wail into Issâm's chest. She stepped behind him and put a comforting hand on his back. "No more tears, Baruti."

Baruti wailed loudly in sorrow, his body shaking. "He toiled for many years in this field, Qamra! He worked hard and he was a good man! He never fought with anyone! He never wished harm on anyone! Issâm didn't deserve to be tortured to death! He didn't deserve it, I say!" Baruti's fist hit the ground angrily.

"E-am! E-am!" Nassar cried loudly.

Amsi rubbed his eyes as he looked at Issâm's body. *He looks happy. Why would he look happy? He was beaten and suffered terribly!*

"He doesn't need to suffer anymore," Nakia sniffled as he wrapped his arm around Issâm's body in an embrace. "Issâm told me once that good men are not dead as long as people speak well of him after their death."

Qamra nodded. "Issâm was a wise man. He never lost his faith."

"Now he is dead," Amsi sighed sadly.

Baruti looked into Issâm's calm, smiling face. "Never have I encountered such a peaceful spirit than yours, Issâm. May you find peace in the Land of the Blessed dead. Anubis, guide him to Osiris."

Nassar sniffled and turned, walking away from the group. Nakia watched Nassar walk away. "I should talk to him."

Baruti stood and held onto Qamra's hand. "We should bury him in the field. His body could bless our crop." Baruti looked at Amsi. "Little Master, you should go to bed. It is late and Kaemwaset may come looking for you if you have not returned."

Amsi nodded and put his hand on Issâm's hand. "May you see the face of Rā."

Amsi ran towards the house when he saw the twins talking by the stables. Nassar was moaning inarticulate sounds and stomping his foot angrily. The teenager fell to his knees and began to cry. Amsi watched as his twin kneeled in front of him and hugged him tightly.

"A-e-ah," Nassar cried.

"Don't cry, brother," Nakia said tenderly. "We still have each other."

Nassar clung to his brother tightly as Nakia looked into the starry night sky. *I will never forget you, Issâm. May you find peace eternal.*

## XXVII

### First Encounter

Nakia held the plate of grapes in his hands as he handed another grape to his master. Amsi sat on his chair looking out of the window sadly, ignoring Nakia's hand. Nassar was kneeling at his feet, rubbing oils into Amsi's feet. The kneeling twin yawned as he began to slump forward tiredly. Nakia put a hand on his brother's shoulder and shook him slightly to keep his eyes open.

*Don't become your father*, Issâm told Amsi before he died. *That is my last wish for you. Don't share his hate. Those were Issâm's last words to me. Now he's dead. Amsi shook his head. He didn't deserve to die that way. He was an old man, an old priest who meant harm to no one.*

"Master?" Nakia asked quietly. "Master Amsi?"

"What is it, Nakia?"

Nakia placed the grape on the glass plate. "Are you hungry?"

"No."

Nakia sighed. "Master Amsi, you need to eat. Please do not blame yourself for Issâm's death."

"I beat him, Nakia!" Amsi screamed. "I hit him!"

Nassar's head snapped up and he looked at his twin.

Nakia swallowed nervously. "Why did you do it?"

"The pharaoh said he would kill me if I didn't."

"Issâm would have wanted you to beat him if it meant saving yourself. I know he's with our mother and father and that he's happy. His soul is at peace and that is what should make us happy."

Nassar and Nakia's head rose when they heard
Kaemwaset growling in the hallway. Amsi gripped onto
the armchairs.

"Pharaoh Runihura killed him and you give me only forty
dînars to compensate me for his death, my Lord Gahiji?
This is my harvest time and my surviving slaves must
work harder for longer to reap the fruits of their labor! I
have to give them one loaf of bread a day to work! This is
unacceptable!"

Nakia looked down solemnly. *Issâm was worth only forty
dînars? Is that the price they place on his life? If Nassar
and I were to die, I wonder how much Kaemwaset would
benefit. How can they put a price on what Issâm meant to
all of us?* Nakia looked down at Amsi and saw the boy's
seat empty. Nakia saw Amsi walking towards the door,
his fists clenched tightly. "My lord!"

Amsi opened the door to his room and saw Gahiji
standing in the hallway before his father holding a small
coin purse. "What are you doing here?"

"I'm paying your father for the loss of his slave during
the interrogation process."

Kaemwaset grabbed the coin purse angrily. "I will take
this as a down payment. I require more compensation for
the loss of one slave."

"Issâm was an old, frail man, Kaemwaset," Gahiji said
with a grin. "What could he have possibly been worth to
you?"

Amsi stepped up to Gahiji. "Issâm was a good worker and he didn't deserve to die!"

Gahiji grinned. "You hit him well, Amsi. Your father would be proud of you."

Kaemwaset looked down at Amsi and put his hand on his shoulder. "I had faith in you, my son. I knew you would follow in my footsteps and continue my great legacy. You have made me proud."

"I hit an old man, father. That is not the mark of a great man!"

"Sacrifices must be made sometimes, my boy. During discipline, you may kill some of them. I'm certain, Lord Gahiji, that the pharaoh will send me an appropriate slave as compensation for my loss."

Gahiji chuckled. "The great pharaoh has none to give you, Kaemwaset. I'm certain you have some house slaves who can be recruited into your field. There are many poor people willing to sell themselves into slavery for a crust of bread. Once we find that boy that your son has befriended, you can add him to your ranks. That is, if the pharaoh gives his permission." Gahiji looked down at Amsi with a grin. "I hear he plans to torture your friend in the most horrible manner possible."

"You leave him alone!" Amsi growled.

Nassar and Nakia poked their heads out from Amsi's room. Kaemwaset turned his head towards the twins and pointed down the hallway.

"The two of you go to the fields! You do not stop harvest until after sunset! Go!"

The twins scurried down the hallway and ran out of the door. Gahiji chuckled as he looked at the teens run.

"They are running skeletons. Very interesting," Gahiji said. "It may do them some good to have a full loaf of bread a day, Kaemwaset."

"They should get more," Amsi said.

Kaemwaset opened the coin purse and counted the money. "Giving the slaves what they need to survive will make them grateful for what little they get. A satisfied slave will work slowly from too much bread, Amsi. You will learn this."

Amsi stepped from between the two men and walked outside. He looked up at the clear sky and sighed. *I'm sorry, Issâm.* Amsi looked into the distance and saw the slaves working in the morning sun. Karida and Laila were tying the bundles of grain. Meskhenet and Khentimentiu were dragging the bundles and separating the grain from the husk. Baruti was cutting the stalks with his scythe.

Amsi saw his mother walk towards the house slowly. He ran to her and hugged her tightly. Imani placed a calm hand on his forehead.

"Good morning, mother."

Imani looked sadly down at Amsi. "My son," she said softly and gently. "What have you done, my boy?"

Amsi released his mother quickly. "The pharaoh threatened my life if I refused to do what he ordered!"

A tear fell down Imani's cheek. "The pharaoh is nothing more than a butcher of men, Amsi. I see that he also makes toys of them."

"*Bedu! Bedu!*" Qamra called as she ran towards the house.

Baruti's head snapped up quickly at Qamra's call. Nakia and Nassar ran towards the entrance to the lands, followed closely by Baruti. The children exchanged confused glances and dropped their tools.

"Amsi, come inside! The *Bedu* are here!" Imani exclaimed.

"Who are the *Bedu*?"

Imani looked down at her son and took his hand. "They are a violent people! They are the enemies of the pharaoh and the people of Egypt! We must get inside before they attack!"

Amsi looked down the path at the fleeing slaves. None of them were carrying their tools to defend themselves. Nakia was running quickly, catching up to Baruti. *If they are so violent, why are the slaves running for the gates? Wouldn't they want to return to their home for safety? If they are enemies of the pharaoh, they should know how to stop him!*

Amsi broke from his mother's grip and ran down the path as he followed the slaves. When he arrived at the gates, the slaves were watching the sight before them.

The *Bedu* were riding camels and horses. Their animals were covered in elaborate blankets with material woven from red and gold textiles. The reigns were decorated with different colored fringes. The *Bedu* themselves were wearing long robes with different colored materials, their eyes only revealed by shiny material wrapping their faces.

Their carts were pulled by horses and carried large vases and many baskets full of apples, dates, pomegranates, gold jewelry, and various material of shiny and immeasurable quality. The women riding their steeds wore long, white dresses which rested just above their ankle. One breast was exposed on each woman as they rode beside the men. Gold rings, bracelets, and jewelry graced their bodies. Several children walked beside the horses of their fathers, guiding a small herd of ten cattle with sticks. They were dressed in long white robes that stopped above their knees.

Nassar pointed at the caravan and shook Nakia's shoulder. "Ah-e-ah! Be-oo!"

Baruti watched the leader of the caravan stop beside the Nile and dismount. Beside the leader there stood a little girl similar to Amsi's age. Her dress stopped at her knees and tied around her waist was a rope of gold. Her body was exposed from her right hip to her left shoulder, revealing her right developing breast. Her long, black hair fell around her shoulders. Around her neck, the little girl wore a necklace of gold decorated with red jewels. Her wrists were decorated with gold bracelets and from her ears dangled earrings of gold. Her lips were colored red as she smiled at the group of slaves.

Baruti looked at the cart and his eyes widened in surprise. "Nakia, those are the *Bedu* who saved you in the desert!"

Nakia gasped as he looked at the large group of men and women. "Do you think so, Baruti? How can you be certain?"

Qamra nodded. "That cart is the same."

Nakia dashed for the group of Bedouin before Nassar could grab his twin. Nakia heard Nassar and Amsi call for him as he ran quickly. "Wait, Nakia! Come back!"

The little girl saw the running slave and pulled on her father's robes. "Father!"

The man dressed in red and gold fabric turned his head and drew his scimitar. "Intruder!"

The other men turned and drew their swords together. Nakia stopped quickly with a frightened gasp.

"Wait!" he exclaimed raising his arms. "I don't want to fight!"

"Then why do you come running for us?"

Nakia swallowed nervously. "Did you save a little boy from the desert eight years ago?"

The men exchanged glances. The leader sheathed his sword. "Yes."

Nakia lowered his hands and fell to his knees, bowing before the group. Nakia's forehead touched the sand as he prostrated himself in front of the men. "Thank you. I didn't get a chance to thank you for saving me."

Amsi put his hand on Nakia's back. "What are you doing, Nakia? They could have killed you!"

The little girl held onto her father's robes as she looked at Amsi. The father put his hand on his daughter's shoulder to calm her. "We see that the gods have spared your life. You are most fortunate."

Nassar arrived beside his twin and punched his shoulder. "Ah-e-ah! Oo moft ki-ah!"

"You were almost killed, Nakia!" Amsi said.

Nakia looked up at the men. "I had to know if it was them. Without them, Master Amsi, I would have died."

Amsi looked at the leader as the other men sheathed their swords. "Thank you for saving my friend."

The little girl smiled at Amsi. "My father is a kind man."

Amsi looked at the little girl beside her father and blushed. She's very pretty. I should do something nice for them for saving Nakia's life. "What can I give you for saving his life?"

"You owe us nothing, child."

Baruti slowly approached the twins and Amsi. "We welcome you back to our lands."

"Thank you for your kind greeting." The leader bowed his head slightly. "It is time we sell our wares and water our herd. The bank here will suffice nicely."

"Do you think Kaemwaset will allow this?" Nakia asked Baruti.

"Kaemwaset does not own the bank of the Nile. He will have no choice. However, the pharaoh may take issue with this."

Kaemwaset and a mounted Gahiji approached the group of slaves quickly. Kaemwaset punched Baruti harshly in the arm. "Get back to work, you lazy bunch of wild asses!"

Nassar growled and pulled back his fists in return, but Baruti caught it quickly before it could contact Kaemwaset.

"You are not welcome on our lands!" Gahiji exclaimed to the Bedouin.

"We are here to water our herds and sell our wares. We mean no harm."

Nakia rose to his feet quickly. "They saved me from the desert, my lord! I came to express my gratitude to them!"

The little girl clinging to her father whimpered as she held onto her father's robes. Kaemwaset punched Nakia's shoulder. "Get back to work, you lazy bunch of bones! I should have them all killed for their kindness!"

"You have a wicked heart, sir," the leader said, holding his daughter close to his body. "We do not treat our cattle with such cruelty, yet you treat another person with contempt and hatred?"

Kaemwaset growled at the group. "You have no business meddling in my affairs!"

"I can certainly do the honors!" Gahiji grinned, removing his sword.

"Stop!" Amsi exclaimed, standing in front of the group with his arms stretched wide. "You will not harm them! They will not cause trouble here!"

Gahiji glared at Amsi. "Step out of my way, young Al-Sakhir!"

"No! Go back to the pharaoh!"

Gahiji glared at the leader. "This is not over, I promise you."

Amsi watched as General Gahiji rode away quickly towards the city. Kaemwaset glared at the men.

"If you interfere with my slaves or my crops, I will not take it lightly."

The leader returned the challenging gaze of the land owner. Kaemwaset broke the glare and shoved Nassar angrily.

"Get back to work, you worthless mule!" Kaemwaset growled at Nassar.

Amsi scowled at his father as he shoved the little children back to the fields. He turned to the leader of the Bedouin and sighed. "I apologize for my father's behavior."

"That is your father?" the little girl asked as she stepped towards Amsi. "My father would never treat anyone like that!"

"Zahra, come back," the father said calmly. "We will settle here for the season of *Shemu*. Thank you for your kind welcome, child."

"My name is Amsi Al-Sakhir."

The leader grinned and bowed his head. "Thank you, Amsi."

Amsi watched as a stone rolled from the reeds and skipped across the ground. *Azizi is here! He made it away from the soldiers! Praise Rā!*

Zahra looked at another rock skipping from the reeds and she slowly crept towards the source of the rocks. Amsi swallowed nervously, fearing that his friend's location would be discovered. *What if they find him? Would they turn him into the pharaoh's hands?*

"You should know something about the banks along the Nile. Please don't tell anyone because it could mean my friend's death!" The leader nodded. "My friend lives along the banks during the dry season and-." Another small rock skipped across the sand and hit Amsi in the foot. "That one hurt! Don't be surprised if you see him."

Zahra stopped her advance on the reeds and looked back at Amsi. "Is he like your father?"

Amsi shook his head. "No, he's not like him. He's an orphan."

The leader nodded. "We shall keep an eye open for the boy. In the meantime, we must prepare camp. Good blessings to you, my boy."

Amsi smiled and bowed his head. He looked at the little girl standing beside her father. He sheepishly waved to her before running towards the home.

## XXVIII

### The Legend of Seth

Azizi grinned as he watched the two girls explore the reeds. He slowly withdrew, careful to keep from their sight. The boy bit his lip as he scurried from the tall reeds. The girls would find no trace of him as he hurried to the safety and anonymity of the city. Azizi wrapped his black cape around him as he entered the city. His eyes narrowed as he moved among the crowd and saw Gahiji racing away on his horse.

*That man killed my mother. I will avenge her someday. Osiris will help me. I know it. First I think it's time to grab a little mid-day meal. I'm hungry.*

Azizi saw men carrying ducks over their shoulders, their bodies laying limp against their backs. One man dressed in fine material held samples of his fine cloth towards the crowd. "The finest cloth in all of Egypt from distant lands! Feel the quality, sir! You cannot make this from papyrus or wool! It's a bargain at twenty dînars!"

Azizi bumped into a man who had stopped to sample some dates. The man looked down at Azizi and grabbed the front of Azizi's cloak. "Be careful where you walk, child, or you could walk into something sharp."

Azizi nodded quickly as the man shoved him away and returned his attention to the date cart. Azizi looked at the cart where dates, raisins, grapes, and spices were priced. The boy sniffed the air and licked his lips longingly. *Fresh bread.* Azizi's attention left the date cart, following the sweet smell of bread. A group of children were hovering outside a bakery looking at the goods within.

Azizi joined the crowd of small children as the bakers removed bread from an oven. One boy, he recognized by a twisted clubbed left foot. Ferryn was one of only few children easily identifiable living on the streets. The little girl beside him sighed longingly as she looked inside. "It looks so good," she groaned as she watched the bakers knead the dough.

"I know, Jamila," Azizi responded to the girl slightly younger than him.

"They want fifteen dînars for that bread! How can we ever afford it?" Ferryn groaned.

Giladi looked around nervously. "Kaphiri will just take it from us."

Azizi turned his head looking around the crowded streets. Kaphiri had continued to take toys and food from the other homeless children of the quarter. "He doesn't appear to be around."

"He's in hiding. He's waiting for us to take the bread and he'll follow us when we get it. He'll steal it from us."

"That's how it happened last time," Ferryn sighed.

One of the bakers turned his head towards the orphans. "Get out of here, you little scoundrels! I won't let you steal my bread again! You know the punishment for stealing!"

Ferryn and Jamila ran away in fear. Giladi stood beside Azizi, shifting closer to him.

"There's no crime in watching you bake!" Azizi protested.

"You stay on the other side of the wall where we can see you!" the baker threatened.

Azizi looked up and down the crowded streets. The bakers were kneading the dough and forming it into loaves. He watched as a baker threw sand into the bread dough.

"Why are you doing that?" Azizi asked.

"This bread is for the poor. It's cheaper. Your mother and father can buy this bread to put into your little stomach."

Azizi narrowed his eyes angrily. *I have to get that bread now! I was going to let him go, but after that comment there's no turning back.*

"Giladi, you may want to run," Azizi whispered to the young boy beside him.

"Why?"

Azizi looked at the nine-year-old. "Because I don't want you to be blamed for my actions. Go."

"What about the bread?"

"You won't go hungry. I know where to find you."

Giladi walked away reluctantly. Azizi watched the bakers focus on their work. He looked above and saw smoke rising from the vent leading to the oven. He took a deep breath and licked his lips with anticipation. *If I can plug that up, the bakery will fill with smoke. Nobody will be able to see me enter. I can't make too much of a commotion during the day. I don't want to be caught.* Azizi chuckled. *I haven't been caught yet and I want to keep it that way.*

Azizi walked to the side of the bakery and looked up at the roof. He crawled on the ground past an opening in the wall to allow light and air into the hot bakery. When he crossed the window safely, he looked up at the roof. It was too tall for him to climb. He needed a boost to grab hold of the roof. Azizi jumped, raising his hands above his head. He tried to grasp onto the roof, but he wasn't tall enough. He grit his teeth and jumped again, trying to grab onto the roof.

The thirteen-year-old looked up at the rooftop with a frustrated growl. Something has to get me up there! Azizi saw nothing between the bakery and the weaver's shop behind him. Azizi walked to the back of the bakery and saw three wicker baskets. He opened the baskets and found them empty, much to his disappointment.

He looked up at the roof and continued to see smoke bellowing from the vent. Azizi crawled on top of the large basket, which quivered under his attempt to climb onto its bulky width. Azizi held his breath as he heard voices between the weaver and the bakery.

"How much for the job, Amari?"

"That woman's spells are dangerous, but I hear she holds the power of a soothsayer. She claims to know the One is living here in Heliopolis."

Azizi held his breath as the wicker basket wavered under him. Azizi moved himself with the basket to keep it steady. *What are they talking about?*

"The pharaoh has increased the price on the boy's head. Kaphiri should know where the boy is located. If we get our hands on that boy, we can easily turn him into the pharaoh's hands for the money. Kaphiri will be unchallenged and he can do as he pleases without the boy intervening. The Seth Clan will rule *Iunu.*"

"Kaphiri is a master thief and he is improving his skill daily. My son has made my heart proud."

Azizi felt the basket begin to tip and lose its balance. The boy gripped the basket's edges desperately. He leaned forward quickly and looked up at the roof of the bakery. *If I can get up there, they won't see me!*

"Amari, Heliopolis is a large city. How will we find the boy the pharaoh seeks?"

"We go to the woman. Aneksi will tell us what she knows. She has to know where the boy can be found. Thirty dînars for her life, Majid."

Azizi felt the basket fall to the side as he jumped for the roof. He looked down as the basket fell, its lid rolling into the alley.

"What was that?" the one man asked.

Azizi heard the men walking towards him. He grit his teeth as he lifted himself onto the roof. Azizi pulled his bare feet onto the roof as the men picked up the lid of the whicker basket. He gasped as he pulled back from the edge of the view of the men.

"It must have been the wind," the one man said as Azizi held his breath anxiously.

*They want to hurt Aneksi! I'll get what I need here and run to tell her!*

Azizi watched the smoke bellow from a metal pipe. A deep, long breath caressed his senses with the smell of fresh bread. The boy took a stone he had carried from the Nile banks and placed it over the pipe, stopping the flow of smoke. Azizi looked down as smoke began to come from the bakery below.

"Something is burning in the bakery!" Amari screamed standing beside the fallen basket.

"Run, Amari!"

Azizi giggled as the two men scurried quickly from the bakery's rear. He looked down and saw the bakers coming out of the bakery coughing loudly.

"The fire was stoked too much, you fools!" the baker growled as he staggered out of the building.

Azizi leaned his head over and slipped into the building via an opening in the wall. He landed on a wooden table and winced as the smoke stung his eyes.

He grabbed two loaves of bread and placed them in a cloth bag. The baker stepped into the bakery, waving the smoke away from his eyes when he saw Azizi through the haze.

"You little thieving dog! I will have your hands for this!"

Azizi gasped and threw the dough at his feet towards the baker. The dough hit the man in the face, making the teen giggle at his skill. *That was close! What a lucky hit!*

Azizi climbed out of the window and landed on his feet. He ran from between the two shops, looking over his shoulder.

"That's the boy who was watching us!" The one baker screamed. "Guards! Thief!"

Azizi faced forward as he dodged through the crowd. His bare feet patted against the hard ground as raced towards a safe place of refuge. He turned a corner and ran into his alley quickly. The boy ran under a cart and covered himself with material.

He clutched the bread against him as he waited for footsteps. He panted heavily from his hasty escape and slowly pulled back the material covering him. The boy breathed a sigh of relief as he broke a piece of the bread and chewed on it with content.

*Aneksi needs me. If I run into Giladi or Jamila, I'll give them some. I already promised Giladi a piece of bread. He has yet to learn the fine art of taking what you need and running away. The pharaoh or Gahiji will not hesitate to punish him if he is caught. Until he can do this on his own, I'll have to help him. Kaphiri bullies that boy terribly.*

Azizi stepped from his sanctuary and slipped into the shadows cast by the setting sun. He wrapped his black cloak around himself and hid behind a large vase as a group of soldiers marched. He held his breath, struggling to maintain his composure, knowing if they caught him, he could forfeit his life at the pharaoh's hands. Azizi put his hands on the sides of his head and grit his teeth angrily.

*"NO!" Khepret screamed. "Don't kill my son! He's only a child!"*

Azizi felt a tear creep down his cheek. Mother. *Why did you have to die?*

*The pharaoh smiled. "I want you to know before you die, that you are to blame for your mother's death."*

Azizi clenched his fists tightly. *No, I'm not! I didn't kill my own mother! Don't say that!*

The boy watched the soldiers march calmly away. He wiped his eyes free of tears as he looked at them with contempt. They were to blame for his mother's death. They watched. They didn't stop Gahiji from severing his mother's head.

Now he was alone.

*I hate you.*

Azizi continued running through the shadows until he came to Aneksi's home. He knocked on the wooden door to her home. No one came to answer the door. Azizi banged on it again, watching around him vigilantly.

The door finally opened and Darwishi stood there. "Boy, what are you doing?"

"Darwishi, let me in!" Azizi exclaimed, running inside.

Darwishi quickly closed the door and looked down at the boy dressed in a black cloak and a beaded linen skirt that was now torn and stained with mud. "I came to see Aneksi. I heard men were talking about hurting her."

"I am here, my boy," Aneksi said as she stepped from the shadows. She looked down at the boy and kneeled before him. She reached out slowly and put a soft hand on his cheek. "You have been crying. What upsets you, our little king?"

Azizi took a deep breath. "It's nothing," he said with a sniffle.

Darwishi grinned. "He can steal well, but he is a terrible liar, my lady."

"Under your instruction, he has learned well, Darwishi," she said with a smile. "I'm afraid there are more lessons which he needs to learn."

Azizi bit his lip nervously. "Aneksi, I heard two men mean to kill you. I wanted to warn you!"

Aneksi nodded. "Darwishi is a good fighter. He will protect me. That is one lesson you must learn, my child. A good fighter is one who is strong of mind and body. Sometimes, you must fight without weapons and use your words and tongue as well as your dagger and sword."

Azizi grabbed Aneksi's shoulders. "You can't stay here, Aneksi! You have to go! Please!"

"I have no fear, my king."

"Why do you insist on calling me your king? I am no king, Aneksi! I'm just Azizi Keket."

The woman smiled at him. "Don't deny your calling, little Azizi. You must believe in who you are to defeat the pharaoh and the growing threat he poses to the people of Heliopolis and the world."

Azizi looked at the woman. "What are you talking about, Aneksi? The pharaoh is mortal. He will die someday."

Aneksi released Azizi and stood up. She walked to a shelf of scrolls and opened one slowly. "According to The Scroll of Thoth, the prophecy reads thus:

> *From the ashes of Iunu, he rises as Aten's light to the dawn. The Agent of Sekhmet strikes at the heart of the Ram. The favor of the Sun God falls*

*not upon his deeds as Sekhmet rides through the streets of blood, flooded by the lust for Death. Rā is blinded by his greatness. The Great Pharaoh's arms shall extend over the land and shower the people with his glorious light.*

"Azizi, the pharaoh lusts for death. He hungers for power unimaginable. He must be stopped." Aneksi unfurled the scroll further and pointed at the hieroglyphics. "Can you read this, Azizi?"

The little boy looked at the scroll by candlelight and narrowed his eyes. "I can read some of it, but some of it I don't understand."

"That is Noble Tongue, Azizi. The Nobility has segregated its language so as to hide the true purpose of the message from those who, in their eyes, are not worthy. Look at this scroll, my boy. Can you read this?"

Azizi rubbed his eyes as he leaned forward to the scroll. His traced the writing with his finger. *I'm not a scribe! How can I possibly read this? Amsi has taught me how to read a few words, but he knows much more than I.* "I'm sorry, Aneksi. I can't read."

Aneksi smiled at the boy. "That is because your tutor instructs you in the language of the Noble Tongue. This is writ in Common Script."

*The Scroll of Osiris does one need*

*For power over death itself*

*For his Scepter to work, one must bleed*

*Over the gold and all its wealth.*

*Deep inside the belly of sand*

*Is where to find the holy relic*

*Where the ram rises over the desert's Red Land.*

Azizi pulled back from the papyrus and touched the scroll with a quivering hand. He felt his heart skip a beat. "Did I read this right, Aneksi? Someone could wield power over life and death? Does that mean that I could bring my parents back from the Land of the Dead?"

Aneksi smiled. "I don't know how the object works, Azizi, but I would assume so."

A tear fell down Azizi's cheek. "I want my parents back, but where is this location? 'The Ram rises over the desert's red land?'"

"Animals cannot jump over the desert. It could mean something allegorical," Darwishi said.

"The Ram symbolizes Osiris," Azizi whispered. "Can a god jump over the desert?"

"The gods can do whatever they wish," Aneksi said calmly. "The gods have blessed mankind with many good things, but soon it came to pass, Azizi, that mankind wanted to be equal to the gods. Let me tell you a story, my Azizi." Aneksi rolled the scroll and replaced it on the shelf. "A long time ago, mankind worshipped the gods. They honored the gods with sacrifices and praised them for all of their good works. Mankind saw Rā grow old with age. They said 'Behold, his Majesty hath grown old, and his bones have become like silver, and his members have turned into gold and his hair is like unto real lapis-lazuli.' Rā gathered the gods together and among those he called was Seth. Seth, the Evil One, heard of the things that mankind was saying. Seth knew that if Mankind were stronger, they could overthrow Rā." Aneksi lowered her head and frowned. "Men are easily manipulated, my child. Seth gave Mankind a chance at Immortality. He handed magical scrolls and magical items to Mankind to allow them to reach godhood. Osiris discovered this and sent his son, Horus, to disperse these scrolls and items so Mankind could never achieve godhood."

Azizi looked at the woman kneeling in front of him. "Why would Osiris want to do that?"

"Power corrupts, my dear boy. Absolute power is an intoxicating elixir, one which Mankind was not yet prepared to imbibe. Powers of reincarnation, mind-control, nature itself are not meant to be controlled by mortals, Azizi."

Azizi and Aneksi looked towards the door as someone banged harshly on the wood. Aneksi looked at the boy and kissed his cheek. "You must leave, Azizi."

Azizi shook his head as he clutched onto her shoulders. "I have to stay and fight!"

"No! You go, my child. I cannot have you killed!"

The door opened quickly as three men entered. Azizi looked at the scimitars in the men's hands. His eyes widened as the Darwishi armed himself with two swords.

"What is it that you want?"

The leader smiled a toothless grin. "We came for the woman." The leader's grin widened further. "The boy would be a nice addition to our list as well."

The two men flew at Darwishi with their swords raised. Azizi grabbed his golden dagger from his belt and stood beside Darwishi.

"You are not ready for combat, Azizi!" The man growled.

Darwishi's swords clashed with the enemy's. Azizi blocked the third man from advancing on Aneksi.

"You leave her alone!"

"Come with me like a good little boy," the leader said tenderly. "And we will spare the woman."

Azizi huffed in defiance, his body tensed as he gripped the hilt of the dagger. "No."

"Then your skin would be a good trophy for the pharaoh," the man said, bringing his sword down. Azizi brought his dagger up to block the man's strike.

*Aneksi's been the closest person I've had to a mother that I can remember. She and Darwishi have taught me how to survive alone. Darwishi taught me how to steal my first grape. I can't let harm come to them!*

Azizi's opponent reached into his belt and grabbed another dagger. The boy jumped back as the blade crossed his path. The thirteen-year-old lunged to the side as the man's sword came down over him. The dagger crossed his path again as he rolled forward. He turned quickly and kicked the man's leg, sending him off balance. Azizi slashed the dagger across the back of the man's leg, making him cry out in pain.

The other two men watched their leader fall to the ground bleeding and screaming in pain.

"You little snake! I'll get you!"

Azizi watched as the man grabbed the front of his cloak and held him in the air. The teen punched the man in the face and brought his knee hard under the man's chin. His adversary fell to the ground unconscious.

The surviving opponent backed away from Darwishi. The fighter grabbed his enemy and held him close. "What do you want with us? Who sent you?"

The man grinned. "Amari wanted the boy dead!"

"Why? Tell me!" Darwishi demanded, holding the blade of his sword to the man's throat.

"Because he is Kaphiri's enemy and if we capture him, the pharaoh would give us enough money to live comfortably for the rest of our lives! We will be granted immortality with his blessing!"

Azizi panted heavily as he stood beside Darwishi. *Everyone wants me dead. I'm not safe anywhere.* "They are members of Kaphiri's clan, Darwishi. The pharaoh speaks with the tongue of a serpent! He promises you immortality when all he will do is see to it that you suffer in his service! He will not give you what he promises and you are fools to believe that he will be true to his word!"

Aneksi calmly walked beside Darwishi. "You are seeking to kill the boy who can save all of us from the pharaoh's wrath. The scrolls have foretold of a Blessed Servant of Osiris, born in *Iunu*, who shall devastate the pharaoh and his plans. This boy is the only hope we have."

"It could be Kaphiri who shall fulfill that prophecy!"

"That boy is selfish. I have seen him intimidate the other children. He does not walk on the side of Ma'at."

Azizi narrowed his eyes at the man. "Kaphiri only cares about himself. He takes all of the best scraps of meat and gives the smaller children the fat. He beats my friends for his pleasure!"

"Your friends are weak!" the man exclaimed, spitting in Azizi's face.

The boy narrowed his eyes and growled. Azizi clenched his fists angrily and punched the man furiously. "I will not let you speak ill of my companions!"

Darwishi looked down at Azizi. "Leave here, boy. I shall dispense justice on him."

"May Osiris damn you!" Azizi looked at the man and at Aneksi, who prodded him towards the door with her hands. "Do you want some of the bread I have, Aneksi?"

Aneksi smiled and shook her head. "No, my boy. You need to eat. You are nothing but bones. Find yourself some shelter. The veil of night is falling fast."

Azizi watched the door close to the home. He slowly walked through the shadows of the streets, keeping his eyes focused on the crowd passing him. He shivered in the night air as he pulled his black cloak closer around him. The teen coughed into his hand and yawned.

His ears detected the sound of sobbing in the dark shadows of one alley. Azizi crept slowly into the darkness. Giladi and Jamila were huddled together in the shadows. One blanket was wrapped around the girl and boy as they shivered. It was barely by the light of the moon that he saw them. The two children looked up at him with smiles.

"Hello, Azizi," Jamila whimpered.

"Did you get the bread?" Giladi asked.

Azizi reached into the bag and removed a loaf of bread. He handed it to Giladi and bowed his head. "I said I would share. Take it."

Jamila grabbed onto the bread and smiled. The eleven-year-old girl broke the bread in half and gave it to her companion. "Thank you very much, Azizi!"

Giladi's teeth tore into the bread hungrily. His stick-thin fingers cradled the bread lovingly in his hands. "Have you seen Kaphiri anywhere?"

Azizi shook his head. "No, I haven't."

"He wants to see you in the pharaoh's jail," Giladi said.

Azizi looked out of the alley. He knew what awaited him if he was unfortunate enough to find himself in the dungeon. He had heard of terrible stories from the streets of those subjected to the cells of the dungeon. Starvation or being eaten alive by rats and even torture were just a few possibilities. Those who found themselves there rarely survived a week after release.

"Don't worry about me," Azizi said with a smile.

Azizi, Giladi, and Jamila held their breath as they heard someone running quickly down the alley. A tall figure appeared from the darkness. Azizi grabbed the hilt of his dagger with a growl.

"Who goes there?!"

The footfalls stopped quickly. "It's me, Azizi! Sekani! I come with news!"

Azizi and the other children relaxed as they watched the fourteen-year-old walk calmly towards Azizi. "You scared us!"

Sekani chuckled and bowed his head. "My apologies, Azizi. I didn't mean to scare any of you."

"Do you want some bread?" Jamila asked, offering a little crust to the other homeless boy.

"Thank you, Mila," Sekani said, taking the little piece of bread.

"What is your news?" Azizi asked.

Sekani quickly ate the small piece of bread. "Hayfa was caught stealing and she's going in front of the pharaoh!"

"Hayfa? She's part of Kaphiri's gang!" Jamila exclaimed. "The pharaoh will hang her!"

Giladi shuddered as he shifted closer to Jamila. "I don't want to be hanged!" The child said, rubbing his throat.

Sekani pat the child on the head. "Stay out of trouble, Giladi and you will be fine. I also heard that the *Bedu* are here! Is it true, Azizi?"

Azizi nodded as he shivered in the cold air. "Yes, they were talking to my friend today."

"The merchants aren't praising their arrival. They are afraid of losing business to them as they should. The *Bedu* have many pretty things that many people in *Iunu* cannot afford."

"Gahiji didn't seem very pleased to see them," Azizi said. "I wonder what the pharaoh will do about their arrival."

Sekani shrugged. "I'm not certain, but I know I have to get back to Saqr and Khalil. I can't leave them alone for long. My little brothers are wondering where I am."

Azizi nodded. "Tell them I said hello."

Sekani bowed his head. "Goodnight, Azizi."

Azizi watched Sekani run away. "I should find shelter. It's cold tonight. You enjoy the bread."

Azizi turned and walked down the alley when he felt a little tug on the back of his cloak. Azizi turned and saw Giladi standing there with a smile. The child shivered as he looked up at Azizi with a smile. "Thank you for the bread."

Azizi pat Giladi on the head. "Get under the blanket before you get sick. Go on."

Giladi disappeared into the darkness as Azizi shivered. His toes curled in the cold night air of the desert permeating the city. Azizi stepped into his alley where the stench of the corpse was intensifying. Wild dogs were sniffing around the alley looking for food and finding only rotten scraps. Azizi wrapped his cloak tightly around him as he continued to find a place to rest. He raised his head to the night sky. Bright, twinkling stars were spread across the sky. The moon hovered above the city, beaming light on the few people wandering the streets.

The boy yawned as he walked through the streets, his head lowered and covered by the black cloak's hood. He felt his tight grip on the cloak weakening as his body grew tired. His eyelids felt as heavy as a bushel of apples as his bare feet tapped against the ground. The Nile was a walk away and offered him privacy and comfort. Tonight, his body craved sleep as soon as possible and knew he would collapse on the street from exhaustion.

*If I fall asleep in the streets, the soldiers would surely find me and take me to the pharaoh.*

Azizi walked beside the bakery and looked into the alley. He shuddered as he walked into the alley. He put his back against the wall and sat on the ground. He covered himself with the cape and shivered, curling his toes from the cold. His arms were wrapped around him underneath the black cloak.  Azizi's congested cough echoed through the alley.

He yawned as his head fell down to his chest.  *Azizi, your mother loves you,* he thought with a smile in the cold, dark alley where he fell asleep alone.

## XXIX

### The Pharaoh's Property

Pharaoh Runihura grabbed Janani by the arms as he deepened the kiss with her.  Janani clenched her fists tightly as she resisted the pharaoh's advances.  A tear fell down her cheek as the pharaoh backed her against the wall of his bed chamber.  She felt his body pressed against him, his stiffened member obvious through the material of his white linen skirt.  His hands slid down to her wrists as he pinned them against the wall beside her head.  The pharaoh moaned into the kiss as he pressed himself intentionally against her.

*If I don't let him do this to me, he'll kill me.  He's done this before and I heard he killed the girl who resisted.  I don't love you, pharaoh! You killed your father!  You are a vicious beast!*

Janani sobbed as the pharaoh kissed her jaw and down her neck, giving the side of her neck a rough bite.  Janani struggled with the pharaoh as he tightened his grip.

"Don't you deny me, Janani! You are denying the Living God your body which I rightfully deserve!"

"I don't love you, my pharaoh! You may take my body, but you will never have my soul or my heart."

Pharaoh Runihura glared at the girl. "You belong to me, Janani! All of you belongs to me! Your mind, your body," Runihura licked his lips. "Your breasts are mine. Your womb is mine."

Janani swallowed nervously. "You are wrong, my pharaoh."

Runihura smiled as he leaned close to Janani's face. "Think what you wish. What you think, what you feel, means very little to me."

A knock sounded on the door, eliciting a groan from the pharaoh. "I am busy! What is it?!"

The door opened and Gahiji walked quickly into the room. The General bowed his head and kneeled beside the pharaoh pressing his slave girl against the wall.

"General Gahiji, I am trying to become amorous with my slave girl and I cannot mate with her if you interrupt me!"

"My lord, the *Bedu* have arrived! They have settled beside the Nile near the Al-Sakhir family lands!"

Runihura released Janani. "You speak the truth, General Gahiji?"

"Yes, my lord! I have seen them with my own eyes!"

Runihura looked at Janani. "Get out of here. I will call for you when I want to use you later." Janani reached for her white robe when the pharaoh grabbed her wrist. "I didn't say get dressed." Janani slowly pulled back and walked out of the room.

General Gahiji stood and looked at Pharaoh Runihura. "They could be here to usurp your power."

"How many were there?"

"About fifty, your Grace. Men, women, and some children were in the group."

Runihura smiled. "The *Bedu* travel far and wide, Gahiji. They may have knowledge that could prove beneficial to me. They are traders and merchants."

"But they are dangerous! They have been known to attack the pharaoh's forces and challenge the authority of your greatness!"

Runihura held up a calm hand. "I can defeat them with Sekhmet's support should it come to a battle. If I could have their support in my search for the legendary items, then the fact that the people fear them would tighten the hold I have over them. They will depend on me to keep them safe. I will appear to be a savior in their eyes. They will worship me. It's to my benefit that we welcome them with open arms."

Pharaoh Runihura stepped onto his balcony and shivered in the night. "The wind is chilled tonight, Gahiji. This is very strange weather."

Gahiji stepped beside the pharaoh. He looked down into the gardens where Hamadi was walking on the path.

"What is that worthless creature doing walking around the gardens at night?"

Hamadi kneeled beside a small campfire and sprinkled herbs into the flame. He folded his hands in prayer and closed his eyes.

Runihura chuckled. "He must be offering the gods supplications for my continued health and my mercy towards him."

"He could be praying that I do not work him to death during battle sparring tomorrow."

The pharaoh and the General watched as Janani walked into the gardens under the cover of darkness. From the pitch-black balcony, they watched Janani slowly walk towards Hamadi.

Hamadi raised his head from the campfire and saw the girl approach him solemnly. "Janani? Where are your clothes?"

Janani looked down, her arms crossed in front of her breasts. Hamadi watched as tears glistened in the fire's light. The teenager stood on his feet and stepped in front of Janani.

He tilted her head up and looked into her sparkling eyes. The pharaoh and General watched as Hamadi slowly leaned down to Janani. The garden slave kissed Janani tenderly on the lips.

Janani whimpered into the kiss, wrapping her arms lovingly around Hamadi's neck. Hamadi wrapped his brown cloak around Janani and held her close. Hamadi's hand reached up and gently caressed Janani's cheek with his fingertips. Runihura's eyes narrowed threateningly as he watched Hamadi kiss Janani.

Hamadi's tender, feather-light kisses worshipped her skin as he kissed her neck. Janani kissed Hamadi's ear tenderly. "I love you, Hamadi."

Runihura's fists clenched angrily as he punched the stone balcony. *How dare he touch what belongs to me!*

Hamadi lead Janani onto the ground beside the fire, their kiss continuing as they laid beside each other. Janani straddled Hamadi's hips as Hamadi wrapped the cape around her to shield her from the cold and the sight of any observers.

"Where is the pharaoh?" Hamadi asked nervously.

"He's talking to General Gahiji. They are in the warm palace," Janani said with a smile.

Hamadi kissed the front of her throat. "Why are you naked?"

Janani avoided Hamadi's eyes. "He was trying to use my body again."

Hamadi caressed Janani's cheek lovingly. "It kills me to see you in the arms of the pharaoh, Janani."

*It will kill you. You are touching what is mine, Hamadi! You will not get away with this, I promise you!* Runihura glared as he watched Hamadi caress his slave girl. *I will kill you, Hamadi!*

Janani sniffled. "He scares me, Hamadi. I don't want to be tossed from the balcony for not pleasing the pharaoh."

Hamadi shook his head slowly. "No, I do not want to see you harmed, Janani." Hamadi added with a smile as he touched Janani out of sight from the pharaoh and General. "I don't want this harmed, either."

Janani smiled. "I want him to know his father."

Hamadi smiled. "You are so beautiful, Janani. I love you so much."

"I love you, Hamadi. You have my heart and always will be the only one to own me."

Hamadi moaned as he felt Janani's hand touch him beneath his linen skirt. Runihura and Gahiji watched as a burst of white breath came from the teen as Janani kissed him, the material hiding their view slightly moving.

Hamadi kissed Janani tenderly on the lips as she rocked against him. The pharaoh heard Janani's whimpers of pleasure as Hamadi welcomed her advances. He glared with malice as Janani moaned and held Hamadi against her.

Janani kissed Hamadi's neck lovingly as she rocked against him under the cover of the cloak. The girl whimpered as she gripped onto Hamadi tightly.

Pharaoh Runihura scowled at the couple. "Hamadi trains twice as hard tomorrow, he gets no food, and he gets tied to the post in the night."

General Gahiji bowed. "Yes, my pharaoh."

"Make certain that he suffers," the pharaoh growled as he watched Hamadi and Janani smile at each other.

Azizi opened his eyes quickly as the shouts of a crowd echoed through the streets. His body tensed as he readied himself for a quick flight should the need arise. He turned his head quickly around the corner and found that he was not being pursued; a crowd of spectators to some unseen event had gathered in front of the alley.

"Get him! Get him!" shouted one woman fiercely.

"Ten dînars on the taller boy!" one man called out as he gathered money for betting on the event in front of his eyes.

Azizi heard General Gahiji's voice call above the crowd for them to stand aside. Azizi swallowed nervously with the presence of the General nearby. The only escape from the alley was through the crowd, making Azizi all the more cautious. Azizi wrapped his black cloak around himself and made certain the hood covered his head.

Azizi stepped into the crowd and looked through the bodies, hiding behind the adults congregating at the only exit from the alley. Two boys were fighting with daggers. Azizi watched as the older boy had disarmed his opponent. Azizi recognized Qasim from Kaphiri's gang of loyal followers. The thirteen-year-old was Kaphiri's friend and was grinning ear-to-ear at his opponent. Azizi gasped when he saw Ferryn holding a knife as he looked up at his slightly taller opponent. The boy struggled for stability on a twisted clubbed foot.

*Ferryn! What in the name of Blessed Osiris did he do to get into this predicament?* Azizi looked around at the adult crowd. He felt his fists clench tightly. *I can't do anything to help him! There's too many people around and General Gahiji will take my head if he finds me! Come on, Ferryn, fight him!*

"Well, Azizi, it seems to me like Ferryn is at a distinct disadvantage," a voice said beside him.

Azizi turned his head and growled at his enemy. "Kaphiri, call off this battle right now!"

Kaphiri chuckled and grabbed Azizi's robe, pulling him close. "I don't think so. When Ferryn is dead, you will be turned into the pharaoh's waiting arms. Only I will rule the streets of *Iunu.* Heliopolis and all its treasures will be mine alone while you rot in the pharaoh's dungeon!"

Azizi and Kaphiri turned their heads as they heard a scream. Qasim held his bleeding hand as Ferryn trembled in front of him.

"It seems Ferryn is not so helpless as you may think, Kaphiri," Azizi said with a smile.

General Gahiji looked at the battle. "What has happened here?"

"The smaller boy stole a handful of dates from my cart!" a man said, pointing to Ferryn. "The other boy began to fight him for the stolen goods!"

Azizi sighed with resignation. *Qasim started an open fight for the food? That is foolish! You wait until you can ambush your prey in private, then you start a fight with him!*

"Let them fight!" Gahiji said with a smile. "It is amusing."

Kaphiri grinned. "Ferryn will pay for his theft with his life, Azizi!"

Azizi shoved Kaphiri away from him angrily. "You made Qasim intentionally start at fight in the middle of the streets, didn't you? You know better than to fight one of your own in the middle of the streets!"

Kaphiri crossed his arms over his chest proudly. "You will soon be one soldier down, Azizi. Watch."

Azizi growled as he watched Ferryn back away from the infuriated Qasim. The thirteen-year-old's eyes darted alarmingly around him. The adults circled around him and there were no exits. Gahiji and two of his soldiers stood waiting to capture Ferryn should he win the battle. *Either way this battle goes, Ferryn doesn't stand a chance.*

Ferryn kicked Qasim in the leg as the teen lunged forward. Qasim screamed in pain as he reached down to rub his leg. Ferryn jumped onto Qasim's back and punched the teen in the back angrily.

"You took my food!"

"That food does not belong to you!"

Gahiji laughed. "This is just as entertaining as watching two hungry rats fight over a piece of cheese! Their hunger is amusing!"

"Ferry, get your dagger!" Azizi called loudly through the crowd.

"My lord, we have to stop this!" One soldier exclaimed as he stepped through the crowd.

"Hamadi, get back in position!"

The soldier watched with pity as the older boy grabbed the younger one by the back of the neck.

"Lord Gahiji, please!"

Gahiji narrowed his eyes at the soldier. "Get back in line, Hamadi!"

"No!" Hamadi called defiantly as he turned to Gahiji.

Gahiji's lip curled in disdain. "You are interrupting my entertainment, boy!"

Kaphiri grinned as Qasim pinned Ferryn to the ground by his neck. "Finish him!"

Azizi's eyes widened as he saw the helpless victim pinned to the ground. "Ferryn! No!"

Qasim plunged the dagger into the victim's chest, making the other boy whimper and tremble. "You die! You die!" The dagger found its way into the victim's chest and stomach until the body lay lifelessly.

The crowd clapped with their amusement. The killer looked at the body of his defeated victim, his eyes and mouth opened wide in a now-silenced scream.

Azizi fell to his hands and knees, his eyes filling with tears. "Ferryn, may the gods take you home."

*Ferryn was a good friend. It wasn't his fault his family abandoned him because of his foot.* Azizi closed his eyes tightly as he sobbed quietly.

"You jackal!" Azizi heard someone call from the crowd.

Azizi raised his eyes at the sound of a familiar voice. He jumped to his feet as he heard Sekani yell angrily. Kaphiri heard the sound of his follower, Chakir, respond angrily.

"Ferryn deserved his death!"

Azizi narrowed his eyes. *I'm not letting another one of my friends die!* Azizi pushed through the crowd. "Sekani!" Azizi called as he found Sekani and Chakir locked in a strangling battle.

"We have another fight!" the same woman exclaimed from the crowd.

People backed away from the fight, revealing Azizi standing beside Sekani. Azizi gasped as Sekani stopped struggling.

"That's the boy the pharaoh wants in his dungeon!" Kaphiri called from the concealing crowd. "Capture him!"

The people lunged for Azizi as Sekani punched Chakir in the face. "Let go of me!" Azizi called. Sekani grabbed Azizi's hand and pulled him away from their grasp. Jamila and Giladi ran in front of the crowd as Sekani pulled Azizi away.

"Get them!" Kaphiri called.

Giladi watched as three teens chased after his friends. "Hairdar! Idogbe! Ini-Herit! Watch out!"

Azizi turned his head to see three teens chase after them with scimitars. "Sekani! They're coming closer!"

"I won't let them get you, my friend!"

"What about Giladi and Jamila?"

Sekani stopped short and dumped a basket of apples onto the ground. "They know where to hide!"

Azizi heard the clash of blades behind them as fourteen-year-old Carim emerged from an alley to battle with Azizi's enemies. Azizi watched as two rocks tied by hide was thrown from an alley. They wrapped around one of the teen's legs and tripped him, making him fall onto the ground.

Azizi chuckled. "Good job, Khalil!"

The little boy found his way to help in the fledgling gang. His toys were his weapons of choice. The seven-year-old was seen scurrying from the alley and throwing a ball into the face of the teen fighting Carim.

Sekani found a black horse tethered to a post. He sliced the rope keeping the animal bound and helped Azizi onto its back. "Ride away, my friend. Worry not about us. I will hide our people." Sekani looked back at the battle between Carim and the other teens. Behind the battle, the crowd, lead by Kaphiri and Gahiji were closing in.

"Ride, my friend!" Sekani said, giving the horse a slap on the hind quarters.

Azizi held onto the horse's reigns as a laughing Sekani charged towards the crowd with his sword held high. *Ever since I saved Sekani from Kaphiri, he's been a loyal companion. Sekani was being beaten by Kaphiri and his companions when I found him. They nearly beat him to death with wooden planks. I can trust he will take care of everyone. He's very protective of the others on our side and he tells wonderful stories. He's never spoken about his parents, so I don't know much about them or why he lives in the alleys. I know he will help Carim and see that Ferryn is removed from the streets. Kaphiri will not get away with this! I swear on the blood of Ferryn that he will not have died in vain!*

## XXX

### <u>Boy Meets Girl</u>

Amsi waited in the reeds closely watching the girl by the bank. His eyes watched her in amazement as she unfurled her long black hair and smiled down at her reflection. *Should I go and talk to her? What will I say? 'Good morning to you!' No, that's been said too many times. 'You're very pretty.' Sweet Rā, even I would hit myself!* Amsi shook his head. *Why am I watching her anyway? Why can't I tear my eyes away from her? She's a Bedouin girl and I'm the son of a rich, Egyptian land owner! Besides, my father intends for me to marry this Ife girl, daughter of another rich land owner. I've seen that girl and I'm not particularly impressed.*

Zahra turned her head to her companion and giggled as they exchanged gold necklaces.

*Amsi, you are going to leave her alone. Right now. Move. Why can't I walk away?* Amsi watched as Zahra applied lip paint to the other girl's lips. *What are they doing? What power are they holding over me? I can't move! I can't go away! Why is my stomach tensing up? They are only girls! It's not like I've never seen another girl before.*

Amsi heard a papyrus reed snap nearby. The two girls stopped suddenly and looked at his direction. Amsi gasped and kneeled lower to avoid detection. Slowly, the girls turned around to face the river. They spoke quietly.

*What are they talking about? What made the reed break nearby? What if it's a dangerous crocodile coming to eat the girls? What if it's-Azizi!*

Azizi leapt at Amsi, knocking into him roughly. The two girls turned quickly to see the two boys roll towards them. They parted screaming in alarm as the two boys fell into the Nile with a splash.

The girls giggled as they watched the two boys swim and surface. Amsi coughed and spit water as Azizi shook his head free of water droplets. Amsi and Azizi watched the two girls laugh at them from the banks.

"So you were the one watching us!" Zahra laughed loudly.

"I-umm-guess so," Amsi said nervously.

Zahra looked at Azizi swimming in place. "Is that the boy you were talking about yesterday?"

Amsi nodded. "Yes. This is Azizi."

Azizi coughed as he swam towards the bank with Amsi. The boys held onto the bank as they looked at each other. "I didn't see you kneeling there," Azizi coughed.

Zahra reached her hand out to Amsi. "I'll help you."

Amsi swallowed nervously as he looked at the dainty, manicured hand reaching out to him. Her fingernails were painted with red, matching the brightness of her lips. The sunlight beamed around her as he looked upwards. He reached out slowly to the hand, who took it gently. Zahra pulled Amsi onto the bank with a laugh.

"Do you need help?" Zahra's friend asked Azizi.

Azizi coughed as he shook his head. Amsi watched Azizi pull himself onto the bank and sit, breathing heavy and looking into the water sadly.

"Azizi, are you alright?"

Azizi coughed again and shook his head. "I lost Ferryn. There was a fight for food and one of Kaphiri's boys killed him."

"Where did that boy run?" Gahiji approached as Azizi coughed again.

Amsi grabbed onto Azizi. "Gahiji will find you!"

Zahra took her veil and wrapped it around Azizi's face and body. Zahra's companion took another piece of fine linen and wrapped it around Azizi's body. "You're one of us!"

Amsi put a hand on Azizi's shoulder as the General approached. "Hello, Lord Gahiji!"

"Master Amsi Al-Sakhir! Did you see that boy around here?"

Amsi looked around. "Boy? I'm talking to the girls here. I'm welcoming them to our land."

Zahra smiled as she approached Amsi. She put a gentle hand on his shoulder. "Master Amsi is telling us everything about Egypt and its hospitality!"

"Your pharaoh is a fascinating person!" the other girl exclaimed with a smile. "Long may he reign!"

Azizi narrowed his eyes through the material.

Gahiji looked at the quiet 'girl.' "Speak, Azizi! I know that is you!"

Azizi swallowed nervously. *If I answer, he'll hear my cracking voice, he'll know it was me. Maybe if I squeal like a girl, he won't notice me. I have to keep my words short.* "Cake!"

Amsi and Gahiji raised a curious eyebrow. *What in the name of Rā is he doing?* Amsi thought as he watched Azizi raise his hands.

"Cake!" Azizi squealed loudly, his voice cracking.

"Our sister has limited vocabulary," Zahra said quickly. "We brought her to the Nile to teach her new words such as-." Zahra looked at Amsi. "Swim! Sister, show us what it means to swim!"

Azizi clapped his hands and jumped into the water. He began to swim downstream. When Azizi plunged into the water, the old linen skirt fell off of him and floated to the surface. Zahra's friend giggled uncontrollably.

"Our sister is swimming away, Amsi! Help us get her back before father finds her naked!"

Amsi bowed before Gahiji. "I have to help them, General Gahiji! Good luck on your search!" Zahra and her friend followed Azizi along the bank.

"One thing before you go, Master Amsi!" Amsi looked up at the glaring General. "If I find that you are harboring Azizi, I will toss you into the dungeon and you will rot until nothing is left of you but dust."

Amsi swallowed nervously and bowed. "Yes, Lord Gahiji!"

Amsi followed Zahra and her friend downstream until Azizi swam to the shore. The girls giggled as Azizi stepped onto the bank. Azizi shook his head free of water as Amsi gasped at his friend's nakedness.

"Azizi! Look down!"

Azizi shivered as he stepped from the water. "What?" Azizi looked down his nude body. The boy screamed as he covered himself with his hands. "I didn't count on this!"

Zahra and her friend watched as Azizi tied the sheer material around his hips to hide his nakedness.

"Are you cold, Azizi?"

Azizi nodded in response, his teeth chattering. "A little."

Amsi looked up at the clear, blue sky. The hot sun was beating down upon everything. "I think you might be sick, my friend."

Azizi coughed as he sat by the banks. "The nights have been cold."

Zahra's friend whispered in her ear. "We can get you some blankets and some medicine! We'll be right back!"

"What made you say 'cake?'"

Azizi wrung his side-lock free of water. "I had to think of something. If I acted maniacal, he wouldn't have had time to become suspicious. You learn to adapt to anything on the streets and I have had to find my way out of difficult situations."

Amsi sat beside Azizi as the boy looked at the ground sadly. "I'm sorry you lost Ferryn."

Azizi sighed sadly. "I hope everyone else is safe."

Amsi sighed. "Issâm died, too. The pharaoh killed him."

Azizi looked at his friend beside him. "Why did the pharaoh kill him?"

Amsi looked at Azizi. "He was asking about the Scroll and Eye of Horus."

"The Scroll of Horus? Aneksi read to me from The Scroll of Thoth! She also had in her possession The Scroll of Osiris."

Amsi raised a curious eyebrow. "More scrolls exist? What does it mean?"

"Do you know anything about these scrolls? Did your teacher tell you anything about them?"

Amsi shook his head. "No, he teaches me mathematics, writing, literature, social grace, and history, but I haven't learned anything about this yet. Soon I will begin my battle lessons."

Azizi shook his head. "I can read only a few words and I can't write. I know how to steal, though."

"I don't think Sawaret will teach me that skill, Azizi," Amsi said with a chuckle.

The boy pointed to his chest. "I can get you anything you want from anyone."

"Why does the pharaoh want to get his hands on the Eye of Horus?" Azizi reached into the water, swirling it with his hands.

"He has the Scroll of Thoth, Azizi. The scrolls are meant to tell of items that can give great power to their owner. He asked Issâm about the items and where they were located. Since Issâm worshipped Tehuti and that he was a priest of Thoth, the pharaoh thought that he would know something more about the scrolls or the locations of the items."

"What does the scroll do? What does it say?"

Amsi shook his head. "I don't know, but he killed Issâm because of it."

Azizi growled as he punched the sand of the Nile bank. "Curses on that pharaoh!"

"Issâm prayed to Osiris before he died, Azizi," Amsi lowered his head. "He was a good man."

Azizi watched Amsi look into the water of the Nile. His friend reached into the warm water sadly and removed a handful of water. He sadly poured the water into the Nile, watching it trickle from his palm.

"I'm sorry, Amsi. Osiris is taking good care of him."

"That's what Baruti says," Amsi smiled. "Baruti said that Issâm has his own group of servants in the Underworld."

"Ferryn was always happy to serve," Azizi added solemnly. "I know he has plenty to eat. He doesn't have to starve. He has been given a place of honor beside Osiris."

Amsi looked up at Azizi. "Maybe the pharaoh can let me see the Scroll of Thoth."

Azizi laughed. "Yes, the pharaoh is just going to let you walk up to it and let you read it like one of your little stories! In case you haven't noticed, Lord Amsi Al-Sakhir, the pharaoh has tipped completely off of his pyramid! He is a dangerous person!"

"Maybe if I ask to learn about the scrolls, he will be willing to teach me!"

Azizi shook his head. "I once asked for an apple because I had no money and the man refused to give me one. Because you ask for something, does not mean that it will given to you."

"What do you suppose will happen if the pharaoh were to obtain great power?"

*The pharaoh would become even more dangerous. The pharaoh told me he wants to become immortal.* Azizi nodded. "Aneksi told me of the Scroll of Osiris. It mentioned a Scepter of Osiris, but it didn't give its location."

"How in the name of Tuat are we going to find it, then, Azizi?"

The boy splashed his hand against the surface of the water. "I'm not sure, but if one possesses it, one can control death." Azizi curled his fingers into claws. The little thief boy grinned wide. "Can you imagine having that type of power, Amsi? Can you? The power to control the uncontrollable and irreversible death would be yours!"

"Does that mean you could kill anyone you wanted?"

Azizi's grin faded and he looked at Amsi. "I would assume so, but I'm not sure. If you can control death and bring someone back from the Realm of the Dead, I wonder if it could work in the reverse."

"The pharaoh has the power over life and death, Azizi. He decides who lives and who shall die."

"I know that all too well, Amsi. I watched him kill my mother."

Amsi sighed as he looked at the Nile. "If the pharaoh could kill anyone he wanted without raising his finger, he could turn the entire city into a desert." The boy shook his head. "I don't want to see anyone else die like Issâm. I don't want to bury Qamra or the twins. They are my friends. I don't want to see you buried, either."

"You're a good friend, Amsi. I wouldn't let him bury you."

"The pharaoh is after the Eye of Horus. We have to find it before he does."

Amsi and Azizi turned their heads to see the girls return with blankets and a vial of liquid. Azizi reached into his black cape and removed a few dînars from the coin purse.

"Don't worry about it," Zahra said with a smile. "There is another way I can be repaid."

"Do you need more money? I can give you more if you want," Amsi said.

Zahra giggled. "No, you get to honor me with one dance at the festival tomorrow night."

Amsi swallowed nervously. "Wait-what?!"

"You get to dance with me at the celebration tomorrow night. It is when we worship the moon goddess and praise the gods for their bountiful harvest."

"I'll give you double the money to make him dance twice with you," Azizi said with a grin.

Amsi kicked Azizi in the shin. "No!"

Zahra giggled. "You have yourself two dances tomorrow, Amsi Al-Sakhir. Goodbye."

Zahra and her friend giggled as they walked away.

Amsi crossed his arms defiantly. "I'm not dancing with a girl!"

Azizi coughed into his hand and laughed. "Yes, you are!"

Amsi groaned. "I don't know how to dance!"

"She'll show you," Azizi coughed as he fell backward on the sand with a sigh of exhaustion. "I'm tired."

Amsi looked over at his sweating friend. "You can't stay here, Azizi. If Gahiji finds you when you are asleep, you'll be easily caught." Amsi grabbed the vial and the blanket. "I'm taking you to my slave house. Qamra will take good care of you!"

"I don't need help, Amsi," Azizi groaned as Amsi grabbed his hands to pull him to his feet. "I can take care of myself." Azizi wheezed and cough to clear his lungs as he stood on shaking legs.

Amsi pulled Azizi's arm around him and watched the other boy stumble unsteadily on his feet. "Yes, you can take care of yourself when you can barely walk."

"What if we're caught?"

Amsi shrugged. "Let me handle it."

Azizi stopped, planting his feet on the ground. "Why are you doing this? You don't have to help me, Rich Boy."

"No, I don't have to do this, but you're sick and you need help, so stop being a stubborn ass and move."

Amsi and Azizi peeked their heads out of the reeds and quickly walked to the Al-Sakhir lands. Laila raised her head to see Amsi helping the other boy into the slave house. She dropped her tiny shovel and ran to the house.

She ran inside and saw Azizi laying on the floor. "Master Amsi, what are you doing?"

Amsi looked around as Azizi laid tiredly at his feet. "Where is Issâm's mat?"

"Baruti wrapped him in his mat when he buried him."

Amsi grabbed another mat and placed Azizi onto it. He covered the coughing boy with a blanket and turned to Laila. "Nobody in the house is to know he's here. Do not tell my father or he will be very, very angry."

"Who is he?"

"He's my friend and he needs my help. Go back to work before my father sees you missing and comes to investigate. I'll tell Qamra he's here so she knows to take care of him."

Azizi coughed. "I don't need to be here. I'll be fine."

Amsi looked down at Azizi shaking his head. "A stubborn ass is what you are."

"I'm not a stubborn ass," Azizi yawned, the boy's eyelids fluttering.

"Get some sleep. The slaves will be home after sundown." Amsi turned his back on Azizi to leave the home.

"Rich Boy?"

Amsi turned his head to see Azizi shivering under the blanket. "Yes?"

"Thank you," Azizi smiled at his friend.

Amsi bowed his head, returning his friend's smile. "You are welcome, Azizi, you stubborn ass."

Azizi chuckled and closed his eyes to sleep. Amsi and Laila left the slave quarters. Amsi ran towards the house and saw Qamra carrying laundry to the large wash basin outside. "Qamra! I need to talk to you!"

Qamra dropped the laundry by the basin and bowed her head with a smile. "Hello, Master Amsi."

"Qamra, my friend is sick and I put him in the slave house. The *Bedu* gave some medicine to him, but I didn't want to leave him in the reeds. Can you take care of him for me?"

Qamra looked at the laundry and at her little master. "I will try, Amsi. Unfortunately, I cannot tend to him while I am working in the home. I have to clean your father's linens before he becomes angered."

Amsi smiled. "Thank you, Qamra! You are the best!"

"You are very welcome, Amsi. You should go practice your studies. Your father wants to see you excel."

Amsi's smile faded into a groan. "I don't like doing them."

"I know you do not, Master Amsi, but if you wish to keep your father from becoming angry with you, I suggest you practice."

Amsi slowly sauntered away. *Zahra invited me to the dance tomorrow night and I don't know how to dance! Maybe Qamra can show me how tonight.*

Hamadi grit his teeth as he struggled with his captors. The two high-ranking soldiers grabbed his wrists tightly as they pulled him roughly across the arena's sandy floor. Hamadi pulled and tugged desperately under the watchful eye of Gahiji behind him. The captive dug his heels into the sand, refusing to move even as the two soldiers pulled his limbs harshly.

Hamadi screamed loudly as Gahiji's whip cracked against his back. Hamadi's resistance quickly faded as the two soldiers dragged him to the post in the training arena. The two soldiers dropped the hungry Hamadi onto the ground. They grabbed his shoulders and pushed him against the post. Gahiji watched as the soldiers tied Hamadi's wrists behind his back against the pole. The General kneeled in front of Hamadi and grabbed the man's throat. He pressed it against the pole making his victim gag. The soldiers tied Hamadi's neck to the pole and left just enough room for Hamadi to breathe.

"You dared touch what belongs to the pharaoh, Hamadi. You should praise Rā that the pharaoh has shown you mercy tonight."

Hamadi swallowed nervously. "I-I love Janani."

"Touch her again, Hamadi, and you will forfeit your life."

Hamadi gasped for air as he looked into Gahiji's eyes. "I would gladly die for her."

Gahiji grinned. "That can be easily arranged, Hamadi. I can promise you that."

"I'm-I'm thirsty, my lord," Hamadi whispered, licking his lips. "Please give me water."

Gahiji punched Hamadi in the cheek angrily. The bound victim's lip began to bleed.

"Your blood will be good enough for you to drink. I can give you something to eat if you are hungry."

A tear came from Hamadi's eye. "No, please!"

Gahiji grinned. "Good boy. If I am in a better mood tomorrow, I may consider feeding you and giving you a drink of water."

Gahiji and the soldiers walked away chuckling. Hamadi's eyes looked up at the stars. His stomach ached with hunger, his blood trickling from his split lip down his throat. *The stars are so beautiful as they twinkle in the sky! I wonder what they say as they look upon our homeland. Do they weep? Do they cry out for vengeance against the pharaoh and his cohorts? Are the stars indifferent to the sufferings of the people below?* Hamadi licked his lips, tasting the bitter blood. *What do the gods say? Is Sekhmet drunk on the shedding of our blood? Does Rā wail in sorrow for what his worshippers have become? Do the tears which created Humankind shed once more in sadness? Great Lords of the Sky, do not shed tears for our sake. Take pity on those who shed our blood. It's not a favor easily asked.* A heavy wind blew around the arena as Hamadi shivered. *My stomach pains with hunger. I pray to the gods that Janani is safe from the pharaoh's wrath. I would endure weeks of this if it meant her safety.* In the darkness, he heard footsteps. His eyes widened as he looked around. The rope tied around his neck restricted his movements and knew if he fell asleep, he could choke himself with the rope. *I can't move! I can't move!*

The footsteps continued closer to him. His palms were covered in sweat, his breathing quickened, and his body began to tremble. He saw two shadowed figures step from an arch and into the moonlight.

Hamadi looked up at the figure of the pharaoh standing before him. Beside him, Janani stood holding a torch. Her face looked down with sorrow and pity at him. "I have discussed with you touching what belongs to me. Am I correct, Hamadi?"

"Yes, my merciful pharaoh."

Runihura glared at the bound soldier. "And yet you continually disobey me. What do you suppose I do about this, Hamadi?"

Two tears fell from Hamadi's eyes as he gasped for breath through nervous, constricting lungs. "I-I love Janani, my pharaoh."

"So my doctors have confirmed," Pharaoh Runihura said quietly.

Janani gave Hamadi a weak smile as she clutched onto the torch tightly. "It's true, Hamadi."

Runihura wrapped his cape around himself. "Janani belongs to me, Hamadi. You do not touch what belongs to me."

Hamadi opened his mouth to protest, but Janani quickly shook her head. "Do not punish Janani, my king."

Runihura reached calmly over to Janani and smiled at her. He caressed her cheek tenderly as she closed her eyes tightly and shivered repulsively. Runihura licked his lips and stepped closer to her.

Runihura took the torch from her and placed it in a nearby stand. He approached Janani with a wicked grin as Hamadi clenched his fists tightly.

Pharaoh Runihura grabbed Janani and pulled her close to him. He put a hand on the back of her hair, squeezing it roughly. He pulled her into a heavy kiss as Hamadi struggled with his ropes to free himself. Janani sobbed into the kiss as she put her hands against the pharaoh. She tried pulling herself away from the pharaoh, but he pushed her to the ground roughly.

"Janani! My lord, do not hurt her!"

"Hamadi!" Janani screamed as the pharaoh hovered over her.

The pharaoh pinned her wrists to the sand below her as her scream echoed through the arena. "I will take my pleasure!" Pharaoh Runihura growled angrily.

"My lord, please don't harm her! She is carrying my child!" Hamadi bellowed.

Janani screamed as she reached for Hamadi, who was slightly out of reach. Hamadi watched Janani helplessly, his heart sinking into his stomach, his tears falling as he would have died to reach and touch her, to whisk her away from the palace. He would carry her on the wind as the swallow flew from the garden. His chest tightened as the ropes which bound him to the post. Hamadi struggled against his bonds.

"You belong to me, Janani! Your body belongs to none other!"

The arena's open field echoed with the screams of Janani and the pleas of the bound man.

# XXXI

## The Scroll of Thoth

Qamra watched Nassar sitting in the corner, his knees drawn up to his chin. The teen's arms were crossed over his knees as he stared into the fire. Nakia took a bite of a carrot as he watched his withdrawn twin sitting in the corner. Baruti was playing with Meskhenet and Khentimentiu on the ground. The father was tickling his son as he writhed on the ground laughing loudly. Meskhenet had climbed on her father's back and was kicking his hips so she could ride him like a horse.

Laila had tried to approach Nassar with a plate of food, but he whacked it out of her hand with an annoyed grunt. She had retreated to the fire silently, sitting with Karida and Azizi.

"Nassar, you haven't eaten all day," Qamra said calmly. "You should eat something."

Nassar blinked silently as he continued to stare into the fire. Qamra slowly lifted her hand and turned Nassar's face towards her. "Eat, Nassar," she said, mimicking the action of eating with her other hand. Nassar shook his head emphatically as his eyes went to Issâm's place beside the wall where the priest would sit and write.

"Nassar may be fasting after Issâm's death," Nakia said. "After a death of a close family member, the family goes on a ritual fast."

"Why aren't you fasting then?" Azizi asked.

"I worked all day and I'm starving," Nakia said, grabbing another handful of lettuce.

Azizi watched Nassar from beside the fire. "Don't be sad, Nassar. Your friend no longer suffers."

Nassar stood calmly and walked out of the home, grabbing the attention of everyone, even the father and his children playing their games.

"I don't think he heard you, Azizi," Nakia said with a sigh.

"Where is Nassar going?" Khentimentiu asked.

Baruti shook his head. "I don't know."

Azizi looked at Qamra after taking a sip from his cup of milk. "Qamra, do you know anything about magical scrolls or items that can give a person powers?"

Meskhenet sat beside her mother as Qamra looked at the orphan. "What kind of powers?"

"Powers which only possessed only by the gods," Azizi responded.

Qamra put her arm around her daughter. "Issâm spoke of The Scroll of Thoth. It was a scroll of prophecy dictated by Thoth himself to his priests. It contains clues as to the location of mystical items, including the of The Book of Thoth, a book that any priest or devotee of Thoth would kill to possess. Within the scroll, the location of The

Book of Thoth is revealed. The book contains magical incantations that are needed to power legendary items. "

"Did Issâm speak of the types of magic that were contained therein?"

Qamra nodded. "Magic can do many things, Azizi. The authors of the Scroll of Thoth hid the book in a secret shrine to The Measurer. Issâm would not divulge the location. He said it was a sacred place and to speak its name meant death."

"How can speaking a name kill someone?" Laila asked from beside the fire.

"Names hold power over people, my child. Here is a story for you. Mother Isis wanted to know the name of Rā to enter the world of the gods. No mortal or god knew Rā's secret name. The Father God had grown old and Mother Isis procured some saliva from the earth and fashioned a poisonous snake from soil and the saliva. She put it in the path of the Father God and he was bitten. Rā assembled all the gods as he was in great agony. Isis told him 'Tell me thy name, Divine Father, for the man shall live who is called by his name.' Rā, fearing the power that Isis could wield over him, stated that he was 'Khepra' in the morning, Rā at noon, and 'Atem' in the evening. The poison burned him worse than before. Rā told her his hidden title and Isis immediately banished the poison from his veins and he became whole again. The man who knows the name of God can kill the living, raise the dead, and perform miracles reserved for the Holiest of Holies.'"

Nakia nodded. "In my tribe, if you knew someone's real name, you owned part of their soul as well as had power over their bodies. If you knew someone's real name, you could do damage to them and prevent their soul from reaching Uala.

Baruti chuckled. "When he first arrived here, he told us his name was Kelile."

"Imani renamed my brother and I when we arrived. My brother never left my side and he was always protecting me from Kaemwaset's anger. That is why she named him 'Nassar.'" Nakia sighed as he stood. "I should find my brother. He looked upset."

Qamra watched Nakia leave the house. "Nakia has such a pure heart, Azizi. He's a loving boy."

"Amsi said the pharaoh has the Scroll of Thoth. I wonder if he reads it if he can find the location of the book. Amsi can read better than I could read it."

Qamra hugged her daughter. "The scroll, as Issâm stated to us, can only be read by one of Nobility. It was not written in Common Script. Only the Enlightened Scholar can read it."

Azizi snapped his fingers. "This means the pharaoh might not be able to read it! Thoth would not be in agreement with how the pharaoh abuses his power, right?"

"I would guess he wouldn't agree," Qamra said with uncertainty. "But the pharaoh would know how to read Noble Script. With all Issâm's education, not even he would be able to have read it."

Baruti looked at Qamra. "Could Thoth himself manipulate who could read the script in the book?"

"What do you mean?"

"Azizi may be on the right path. If Thoth himself does not agree with the pharaoh's agenda, would the god be able to make the script illegible to the pharaoh?" Baruti said bringing his son onto his lap.

"The pharaoh can read the Scroll of Thoth, so he might be able to read The Book of Thoth," Azizi said.

"The pharaoh would not hesitate to wield such power if he possesses it," Qamra said. "We would have experienced his wrath had he the book in his hands."

"What about the Eye of Horus? Amsi said that the pharaoh is after the Scroll and Eye of Horus."

Qamra shook her head. "I know not of either relic."

Khentimentiu yawned in his father's lap and fell asleep against him. Meskhenet fell asleep beside her mother. Qamra looked at the entrance to the home. "The twins haven't returned."

Azizi stood up and walked away from the fire. "I'll look for them."

Azizi stepped into the night and looked around at the empty path. He heard voices coming from the field. He followed the path to the voices, stepping quietly through the rows of tall plants.

"Nassar, I'm worried about you. Please don't cry," Nakia said to his brother.

Nassar's head lowered as his shoulders sagged. Nassar's hands touched the ground beneath his knees.

Nakia put his arms around his brother's shoulders. *I know he can't hear me. He can't watch my lips in the night to know what I am saying. He can't talk to me and tell me what is running through his mind. I know, Nassar. I don't need you to say one word. I know what you are thinking.* "I hate to see you cry, brother."

"Ah-e-ah," Nassar whimpered as he buried his face into Nakia's chest. Nakia wrapped his arms around his brother protectively. He looked up at the stars. "One day, Nassar, we'll be free like Issâm." Nakia's face lit up with a small smile. "Freedom, Nassar. I remember when I would ride father's warhorse into the field. The wind flew through my hair and I was One with the wind. Nothing else mattered to me but to be able to ride my father's horse and to tend the flocks of the Enzi tribe."

Nassar sighed with his head against Nakia's chest. *I sparred with our father. Learning the art of warfare was my path to freedom. He was teaching me how to fight in great battles. He was teaching me how to track enemies through the forest using broken twigs and footprints. I wanted to become a warrior, to protect our people...to protect you, my brother. The medicine man told our father that I was the Shadow of your Warrior Spirit. The fire of warfare runs not in your blood, Nakia. Mbwana always said we were one complete person split into two different beings.*

A little chuckle escaped the teen as he leaned into the ear that his brother was able to hear him slightly. "Do you remember when we were little and we would run through the forest? You brought back a frog from the lake and put it in Ngenge's bed? Ngenge screamed and ran from his hut."

Nassar giggled as his head was lowered. "Ngenge wa-an-ee."

"Ngenge was so angry with us! He called you my evil shadow, do you remember?"

Nassar nodded his head and laughed. He looked up at his brother with a mischievous smile. "Kam-wa-et,"

"Kaemwaset would be insanely furious if you put a frog in his bed. It would be funny, though."

The twins shared roguish laughter between them. Nassar looked up at his twin as he laughed. *Nakia, you always knew how to make me feel better. Even in the dark, you always seem to find a way to bring in a glimmer of light. You've always taken care of me and I've always protected you. I love you, brother.*

Azizi stepped on a leaf of a plant, making it snap. Nakia turned his head in alarm and clutched onto Nassar tightly. The twin breathed a sigh of relief when he saw Azizi standing before him. "Sorry, didn't mean to scare you. The others were wondering where you were."

Nassar looked over Nakia's shoulder and dug his fingernails into Nakia's skin.

"It's okay, Nassar, it's only Azizi. We should be getting back to the home. I had to cheer up Nassar."

Azizi looked at the mound on the ground and knew why the twins had come. "I should be returning to the city."

"But you are still sick, are you not? Master Amsi would want you to stay with us until you feel better."

"I'm not accustomed to being in a home. I sleep by the Nile or in the streets of *Iunu*. Besides, I have to check on Sekani and the others and I have to bury my friend."

Nakia nodded. "We will give Master Amsi your best wishes."

"Before I forget, tomorrow night the Bedouin are having festivities. Amsi is going to be dancing with a girl, so you should come and watch. It should be amusing to say the least," the poor boy said with a grin.

"Master Amsi doesn't know how to dance," Nakia said.

Azizi laughed loudly. "That's why it will be amusing! I will see you there! I wouldn't miss it for the world! Goodbye, Nakia and Nassar!"

Nakia watched the boy run away. "This will be entertaining."

Nassar looked at his twin quizzically. "Wha?"

"Amsi is going to dance with a girl tomorrow night! We have to go!" Nakia screamed in Nassar's ear.

Nassar stood and pulled Nakia to his feet. He took
Nakia's wrist and tugged. Nakia turned his head as he
and his brother walked from Issâm's grave. The teen
walked beside his brother as they entered the home.


Azizi approached the city gates with his black cloak
wrapped around him. His eyes shifted around him
cautiously as he coughed. In front of the city entrance, he
saw Jamila and Giladi kneeling beside Ferryn's body.
Azizi approached slowly as they turned their heads.

Jamila wiped the tears coming from her eyes. "Carim is
digging a grave for him now."

Azizi put a comforting hand on Giladi and Jamila.
"Kaphiri won't get away with this, Jamila."

Giladi put his hand on Ferryn's body. "We have nothing
to put in his grave."

Carim approached the two young children and saw Azizi
standing behind them. "My friend, welcome," Carim
bowed.

"I'm glad to see you escaped from that mob chasing after
Sekani and I."

Carim nodded. "I am glad to see your escape as well, my
friend. Ini-Herit will learn not to meddle with me again."

Carim picked up the body of the dead boy and walked it
over to a nearby grave dug into the sand. Jamila and
Giladi followed Carim and Azizi. Carim carefully laid
the body in the grave and sighed.

"May Horus avenge you, Ferryn," Carim prayed.

Giladi held onto Jamila's hand as Azizi sprinkled a handful of sand over the body. "May Osiris welcome you home."

Carim shoved the rest of the sand onto Ferryn, burying the body as the younger children watched. When the body was buried, Azizi lead the others through the streets of the city.

Azizi saw Saqr and Khalil wandering the streets holding hands. They were looking around frantically and appeared agitated. *What are they doing roaming the streets at this time of night?*

"Saqr! Khalil!" Azizi ran up to the little children, who looked up at him sadly. "Why are you walking the streets so late at night? Can't you find a place to rest? Kaphiri's loyal followers would beat you if they found you roaming the streets by yourselves."

Khalil rubbed his eye. "Hairdar and Marid stole the cart where we sleep. They told us not to enter the alley or they will kill us."

"That's awful!" Jamila exclaimed.

"Where is your brother?" Carim asked the two little boys.

Saqr began to cry. "Gahiji took our brother!"

The children gasped. Azizi swallowed nervously as he looked at the looming palace. *If Gahiji has him, he won't have a chance!*

"Our brother is to be executed tomorrow as a warning to all of us not to disturb the peace."

Saqr kneeled before Azizi and grabbed his hands. He pressed his forehead to Azizi's hand in supplication. "Please, Azizi! Save our brother! Please!" the child cried

*Saqr and Khalil are as young as when I lost my mother. I can't let them see their brother hanged. People when they hang, they don't always die right away. They struggle. Their tongues creep from their head like a snake from the desert sands. Their eyes bulge and almost pop out. It's a horrible death unless it is immediate. Sekani is a good friend and he's innocent of any crime.* Azizi clenched his free fist angrily. *I won't passively stand by and watch an innocent boy be murdered like my mother! Kaphiri wanted to lure me out of hiding. I won't watch Sekani die!* "I won't have it!"

Saqr and Khalil raised their heads suddenly at Azizi's cry of anger. "But what can we do, Lord Azizi? There will be many people there and many soldiers!" Saqr exclaimed.

"We're just children, Lord Azizi! What can we do?"

Azizi chuckled. "The pharaoh has been trying to catch me for many years and he has not caught me. I should be no match for him, but he doesn't stand a chance against me. I will avenge the death of my parents and I will not stop placing myself in his way! Khalil, tomorrow, bring your toys. Giladi, bring your rope. Carim, find something for Jamila to defend herself."

Azizi felt his heart leap into his throat. The thought of the quarter watching the hanging, cheering, some silent, filled him with repulse and fear. If he was caught, the gallows were readily available. Many soldiers would be there, armed and waiting for the rescue party. The pharaoh's dark eyes burned into his soul. "Meet in Sekani's alley and we will progress from there."

Khalil wrapped his arms around Azizi's hip tightly. "Thank you, Lord Azizi! Thank you!"

"Why are you calling me that?"

Saqr looked up at Azizi, the moonlight illuminating his body. Saqr's eyes were wide and venerating. "You have helped my brothers and me when we needed you. You are going to save our brother from the hands of the pharaoh! Many people would be too afraid to stand against him with such impossible odds!"

"I'm not going to walk away from my friends, Saqr."

Khalil looked up at Azizi wide-eyed. "You are very brave!"

"This is what one does for a friend. I have to try, even if it means risking myself in the process. I'm not afraid, my friends. Meet me in Sekani's alley and we will save him."

"Hail, Lord Azizi!"

Carim bowed before the younger child. "I will keep Saqr and Khalil with me tonight so they may sleep in peace."

"Thank you, Carim. Now, if you will excuse me, I have to gather some reinforcements."

Azizi walked away calmly from the cheering little boys. Azizi swallowed anxiously as he tried to push his fear into his stomach. *I have eluded the pharaoh thus far. I have lived on the streets since the age of five. I have showed compassion to the other children of the streets. I have survived the near-destruction of Iunu. I sleep in the alley filled with garbage and death. My home is the reeds on the banks of the River Nile. What have I to fear?* Azizi looked up at the gallows as he walked to Aneksi's home. *I am afraid, but I cannot live with watching my friend die. It is better to try and fail than to do nothing and feel regret. The gallows thirst for blood. They are awaiting their next victim who lingers in the dungeon of Pharaoh Runihura.* Azizi looked up and saw the balconies of the pharaoh's palace. *From there, he could watch the public executions in safety like a falcon hovering over his intimidated populace. I won't let you kill Sekani, pharaoh.*

Azizi ran towards Aneksi's door and hit it. "Aneksi!"

Darwishi opened the door and looked down at the child. "What are you doing awake this late, Master Azizi? You are young and you-."

Azizi pushed past Darwishi and ran towards Aneksi, who was sleeping on her reed mat. "Aneksi! Aneksi! Wake up!"

Aneksi groaned as she opened her eyes. "Who is there?" she asked in the darkness.

"It's me, Azizi! Aneksi, I need your help."

Darwishi closed the door and lit the fireplace. "Master Azizi, it is late and you should be sleeping."

Azizi turned his head and looked up at Darwishi. "Sekani is to be executed tomorrow and we have to stop it!"

Aneksi sat on her reed mat and yawned. "My dear boy, it is early."

"Aneksi, Sekani is going to be executed tomorrow and I need your help! Please!"

Darwishi sat beside the infant fire and looked at Azizi. "Which one is Sekani?"

"He's older than me and he's the brother of Saqr and Khalil. I have to stop this execution, but I need your help, Darwishi."

"Are you mad, child?" Darwishi exclaimed. "What you are proposing is suicide!"

Aneksi yawned again. "My boy, there will be many guards. It will be very dangerous."

"I don't care about dangerous! I know it will be dangerous! I need your help to save him, Aneksi."

Aneksi rubbed her eyes. "When is this execution to take place?"

Azizi sat beside the fire. "I don't know. When all executions happen, I believe. High-sun is the time."

Azizi looked into the fire as Darwishi moved the wood. *I can only imagine what is happening to Sekani. Stories from the dungeon are few since not many escape alive. It is said that the bodies which come from there are tortured most horrendously. I hope Sekani survives. I don't want to bury another friend like Ferryn. There was no reason for him to die. It was only for Gahiji's twisted entertainment.*

"Why do you wish to rescue him?" Aneksi asked.

"How could I not try? Sekani is my friend and when you live on the streets, you need every friend you can obtain! Besides, Sekani is innocent! He was angry at Kaphiri's gang for Ferryn's death! I don't want him to die!"

Aneksi smiled. "You are a kind boy."

"Or is he a very foolish one?" Darwishi added.

Azizi narrowed his eyes angrily. "What are you saying, Darwishi?"

"It's suicide for you to attempt this, Master Azizi. I don't think Sekani would approve of you placing yourself in harm's way for him."

Aneksi looked over at Darwishi calmly. "If Azizi can accomplish this feat, he will have earned his title as King of Thieves. He will have accepted his fate that Khnum has laid before him when fashioned on his potter's wheel."

"My boy, I have doubts that you can accomplish this successfully and without bloodshed."

"I want to avoid the bloodshed of my friends," Azizi said.

Aneksi reached over and touched the boy's shoulder lightly. "You are very brave, Azizi. Not many people would throw themselves into the jaws of the jackal for the sake of another."

"I won't say I'm not afraid, Aneksi. What do I have to lose? Sleeping in the alley and beside the Nile? Going hungry some days and only eating when my friend finds me some crusts of bread? I am doing this for Saqr and Khalil. Do I have your help?"

Aneksi bowed her head. "Yes, my king."

"Darwishi?"

Darwishi glared at the child and shook his head. "If we emerge alive from this day, I will praise Amun-Rā almighty."

"Aneksi, may I borrow some of your sacred herbs? I will replace them."

Aneksi handed Azizi a handful of herbs. "There's no need, child. Make your offerings and rest."

Darwishi watched as Azizi sprinkled some of the herbs into the fire. Azizi's eyes raised as he saw Darwishi watching him intently.

"Why are you looking at me?"

"I am trying to decipher what manner of creature are you."

"Darwishi, I need your help tomorrow. I need the help of the other thieves and I know you know them."

Darwishi smiled. "The others have been watching you. They are impressed with your skill, but you still have much to learn, young one."

"I won't let Sekani down. I am going to do the best I can." Azizi looked into the fire and sprinkled a pinch of herbs into the fire. "Hail, Lord of Abydos, king of eternity, lord of everlasting, Un-Nefer, I beseech your aid. Glorious are you before the gods, great is your mighty hand!" Azizi sprinkled more herbs into the fire. "Your humble servant glorifies your name in the Land of the Blessed Dead. Grant me the strength of your son, Horus, so that I may find victory in battle against my enemy. Shield me with your grace and guide my blade so that I may please you. Great is your name, Lord of Eternity, Un-Nefer! Your faithful servant calls upon you," Azizi said, sprinkling the rest of the herbs into the fire. "Beautiful is your name, Osiris! Grant me your aid and your blessing in my hour of need."

## XXXII

### The King of Thieves

Nakia and Nassar entered the home beside Qamra. Imani greeted the slaves as they stepped into the Reception Hall. "Kaemwaset wishes to see the twins in his office. Come with me, boys."

Nakia and Nassar exchanged wary glances as they followed Imani. Qamra watched Nakia tell Nassar to follow Imani. The twins slaves followed Imani to the office where Kaemwaset was smiling and standing beside the window.

"Today is another glorious day in the land of Egypt, my slaves. Do you know why?"

Nakia and Nassar looked at each other with confusion. Nassar pointed to his ear and shook his head. "Wha-e-ay?"

"Why would that be?" Nakia asked.

Kaemwaset grinned. "Today a criminal, a thief, an enemy of the pharaoh, shall hang from his neck until he dies."

Nakia swallowed nervously. *Did they catch Azizi? Oh no! Master Amsi will not take that news lightly!*

"We have been personally invited to watch this entertaining spectacle at the pharaoh's side. Nakia and Nassar, you both will come with me. Attend to his body and be ready by high-sun."

Nakia bowed his head. "My lord, did they find that boy? The one who has eluded capture by the pharaoh?"

Kaemwaset slowly approached Nakia. The large man looked down at the frail, bony teen. "You will have to just wait and see, Nakia. Go do as I say or you will join the condemned."

Nakia nodded quickly. "Yes, sir." Nakia grabbed Nassar's arm and pulled him out of the room. Nakia stopped outside the door and turned to his brother. "If Azizi was captured, what are we going to do, Nassar?" Nassar shrugged his shoulders and looked at his twin questioningly. Nakia sighed. "You can't hear me, can you? What can we do?"

Nassar sighed and shook his head.

"We'll think of something, brother. Let's tend to Master Amsi."

The twins walked into Amsi's bedroom and woke the pre-teen from his slumber. "We must prepare you for the pharaoh," Nakia explained.

Amsi yawned and rubbed his tired eyes. "The pharaoh? Why am I going to the pharaoh?"

"Because there is to be an execution of a criminal today, my lord. You are to witness the execution with your father."

Amsi's eyes widened suddenly as he looked up at Nakia. "Are you certain? Is it Azizi?"

Nakia lowered his head. "I cannot say, my lord. I do not know."

Amsi looked down worriedly. "What if it is Azizi? How can I save his life?"

"I don't think there is much you can do, Little Master," Nakia said as Nassar left to retrieve some water from the kitchen.

Amsi gripped his bed linens tightly. "What am I going to do? I have to do something for him!"

Nakia sat on the bed beside Amsi and took the boy's hand. "No matter what happens, Master Amsi, Nassar and I will be there for you."

"Azizi paid that girl to dance with me tonight. I can't go to that dance if he's killed today!"

"Hopefully it will not be Azizi tied to the end of the hangman's noose."

Amsi sat quietly beside his father as the carriage rode quickly towards the palace. Nassar stood at the back of the carriage holding the feather canopy over the head of his master. Nakia gripped Hadi's reigns tightly as they raced through the city quarter. As they passed Azizi's alley, Amsi looked quickly, hoping to find his friend. Unfortunately, he did not see Azizi in the alley.

He looked at the empty gallows as they passed. *Rā, please don't let Azizi hang! I will do anything you ask of me, just please do not let Azizi swing!*

"You are quiet, my son. Why do you look heavy with worry?"

Amsi swallowed nervously. His father couldn't know the true nature of his apprehension. "I…I'm worried about my studies with Sawaret. I do not want to miss them, father."

Kaemwaset smiled and put his arm around his son. "No need for worry, my boy! Your studies are progressing well. Sawaret tells me that you are excelling in your reading and writing requirements."

Amsi bowed his head. "Yes, father. I have been studying, though it is difficult without the help of Issâm."

"He would have only steered you into the wrong direction. Now you can learn from a master scholar without interference. I am proud of you, my son. Continue excelling in your studies and you will have brought pride onto our family."

Amsi saw a small figure dressed in a black cloak sitting in the shadows. Around the figure's neck hung a necklace of bone in the shape of the djed pillar, the backbone of Osiris. The unseen figure slid the cape over his shoulder, revealing a tattoo on his right arm. His heart leapt into his chest as he tried to see the figure's face. *Does this mean that Azizi isn't the one being hanged?* The figure's head raised as the carriage passed. Amsi watched as a smiling Azizi stood on his feet. *It is him! Praise the Sun-God! He's safe! Amsi watched as Azizi retreated into the alley as the carriage passed him. If Azizi isn't being hanged, who is?*

The carriage approached the palace as the two guards opened the gates for the Nobleman. Nakia coaxed Hadi inside as the horse reluctantly passed through the threshold to the palace. Amsi watched as lines of armed soldiers were marching towards the gate. Amsi turned his head backward. *Azizi, what are you scheming?*

Nakia stopped the carriage outside the palace. Kaemwaset stepped down from the carriage and turned to the teen. "You will both come with us and keep silent." Nakia bowed his head.

Amsi walked beside his father past the pleasantly-scented garden and into the pharaoh's palace. Kaemwaset's heavy footsteps sounded against the marble floor as they walked down the elaborately decorated hall covered with murals of the pharaoh's mythical birth. Amsi looked along the walls as they passed and found Pharaoh Runihura springing from the womb of Sekhmet, the goddess of destruction. In his hands he bore a sword and a club. In another mural he was smiting some indistinguishable foe with a face that had been carved away.

Nakia's eyes went to yet another mural where Pharaoh Runihura was bathing in the blood of enemies and taking a bite out of a human heart. He shifted uncomfortably towards his brother, who either seemed indifferent to the savage imagery or who was simply not seeing what was before his eyes. *I have seen cave murals that depict the same images. The Enzi's enemies participated in human sacrifice and drew images similar to these.*

Kaemwaset lead the teens and his son through the doors to the pharaoh's throne room. Pharaoh Runihura smiled pleasantly from his throne as Gahiji stood over the bound Sekani on his knees. "You will tell me where I may find the boy."

Sekani looked up at the pharaoh defiantly. "You're going to kill me anyway no matter if I tell you or not. Why would I give my friend up to your slimly claws?"

Kaemwaset chuckled as he entered the room. "They're a challenge to break sometimes, my pharaoh."

Runihura held an empty cup in his hand. His slave girl, Akilah, poured him a fresh cup of cool water. "They may be a challenge, but that can also be pleasurable to break them and their spirit. Your renegade parents experienced that first-hand, am I right, Akilah?"

The little girl lowered her eyes as she stood beside the throne.

Pharaoh Runihura turned his head. "Kaemwaset Al-Sakhir, I am pleased that you have agreed to join me this day! It makes my heart happy to see you as well, my young Al-Sakhir. Does the love of the poor still cloud your eyes to their savagery and corruption?"

Amsi watched as the teen prisoner kneeled before the pharaoh. His hands were tied helplessly behind his back, a metal collar bound around his neck. "I do not see his savage nature right now, my good pharaoh."

Pharaoh Runihura stood on his feet and descended the three marble steps to the prisoner's level. He placed a kind and gentle hand on the top of the trembling teen's head. "This boy is bait. He will lure your friend into the open and I will cease your repulsive affection for those who are inferior."

"You have nothing to fear from my son, my pharaoh. My son will soon learn to delight in his social station."

"This boy claims he has no knowledge of the relics of Horus. I believe he is lying to me and for that I should take his tongue," Runihura said with a smile. "I will find what information I need soon enough. He will not divulge the location of Osiris' Servant, but he will not need to if he is a companion of the boy. I will make the boy come to me."

Amsi watched as the pharaoh returned to his throne. "My lord, could you tell me more of The Scroll and Eye of Horus?"

Runihura grinned. "Why do you wish to know? You are corrupted, my young Al-Sakhir. You do not approve of my reign and you seek to work against me. Why would I give you sacred knowledge which you could use to destroy me?"

Amsi swallowed nervously. "I wish to learn of the ancient mysteries of which Sawaret speaks."

"My boy craves knowledge, my pharaoh," Kaemwaset said. "He will make you a proud student."

Pharaoh Runihura raised a suspicious eyebrow. "We shall see in time. Your loyalties are questionable, my young Al-Sakhir."

"My pharaoh!" a familiar voice called from the door.

Amsi and his father turned and saw Mahoma approaching with his daughter, Ife. Nakia felt Nassar grab his shoulders and step against his back protectively.

"Mahoma Re-Nefer, you please me with your presence," the pharaoh said with a grin. He descended the three steps and walked towards the other Nobleman.

Mahoma bowed his head as Pharaoh Runihura grabbed his arms. "The honor is all mine, my great pharaoh, to be in your presence. Health, Life, and Happiness to you, my great king!"

Ife smiled at Amsi and waved. "Hello, my future husband. You are looking well."

Amsi smiled slightly. "You are looking well, too, Ife."

498

Ife looked at Nassar standing behind his twin. "I see you still have the dog-slave. Haven't you put him to sleep yet?"

Nassar narrowed his eyes at the girl and put his arms around Nakia's shoulders. Nakia coughed as he felt Nassar squeezing his chest.

"Nassar isn't a dog, Ife."

"When you take me as a wife, I don't want him near me! I may catch the fleas on his body."

Nakia heard a low growl come from his twin brother. "Nassar, no. You're choking me," Nakia coughed as he gagged from the force of Nassar's protective squeeze.

"Kaemwaset, why do you still possess that barbarian?" Mahoma asked.

"He has a good back," Kaemwaset answered casually. "Nassar has the back of a mule. It is just a shame that he has the mind and manners of one as well."

Ife walked up to Amsi with a smile. She wrapped her arms around Amsi in an embrace. "When you take me as your wife, we won't have a need for him. His brother is handsome, though. We could keep him."

Nakia blushed and felt revulsion for the girl simultaneously. *I don't know whether I should be flattered or sickened.* "Nassar, you're hurting me!" Nassar released his tight grip on his twin slightly.

Amsi swallowed nervously as he felt Ife's arms around him. *I wonder if Zahra is going to do this tonight. That's right! I have that dance tonight! I don't know how to dance! What am I going to do?*

"My daughter is anticipating her intended marriage to Amsi Al-Sakhir, my pharaoh."

Runihura looked at the boy. "She will remove the blinders covering his eyes to the threat these people pose to the Nobility. In the meantime, we shall enjoy some entertainment," Runihura said as he looked down at the condemned teen.

Azizi stepped through the crowd wearing his black cloak. Saqr and Khalil were standing beside him looking nervously up at the gallows. Saqr rubbed his teary eye as he tightly grabbed onto Azizi's cloak.

Azizi glared at the imposing structure, hoping his late-night activity was enough to weaken the wood at the top. He had returned the tools to the woodshop under the cover of the early dawn before the workers noticed their bronze tools missing. Azizi swallowed nervously as he looked up at the pharaoh's balcony and saw Pharaoh Runihura standing in plain view. Beside the pharaoh stood Kaemwaset and Amsi, as well as a couple that Azizi couldn't recognize.

*I hope Giladi and Darwishi can prevent the soldiers from swarming this place like a bunch of flies. There will already be too many to fight all at once. I don't have the best army with the best weapons, but I refuse to let Sekani swing without a fight. Amsi, whatever you do, don't interfere.*

Azizi looked to the right and saw Carim standing nearby, his scimitar sheathed at his hip. Carim kept his eyes sharp looking for signs of Kaphiri and his gang. Carim turned his head to Azizi and nodded silently.

"My people, today your eyes will bear witness to the execution of one who disturbs the peace of *Iunu*! Let the shedding of his blood remind that disruption of the peace is a crime punishable by death! I will not have my kingdom ruled by chaos and disorder! Today, the death of this boy will be a lesson to all of you! Bring out the condemned!"

Saqr and Khalil watched anxiously as they shifted towards Azizi. Carim moved towards the edge of the gathered crowd.

Azizi looked at the bottom of the gallows where two holes had been dug beneath the sands. Jamila was hiding beneath there to wait for the dropping of Sekani's body. That was her signal to demobilize the soldiers standing watch at the base of the gallows. To protect her, Darwishi had assigned Halimah, a female thief whose expertise included the scythe as a weapon. The young woman kneeled beside the young girl, waiting nervously and hoping that Azizi had cut the wood deep enough to allow the hanging of the teen to fail.

Giladi waited behind the crowd forming a noose at the end of a rope to trip the guards. The nine-year-old looked around him nervously for signs of Kaphiri's gang. Carim casually approached Giladi, but turned his back to them.

"The procession has started, Giladi. Prepare yourself."

The little boy's hands quaked as he clasped onto his rope tightly. "Do you think this will work, Carim? What if we see Kaphiri's gang?"

Carim clutched the hilt of his scimitar tightly. "We must not allow them to interfere with the operation. We must assure a clear retreat for Azizi and the others."

"Do you think that Azizi is the Chosen One, Carim?"

"I am no soothsayer, but the Oracle seems to think so," Carim answered.

Giladi looked up at his assigned protector. "Azizi is mad if he thinks he can confront the entire army of the pharaoh."

"If he can succeed in this endeavor, then he would have gained the respect of every thief and criminal in *Iunu*. Heliopolis shall either bow before him or raise the bounty on his head." Carim crossed his arms as he leaned against the wall of a home. "I bet you even Kaphiri will be impressed if Azizi can succeed."

Giladi nodded. "If any of us lives through this, it will be a blessing from Rā."

Darwishi approached the two boys. He slipped beside Carim and handed the boy a bow and arrow. "Should the wood not break, use it. You get one shot before the soldiers come to slit your throat."

Carim nodded. "I will not miss."

"It would be in your best interests not to be in error. The soldiers will cut you."

Giladi swallowed nervously as he watched Darwishi walk away. Qeb whistled to them from above the building. "The procession has begun! Ready yourselves, boys!" The archer tightened his grip on his bow, his black cape fluttering behind him as he kneeled on the rooftop.

Giladi stood beside Carim and gripped his rope tightly. "There's no turning back, Carim."

Carim heard the drums beat solemnly as the condemned was escorted in chains towards his death. "It begins."

Saqr and Khalil watched their brother climb the steps to the gallows. Saqr closed his eyes as he started to cry as Sekani stood on a stool. Azizi put a comforting hand on the boy's shoulder. "Our brother's going to die, Azizi."

Azizi tightened the grip on the hilt of his dagger as he looked up at the pharaoh standing on his balcony. He focused on the pharaoh and his companions when he noticed Kaemwaset standing beside the pharaoh. Azizi grit his teeth in fury. *That snake is no better than the pharaoh,* Azizi thought to himself.

Carim held his breath as he saw the rope pulled over Sekani's head. Giladi's hands quivered as he held onto the rope, ready to throw it on the signal given. Darwishi slowly reached behind him for an arrow, the bow gripped tightly under his black cloak.

Saqr's eyes looked at the base of the gallows where he knew the two women were hiding, ready to stop the interference of the soldiers.

"Please don't hang me! I have two little brothers who need me! They'll starve without me!" Sekani pleaded.

"Then you should have thought of them before you started that fight in the streets!" Gahiji growled.

"You killed Ferryn! He was only a child!"

Gahiji grinned. "That is a poor excuse for the disruption of civil peace!"

"You're a murderer! Long live Azizi, The King of Thieves! Death to Pharaoh Runihura!"

Azizi looked up at Aneksi. "Get ready, Aneksi." *I hope I carved that wood loose enough so Sekani falls.*

The woman placed Khalil on her shoulders as the boy held his toy ball. The child swallowed nervously as Aneksi held his ankles. "Remember, my child. Aim for Gahiji. You have one shot and you cannot miss."

"Sekani, we're going to save you," the little boy whimpered.

Gahiji glared at the teen hanging. "May Ammut devour your soul, boy!" Gahiji punched Sekani in the face, making the teen fall backwards off of the stool. Azizi watched as the teen began to hang. The wooden structure tipped slightly, but did not snap like he expected. Sekani gagged and kicked his legs as his body dangled from the rope.

"Sekani!" Saqr shrieked in horror.

"Khalil! Now!" Azizi cried out, pushing his way through the crowd.

Halimah and Jamila listened for the sound of the dropped body, but only heard Azizi calling out. "Qeb! Darwishi!" Halimah told Jamila with a smile as she grabbed her dagger. Halimah stuck her hand from under the gallows and impaled her blade through the foot of one of the guards.

Jamila heard the soldier scream as she repeated the action on the guard standing before her. Jamila heard the guard scream in pain as she pulled back her hand quickly.

"Grab your dagger, sweetheart!" Halimah exclaimed.

"What is going on here?" Gahiji asked above them.

Halimah gasped. "There's no time, Jamila!" Halimah grabbed Jamila's hand and escaped through the trap door on the side of the gallows.

"It's an ambush!" Gahiji exclaimed as he saw the woman and the girl emerge from the bottom of the gallows.

The crowd's voices raised in alarm and confusion. The guards were mingled with the masses, searching for the source of the confusion.

One guard dashed after the woman, who removed a scimitar from under her robes. She swiftly cut through the guard, making him fall onto the ground.

Halimah heard a loud bang as Sekani fell onto the deck of the gallows, gasping and twitching. An arrow embedded itself in a guard standing on the deck of the gallows. Halimah smiled as she saw Sekani struggling for air.

"You will die with your friends, you dog!" Gahiji exclaimed, removing his sword.

"Now, Khalil!" Aneksi exclaimed.

Khalil threw his ball at Gahiji, making it pass in front of Gahiji's face. Gahiji turned his head, distracted from his target. The General glared at the boy and pointed his sword towards him.

"Get that child!"

Khalil gasped as he grabbed tightly onto Aneksi. "Soldiers are coming!"

Aneksi felt a pair of hands on her. She turned to the crowd trying to grab onto her and slammed her fist into the men's faces. She removed her club and smashed it against a man trying to push her towards Gahiji. The man fell onto the ground, eliciting panic from the middle of the crowd.

Azizi ran to the gallows and found Halimah. "Get Sekani to Aneksi's home." Halimah smiled at the boy and bowed her head. Azizi climbed onto the deck of the gallows and glared at the General. "I won't let you harm one of my own!"

Gahiji glared at the boy in front of him. "You insolent street-rat!"

Azizi tightened his grip on the hilt of his dagger. "You killed Ferryn!"

"They're part of Azizi's gang! Get them!" Kaphiri called from among the crowd.

Azizi watched as Kaphiri lead his gang towards Azizi's friends. The screams of the crowd intensified as swords clashed between the opponents. Azizi saw several imperial guards trip, falling onto the sand. *Giladi, good job.*

"There was no loss in his death, child."

"My name is Azizi!"

Gahiji grinned. "The pharaoh will enjoy watching you suffer!"

"General Gahiji! Bring him to me!" Runihura bellowed from his balcony.

General Gahiji lunged at the boy, reaching for him. Azizi pulled his dagger from under his black cloak and stabbed through Gahiji's arm. The General screamed in pain as he fell to his knees.

"That is for the death of my parents!" Azizi growled.

"Azizi! We need you here!" Darwishi exclaimed.

Azizi turned and saw Kaphiri running behind Gahiji. The other thirteen-year-old boy glared at Azizi as he stood in front of him with twin swords. "Kaphiri!"

"Hello, Azizi, you fell into my trap!"

Azizi grinned. "I think it's the other way around, my friend."

Kaphiri lunged at Azizi, who charged towards his nemesis. Azizi blocked the strike of Kaphiri's dagger and kicked Kaphiri's leg. The slightly taller boy crossed his swords and pushed hard, knocking Azizi off of the gallows and onto the ground below.

Azizi looked up and saw the sunlight illuminating Kaphiri. The boy jumped off of the gallows and stabbed the ground beside Azizi's head, trapping the boy between the blades.

"Your head will be a worthy trophy! Then *Iunu* and all of its treasures ripe for the stealing will belong to me!"

Azizi watched as a rope fell around Kaphiri's neck and tightened quickly. Giladi was standing nearby holding the end of the rope. Giladi pulled roughly as Kaphiri fell over onto the ground. The child smiled happily at his leader. Azizi stood and grabbed one of Kaphiri's swords.

"Good job, Giladi," Azizi said.

Giladi stood beside Azizi and gripped the rope tightly.

Azizi pointed the other sword at Kaphiri's neck. "Call off your attack!"

Kaphiri glared at his enemy and spit in Azizi's face. "You are a dead man!"

"Azizi! Watch out!" Darwishi called.

Giladi gasped as he saw Azizi grab his upper arm and scream. An arrow protruded from the boy's arm. "Azizi!"

Kaphiri took advantage of Giladi's momentary distraction and laughed as he pulled on the rope around his neck. Giladi fell forward onto the ground, releasing the rope. Kaphiri lunged for Azizi, stepping over Giladi.

Pharaoh Runihura glared at the battle below. "Guards! Get that boy!"

"The gate will not open!"

"That boy is making fools of your army!" Mahoma shouted.

Runihura glared at the garrison waiting below. "Open that gate, I say!"

"The gate is chained shut!"

Nassar and Nakia listened to the sound of mayhem below. People were screaming and howling in pain. Cries of fear rose into his ears. Nassar suddenly found himself knocked into by his brother. Nassar looked down and Nakia buried his face in his chest, trembling.

"It's what we heard in the village, Nassar! People screaming! Can't you hear it, brother? Make it stop! Make it stop!"

Nassar wrapped his arms around his shaking twin. *Nakia, it's going to be alright, I promise. Nakia never forgot about that day. He was terrified. Nakia was sprayed with our mother's blood. I did everything I could to keep him safe that day, but it wasn't enough. Ever since that day, Nakia gets startled by the sounds of mass panic. Nakia is sensitive and easily terrified when many people raise their voices in fear or anger.*

"I can hear our mother and father! They're screaming!" Nakia's mouth opened and wailed loudly. "They're all going to die, Nassar!"

Nakia went weak in the knees as Nassar guided him onto the floor. Nassar kneeled in front of his twin, holding him tightly as the sounds of mass hysteria echoed around them. "I can hear them, Ulan! Mother and Father!"

Kaphiri reached for Azizi, but the boy caught Kaphiri's fists in his grip. Kaphiri pushed Azizi onto his back with a furious growl. "*Iunu* is mine!"

Azizi's muscles tensed, making the pierced arm burn. With a sudden burst of strength, Azizi bucked Kaphiri off of him and rolled on top of him. Azizi clenched his fists and punched Kaphiri harshly. Kaphiri went limp as he lost consciousness. Azizi looked over and saw Giladi grabbed by Chakir.

"Azizi! Help!" Giladi called.

Azizi grabbed Kaphiri's sword and chased Chakir through the scattering crowd. He saw Giladi kicking and punching his assailant. Darwishi watched as Chakir knocked him down, plowing into him harshly. Azizi followed Chakir and grabbed the hilt of his dagger.

*Osiris, guide my dagger!*

Azizi threw the dagger with his good arm and it landed in the back of Chakir's leg, sending Chakir and Giladi collapsing onto the ground. Azizi ran to Giladi and found the boy holding his throat and gagging.

"Let me see, Giladi," Azizi pleaded, pulling the boy's hand away from his neck.

Azizi breathed a sigh of relief when he saw only bruises around the boy's neck.

"He was choking me," Giladi gasped for breath, holding onto Azizi. Giladi looked at the arrow protruding from Azizi's arm. "You're hurt, Azizi!"

"Go to Aneksi's home."

Giladi clutched onto Azizi tightly. "You need help!"

Azizi shook his head emphatically. "I need you to be safe. Go to Aneksi's home and protect Sekani and the women."

The nine-year-old nodded and stood on his feet. Azizi watched him run away. Azizi returned to the battle and saw Saqr being kicked by Ini-Herit. Azizi raced towards Ini-Herit with a snarl and his dagger revealed.

"Leave him alone!" Azizi called out as he plunged the dagger into Saqr's assailant. The boy fell over with a scream, holding his side.

"Kaphiri is unconscious!" a cry from the crowd sounded.

"We must protect him!"

"Retreat!"

Azizi fell to his knees beside the unconscious five-year-old as he watched the enemy scatter, leaving him and his friends alone around the gallows. Azizi gathered Saqr into his arms and pressed his cape onto the boy's open wound on his head. "Hold on, Saqr. Your brother awaits you."

"Boy, I will get you!" Pharaoh Runihura exclaimed in fury.

"Azizi!" Amsi called from beside his father.

Azizi looked up at the sound of his friend's cry of alarm. Darwishi approached the two boys. "You are hurt, Lord Azizi. We must leave before they remove the chain to the gate!"

Qeb rushed beside Darwishi. "The chain is nearly broken! We must leave!"

"Qeb, grab Saqr!" Darwishi demanded.

Qeb reached for Saqr and carefully brought the boy into his arms. "Hurry, my king!"

Darwishi took Azizi's hand and lead him from the quarter square.

"I'll get you, Blessed Servant of Osiris!"

Azizi growled as he turned his head. *I am not afraid of you! Our war is not yet finished!*


Aneksi opened the door at Darwishi's command. She secured the door behind them and turned to the injured boys. Qeb placed Saqr on a reed mat and quickly set to cleaning the boy's injuries. Aneksi and the others watched quietly as Azizi fell beside the fire, holding his arm in pain. The boy's face was covered with sweat.

Azizi sat beside the fire, whimpering as he held his arm. His eyes went to Sekani laying on the opposite side of the fire. "Sekani?"

Sekani's eyes opened slowly. "Yes, my lord?"

"Are you alright?"

Sekani nodded slowly as Khalil snuggled against him. "Thank you, Azizi. I owe you my life."

Aneksi kneeled beside Azizi and grabbed the arrow slowly, making the boy scream. "Prepare yourself, my king."

Aneksi pulled the arrow from Azizi's arm as the boy bellowed with pain. "It was stuck in your bone."

Darwishi kneeled beside Azizi and cleaned the wound with honey. He wrapped Azizi's arm, placing a healing amulet in the wrappings. "You are very brave. I offer my apologies for having doubted you, my king."

The thirteen-year-old boy looked up into Darwishi's eyes. "You have my gratitude for your help in saving Sekani from the grave."

Aneksi smiled at Azizi and caressed the boy's cheek tenderly. "What you have done today, not many would undertake."

"Sekani is my friend. I couldn't let him die."

"You are a blessing, Azizi. You are his savior."

Halimah offered Azizi a cup of water. "You must be thirsty."

Azizi took the cup of water from Halimah and bowed his head. "Thank you." Azizi drank the water with great thirst. When he lifted his head from his cup, he saw Qeb and Giladi bowed before him.

"Long live Azizi, King of Thieves!"

## XXXIII

### Runaway

Amsi watched as Azizi retreated with the large, cloaked figure. Beside him, Pharaoh Runihura was shaking with fury. The pharaoh's teeth were clenched tightly together and glared with a deadly look towards the quarter's square. If eyes could throw daggers, the pharaoh was throwing millions of them through his narrowed, eagle eyes. *I can't believe it! Azizi fought the pharaoh's forces and won! I don't know who those other people were, but Azizi beat them, too! I wanted to run and help him when I saw him hurt, but if I do anything, my father and the pharaoh would surely stop me. What a battle!*

"Who was that boy?" Mahoma asked.

"That boy," Pharaoh Runihura snarled through clenched teeth. "That boy is a disease! That boy is vermin to be exterminated!"

Kaemwaset looked at the chained gate that the royal blacksmith was attempting to break. "What happened to the guards at the front gate?"

Runihura growled. "I don't know, but when I find them, their carcasses will be food for the dogs!" The pharaoh looked down at Amsi. "Boy, did you have something to do with this?"

Amsi swallowed nervously as he stepped backwards. "No, my pharaoh! I had no idea this was going to happen!"

Kaemwaset pointed an accusatory finger at Amsi. "You told him this was to happen, didn't you, Amsi?"

Amsi shook his head. "No, father! I haven't spoken to him!"

Mahoma spit on the ground in revulsion. "You converse with those creatures, Amsi? You should know better."

Ife wrinkled her nose. "I hear those people eat their own young!"

"That's not true!" Amsi protested.

Kaemwaset glared down at the boy menacingly. His fists clenched tightly as his lip curled in disgust. "Boy, you are severely trying my patience. I never thought that the boy I loved would blatantly disobey my orders. I am very disappointed in you, my son. Convince me that you were not involved in this raucous!"

"Father, I didn't know that Azizi was going to be here or that he was going to save the condemned!"

"How can I believe you?" Kaemwaset asked.

"The flames! The flames! Run! The blood flows in rivers!" Amsi heard a shrieking voice. Amsi ran inside the throne room and found the doors burst open and Nassar looking down the hallway. "Nassar, where is Nakia?"

"Ah-E-ah," Nassar said, pointing down the hallway.

"He ran that way!" Akilah cried out loudly.

Kaemwaset narrowed his eyes. "He's trying to escape!"

"No, he's not! You know how he gets when he hears people screaming!" Amsi exclaimed.

"I've had enough of his foolishness! Nakia! Get back here, you little whelp!" Kaemwaset screamed, walking out of the throne room, his feet stomping angrily against the polished floor.

"Guards, capture the renegade Al-Sakhir slave!" Runihura bellowed. Runihura turned towards Akilah standing by his side. "Why did you not try and stop him?"

Akilah took a step away from the pharaoh's side. "I'm sorry, my lord! He was too fast!"

Runihura growled. "If that boy is trying to escape, I'll make sure he can never walk again!"

Amsi grabbed onto Nassar. "We have to find your brother!"

"Ah-e-ah scream," Nassar said, his throat gurgling to speak the full word.

Amsi ran out of the door, followed by Nassar. "Nakia! Nakia, where are you?!"

Nassar followed Amsi down the hallway. Kaemwaset and the pharaoh ran outside. "He has to be somewhere around here," Amsi said, looking anxiously for his missing slave.

Amsi stopped as he heard sobbing nearby. The connecting hallway was empty. "Nakia?" Amsi stopped and looked both ways down the hallway. "Nassar, do you see him?" Nassar looked at Amsi blankly. *He can't hear me.* Amsi grabbed Nassar's arm and gave it a light tug. He walked down the left hallway and looked along the walls. Pharaoh Atenhotep's image had been removed from the walls. His name was chiseled from the hieroglyphs chiseled into the stone.

Nassar's eyes widened as he pulled back on Amsi's grip. He looked up at the mural before him.

"What is it, Nassar?"

"Home," Nassar said with a guttural sigh.

Amsi looked up at the mural. Huts were burned and Nubian prisoners were being rounded into groups. Pharaoh Atenhotep's figure was replaced with Pharaoh Runihura. Nubians in chains were being paraded behind Pharaoh Runihura's image. Above the pharaoh, the image of Rā was replaced by Sekhmet. Under the pharaoh's chariot, people were laying prostrate.

Amsi watched as Nassar slowly approached the mural and reached out to touch it. Nassar's fingers slowly glided over the image of a kneeling Nubian, the pharaoh holding a club, ready to strike his captive dead.

Nassar lowered his head as he touched the kneeling Nubian. "Poor Ge-ge."

Amsi turned his head and gasped. Sekhmet was standing in the middle of a field of bodies. Prostrate bodies of the dead were piled high while flames burned the land barren. The lioness raised her bow and arrow high with a wicked grin. Beside her, the creature Ammut was waiting to devour the souls of Sekhmet's victims. Pharaoh Runihura was kneeling beside her offering gifts of bread and a chalice filled with human blood.

Amsi walked to the mural and read the hieroglyphs. *May the Goddess Sekhmet grant me protection and power and in return shall I give her the flesh and blood of my enemies to feast upon.* "The pharaoh is mad, Nassar!"

"Am-i," Nassar said, tugging on Amsi's skirt. Amsi turned his head and allowed Nassar to lead him to the mural beside him. Amsi's eyes widened when he saw the image of a grand army. Thousands of people armed with weapons stood in front of two figures. Pharaoh Runihura led the army with Sekhmet hovering above him.

Nassar pointed excitedly to the two figures opposite of the army. Rā and Osiris hovered above two figures, both of which had been carved away.

"What is this, Nassar?"

Nassar shook his head and touched the mural.

Amsi looked closely at the writing. "'The Blessed Servant of Osiris and the Anointed Companion of Rā shall-.'" Amsi pulled back. "The letters have been chiseled away. It looks like it should say 'find victory over the Embodiment of Evil,' yet it reads 'shall fall under my mighty fist!'" Amsi jumped back. "Could this mean that one of these figures is me?" *Azizi worships Osiris! What is this all about?*

"Nassar!" Amsi heard a voice screeched from down the hall.

"Ah-e-ah!" Nassar called loudly.

Amsi turned his head and saw Nassar running down the hallway. "Nassar! Wait!" Amsi watched as Nassar turned the corner. *This place is like a maze!*

Amsi turned the corner and found Nakia kneeling in front of a mural. The teen's head was raised as he looked up at a mural of Pharaoh Atenhotep that had remained intact. The image of the pharaoh was sitting on the throne as he held the crook and flail in his hand. Nassar and Amsi watched Nakia looking blankly at the mural. The pharaoh was pardoning two prisoners of war, the figure of Ma'at was hovering above the pharaoh's head. Amsi watched Nassar kneel beside Nakia and put his hands on his brother's shoulders. Nakia wavered on his knees and covered Nassar's hand with his own.

"Brother."

*Nakia, you worried me! Why would you go off on your own? Master Kaemwaset will be furious with you!*

"Nakia, are you alright?"

"Why, Master Amsi? Why?" Nakia whimpered as he sadly looked up at the mural. "I wanted to ride the horses. I wanted to catch the *Banu* fish and feed my family." A tear crept down Nakia's cheek and a lump formed in the teen's throat. "I wanted to hunt the gazelle and run in the open field like the wind. Nassar and I were to marry twin girls and start families of our own. Why did this have to happen?" Nakia's hand went slowly to the tattoo on his arm. "Why did I have to become a slave?"

Amsi walked towards Nakia slowly and put his hand on Nakia's shoulder. "You will be free someday, Nakia. Then you can do everything that you want. You can hunt and fish. You can have a family."

Nassar looked down at his twin. *Who will want a man who cannot speak and cannot hear? How can I pleasure her? I cannot speak words of love. I cannot hear her say that she loves me. It will appear to her nothing more than a whisper. Who will want a man with whip lashes torn into his skin?*

"Kaemwaset won't free me and my brother. The only way we will probably be freed is the same way Issâm was set free," Nakia said as sadness plagued his voice.

Amsi sighed. "I'm sorry, Nakia."

"It's not your fault, Master Amsi. I do not set blame on you."

"There you are, you little pest!" Mahoma exclaimed, hovering over Amsi and the twins. "So you think you could escape from your master?"

Ife stepped beside Amsi and glared at Nakia. She pointed an accusatory finger at the twin. "You are in big trouble! You are naughty!"

Nakia lowered his head passively. Amsi stood in front of Ife and pushed her backward. "Nakia is not naughty! He was startled by the people screaming! He was afraid!"

Mahoma stood over the twins and crossed his arms sternly. "You should be severely punished for this!"

Nassar wrapped his arms around Nakia protectively. Nakia kept his head lowered submissively.

"Your master feeds you and clothes you! He gives you bread and allows you to continue your miserable existence. This is how you repay him for his gratitude? Shame on you, Nakia! You are a wicked boy!"

Nakia closed his eyes tightly and sobbed. He buried his face in his hands and cried softly. Amsi looked up at Mahoma. "Leave him alone! His only crime is being afraid of that crowd outside the palace gates!"

"He cries!" Ife laughed. "How amusing!"

Nassar heard Nakia's lungs begin to wheeze. The twin shuddered as he struggled for breath. *Brother, breathe! Don't listen to them. They are savage dogs harassing a tiny, cornered rabbit.*

Nassar narrowed his eyes and growled at Mahoma angrily. *I've had enough! If you want to bully someone, mock me!* He stood up and looked the Nobleman in the eye. "You wa pick of Ah-e-ah, pick of me!" Nassar tightly closed his fists.

Ife giggled. "You talk funny!"

"Nakia! Nassar!" Kaemwaset growled as he stepped beside Mahoma. "Boy, did you think you could escape me here in the royal palace?!" Nakia shook his head silently.

Pharaoh Runihura looked down at Amsi. "You should discipline him."

Amsi looked at the teen who rubbed his eyes and kept his head lowered. His sobs had diminished to sniffling. "He was afraid of the crowd, my lord. That is why he ran."

"He could have escaped."

"If Nakia wanted to flee, he would have done so when we left the palace. He would not run from inside where there is no escape."

Pharaoh Runihura glared down at the teen. "I should crack your neck with my club, you disobedient little swine!"

Nassar put a comforting hand on his brother's shoulder. Nakia blinked silently and leaned over, exposing more of the back of his neck to the pharaoh. *One day I will be free just as Issâm. Please set me free.*

"Get to your feet, boy! You have embarrassed me enough in front of my friend and the pharaoh!" Kaemwaset grabbed Nassar's arm and pulled him from his brother. "You deaf and dumb mule, get off of him!"

Amsi glared at his father as he clenched his fists angrily. "Nassar is not deaf and dumb!"

Kaemwaset raised his fist to his son. "Do not correct me, my boy!"

Ife pointed at Nakia. "You are very, very bad! Bad dog!"

Kaemwaset pulled Nakia to his feet. "You ride with me and my son! Nassar, you drive the carriage! I offer my apologies, my pharaoh, for my slave."

"Do not apologize. It is your son who must apologize for not keeping his slaves obedient."

Amsi looked up at Runihura. "I'm sorry, my lord."

"Get out of my sight."

Kaemwaset gripped onto Nakia's upper arm tightly as he pulled the teen down the hallway. Amsi looked into Nakia's tired face. The teen looked ready to sleep as his lungs wheezed. Nakia's hand went to his chest as he began to slow his steps. Kaemwaset tugged harshly on Nakia. "I don't know why I keep you, Nakia. Come on, lazy bones, walk faster!"

Nakia closed his eyes tightly as his lungs began to whistle. The gaunt teen slowed his pace as he grabbed his chest tightly.

"Father, Nakia can't breathe!"

"Then that will give him an incentive to move faster!"

Nassar ran beside his twin and took Nakia's free arm. Nakia turned his head towards his brother and looked into his eyes. "Nassar, I can't breathe," Nakia whimpered.

Nassar took a deep breath and pointed to his brother. *Breathe with me, brother. Do as I do.*

Amsi looked up at Nakia with concern. The teen stumbled over his own feet as he was pulled beside his master. Nakia was breathing in unison with his brother as they approached the carriage. Kaemwaset threw Nakia against the carriage. "Get in! Now! Nassar, take us home!"

Amsi jumped into the carriage and helped Nakia into the seat. Amsi sat between Nakia and Kaemwaset. Amsi watched Nakia close his eyes and steady his breathing as Nassar pulled the reigns roughly. Kaemwaset crashed against the side of the carriage as Nassar pulled Hadi around.

"Be careful, Nassar!" Kaemwaset growled. "I will not have my carriage ruined!"

Nakia and Kaemwaset held onto the sides of the carriage as Nassar shook the reigns quickly. *Nakia needs to get home. He needs to rest. I have to get him there as fast as I can, no matter what I have to do! I'll break down that gate with my bare hands if I have to!*

Nassar saw the blacksmiths pounding at the gate with their hammers. The chain broke free as the soldiers watched the carriage approach the gate quickly.

"Nassar! Watch out!" Amsi called out loudly.

"Brother! Stop!"

Kaemwaset watched wide-eyed as the carriage approached the gate. The soldiers were scrambling to open the gate before the carriage could collide with the black iron gate. The Nobleman's heart raced wildly as Hadi's cry rose above the panicked screams of the soldiers. "Nassar, you foolish boy!" Kaemwaset screamed and covered his eyes, bracing for impact.

Amsi watched as the gate was pushed open quickly for the advancing carriage. Nassar snapped the reigns against Hadi's back with a grin. "Nassar, you are insane!"

Nassar turned his head slightly as he looked at Amsi. *I may be insane, but I am not going to let anything happen to my baby brother!*

Nassar raced through the streets as Kaemwaset raised his fists and threatened him if he refused to slow the carriage. Nassar snapped the reigns again and Hadi ran faster through the quarter.

Nakia raised his head as he watched his older twin handle the reigns. *Now I know why the horses like it better when I am in control. Nassar's treating Hadi like a war horse!*

"Nassar, Hadi isn't a horse to race! Go easy on him!"

Amsi saw a boy standing in the streets. He quickly leaned forward and grabbed the reigns in Nassar's hands. "Don't hit him!"

Nassar struggled with the reigns as the child jumped out of the way quickly. People scrambled out of the streets screaming as the carriage swayed to and fro as Amsi tried to wrestle the reigns from Nassar's hands. "Give me the reigns!"

"Nah!" Nassar protested, pulling the reigns to the side.

Nakia saw Kaemwaset screaming in the seat beside him. The Nobleman's face was red with fury. Nakia grabbed the seat in front of him and lifted his leg to climb into the front seat. "Nassar! Let me do it!"

The carriage swayed to the side, knocking Nakia off balance. The teen gripped onto the seat tightly as his feet lost their stability. He looked at the ground moving quickly beneath the carriage. *I'm going to fall!* Nakia grabbed onto Nassar's arm tightly. "Nassar! Keep Hadi steady! I'm falling!"

Nassar turned his head and saw Nakia holding onto his arm and the front seat tightly. His body was hanging off the side of the carriage. Nassar reached over and grabbed the back of Nakia's neck to pull him into the carriage.

"Nassar! Don't grab me there!"

Amsi grabbed onto Nakia's skirt and tugged, pulling the slave into the front seat to sit beside his brother. Nakia grabbed the reigns from Nassar and tugged. "Steady, Hadi! Good boy!"

The horse shook his head as he slowed his gallop to a steady canter. Nakia leaned back in the seat, his head hanging backwards in relief. He held the reigns in his shaking hands as he took deep breaths.

"Nassar, you almost had us all killed!" Kaemwaset snarled angrily. "You worthless insect!"

Nassar watched his brother, ignorant of Kaemwaset's insults. *Nakia? I'm sorry. I was only trying to help you.*

Nakia felt a hand on his thigh and looked at Nassar with a smile. "That was quite a ride, brother." Nassar returned the smile with a chuckle. "Now I know why the horses get skittish around you. You would have made a good warrior riding into battle, brother. Father taught you well." Nakia sighed tiredly and put his head on Nassar's shoulder.

Azizi returned to his seat beside his father. "That was scary, wasn't it, father?"

Kaemwaset crossed his arms angrily. "I am not shielded from the rays of the sun. If I get a burn, Nassar will feel my whip for a week!"

Nassar looked down at Nakia and licked his lips. "Ah-e-ah?"

Nakia lifted his head and looked at his brother. *He's trying to talk to me?* "What is it, Nassar?"

"Am g-at-oo be yu-oh buffah."

Nakia raised an eyebrow. "What?"

"Am," Nassar said pointing to his chest. "Happy," Nassar said with a smile. "Yu-oh," Nassar said pointing to Nakia. "Buffah."

Nakia stared at Nassar and blinked quietly. "Thank you, Nassar," Nakia said with a smile. *He's trying so hard to be understood. I know it gets him angry if he can't be understood. Let's get home, Nassar. I don't feel very well.*

Amsi watched as the carriage passed the city gates. Kaemwaset breathed deeply as the carriage crossed the threshold of the city. "You and Nassar will help Najam in the kitchen. If I hear that the two of you are being lazy, you both will feel my wrath! Do you hear me, you lazy bunch of bones?"

Nakia nodded his head. "Yes, sir." Nakia sighed tiredly as he rubbed his bare chest. The teen coughed hard as his body trembled. Amsi leaned forward and saw Nakia coughing red into the palm of his hand.

"Father, Nakia should return to the home and rest. He's coughing blood again."

"He can still clean dishes."

Nassar watched as Nakia leaned forward in his seat. He extended his arm, blocking Nakia's body. *You are in no condition to work, brother. I will speak to Najam and she can give you something unimportant to do.*

Amsi looked at the Bedouin settlement beside the Nile. Zahra lifted her head from her potter's wheel and smiled at him. Amsi blushed as she waved at him with a wink.

He nodded quietly, his father sitting beside him and watching him closely.

Nakia pulled onto the Al-Sakhir lands and drove towards the stable. Kaemwaset stepped off of the carriage and tugged at his white tunic.

"Get Hadi in the stable and get to Najam. Make yourselves somewhat useful around here."

Nakia bowed his head. "Yes, sir."

Kaemwaset walked away as the twins glared at him angrily. Amsi stepped off of the carriage and looked up at Nakia.

"Tonight the Bedouin settlement is having a dance. Would you two like to come with me? I have to dance with a girl and I don't know how to dance!"

Nakia chuckled. "Azizi has already invited us and we have already accepted his invitation. Nassar knows how to dance."

"Wha-?"

"You know how to dance!" Nakia yelled at his brother.

Nassar focused on Nakia's words and nodded slowly, barely hearing his brother's bellowing yell.

"If you're not well enough to attend, Nakia, I'll understand."

Nakia shook his head. "I can probably come for a little while. This place gets boring and all we do is work, eat, and sleep. There's not a lot of time for play." Nakia smiled. "We may even meet a pair of twin girls to dance with. Nassar, would you like that? Girls?"

"Wha-?"

"Girls! Girls!" Nakia screamed as he pointed to his chest and held his hands slightly away from them.

Nassar focused on Nakia and his eyes lit up brightly. He nodded quickly with a chuckle. "Gir-w! Yef!"

Nakia laughed. "We'll find some nice twin girls to entertain ourselves. You go to Najam, Nassar! I'll get Hadi fed and watered. Come with me, Hadi. You're a good boy."

The horse nuzzled Nakia when he freed him from the carriage. "I know you don't like that, boy. Nassar was a little rough on you, wasn't he? It's alright. Nakia will take good care of you."

Amsi followed Nakia into the stable. He watched as the teen placed Hadi in his stable. Nakia grabbed a carrot and placed it in Hadi's feeder. Nakia grabbed a brush and brushed the horse's coat gently. "You're a good boy, Hadi."

Amsi stood at the entrance of Hadi's stable. "Nakia? Do you believe everything that my father said?"

Nakia stared blankly at the horse and caressed the horse's coat with his open hand. "Maybe he's right, Master Amsi."

"Don't believe him, Nakia. You're not bad."

Nakia lowered his head as he gently brushed the horse. "It's kind of you to say so, Master Amsi. I don't believe I am wicked." Nakia sat beside the horse on a wooden stool. He sighed with his shoulders sagging. "I kept thinking of what Pharaoh Atenhotep took from me. Whether you want to admit it or not, Master Amsi, he has taken from you, as well."

"What do you mean? He died when I was an infant."

"Pharaoh Atenhotep was a good man, despite his military campaigns. He cared for his people. He made edicts that no harm could come to slaves. We were able to own our own property and we could leave our masters if we were not satisfied. We cannot do that now because of the pharaoh's death. He could have killed my brother and I." Nakia looked at Amsi in the eyes. "He spared us. We were little children. We couldn't fight. Nassar wanted to, but he didn't want to leave my side. You must bear the burden of living up to the expectations of the new pharaoh."

Amsi narrowed his eyes. "He wants to kill my friend and he killed Issâm! I don't want anything to do with the pharaoh!"

"Your father would beat you if he heard you speak those words," Nakia stood and continued to brush Hadi.

"Do you think Nassar can show me how to dance?"

Nakia giggled. "I don't think Nassar knows how to do the kinds of dance a young lady would ask you to dance. Unless she's dancing for rain, worshiping a god, dancing before a battle, or doing a mating dance, Nassar can't help you with the types of dances he knows."

"The Bedouin are praising the moon goddess!"

Nakia raised an eyebrow as he grabbed a bucket. "Nassar may be able to help you with that dance, but there's a difference between dancing with a girl and dancing to honor a war god."

"Really?"

Nakia laughed loudly. "Yes, my young Al-Sakhir. There is a big difference."

"How so?"

"You don't cover yourself in war paint and blood when you dance with a girl. Nassar and I will be there. I might be able to show you some dance moves while we are there."

Amsi watched as Nakia filled the bucket with water and place it in Hadi's stable. "Were you and Nassar supposed to marry twin girls?"

Nakia nodded. "Yes. In our tribe, surviving a twin birth was extremely rare. Twins are considered one person split into two bodies. According to my tribe, I am not a complete person. I am only half of a complete person. Only twins can complete other twins, so only twins can marry twins. If there are no other twin pairs in the tribe, the babies are abandoned in the jungle or slaughtered by the tribal medicine man."

Amsi looked at Nakia in shock. "What if one twin dies during birth?"

"The other is slaughtered without question since that baby is only one side of a complete soul. There were twin girls living in our village at the time of our birth. Our parents were hoping I would live so they would not need to kill Nassar." Nakia coughed hard as he held onto Hadi for support. "We were to marry them when we turned thirteen. They didn't survive the raid of Pharaoh Atenhotep."

Amsi watched as Nakia closed the door to Hadi's stable. "I'm sorry, Nakia. You are one of the best people I know."

Nakia smiled. "Don't be sorry, Master Amsi. You rest for tonight. Nassar and I will be there. Maybe Qamra and Baruti would like to come along."

Amsi nodded with a smile. "Be careful my father does not see you and your brother leave the grounds."

"I will see you later, Master Amsi," Nakia said with a deep bow. He ran out of the stable and towards the house.

Amsi walked out of the stables and watched Nakia run. *I hope Nakia and Azizi will be alright. Maybe Nakia's right. Dancing with a girl can't be too difficult, can it?*

## XXXIV

### <u>Nightfall Twin Dance</u>

Amsi peeked his head outside of his room. He looked
carefully up and down the hallway, holding his breath,
waiting for his father to enter the hallway and scold him
to return to his bed. His father had retired to his
bedchamber for the night. Amsi wondered why his father
was not wandering the halls at night as usual. His
father's heavy snoring sounded from his bedchamber. *It
sounds as if a herd of stampeding elephants wouldn't be
able to wake father!*

Amsi crept from his bedroom slowly, his ears and eyes
sharp for the sounds of anyone in the hallway. His long,
ankle-length robe hovered just above the floor as his
sandaled feet walked carefully along the floor. He held
his breath suddenly as he felt his father's voice moan
from the bedroom and the snoring resume.

Amsi quietly opened the door and closed it behind him
carefully. He ran down the path into the moonlit night.
The red-orange light in the distance testified to the
location of the Bedouin camp. A large cloud of smoke
rose into the night as well as loud clapping and cheering.
Amsi met the twins at the end of the path. They ran
towards the celebrating Bedouin tribe together.

Amsi ran towards the Bedouin settlement. Tents were
grouped together, circled around a large bonfire. Zahra
greeted Amsi with a smile and a wave. "Hello, Amsi. It is
nice to see you again."

Amsi blushed as Zahra kissed both of his cheeks in a friendly greeting. "He-Hell-Hello, Zahra."

The girl giggled as she stood in front of the Noble boy. "Your friend has yet to arrive. I hope that he still intends on coming to our celebration. I see you have brought two friends with you."

"I'm Nakia and this is my brother, Nassar."

Zahra smiled and kissed the twins on each cheek. Nassar swallowed anxiously with a smile. "Please help yourselves to our beer and lamb. You both look very hungry."

Nakia and Nassar's eyes opened wide to see a barrel of beer opened beside the fire. Two Bedouin men were scooping cups full of beer and handing them to the celebrants.

Nakia smiled and cheered happily. "Meat! Nassar! Food!"

Zahra and Amsi watched the twins run for the lamb. "They behave as if they have never seen food before."

Amsi sighed. "My father didn't feed them today."

"It appears that two of your other servants have arrived and they said that they haven't seen lamb or beer in many moons."

Amsi watched as Baruti was dancing with Qamra beside the fire. "Baruti! Qamra! I'm glad you came!"

Baruti smiled as he raised the cup in his free hand. "Long live the *Bedu*! They have given us food and drink! Neither of which we have seen in many suns!" Baruti danced with Qamra to the sound of flutes and lyres.

Zahra looked down at Amsi. "Your father must not treat his servants very well. Our beer, bread, and lamb are theirs to share."

"Thank you, Zahra. You are very kind to share what is yours."

The girl looked down at Amsi, who was slightly shorter than she. Her hair was weaved intricately around itself, ending in a lock of hair falling slightly over her forehead. The gold around her neck shimmered in the fire's light. Her rose-red lips smiled at him. She looked at the golden ankh hanging around his neck. "You worship the Sun God, Amsi?"

Amsi looked at his necklace and smiled. "I believe that Rā watches all of his children and will return our society into the glory it had been for many years."

Zahra looked up at the moon. "The moon goddess showers us with her light tonight, Amsi. She looks down upon us and smiles. Her blessings have been many. How else could we allow so many strangers into our tribe to celebrate her glory?"

"Nassar, I get the leg!" Nakia protested.

"My -eck!" Nassar growled, pulling on the bone in a tug-of-war with his twin.

Zahra watched Nassar pull the leg of lamb from his twin and settle beside the fire biting into it hungrily. "There are more legs of lamb, Nakia. There is no need to fight."

"They're all so hungry," Amsi said.

Zahra nodded. "When your other servants arrived, they were just as desperate for food."

"I thank you again, Zahra."

The girl smiled at the boy. "Please help yourself to the meat, Amsi."

Amsi walked to the lamb where he found Nakia cutting through some ribs. "There's plenty of food here, Nakia. Take whatever you want first."

Nakia cut some ribs and hacked another leg off of the lamb. "Mine," Nakia growled with a wild ferocity in his eyes that Amsi had never seen. *My father should feed them more. They're starving to the point of beating each other up for food.* Nakia sat beside his twin, biting into the meat ravenously. Amsi watched as the twins tore at their meat with their teeth like rabid dogs. Nassar wiped the drool falling from the sides of his mouth as he tore meat from the leg bone.

Amsi stood beside the lamb and cut himself a piece of meat. He looked back at Zahra, who was standing beside the fire, clapping with the beat of the music. Amsi placed the meat on a clay dish and walked it over to her. Zahra stopped clapping as she saw him approach her. "Zahra, this is for you."

The girl smiled as she held her hands up slowly. "Amsi, you do not need to serve your host. Please, you take it. Sit down and enjoy the celebration."

"Well, well, if it isn't my Noble friend, Rich-Boy Amsi Al-Sakhir," Amsi heard from behind Zahra. Amsi looked at Azizi approaching from behind Zahra. "Did you enjoy the entertainment this afternoon?"

Amsi watched as Azizi stepped into the firelight. The other thirteen-year-old boy wore a plain white skirt and his black cloak hung slightly over his shoulders. A bandage had been wrapped around his left arm. "Are you hurt badly? I was worried about you!" Amsi reached out and embraced Azizi. The thief returned the tight hug.

"My friend is safe. That is all that matters to me."

Amsi looked at a gold band around Azizi's upper right arm. "Where did you get that?"

Azizi looked at his arm and slid the band slightly lower. "I found this band on one of my exploits. This is a tattoo designates me as a follower of Osiris. Every criminal in *Iunu* bears a tattoo. Kaphiri's followers bear the mark of Seth, the god of destruction." Azizi slid the gold band higher onto his arm, hiding the tattoo. "Are you ready to dance with Zahra here?"

Amsi looked at Zahra and swallowed nervously. "Azizi, I don't know how to dance!"

"Come with me, Amsi! I will show you! Azizi, help yourself to beer and lamb!"

Azizi took the plate of meat from Amsi's hands. "I'll take this. You go dance."

"What?! That's mine!"

Azizi chuckled. "You have a dance to do, my friend!"

Amsi watched as Zahra lead him beside the fire. Azizi sat beside the twins and happily chewed on the meat. Zahra took Amsi's hands as the music continued to play.

"The girl has chosen her partner!" one man called out happily.

"The leader will be pleased! Bring him so that he may watch his child dance!"

Zahra smiled at Amsi. "Follow my lead."

Amsi watched as Zahra pointed her toes and lifted their hands in a bridge. She spun herself between their raised arms and smiled. She stepped closer to Amsi, then backed away. Zahra stepped around Amsi, keeping her grip on Amsi's hands lightly.

"My daughter dances! Dance, my girl!" the leader cried out happily, raising his cup of beer.

The couple spun in front of the fire as Zahra twirled Amsi under their joined hands. His footsteps tried to match hers as she lead him through the traditional dance.

"Dance, Master Amsi!" Qamra smiled as she cheered and clapped.

"May our music reach the gods and celebrate their bounty!" Baruti cheered, gulping more beer.

Meskhenet and Khentimentiu danced with the other dancers, joining their hands together and laughing happily. Karida and Laila were talking to two Bedouin boys beside the fire, giggling and feeding the boys pieces of meat.

Zahra spun with Amsi as the boy caught her before she could fall. Zahra giggled happily as Amsi smiled. The gold anklets and bracelets jingled as she stepped lively.

"Dance, my girl!"

Amsi took Zahra's hands and followed her unsteadily until he caught the rhythm. He spun her under his arm and skipped with her under a bridge of joined hands. Amsi spun Zahra under his arm as the girl laughed.

Two drums made of animal hide were brought beside the musicians.

Nassar stood up and tugged at Nakia's arm. "Ah-e-ah! Gan-ke!"

"You want me to dance with you?" Nakia asked.

Nassar pulled Nakia on his feet before the twin could reject the offer. Nassar began moving to the beat of the drum. His hands and his feet danced wildly as he shrieked with joy.

Amsi watched as the twins dominated the fire dance. Nakia smiled as he watched his twin move with the motions of the warriors after a successful battle. Nakia joined his twin in jumping up and down wildly. The brothers linked arms whooping and howling.

Nassar's feet dug into the sand as he lifted his head to the starry sky. "Talai-he-la-hey-ha!" Nakia called into the sky. "Bu-ma-let-ta-ka-yay-na!" Nakia called again.

Nassar jumped high off of the ground and landed, squatting over the ground. "Ah—na-E-am!"

Nakia stepped on Nassar's leg and somersaulted over the fire. "Kelile!" Nakia flipped over the fire and landed on his feet. He turned and watched his twin jump over the fire. "Ulan!" Nakia called as Nassar jumped over the flames and landed beside his twin.

Amsi clapped as the twins continued their dance around the flames. *I can't remember the last time that I saw Nassar that happy. I haven't seen that smile on Nakia's face in a long time either. They must be happy to do the dances of their people.*

Zahra laughed as she clapped. "I'm glad you came to celebrate with my people, Amsi."

Amsi looked at the girl sitting beside him and swallowed nervously. He rubbed his sweaty palms on his robe and chuckled uncomfortably. "It is my honor. I'm grateful for your hospitality."

The twins stopped their dance as they panted heavily. Nakia laughed as he put his arm around his older brother, hugging him tightly. The twins walked to the barrel of beer to grab more drink and food.

Zahra looked up at the starry night. "The gods have blessed us with perfect weather for tonight's festivities. Wouldn't you agree?"

Amsi nodded. "The wind is calm and gentle. The sky is clear. It is the perfect night to celebrate."

Azizi brought a plate of meat and bread to Amsi. "I took your food earlier. Eat, for you owe Zahra one more dance, my friend."

Amsi took the plate with a polite bow of his head. "Thank you, friend." Azizi sat beside Amsi and watched Baruti kiss Qamra off of her seat and onto the ground. The slave woman giggled under her mate as he kissed her deeply. Baruti laughed mischievously as he began to tickle and kiss Qamra simultaneously.

"I believe Baruti is enjoying himself," Amsi snickered.

"I believe that is an understatement," Azizi said, leaning back to watch the couple kiss.

Zahra smiled. "This is a night of celebration. This night we honor the gods and goddesses for their blessings."

Amsi watched as Laila kissed the teen boy with whom she shared her food. He turned to Zahra, who was smiling at him. "My father said that you and your people were dangerous."

"We pose no threat, Amsi. We are merely innocent travelers selling our wares that we make with our hands. We are merchants, nothing more and nothing less. I want to give you something." Zahra unclasped a golden necklace with golden rays spiking from the chain. Zahra removed it from her neck and clasped it around Amsi's. She moved the rays so they laid flat against Amsi's chest and shoulders. "That is my gift to you on this night."

"Were we supposed to exchange gifts? I didn't know. I don't have anything for you."

Zahra placed a calm hand on his. "Don't worry. You need not bring me anything. You have brought yourself and your friends. Have you ever danced before, Amsi?"

Amsi shook his head. "No. I've seen the twins dance and the others dance before around a bonfire, but I never learned how to dance."

Azizi smiled with a chuckle. "You owe her one more."

"I know, Azizi!" Amsi said quickly.

Zahra giggled. "You seem an unlikely pair."

"He brought me food when I was alone and my parents were killed," Azizi said. "He's not like the other rich people around here who close their doors to vermin such as myself."

Zahra smiled. "That's very nice of you, Amsi."

"Well, as I see it, I've never been hungry and I have all of my needs satisfied. I've seen my slaves starve and collapse from hunger. I've seen them mistreated. They feel what I feel, so I don't see them as disposable, unlike my father. Azizi is my friend. That will never change."

The girl looked at the fire. "Many people want to keep us at a distance. They fear us and yet they do not know us.

My father trusts no one. That is why when your servant was running towards us, my father reacted with hostility. It's difficult knowing who is friend or enemy."

Azizi looked at the girl from his plate of food. "You're right, Zahra. The pharaoh's guards want to arrest me. The rival gang of *Iunu* wants to see me dead so they can have free reign on the goods of Heliopolis. They want to be the only gang of thieves in the quarter. It's a territory war. People like Amsi's father would rather run me down with their large, gold carriages." The thirteen-year-old boy looked at the boy decorated in gold sitting beside Zahra. "It's hard to know sometimes who is a true friend."

Amsi looked down at the sand. *It has to be hard for him to be constantly hiding in the shadows. He can't trust anyone. Azizi is right.*

"Amsi, you owe Zahra another dance. Go entertain me, Rich Boy!" Azizi exclaimed with a smile.

"Stop calling me that!" Amsi exclaimed. "Stubborn ass."

Azizi chuckled as he rubbed his hands before the fire. "Dance, Master Amsi!" Laila and Karida clapped and cheered.

Amsi looked toward Baruti and Qamra's direction and noticed that both of them had wandered away. "Shall we? I guess they want to see us dance again."

Zahra smiled as she took his hand. "We should give our guests what they desire."

Amsi and Zahra stood among clapping and cheering. People raised their cups of beer high with smiles. Azizi snickered mischievously as he watched his friend get to his feet.

The couple stood beside the fire as the music began to play. Drums, the lyre, and flute played as Zahra and Amsi jumped and spun around the fire. Amsi tried to remember the dance moves of the entertainers who performed for the royal court. Kaemwaset had taken Amsi to the feasts held by Pharaoh Runihura. Many dancers bent themselves and raised their hands in unison. His father had also brought professional dancers to entertain him during some meals. Qamra had been a candidate on several occasions. He demanded that she dance for him. His mother demanded that Kaemwaset cease his request for this after discovering that Laila was fathered by her husband.

Amsi followed Zahra's lead as the group clapped and cheered. Nakia and Nassar drank from their cups of beer when they were both poked on the shoulder. The twins turned together and looked at the pair of twin girls smiling at them. The twin boys' eyes widened and Nakia dropped his cup in surprise.

"Hello," the twin girls said together. "What are your names?"

Nakia swallowed nervously as he pointed to his chest. "Nakia. This is my brother, Nassar."

The girls giggled. "Shera. This is my sister, Sumati."

Nassar took Sumati's hand and smiled. He pointed to the musicians and back to her.

"I think he wants to dance with you," Nakia said.

Sumati looked at Nassar with uncertainty. "Can't you speak?" Nassar shook his head slowly.

"The pharaoh and our master removed his tongue when he was a child. He can't say very much."

Sumati tugged Nassar towards the reeds, leaving Shera with Nakia. "It is a nice night to celebrate the moon goddess and her blessing."

Nakia nodded. "It is a fun night. I can't remember the last time that we had such an abundance of food and drink. You have blessed us and saved us from the hunger which keeps us awake at night. You have my sincerest gratitude."

Shera looked at the scarab tattoo on Nakia's right arm. "What does this mean?"

"It marks Kaemwaset's slaves as his property," Nakia said, touching the tattoo lightly.

"What about the mark on your chest?"

Nakia pointed at the lines and dots on his right chest. "This marks me as a member of the Enzi tribe. The other set of twins in our tribe had the same mark. It could be the mark of being a twin. Very few people survived the attack on our village, so there's nobody around I can ask."

Shera took Nakia's hand lightly and sat beside the fire. "Let's watch them dance."

"That is my master," Nakia said, pointing to Amsi.

Shera watched Amsi dance with Zahra, spinning her around. The girl twin laughed as she saw Amsi slightly stumble. "Your owner doesn't dance much, does he?"

"I've hardly seen him dance. Sometimes he comes to the bonfires that we have behind our slave home, but he doesn't participate that often."

Shera smiled. "I saw you dance. You can tell that you are twins. You move the same way."

Nakia smiled and cleared his throat. He swallowed nervously as he rubbed the back of his head. "We haven't danced to drums since the night before the attack. All the children would gather around the fire after the adults had finished their dance. The tribe loved to watch the Nightfall Twin Dance. It was freedom in the night, a night where two souls merged as one. Two souls were to unite into one during the Nightfall Twin Dance. Nassar and I would dance along with the other pair of twins and it was nothing like I can describe."

Shera nodded. "My sister and I are similar, yet different."

Nakia chuckled as he thought of the morning's adventure, holding onto the carriage as wild Nassar made the carriage zigzag through the streets and almost throwing him from the carriage. "My brother doesn't have a way with the horses. They will listen to him, but they are skittish around him. The animals respond better to me than to my brother."

Shera smiled. "I tend to the goats. I know everything there is to know about the goats. My sister is skilled at jewelry making. She made the bracelets around Zahra's wrists. I cannot make jewelry like her."

Nakia took a deep breath and began to yawn. He rubbed his chest as he leaned his elbows on his legs. Shera put her hand on his back as she watched the twin waver on the mat where they were sitting.

"Are you alright?"

Nakia sighed tiredly as he nodded. "I'm very tired." Nakia coughed hard as his hand gripped the sand. His body shuddered as he did so. Shera watched the gaunt figure wheeze and cough. "I'm so very tired," Nakia groaned.

Shera rose to her feet and brought Nakia a cup of water from the Nile. "Drink this. You must be thirsty."

"Thank you," Nakia said, taking the clay cup and drinking thirstily. Nakia licked his lips as he watched Amsi and Zahra finish their dance.

"Are you ill?"

Nakia shrugged his shoulders. "I've always had bad lungs. My parents didn't think I would survive the first month. They fed me herb tonics made by the medicine man." Nakia snickered. "They even had a tribe-wide ceremony to ensure that my soul would not escape into the jungle. Father said they sacrificed the best calf to the Creator to ensure my continued survival."

Shera smiled at Nakia. "So you have been a slave for a long time?"

Nakia nodded. "Yes, since I was five-years-old. I have Nassar. My brother is all I have left of my people."

"Have you ever kissed a girl?"

Nakia gasped and swallowed hard. *I hope she can't see me blush.* He chuckled uncomfortably. "No, I have never kissed a girl. I mean, I kiss my brother, but not in a romantic way. That is to say, I-I love my brother, but not in an amorous way." Nakia felt his palms become sweaty as he looked into the eyes of the Bedouin girl. "I mean, I would like to kiss you, but I don't really know how. I don't have much-."

Shera leaned into Nakia slowly and pressed her lips against him lightly. Nakia's eyes widened in surprise as he felt the girl's soft lips lightly touch his own in a gentle kiss. Nakia felt the girl's hands lightly touch his bare shoulders. The teen slowly closed his eyes and pulled the girl closer to him.

Amsi watched as Nakia kissed a girl beside the fire. *It looks like Nakia is enjoying himself. Where did Nassar go?* Amsi looked at Zahra, who smiled at him and took his hand. "You dance very well, Zahra."

"And you dance very well, though you lost a little grace when you stumbled."

Amsi blushed. "I guess I have two left feet."

"You will learn. Dance with your servants. I'm sure they can show you some moves for the next time we arrive."

Amsi's jaw dropped. "'Next time?'"

"We are nomads. We wander the desert for long distances, but we have our favorite spots for celebrating certain occasions. I would like to dance with you again."

Amsi watched as Zahra winked at him and walked towards the reeds. She stopped and waved back at him before disappearing into the brush. Amsi waved back slowly, swallowing nervously, but with a smile on his face. *I think she likes me.*

"Amsi?"

*She moved perfectly. She moves like a water goddess. My knees feel weak. Why am I feeling so tense? My palms sweat. I've never met any girl like her. Ife is loud and so tempestuous. Zahra has the smile of Isis.*

"Amsi? Azizi to Amsi! Hello!" Azizi called as he stood before his friend waving his hand in front of Amsi's face.

*Ife is so cruel to our servants. I have seen how she treats her own. When I had seen her last year at the Festival of Bastet, I saw her kick her servant. Her loud shrieks could be heard from a distance. Her servant trembled at her feet, afraid of her and her father's wrath. If I must take a wife, I do not wish someone so much like Seth. I went to her servant's side and pushed her back. Mahoma was disgruntled with me.*

"Azizi calling Amsi! Amsi Al-Sakhir, are you in there, Rich Boy?" Azizi asked, snapping his fingers on either side of Amsi's head. "Answer me!"

*My father is very insistent that I marry Ife. He wants me to have a family and become overseer of his lands upon his death. I have seen what prosperity has brought my father. I have seen what it has done to him. His wealth relies on our slaves. They work from sunrise to sunset with one loaf of bread and a bucket of water for drink. I have seen the cruelty with which my father treats the poor and the slaves.*

"Hello?"

*How can I obey his wishes? I do not know how to work the earth. I do not know how to be a baker, a blacksmith, or a farmer. I can read and write, which are valuable skills, but they are skills to serve the pharaoh and to serve the wealthier interests of the Nobility. Zahra may not know how to read or write, but she can certainly dance.*

*What is wrong with me? I never paid this much attention to a girl before. My gut never felt so tight. What is going on? Why am I feeling this way? Why-*Ow!

"Hey, snap out of it, Amsi!" Azizi exclaimed, hitting Amsi in the arm.

"What was that for?" Amsi growled.

Azizi crossed his arms. "I hit you because you wouldn't answer me. You were looking at that girl as if she were some kind of goddess."

"No, I wasn't!"

Azizi laughed loudly, bending over holding his sides. "You can't lie to me! Your eyes went as large as the moon itself!"

"I just-. She was-." Amsi sighed with resignation. "Alright. I was captivated. There, are you happy?"

Azizi chuckled. "Possibly. I'm more entertained than anything."

Laila walked towards Amsi and bowed. "My master, we should be returning to the lands. If your father awakes and sees us absent, he will be very angry."

Azizi yawned and stretched. "Yes, I should be finding a place to sleep tonight." A twin pair of chuckles rose from the reeds. "I see that the bank is occupied."

"I heard the others speak of an oasis. It's located south of the city. They said it was unoccupied and very welcoming."

Azizi smiled as his eyes lit up with anticipation. *An oasis in the middle of the desert would make a perfect home! No people would be there to chase me. There would be food and water! I could use the trees for shelter. I would be alone. Depending on the distance, pharaoh's soldiers won't be able to track me down in the desert. They would be searching for years if they knew I was hiding in the desert. Everyone is afraid to travel there except for the Nuu. It would be the perfect sanctuary.* "It's located to the south?"

Laila nodded. "Yes."

"And they claimed it was unoccupied, correct?"

"Yes."

Azizi smiled. "I'll have to find a way to search for it. I'll find a way to get there."

"Don't tell me you are going to begin wandering the desert on foot," Amsi groaned.

"No, I'm resourceful. I'll find a way to get what I need."

Amsi sighed. "As long as you don't get yourself captured by Runihura or Gahiji or any of the other soldiers, for that matter. Be careful."

Azizi smiled. "I'm always careful. It means the difference between a full belly or a severed one. I must go into the night, my friend. May Osiris bless you and keep you safe." Azizi took a hold of Amsi's wrists.

Amsi bowed his head and held Azizi's arm. "May Rā's light shine upon you and keep you safe, my brother."

Amsi watched as Azizi walked away slowly. Laila took Nakia's arm in her hand and tugged.

"Nakia, it's time to go before the master discovers us missing."

Nakia pulled back from his kiss with Shera with a disappointed groan. "I don't want to!"

"Nakia, let's go!"

Nakia put his head reluctantly on Shera's shoulder. "I'm afraid I must go, Shera."

Shera sighed and caressed Nakia's head tenderly. "I understand."

Nakia stood and looked around. "Nassar?"

"He must still be with my sister," Shera said. "I'll get them."

Nakia looked up at the moon as Shera disappeared into the brush. "This is a night I won't forget for a very long time, Laila."

Laila smiled. "I can't remember the last time we were able to have fun."

Nassar and Sumati were heard squealing from the brush. Nakia chuckled. *I think my brother is enjoying himself more than he probably should.* Nassar and Sumati ran from the reeds, giggling mischievously.

"Brother, what were you doing?"

Nassar giggled, shaking his head. *If you only knew, brother.*
"We have to get back to the home. We have a long day of work ahead of us and we must be rested."

Nassar turned to Sumati and looked back at Nakia. The twin shook his head.

"What do you mean by that? We have to return."

Nassar narrowed his eyes and stomped his foot defiantly. He held onto Sumati's hand tightly.

"Do you remember when Tabari and Sabi ran? Do you remember the beating you received? Do you want me to suffer the same punishment? What about Khentimentiu or Meskhenet?"

Nassar looked down at the ground and towards the fire. The large fire burned, illuminating every person sitting around the fire. People were feasting on the sacrificial lamb and imbibing their beer. There were no whippings. There was plenty to eat and drink. Sumati had accepted him, despite the fact that he was mute, deaf, and scarred.

"Nassar, let's go," Amsi said. Nassar growled defiantly at Amsi, making the teen turn his head. "Nassar, we have to get back before my father awakes! You have to come with us!"

"N-ah!" Nassar screamed.

"Stop this foolishness, brother!" Nakia exclaimed so his brother could hear him. "We must go home!" Nakia grabbed Nassar's wrist. "Let's go!"

Nassar turned to Sumati and kissed her deeply. Nakia tugged on Nassar and the twin followed him reluctantly. Nassar turned his head back to see Sumati waving goodbye to him sadly.

*I'm sorry.*

## XXXV

### No Fear

Pharaoh Runihura read the Scroll of Thoth in front of Gahiji. The General stood beside his king as a battalion

of soldiers stood still before them. Hamadi's eyes
watched the wicked grin on the pharaoh's face as he
chuckled. Hamadi swallowed nervously as the pharaoh
pointed to a location on a map and spoke quietly to the
General beside him.

*What is the pharaoh after? Why has he assembled our
troops? Are we marching into war? I won't have a
chance to say goodbye to Janani if I do not return. I'm
sorry, my love.*

"King Nesebi was buried in the cliffs to the south.
Beyond the mines lay the ancient burial sites of the kings
of Egypt. It will take us some time to ride there and
obtain the Eye of Horus."

"Is the Eye of Horus buried with Nesebi?"

"That is what Heh claims. The priests at Edfû have told
him this. I do not know what dangers lay before us in the
mountain cliffs. I have asked Heh to accompany us. He
knows what lies beyond the Zeniah."

Heh bowed before his pharaoh. "I will lead Your Grace
into territory most dangerous. But you need have no fear.
My men will protect you until our last breath and ensure
your success."

Pharaoh Runihura glared at the *Nuu* explorer. "Failure is
not an option. I will not tolerate cowardice or failure
within my ranks."

Gahiji looked at his troops in formation. "You have the
finest army assembled here, with a few notable
exceptions," Gahiji glared at Hamadi.

"Your men are prepared, Gahiji?"

Gahiji bowed his head. "Yes, my pharaoh. My people are ready to ride when you give the order."

The pharaoh's eyes gazed over the small battalion of warriors. Pharaoh Runihura slowly walked around the table and advanced to the soldiers slowly. He stood at the end of the front line and looked each of the standing soldiers in the eye. Their gaze continued forward, hiding any intimidation from their god-like leader.

Pharaoh Runihura stood in front of Hamadi with a grin. "Are you certain you wish to come with me, Hamadi? Do you know how dangerous the wilderness of the desert can be?"

Hamadi swallowed hard. "Yes, sir!"

"If you must take an arrow to the chest for me, would you do so willingly?"

Hamadi's bottom lip trembled slightly. "Yes, my lord!"

Runihura chuckled. "I know you do not mean that. You would lie to your god?"

"No, my pharaoh!"

Runihura reached towards Hamadi's cheek and touched it lightly with a wicked smile. "Will you not obey my every command?"

"Yes, my pharaoh."

Runihura chuckled. "Good boy. You know what will happen if you go back on your word, correct?"

"Yes, my lord," the soldier cringed.

"Good boy," the pharaoh smiled, indulging in the cringing soldier's fear. "Prepare my steed, Gahiji! We ride when it has been appropriately attired!"

The pharaoh turned his back on Hamadi, who raised his eyes to see Janani standing on the balcony of the pharaoh's throne room. He saw her look down at him with a small smile. She blew a kiss at Hamadi and mouthed a quiet 'I love you.' The soldier returned the smile briefly should Gahiji or the pharaoh discover his forbidden moment of happiness.

*Janani, I will return to you. I love you.*

"You heard the pharaoh, Hamadi! Prepare the pharaoh's steed for our journey!"

Pharaoh Runihura grinned. "Soon I will be one step closer to realizing my dream, Gahiji. I know why the gods breathed my life into my mother's womb. I was meant to be immortal and the greatest pharaoh of all time. I will achieve my dream, Gahiji. I will not fail."


Azizi waited in the shadows as he saw drunken men stagger from Mbizi's bordello. Maysun and Oraida stood in front of the building, smiling and waving at potential customers. Azizi looked up at the window above him where he heard a woman screaming in pain. He narrowed his eyes as he glared at the window.

*When I was a child, these women were nice to me. When Kahla was allowed to take a short break from her duties, she and I would play tag and hide-and-seek when we were children. They held me on their knees and told me stories. They gave me what little they could behind Mbizi's back. Mbizi doesn't care what kind of men use his women. All he cares about is the money which the lust-filled men give to him.*

"Please slow down! That hurts!" the woman cried.

"Stop your complaining, you filthy whore! Lay on your back and let me get my money's worth!"

Azizi looked at the drunken, staggering men and back towards the window. *I was going to steal Mbizi's horse, but I guess that is going to have to wait.* Azizi looked along the wall and found a slight protrusion from the wall which opened into the waiting room. He looked inside and saw Rida and Tabora sitting on either side of one man. They were kissing him simultaneously and sensually. Rida opened her eye and saw Azizi staring at them. She gave the boy a wink and a subtle wave of greeting.

Azizi pointed above him and at the group kissing. Rida winked again and straddled the man's hips, blocking his vision of the opening. Azizi grinned. *Rida remembers our signal. I used to use it on the cold nights where I had nowhere else to sleep. She would go upstairs and help me onto the second floor. I'm thirteen now and she's almost fifty-years-old. She can't lift me up as well.* Azizi climbed into the opening of the wall and looked over at Rida and Tabora. He looked above at the window. With a quick leap, he would be able to reach the ledge.

Azizi stood up carefully, looking backwards at the ground beneath him. *If I fall, this could be both painful and embarrassing.* Azizi's body stood at a slight angle as he leaped into the air. Azizi's hands grasped onto the opening of the next floor as his legs dangled in front of the window below. Azizi looked towards either side of the alley for the pharaoh's soldiers.

"Please stop!" the woman cried again.

Azizi growled and pulled himself through the opening. Azizi parted the blue and gold curtains as he pulled himself into the room.

Azizi pulled his leg into the room as he watched Kahla crying underneath her assailant. Azizi grabbed the man by the back of the neck and punched him. "Get off her!"

The man turned his head angrily and put his hand up. "What are you doing here? I paid for this whore's services!" The man on top of Kahla growled and pulled back from the girl. Azizi swung his fist quickly, punching the man in the face.

"Are you jealous because I'm with your girlfriend?" the man chuckled.

Azizi glared at the man. "You are hurting her and I won't let you get away with it!"

Kahla watched as the man lunged for Azizi, wrapping his hands around the teen boy's throat. Kahla curled into a protective ball against the pillows as she watched Azizi kick her assailant in the stomach. The older man doubled over as Azizi kicked the man's face, knocking him onto the ground unconscious.

Azizi glared at the man, his body trembling with anger. "Your best isn't good enough!"

Mbizi had told Khepret before he attacked her, grabbing her throat. *Mbizi kicked me that day. I was trying to protect my mother. I saw how those men treated my mother. They kissed her, they touched her breasts. They used her body. It hurt to see my mother so poorly treated. I won't let any other woman fall under that same abuse again.*

Azizi turned to Kahla curled up on the bed crying. He slowly walked towards the bed and sat beside her. He raised his hand slowly to her face and cupped her cheek lightly.

"I took care of him, Kahla. Don't cry."

"Azizi!" Kahla exclaimed as she wrapped her arms around him tightly in a trembling embrace. Azizi caressed her hair and held her calmly. "I was so scared!"

Azizi rubbed her back reassuringly. "I know. It's all over now."

"I asked him to stop, Azizi! It's my first time and he hurt! He called me a filthy whore!" The girl sobbed, her body quaking.

Azizi pulled back and looked into her green, sparkling eyes. His thumb lightly brushed away a falling tear. "You are not a filthy whore, Kahla. You've always been a good friend to me. You are a good person."

Kahla lowered her head and shook it slowly. "No, Azizi. I'm not."

Azizi tilted her head upwards slowly. "You'll never convince me of that, Kahla," he said with a smile.

The girl smiled slowly and touched Azizi's face. "Thank you for saving me."

"I won't let anything bad happen to my friends. The next time when Mbizi sends you on the streets to offer your services, I want you to find me in my alley. I'll take you to the Nile and you can just relax."

"What if Mbizi asks about the money I made?"

Azizi released her and approached the unconscious man's clothing. He found twenty dînars in the man's pocket. He grabbed onto the money and slipped it into his own money pouch. "That's a good start. I'll keep this separate so you can take it when you come to the Nile with me. Do you promise?"

Kahla watched as Azizi sat beside her again. "I don't know, Azizi. What if Mbizi finds that I am not working on the street but I am relaxing with you?"

Azizi chuckled. "Nobody will know. If you don't want to join me, I will understand."

"Well, you saved me today, so I do owe you something."

Azizi shook his head. "I don't want the money. I am holding it for you because I know Mbizi forbids you to carry your own money."

"Thank you, Azizi," Kahla smiled at him. Kahla leaned over and kissed his cheek tenderly.

Azizi returned the kiss with a grin. "Do I owe you one dînar for that kiss?"

Kahla giggled. "You have just earned yourself a lifetime of free kisses."

"That must cost many dînars."

"You're a good friend, Azizi. Thank you."

The man on the ground began to groan as he slowly regained consciousness. Azizi kissed Kahla's hand. "Please allow me to rid this room of garbage."

Kahla watched as Azizi grabbed the man's clothing and tossed it through the window of the room.

"Get up, horse's ass!" Azizi growled as he kicked the man on the ground. "How do you enjoy being kicked when you are down?" The man groaned as he rolled. Azizi grabbed the man's wrists and dragged him from the room. The narrow hallway led to a wooden staircase nearby. Numbered doors lined the box-shaped hallway as Azizi dragged the man towards the stairs.

"Look out below!" Azizi called as he pushed the man down the stairs. The semi-conscious body quickly became silent as it crashed against every stair. The man landed at the bottom of the step silently.

"What was that?" a man asked from below.

"Azizi! Is that you?"

Azizi calmly walked down the stairs, brushing his black cape behind his shoulders. He stepped onto the man at the bottom of the stairs as he calmly approached Rida and Tabora with a smile. "Greetings, my pretty ladies!"

The three kissing adults stopped and turned their heads towards the new arrival.

"Hello, Azizi," Rida and Tabora said with a giggle.

The man under Rida looked at the teenage boy. "What are you doing here? You're interrupting my time with these fine ladies!"

Azizi grinned as he approached the long couch. "Yes, these are fine ladies. If I hear that you are mistreating them, you will find yourself in a similar accident as that horse's ass."

The man laughed. "You're only a boy! What can you do to me?"

Azizi removed the golden dagger from below his cloak with a grin. The blade of the knife pressed against his finger. "You would be surprised what a thousand little cuts would do to a person."

"Now, Azizi, Hessemet has been treating us nicely," Tabora said with a smile.
"That's what I like to hear."

"What's the meaning of this, Azizi?" a loud, bellowing voice sounded from the entrance.

Azizi turned his head and saw Mbizi step through the threshold. The large man rushed to the unconscious man laying at the foot of the steps. "What did you do to Râteb, you little runt?" Mbizi pressed his fingers to the man's neck.

"He was hurting Kahla."

Mbizi stood up, his face red with anger and his large hands clenched into angry fists. His upper lip curled into disgust as he glared at the teen. "Râteb is one of my best customers!"

"I wasn't going to let him hurt Kahla!"

"She was earning her keep! Now she has to work twice as hard!"

Azizi narrowed his eyes and tossed the golden dagger towards Mbizi. The golden dagger buried itself into the wall beside Mbizi. The teen lunged at Mbizi and grabbed a hold of his purple and gold tunic. He shoved Mbizi violently against the wall and growled at him.

"Kahla is only a fourteen-year-old girl! How dare you make her service a man twice her age!"

Mbizi grabbed onto Azizi's wrists, trying to shove his assailant away from him. "She does as she is told! She has no more choice!"

"It's all about coin, isn't it, Mbizi? That's all my mother was worth to you! You wanted to see me dead! From that day, I promised never to let you forget that I still live! I will not stand idly by as Kahla suffers at your hand!"

Mbizi grinned. "What are you going to do, Azizi? Are you going to go to the pharaoh? I know the bounty on your head is quite rewarding."

Azizi grinned. "Try to turn me into the pharaoh and I will turn you into alligator food!" Azizi released Mbizi and grabbed the dagger from the wall. "I have no fear of you, Mbizi, but you have every reason to fear me."

"Get out of here, Azizi! Ride away on the high horse which carried you here!"

Azizi grinned. "Don't mind if I do. That sounds like a good idea to me." Azizi turned to Rida and Tabora. "Have a good day, ladies."

"Behave yourself, Azizi Keket."

Azizi chuckled with a wink. "I'm a good boy."

Azizi walked calmly out of Mbizi's Bordello and saw Maysun and Oraida greeting men. They both turned with shock to see the teenager emerge from the building.

"What are you doing here? We didn't see you come in!"

Azizi chuckled. "I took the scenic route." Azizi calmly went to Mbizi's black horse and grinned. The horse reared as Azizi removed the rope binding the horse to the wooden post. Azizi put his hand on the horse's shoulder. "Calm down, beautiful."

The black horse looked at Azizi and snorted. Azizi grabbed the horse's leather reigns and mounted her back. "She's comfortable."

"Azizi, that's Mbizi's horse," Oraida said.

Azizi removed a twenty-dînar coin and flipped it towards Oraida. "That's for you, lovely. Goodbye, ladies!"

Oraida and Maysun looked at the coin. "Did Azizi just steal Mbizi's horse?"

"That boy is still as naughty as he ever was," Maysun sighed. "Will he ever learn?"

"Only Rā knows for certain, Maysun. Hello, sir, ten dînars will bring you pleasure beyond measure."


Azizi rode through the gates of the city. He pet the black horse's thick neck as its hooves thundered against the ground. Azizi held the reigns tightly as he passed the Bedouin settlement. Zahra and her twin companions waved to him as he passed. He turned his head and saw the Al-Sakhir slaves toiling in the field.

Past the Al-Sakhir lands laid the edge of the desert. The horse's hooves dug deep into the sand as she ran. Azizi smiled and cried out loudly into the open desert air as his new steed carried him into the hot land. He heard a return call and saw a pair of horses in the distance.

*That sounds like Nakia the other night when he was dancing beside the fire. Let me see.* Azizi repeated his call and the series of shrieks were returned in the same pattern. *That has to be Rich Boy out for his daily horsemanship lesson.* Azizi pulled the horse's reigns to the left as the horse began to shift towards the left. The forms of Nakia and Amsi slowly came into focus.

"Where did you get that horse?" Amsi asked Azizi.

Azizi grinned. "I said I'd find a way to get what I needed. I'm resourceful, remember?"

Amsi shook his head. "One of these days, your luck might run out."

Azizi nodded. "Yes, maybe someday, but not today, my friend!"

"Who owns the horse?"

"Me."

Nakia shook his head. "No, I mean from whom did you take it?"

"Mbizi, the brothel owner."

Amsi gasped. "Mbizi? Azizi, you need to return the horse!"

"Why? He has a lot of money. Those women work hard and he pockets of the money. He can pay for his own horse." Azizi looked at Amsi. "Sit up straight, Rich Boy. You're going to put strain on the horse's back if you sit that way."

"Hey, I'm the tutor here," Nakia said with a grin, pointing to his chest tattoo.

"Then show him the right way to ride the horse. It could save his life someday if he falls off."

Amsi narrowed his eyes. "I won't fall off! I ride well!"

Azizi chuckled. "We'll have a race someday to test your skill. I'm off to find the oasis that the Bedouin mentioned."

"Do you know where it is?" Nakia asked.

"No."

"Do you know there are dangerous animals and thieves in the desert, Azizi?" Amsi asked.

"There is danger everywhere. Why should the desert be any different? The thieves will not bother me." Azizi touched the golden band around his right arm. "I bear the mark of the Osiris Clan of *Iunu*."

Nakia pointed to the open desert. "The *Nuu* are out there. I have seen them. There have been many exploring the desert. They are looking for something."

"The Eye of Horus," Azizi looked into the wilderness of the desert. The rolling hills of dunes and seemingly never-ending sand lay before him. *The pharaoh is after power. He knows the* Nuu *are expert trackers and know the placement every grain of sand in the desert. They are searching for the pharaoh's desire.* "Amsi, has the pharaoh found the Scroll or the Eye of Horus?"

Amsi shook his head. "No. When you rescued your friend, he was furious. He didn't say that he had acquired them yet. He must still be searching for them. Your friend told the pharaoh he knew nothing of the scroll or the eye."

"The pharaoh must be still looking for both of those relics."

"If I hear anything, I will let you know, Azizi."

Azizi nodded his head. "Thank you, Amsi. I should be going. Farewell."

"Please be careful, Azizi."

Nakia and Amsi watched Azizi ride away. Nakia watched with a sigh, envious of the orphan boy's freedom. Azizi held the reigns tightly as the black horse ran swiftly. The teen's eyes darted around the sands in front of him, searching for the *Nuu* or the bandits which plagued the desert's wilderness.

*This is the life! No guards are chasing me! I don't have to fear an attack from Kaphiri's gang! It's just me and the open sands!* Azizi smiled happily as he continued to ride.

*If Amsi thinks he can defeat me in a contest of horsemanship, he's sadly mistaken.*

Azizi narrowed his eyes as he saw figures racing towards him in the distance. Azizi watched as the group of men began to scream when they saw him. They approached him faster, removing their weapons from their sheaths.

*These must be the desert bandits!*

The group of men began to separate, to prevent his passing as they continued their forward gallop. Azizi gripped the reigns tightly and tugged towards the right. The horse began to run to the right as the group followed him. Azizi looked over his shoulder and saw the gang of people quickly approaching him from behind.

Azizi looked forward, his eyes frantically searching for some means of shelter. *Hurry up, sweetheart, they're gaining on us!* Azizi heard the hoof beats become louder and closer. *If they want to take me, I'm not going down without a fight!*

Azizi turned the horse and removed his golden dagger from its sheath. He glared at the men approaching and shielded his eyes from the bright rays of the desert sun.

The men approached him, laughing. "Well, look, my men! We caught a boy!"

The men laughed as they pointed their scimitars and swords at him. "He doesn't look like he has a lot of money on him, Nefertum."

"How much is your life worth to you, my son?"

Azizi grinned, the corners of his mouth curling defiantly. "You try and take my gold and I will take your hand!"

The men laughed, some of them to the point of tears. "There are ten of us and one of you, boy! You are young and a simple target for our arrows! What makes you so confident that you will be able to defeat all of us?"

Azizi tightened his grip on the hilt of the dagger. "I have faced the pharaoh's army and lived! I wounded the face of the god himself!"

The men's laughter slowly ceased. One of the men leaned over to his companion.

"Could this be the child?"

Azizi glared at Nefertum, who had leaned back in his saddle to listen to the murmurings of his men.

"What is your name, boy?"

"Azizi Keket, son of Ghazi of *Iunu*," Azizi lowered the gold band on his arm, revealing the tattoo of Osiris' backbone, the djed pillar.

The leader pulled his horse backward two steps. "You are the boy who scratched the pharaoh and rescued his friend."

Azizi tensed, ready for the leader to issue an attack.

"We have heard much from the bandits of *Iunu*. They have told us of your deeds. I thought you were just a legend, a hope and nothing more."

Azizi kept a sharp eye on the actions of the men ahead of him. The men lowered their weapons and bowed their heads.

"They have informed us of the power which the pharaoh seeks and it is dangerous indeed, Azizi."

Azizi slowly relaxed in his saddle. "I'm going to stop him. No matter what I must do, no matter where I must go, no matter what blood must be shed, I will stop him."

Nefertum bowed his head. "You are a brave child."

"I'm thirteen-years-old! I'm not a boy anymore!"

Nefertum grinned. "You still have your side-lock. You are still a child and without the ritual circumcision, you have not yet become a man."

Azizi narrowed his eyes. *I cannot afford the Rite-of-Passage ceremony. The temples have raised the money required to perform the ceremony. I'll show them who is not a man!* Azizi grabbed his side-lock and placed the blade of the golden dagger near the top of his head. With a single swift cut, he severed the side-lock. He held the severed hair for the men to see and opened his hand. The hair flew into the desert wind as he lowered his arm. "Do not call me a child anymore."

"What has brought you into the vast desert, Azizi?"

"I am searching for an oasis which the Bedouin say is located to the south of Heliopolis."

Nefertum pointed to the left of him. "Continue on your way. The Zeniah Oasis lays ahead towards the mountains."

"Thank you. Do you know why the *Nuu* have been so active lately in the desert?"

"The *Nuu* are searching for the relics sought by the pharaoh. We have been searching for them, but we do not have any clues as to where they may lay. We have seen them in the distant mountains. We recently captured one of them and questioned him. He told us that the pharaoh possessed the Scroll of Thoth and was searching for the first relic mentioned, The Eye of Horus." Azizi watched as Nefertum pat the money pouch on his hip.

"The *Nuu* was paid handsomely by the pharaoh and now we carry the pharaoh's gold."

Azizi wiped his sweaty brow. "The Eye of Horus, you say?"

"The pharaoh needs to locate the Scroll of Horus to give power to the Eye of Horus. The *Nuu* refused to say anything more, so we permanently silenced him."

Azizi sighed as he looked into the desert. "How are we going to find it before he does? We can't let him get his hand on any of the items he seeks!"

"What do you suppose we do? Fight the pharaoh's army to gain possession of the items? That is madness!" one of the bandits exclaimed.

"If that is what we must do, Hakizi," Nefertum said calmly.

Azizi glared at the man. "Are you afraid?"

"It is foolish to fight an entire army by yourself."

"That man killed my parents! That man tried to kill one of my best friends! He is a cruel tyrant, killing women and children for his own entertainment! I will not let him become immortal! I won't let Sekhmet triumph!"

Nefertum held up his hand. "If we can be of any help to you, Azizi, you have only to ask."

"I am not serving a child," Hakizi growled defiantly.

The other bandits looked at Hakizi. Some of them moved their horses slowly away from him.

"Hakizi, this is Azizi Keket, the King of Thieves! He has helped the poor and the orphaned. He has evaded capture by the pharaoh. He has risked his neck to save those who are in need. He is the One, chosen to battle Sekhmet in the ancient scriptures! Desta has spoken to Aneksi and the Oracle has told her that Azizi is the longed-for King of Thieves."

Azizi straightened in his saddle. "You know Aneksi?"

"Desta goes to the town to get supplies for us. She gives Aneksi some of our earnings in exchange for necessities. Nobody would suspect that she is one of us."

Hakizi chuckled. "We can't exactly walk through the front gates of *Iunu* and go shopping. When you are a thief and everyone knows you, you must be careful."

Azizi nodded. "I know. That is why I have my cape."

"The desert is vast. The pharaoh and the *Nuu* will have a difficult time finding you here. I will tell no one that you seek the Zeniah Oasis."

"Where can I find you?"

Nefertum bowed his head. "We have operatives everywhere."

"Amsi Al-Sakhir at Heliopolis knows me. If you need to find me, go to him, but do not let his father see you."

"Yes, our king."

Azizi and the group turned their heads as they heard the loud neighing of horses. Azizi shielded his eyes from the rays of the sun as he looked into the distance.

"Could that be a Noble caravan ripe for the plucking, my men?" Nefertum asked.

"That is too numerous to be a Noble caravan or a merchant. Merchants do not have chariots of gold."

Azizi gasped. *Chariots of gold! Only one person can afford that!* "That must be the pharaoh's caravan! He must be searching for an item! Perhaps the pharaoh has found the location of the Scroll of Horus!"

Nefertum narrowed his eyes and focused on the army. "There are many men."

"I must not lose them!"

"May Osiris, Lord of Eternity, keep you safe, Azizi Keket," Nefertum said, bowing his head.

Azizi bowed his head. "May Osiris guard your path through Deshert." Azizi turned his horse and rode following the army at a distance. He turned his head and watched them, careful to keep a sharp eye on their location. *I won't lose the pharaoh. He's not going to succeed!*

Azizi focused on the army. Horses pulling chariots and armed soldiers followed a pair of golden chariots, one of which carried the symbol of the pharaoh. The feathers hovered over the pharaoh's image as he whipped his horses quickly.

Azizi heard the yipping of jackals as they chewed on a mid-day meal. The jackals tore the carcass apart as they fought for the best pieces of meat. Azizi watched as one of the jackals fell to the ground, an arrow protruding from its neck. The jackals scurried away from the carcass quickly. A cry of victory from the pharaoh made him growl.

"Die, Anubis!" the pharaoh laughed as he handed his bow to one of the occupants of his chariot.

*You're not going to get away with that, pharaoh!* Azizi growled as he clutched the reigns of his horse tightly. His eyes looked at the fallen jackal in the distance as he rode. *That pharaoh is nothing but a beast!*

Azizi followed the group and saw an oasis approaching him. Tall palm trees and bushes lined the circular oasis. Azizi's eyes lit up with happiness as he saw the lush ground and foliage. The leaves of the palm trees swayed calmly in the desert air. *I found it! I found my new home!* The teen's ears rumbled with the sound of the pharaoh's army. *Too bad I can't enjoy it now. I must follow the pharaoh and see what he plans!*

The sun began to set as Azizi saw the army cease their pursuit. The large group of men settled and began to build a fire and set up tents. Azizi rode a distance away to prevent the pharaoh's army finding him.

## XXXVI

### <u>The Scroll of Horus</u>

The land raced under his eyes. The Zeniah Oasis rushed past him as fast as a shooting star. He rushed over sand dunes and valleys. The mountains hastily approached him as he flew into a cavern on the top of the mountain. The cavern's passages twisted and turned into a large room. He flew down the stairs as he saw a golden altar with a golden box sitting upon it. Flames burned on either side of the altar, lighting the dark room.

*This is what you seek,* a female voice said seductively. *Use the Scroll of Horus to discover the incantation to give the Eye its power!* The room shifted towards an altar overshadowed by a large hawk. The room was brightly lit as he looked up at the hawk. Its wings were stretched wide, it's beak open in a silent, piercing screech. Its eyes glared down at him menacingly. *Horus waged war against the night and darkness. Use the Scroll of Horus in Edfû to give the Eye its power! Out of myth comes the power of the scrolls. Beware, Pharaoh Runihura!* The eyes of the hawk glowed red and the wings flapped menacingly. The female voice deepened into a deep, masculine growl. *I avenged my father's murder. My eye was torn to pieces by the wicked Seth. I harpooned the evil Seth, the embodiment of darkness. I will not abide evil in my domain. Beware, Pharaoh Runihura!* The hawk closed its beak and screeched at him with an ear-piercing shriek. The talons opened and closed tightly around the box. A blinding light appeared behind the hawk as it reached for him with sharp talons. *Stay away*

*from my domain! You come with evil intent! I will
vanquish you like my uncle, Seth! I shall not let a
powerful amulet such as my Eye be taken easily. I will
avenge my father! Turn back, Pharaoh Runihura! Turn
back or you shall perish under my fierce hand! I shall set
a harpoon through your chest in the name of my father,
Osiris!* The hawk lunged his beak towards him.

Pharaoh Runihura opened his eyes and sat up quickly.
His chest rose up and down swiftly as he wiped away a
thick layer of sweat from his forehead. His head darted
around the tent quickly. Gahiji was sleeping in his
separate tent. The occupant of his chariot held onto an
arrow against her shoulder and stared into a bowl of
water longingly.

"Akilah!" Runihura growled, making the young girl
startle. "Bring me the water!"

The girl nodded quickly and dropped the arrow. He took
the bowl in her hands and walked towards the pharaoh.
Runihura grabbed it and drank the water quickly. He
shoved the empty bowl back into the eight-year-old's
hands. The child looked down at the empty bowl and
back at the pharaoh quietly.

"What were you doing while I was asleep, girl?"

"I was looking at the water. I'm thirsty, my pharaoh."

Runihura chuckled as he stood on his feet. "You must
earn your drink, girl."

"Did you have a bad dream, my king?" the girl asked
timidly.

Runihura glared at the child. He folded his arms sternly. "If Horus believes that he can stop me from obtaining the power of the immortals, then he is sadly mistaken. I am not afraid of the wrath of the gods. They will be bowing before me someday." Runihura grinned. "They will be bowing before me just as your parents did eight years ago. I showed them no mercy!"

The little girl looked down at the sand below her feet sadly. "I know, my pharaoh."

"Kaemwaset would have not shown them any mercy had he recovered them! I did them a favor by letting them languish in the dungeon! You should be thanking me for my generosity towards them! Am I not a merciful pharaoh?"

The little girl's shoulders sagged. "Yes, my lord." *My mother died first. My mother starved to death. She was hungry. I heard her cries for bread. I have never seen the world beyond the dungeon. I never knew there was a wide world beyond the metal bars. My father's screams echoed through the dungeon. I saw him dragged from his cell. His lifeless body was light as a feather as I helped carry him up the stairs.*

"I should return you to Kaemwaset when we return to Heliopolis. Kaemwaset ordered your birth, so it is fitting that you belong to him."

Akilah bowed her head. "Yes, my pharaoh."

Runihura dressed and placed his sword and dagger into their sheaths. He stepped outside to the morning light and saw Gahiji readying the soldiers. "Gahiji, we are to march at once!"

"Yes, my pharaoh! We should be near the mountains very soon. According to our map, we should be able to find the city of Edfû to the south-west along the banks of the Nile."

Runihura looked at Gahiji. "We are in the middle of the desert. How are we going to follow the Nile?"

"Memphis lies to our west. We can command a barge there and sail to Edfû."

"Very well." Pharaoh Runihura took the map in his hand. "There is no mention of a mountain range here, Gahiji! Are you certain that is what we will find?"

Gahiji rolled the map. "The *Nuu* said that the riches are stored high. It is possible that the map was made to hide the true location of the cavern. It could also be referring to cliffs hanging above the ancient cemeteries." Gahiji noticed Runihura rubbing his forehead tiredly. "Did you not sleep well, my pharaoh?"

"Sekhmet spoke in my dreams. Horus warned me not to enter his domain. I am not afraid, Gahiji. I have set my sights on godly powers. I will not let fear stop me. I will continue! I must continue! Akilah! Come!"

The men disassembled the tents and extinguished the fires from the night. The soldiers grabbed their weaponry and their gear. The battalion formed their lines and began to march behind the pharaoh's golden chariot.

Azizi yawned as he rode a distance away, still extremely cautious not to travel too closely to the royal army. *I wonder if the pharaoh even knows he is being followed. It's too bad that they had sentinels keeping watch. Otherwise, I could have grabbed some of the gold and some pretty jewelry for Kahla. I'm sure she would have appreciated something nice and shiny. What girl wouldn't want a new piece of jewelry, especially if it belonged to the pharaoh? I could have also killed the pharaoh in his sleep and finished his reign of terror.* Azizi glared at the royal entourage. *If only I could have avenged my parents here! I will not stop pursuing him until he has paid for the bloodshed he has caused! My parents, Ferryn, they died because of him! They died painfully. I won't let him make anyone else suffer!*

A tall range of cliffs entered into his line of sight. They towered over the sands, casting a wide shadow over the sunken valley below. A bright light twinkled from the mountain top high above him. *What could that be?* Azizi pulled on the reigns of the horse, making the animal come to a reluctant stop. His eyes watched the frequency of the bright twinkle, searching for a pattern. *Could it be the Nuu trying to communicate?*

He shook the reigns slightly, coaxing the horse into a quick trot. The shimmering light ceased. *What is this?* Azizi stopped the horse and the light began to flicker again. *Are they trying to communicate to me? Is this the location of one of the legendary items or scrolls that the pharaoh wishes to obtain? I can't let it fall into his blood-stained hands!*

Azizi watched as the pharaoh's party raced towards the cliff. Azizi turned the horse towards the mountains. The teen watched as the cliffs loomed higher over him as he advanced. The cliffs were steep. The absence of green attested to the barren nature of the path ahead.

The battalion suddenly stopped. The frightened whinny of horses and Runihura's angry voice told him that the pharaoh's horses were afraid of the path ahead of them. "You foolish beasts! What are you afraid of?"

"The horses know there is danger ahead!" Hamadi called to the pharaoh. "They will not move!"

Runihura turned his head angrily. "Then you will make them move, Hamadi! Get ahead of the chariot and pull the beasts ahead!"

Hamadi swallowed nervously, seeing the two white horses stamp their feet emphatically and shake their heads in refusal. Hamadi slowly walked in front of the frightened horses and took their reigns. "Let's go, girls. I'm right here," he said reassuringly. The horses whinnied loudly as Hamadi tried to pull them. "Please, girls! The pharaoh will become-."

"Get going, you worthless mules!" Runihura cracked the whip, snapping against Hamadi's back. Hamadi screamed and fell to one knee as his back began to bleed. "My pharaoh!"

"Get on your feet, Hamadi!"

Hamadi struggled to his feet, his legs quaking under him. The horses slowly began their ascent up the cliff's path.

Hamadi watched his feet as he walked along the pebble-laden path. The desert wind blew as he cajoled the horses to continue along the steep cliff. The barren path was soon replaced by one lined with papyrus plants.

Pharaoh Runihura shielded his eyes as a bright light emanated from the top of the cliff and abruptly faded. "Gahiji, did you see that?"

"Yes, my lord! I wonder what that could be!"

Runihura looked beside the chariot as papyrus lined the road. Isis hid Horus in the papyrus reeds beside the Nile so Seth could not find him. A strong northern wind blew around them. Hamadi held his arm up to shield his eyes from the flying sand and pebbles. The pharaoh wrapped his cloak around him to shield his mouth and nose from the flying debris.

Hamadi felt his feet crunch upon papyrus reeds as he pressed forward. The horses allowed their handler to move them steadily across the reeds of papyrus. The wind had died as they advanced carefully along the narrowing path. Hamadi lifted his head to see the entrance leading inside a cavern. The papyrus in front of the entrance blew briskly, a wind streaming from the entrance, sending pebbles flying off the cliff.

The horses reared suddenly, vocalizing their hesitation and fear. Akilah and Runihura fell backwards off the chariot with the sudden motion of the frightened creatures. Gahiji jumped off his horse and ran beside the fallen pharaoh. "My great king, are you alright?"

Runihura glared towards the horses angrily. "How dare they throw me from my chariot!"

"The horses are too afraid to continue, my lord. We should leave them here and continue without them."

Runihura stood on his feet, ignoring his slave girl standing on her own. "Leave them. The chariot appears too small to enter the cavern." Runihura walked around the side of the chariot carefully, looking at the ground far below him. He stepped beside Hamadi and pushed the soldier angrily against the rocky cliff. "How dare you make me look like a fool in front of my army!"

"My lord, the horses were afraid! I tried to control them!"

"That had better not happen again or I will toss you off of this cliff and the jackals will eat you!"

"Yes, my lord!"

Runihura tossed Hamadi onto the ground furiously. "You will proceed first into the cavern!"

Hamadi slowly regained his footing and looked at the wind flying out of the cavern. Hamadi swallowed nervously as he looked back at the pharaoh. Runihura unsheathed his sword and held the tip of the blade against Hamadi's ribs. The nervous teen turned towards the cavern. *Great Horus, I mean you no disrespect. I mean you no harm. My tongue speaks not against your greatness. I do not wish to help the pharaoh, but if I do not, he will slay me and I will not see the birth of my child. Janani, I hope you are well. Our child may have a chance of survival if the pharaoh is away from you.*

Hamadi held his shield in front of him as he approached
the mouth of the cavern cautiously. He held his breath
nervously as he felt a bead of sweat caress his cheek.
The wind continued to blow as he stood at the edge of the
cavern. Hamadi looked into the dark, sweet-smelling
cavern. *Why would the cavern smell sweet? Little light
can penetrate deep into the rock. This is holy ground.
The pharaoh defiles it with his footsteps.*

The rockface appeared smooth, unlike the rocky surface
of the sides of the cliff. The rock appeared polished
inside, speckled with hues of green, blue, and red circles.
Sand had covered the floor of the cavern. Hamadi
looked closely at the walls, much to the impatience of the
pharaoh behind him wielding his weapon at the ready.
Eyes! *These are eyes! The Eye of Horus lines the walls!
There must be thousands of them!*

"What are you waiting for, you frightened child?"

Hamadi turned to the pharaoh. "There are paintings of the
Eye of Horus, my king! There are countless numbers of
them!"

Pharaoh Runihura stepped beside the soldier and ran his
hand across the wall. His eyes roamed from the floor to
the ceiling of the cave.

"My lord, there is writing above us!" Hamadi exclaimed.
"What does it say, my king?"

Pharaoh Runihura's eyes scanned the hieroglyphics.
"Beware, Seth! Should you enter with evil in heart, once
more shall I remove your eye! I will avenge my father's

murder-." Pharaoh Runihura glared at the wall. *I was the one to place the venom of the scorpion and the deadly herbs inside my father's last meal. I murdered my father. Horus, you will not punish me for my deed!*

Runihura grabbed Hamadi by the back of the throat and shoved him onto the floor inside. "Get inside there!"

A bright light flew from the back of the cavern. Runihura screamed as he shielded his eyes from the brightness of the light. Hamadi crossed his arms in front of him as he looked down into the dirt to avoid the light. *It's the light of Horus, the avenger of his father!*

Runihura's eyes burned with the brightness of the light as he turned his back. A great heat surrounded his eyes as his shrill scream echoed over the cliff.

Hamadi slowly opened his eyes and cautiously looked towards the light. The warm, gentle light caressed his face. The pained scream of the pharaoh shrieked behind him. Hamadi looked upward towards the ceiling. 'Should you enter with evil in heart, once more I will remove your eye.' The pharaoh pushed me to the ground and that is when the light began. *If the pharaoh commits any evil deed within this shrine of Horus, he will be punished! Great Horus, I praise you!*

Hamadi looked at the illuminated cavern walls. Countless eyes looked at him from the walls, protecting the sanctuary against evil, destruction, and violence. The winged disk on the ceiling contained the warning to any who enter. The soldier kneeled before the light and bowed his forehead to the ground. "Great Horus, we praise you for your goodness and your greatness! You stand at the right hand of Rā, the Sun God. Great is your glory, avenger of his father, Osiris!"

The light diminished as Runihura rubbed his eyes with pain. Runihura's hands trembled with pain as he looked at his twitching fingers. His body quivered as the heat surrounding him diminished. Gahiji ran beside the pharaoh's side and put his hands on his shoulders.

"My pharaoh! My king, are you injured?"

Runihura pulled his hands from his eyes as he breathed sharply. "The light...burned!"

Gahiji turned his head towards Hamadi kneeling on the ground. "What did you do to our pharaoh, child?"

Hamadi turned his head as he straightened his back. "Nothing, my lord! The pharaoh shoved me to the ground and the beautiful light appeared."

"Beautiful?! Beautiful?" Runihura screeched with anger. "That light was oppressive! It burned with the fire of thousands of suns!"

"My king, you threw me to the ground," Hamadi said as he stood on his feet. "The warning above the entrance says that no evil heart shall enter the sanctuary."

Runihura opened his eyes; his vision was cloudy as he opened his eyes to the sands below. Gahiji held onto the pharaoh tightly as he wavered unsteadily on his feet.

"I will let no harm become of you, my great king!" Gahiji growled as he looked at his troops. "You will follow us inside!"

Akilah ran towards the pharaoh. "My king, are you hurt?"

"Get inside the cavern, Akilah! You are to walk beside Hamadi! You both are no better than human shields!"

Akilah turned to Hamadi and cautiously stood beside him. The teenaged soldier looked down at the little girl standing beside him. Akilah looked into the darkness of the tunnel. She shivered in the dampness, the chill biting her and the barely-clothed soldier to the bone. She stepped closer to Hamadi and took a timid hold of his wrist. The seemingly endless darkness loomed in front of them as the few rays of the sun illuminated just beyond the entrance.

"Master Hamadi? I'm afraid," she said, pressing her cheek against his arm.

Hamadi swallowed hard. *If that beam of light was the work of the gods, what have we to fear, Akilah? The gods protected me from further abuse of the pharaoh. If we continue to be humble in his sight, Horus shall protect us. Hamadi felt a drop of cold sweat trickle down his chest.* "Don't be, Akilah. Stay beside me."

Akilah nodded. "Thank you, Hamadi."

Hamadi took the little girl's hand with his left hand. He held onto it tightly as he grabbed his sword with his right hand. "Do not let go of my hand."

Akilah and Hamadi took one step as a light illuminated the cavern. Akilah squealed in surprise and held her breath. Hamadi turned his head to see Pharaoh Runihura standing beside him with Gahiji.

"Get going!" the General growled.

Hamadi and Akilah cautiously walked down the lit hallway. Eyes decorating the sides of the wall looked at them as they passed. Akilah shivered as she watched them looking at her. The eyes outlined in blue blinked at her, making her scream and jump against Hamadi.

"I want to go out! I want to go out! I'm afraid!" the little girl cried. "The blue eyes are blinking!"

"Don't be foolish, girl!" Runihura groaned. "The eyes are painted onto the surface of the rock. They are not alive!"

A screech heard from the back of the cavern made Hamadi hold his breath. Akilah watched the red eyes blink repeatedly along the wall. "The red eyes are blinking!"

Hamadi watched as a harpoon flew from the back of the cavern. Hamadi sunk to his knees quickly as the harpoon flew over Akilah and between Gahiji and Runihura. A series of painful screams behind him and the sound of falling bodies made him tense.

Akilah turned her head to see several soldiers had fallen to the ground. The harpoon had speared several soldiers through the skull.

Hamadi looked down at the ground and saw Akilah's foot had sunken into the sand. He reached for her foot and brushed aside the sand. "Akilah, move your foot." Hamadi brushed the sand away as Akilah moved her foot away cautiously. He touched a depressed tile on the floor. "My king, the floor has been covered in sand!"

"Akilah, did you make that harpoon fire at me?" Runihura scowled at the little girl.

"I'm sorry, my lord! It was an accident!"

Hamadi held up a hand towards the pharaoh. "My king, Horus becomes angry when you speak with anger. Remember the warning writ on the ceiling. Entering here with a heart of evil will kill us all."

Runihura grinned. "I care only for obtaining the Eye of Horus. Continue!"

Hamadi stood on his feet and cautiously tested each step forward. *Horus harpooned Seth in the form of a hippopotamus. Horus is striking at the heart of evil, but he is striking at the wrong target. Those soldiers were following the pharaoh because they had no choice. They paid for their blind allegiance with their lives. I know the pharaoh feels no remorse for their loss.*

Akilah whimpered as she held onto Hamadi's hand. Her sight brushed against the walls as she watched the blue eyes blink at her again. "Are you watching us, my lord?" the little girl asked the eyes. The eyes blinked in response. "Please don't hurt Hamadi or me."

The blue eyes blinked at the group as they passed deeper into the cold cavern. A shriek from a hawk echoed through the cavern. Gahiji held his hands to his ears as the pitch pierced his eardrums. "That infernal cry is beginning to irritate me!"

Runihura narrowed his eyes deep into the cavern as he pointed his sword ahead of him. *I'm willing to fight*

*anything that interferes with my goal! I will not let
anything stop me from obtaining glory! Come to me,
Horus! I will fight!*

Hamadi watched as the light diminished from the
hallway. Darkness crept from the end of the hallway,
covering the passage in darkness. Runihura watched as
the darkness enveloped him. He turned and saw nobody
beside him. "Gahiji!"

"I'm right here, sir!" Gahiji called as if from a great
distance away.

The pharaoh felt the General's tight grip on his arm. He
took a cautious step forward and bumped into Hamadi.
"Continue!"

"But, my lord, I cannot see anything ahead of me!"

"Do not give any excuses! March, soldier!"

Hamadi took a step forward, his breath coming in sharp
gasps as the air became thinner. He could still feel Akilah
gripping onto him tightly. Her little hand trembled in his
as she shifted closer to the soldier. Hamadi could hear
the labored breathing of the soldiers and pharaoh alike as
they stepped gingerly behind him. The sharp point of the
pharaoh's sword touched between his shoulder blades,
making him tense.

"I do not suggest you stop, Hamadi. It could be hazardous
to your health," the pharaoh's whispered words sounded
quietly in the darkness.

Hamadi continued forward in the void of darkness as the
ground beneath him began to descend. "The floor slopes

downwards, my pharaoh! We are venturing deeper into the cliff!"

"Perfect. Keep moving, Hamadi."

Hamadi proceeded at the slight decline of the floor. A ray of light twinkled from the end of the hallway, its brightness illuminating the floor before them. "Horus, destructor of darkness, his eyes are of the sun and the moon, his presence is here. Do you not feel the presence of the god, Horus of the two horizons, my lord?"

Runihura looked into the bright light ahead of him. "The light waxes and wanes. The light fades and it returns. What sorcery is at work here?"

Hamadi looked into the light, his skin warming from a gentle breeze. The light warmed his skin as he stared with wonderment at the twinkling light. "This is not sorcery, my pharaoh."

Runihura squinted his eyes and held his hand in front of him to block some of the harsh light. *I remember seeing this place in my dream. Was it truly a dream or a vision given to me by Sekhmet herself? Was she trying to warn me of impending danger? No, she was telling me use the scroll. She wants me to be as powerful as she! Sekhmet, give me strength.*

"Hamadi! Help!"

Hamadi felt Akilah tug on his hand as she fell through the floor. A trap door had opened under her feet and the little girl was dangling from Hamadi's hand. Hamadi dropped his weapon and grabbed the girl's arm with both hands.

"Hamadi! Don't let me fall!" Akilah screamed as she dangled from Hamadi's grip.

Hamadi pulled her to the surface and set her on her feet. Akilah wrapped her arms around Hamadi and quivered with fear. Hamadi returned the embrace and looked at the light ahead. He released the little girl and looked her in her brown eyes. A gold collar around her neck sparkled in the light, bearing the hieroglyphs 'Pharaoh Runihura's property.' Hamadi touched the little girl's face lightly. *I wonder if my child will look like me.* "I won't let anything happen to you, alright?"

Akilah nodded as her bottom lip trembled. "I want to leave here, Hamadi."

"I know. Be brave," he said smiling for her. *I can't let her see my own fear. We are within the sanctuary of a god. We have already hit two obstacles in our attempt to reach the ancient relic. What other dangers await us ahead? Maybe I shouldn't ask that question. We'll find out soon enough.* "Let me see your smile."

The little girl struggled to lift the corners of her mouth in a smile.

"Good girl. Let us do what we must so that we may return to the palace."

Akilah nodded as she looked towards the light.

"I do not have my entire lifetime to wait for you, Hamadi Nefer-Aten!"

Hamadi stood and took Akilah's hand. He continued forward, testing his steps against the sand. The cavern walls began to close against the intruders. Akilah watched as the walls came closer to her, narrowing the passage ahead. Hamadi continued to hold her hand as she was forced to walk behind him.

Runihura shielded his eyes from the harsh light as they entered a large room. He heard Akilah scream as they emerged from the cavern passage. Runihura uncovered his eyes as they stood in a large room. The smell of death and decay permeated his nasal cavity. He opened his eyes to see skeletons and decaying bodies scattered around the floor of the room. The bright, harsh light had diminished into a series of torches lining the walls and on pedestals.

Gahiji's eyes scanned the room as he felt a wind brush against his face. "What is this place?" The General parted from the pharaoh and stepped towards the wall. His hand brushed against the wall as he read fading hieroglyphs. "Who has lit these torches and writ these words?"

Runihura slowly approached one of the decaying corpses. He kneeled before the body, frozen in an eternal position of agony. "What killed these men? They wear Noble Egyptian garb."

Hamadi walked to a skeleton clutching an amulet. Hamadi reached for the amulet and examined it in the light of a torch. "No poor man could afford this type of jewelry."

Gahiji took a torch from a pedestal and held it to the wall to examine the images. A mural of Horus spearing Seth in the form of a hippopotamus decorated the wall. The next mural was Seth taking Horus' eye and tearing it into many pieces. Horus standing as a sun god being worshipped by the poor and rich alike adorned the ceiling. "These images are ancient."

Hamadi abandoned the decaying corpse and looked upon the wall opposite of Gahiji. Pharaoh Atenhotep! He is here! Pharaoh Atenhotep stood before Osiris and Horus. Horus was placing a blessing onto Pharaoh Atenhotep for protection. "My pharaoh! I have seen your father on this wall!"

Runihura turned his head and casually walked towards Hamadi. He looked up at the blessing that Horus had given Pharaoh Atenhotep. "Long life to he who is merciful and just. Glorious is he who upholds the will of Ma'at! Long may he reign!" Pharaoh Runihura chuckled. *He could have lived longer had he lived by the will of Sekhmet! She protects me and I will rise to her level of greatness!*

"My pharaoh, look!" another soldier exclaimed.

Runihura, Hamadi, and Gahiji turned towards a soldier standing near the entrance. Runihura's eyes widened as he saw a large snake standing beside the pharaoh. Below the snake carved the inscription, 'Wadjet serves the pharaoh.' An image of a vulture stood on the opposite side of Wadjet. Pharaoh Runihura looked at the pectoral hanging around his neck. Wadjet and Nekhbet stood beside the Eye of Horus. Nekhbet and Wadjet are protectors of the pharaoh, the Living Horus. Wadjet protected the infant Horus on the island of Khemmis.

A great gust of wind brushed against his head and he turned quickly. "How could wind appear in a place so deep into the cavern?" Hamadi asked as he turned his head slowly.

"My pharaoh," Akilah whimpered as she threw herself at the pharaoh.

Akilah grabbed onto Runihura's white skirt tightly. She pressed her cheek against his ribs. Runihura glared down at the trembling girl. "How dare you touch me with your filth, you bad, dirty, pathetic girl?!"

Hamadi turned and gasped in surprise. "My king! Turn around!"

Runihura turned his head and saw a cobra slither from an opening at the other end of the room. The cobra slithered and stood, its teeth barred menacingly towards the group of men. "Wadjet," Runihura whispered.

"My pharaoh, be careful," Akilah whimpered.

Runihura grinned as he stepped forward. "It won't harm me. I am the Living Horus."

"There, you are wrong!" a voice echoed from across the room. "You profane his name with your tongue and title."

Runihura raised his head to see a vulture descend quickly and land upon one of the soldiers. The creature pecked at the soldier's face as the man screamed. He swatted at the vulture with his hands as the other soldiers scattered away from the man.

Hamadi watched as the man fell to the ground as the vulture tore the man's eye from its socket. Hamadi watched in horror as the vulture turned his head towards him.

Runihura watched as a man stood at the other end of the room. "What are you doing here?! If you think you are going to obtain the Scroll of Horus, you are sadly mistaken!" Runihura removed his sword from its sheath and held the blade in front of him.

The cobra hissed at Runihura as its slithery body slid across the sandy ground.

Gahiji stood beside the pharaoh. "You will not stand in the pharaoh's way! Bow before your king!"

The man dressed in a long, white robe chuckled quietly. "He is not my king," the man said calmly. "He is only a mortal. His stele shall never stand the tests of time."

Runihura's face grew red with fury. "How dare you!"

"How dare I speak the truth?"

Gahiji stood in front of Runihura. "Show some reverence to the Great Runihura!"

"I shall not do so, Lord Gahiji."

Gahiji narrowed his eyes. "How do you know my name? Who are you? Speak, you common dog!"

The man reached a hand towards the cobra. "I am not a common dog, I assure you."

Hamadi watched as the vulture flew towards the man. The vulture perched upon the man's shoulder. "Are you a god? Are you the human embodiment of Horus?"

The man smiled at Hamadi as the cobra and vulture stood beside the man. "I am not a god, but a cursed man here to give you warning. Do not continue on your quest, Pharaoh Runihura."

Gahiji tightened his grip on the hilt of his sword and walked angrily towards the man. "I have had enough of you!" Gahiji pierced the man's stomach with his sword. The man continued to stand before Gahiji. The General's eyes widened in surprise. A mortal would have fallen in agony.

"That was most unkind, General," the man said calmly and quietly. "That is painful. Please remove your sword from my belly."

Runihura and the men watched as Gahiji twisted the sword in the man's stomach. *What manner of creature is he? Why do I not hear his beautiful screams of death?*

The man looked casually at the sword stabbing through his stomach. "Please remove your sword. That is slightly uncomfortable."

Gahiji removed his sword with an annoyed growl. "Why won't you die?"

"You cannot harm me," the man smiled at Gahiji calmly. "Because I'm already dead."

The men stared in amazement at the specter before them. Hamadi looked down at the man shrieking in pain from the loss of his eye. Akilah whimpered as she ran to Hamadi.

"How can you be dead? You stand before us!" Runihura exclaimed loudly.

"I have been given the curse of immortality. You do not wish to bestow this curse upon yourself. We are doomed, my pharaoh, to walk the earth eternally. Do not proceed."

Runihura chuckled as he approached the man. "You feel no pain?"

"I do feel pain. Your General hurt me when he stabbed me. I will heal in time. Heed my warning, pharaoh. Do not anger Horus with your continued defiance of his word. Turn back before you live forever, doomed to a life of eternal unrest."

"I have come this far on my quest, stranger. I will not allow you to stand in my way."

The vulture looked down at the pharaoh and spread its wings. It flapped its grand wings and screeched, making the soldiers behind him step backwards in alarm.

Runihura sliced his blade across the man's chest. The man's blood speckled the sand red at his feet. The man grabbed his chest as red blood slipped between his fingers. "The god will not allow his relic to be taken easily! Nekbet! Attack!"

The vulture opened its beak and darted towards the pharaoh. It screeched as Runihura held his hand up to his face, blocking the vulture's attack. The sharp talons reached for the pharaoh's eye as Gahiji swatted at the vulture with his sword.

"Horus removed the eye of his enemy! He will do so to you who defy his will!"

Hamadi watched as the cobra hissed, slithering towards the soldiers. The soldiers scurried back through the tunnel in alarm. Hamadi watched as the cobra turned its head towards him and Akilah. The snake slowly slithered, its tongue flicking the air ahead of it.

Akilah shivered as she backed away with Hamadi. "Hamadi, what shall we do?"

Hamadi held his sword in front of him. "Stay with me, Akilah."

Runihura reached ahead of him and grabbed the leg of the vulture as it clawed at his face. Runihura threw the vulture to the ground. "Wadjet! Your master summons you!"

The cobra ceased its advance on the soldier and the little girl. It turned his head and slithered towards the pharaoh. The vulture regained its footing as it shrieked angrily at Pharaoh Runihura.

"Attack those who threaten your master!"

Hamadi and Akilah watched as the cobra struck the vulture with its teeth. The vulture's shriek was muted by the cobra biting into its neck. Hamadi watched as the cobra spit venom at the bird. *Wadjet serves the pharaoh. According to the religious texts, Wadjet protects the pharaoh. That is why the pharaoh wears the pectoral. But why does Nekhbet not obey the pharaoh?*

Runihura and Gahiji watched as the vulture sunk to the floor silently, the venom of the cobra racing through its veins. The man stepped backward from the cobra. "You fear the cobra," Runihura said with a smile. "Nekhbet challenged my dominance. Wadjet obeys my commands. Wadjet, silence him!"

The cobra struck quickly at the man's ankle. The man screamed in pain and collapsed on the sandy floor. Runihura grinned as the cobra sunk its teeth hungrily into the man's flesh.

"You may not die from that bite, but you will suffer like a mortal until you heal," Runihura grinned.

Gahiji turned back and found his soldiers had run in fear. "Those fools have ran, my pharaoh! Only Hamadi and the girl remain!"

Runihura chuckled. "I care not. When I obtain the Eye of Horus, my enemies will unite against them. They will not stand a chance against the masses who call for the spilling of my blood. My loyal subjects will be even more willing to die for me and sacrifice their lives at my whim. My strength will surpass mortal capacity."

Gahiji approached Hamadi and Akilah. "You will lead us through the tunnels ahead! Move!"


Azizi looked into the dark tunnel, laying seemingly endless before him. The dark and quiet loomed in front of him, a terrible monster to be confronted. Azizi swallowed nervously as he stepped into the tunnel cautiously. His eyes gazed at the decorations painted onto the walls. When the green eyes blinked at him, he jumped, ceasing his movements. *What manner of sorcery is this? Is this the work of the gods or are human hands?*

Azizi felt the ground shaking beneath his feet as screams of terror pierced the air. A battalion of Egyptian soldiers raced towards him. Azizi screamed and turned suddenly, jumping out of the cavern and into the papyrus reeds to the left of the cavern. He watched in amazement as the men flew out of the tunnel's mouth, screaming and raising their hands in fear. Azizi looked into the tunnel and swallowed nervously. *I don't like the looks of this.*

Azizi crept into the mouth of the tunnel again slowly. The green eyes closed suddenly, making him gasp in surprise. *What is going on here?* Azizi brushed his fingertips lightly across the rock face. "It's smooth."

The screeching of a hawk pierced the air around him, making him hold his ears. He closed his eyes against the intensity. *King of Thieves, I know you have come.* Azizi opened his eyes to the empty hallway. *Seek not to steal the relic hidden within.* Azizi staggered forward as he held his ears. His feet sunk into the sand as he staggered forward. *Do you come with an evil heart, Seth?* Azizi felt the tunnel descend as he cautiously made his way down the decline. A bright light glistened at the end of the tunnel. Azizi felt his leg slip as he fell on one knee. His other knee dangled over a chasm. "Someone is very focused on keeping the treasures contained within this sanctuary. I won't let the pharaoh win!"

Azizi stepped into a large room decorated with murals. Torches lit the room. Azizi heard the hissing of a snake, his skin crawling in response. He grabbed a torch and gagged as the smell of death circled around him.

"My eyes! Help me!"

Azizi looked at the only moving body on the ground. Blood poured from between the man's fingers as he covered his empty eye socket. "What happened here?"

The man looked at Azizi with his good eye. "Beware of the vulture! It took my eye!"

Azizi held the torch in the air and saw a vulture laying motionless on the ground beside a slithering cobra. A trembling body laid beside the other archway out of the room.

Azizi jumped over a decaying corpse and ran beside the man laying on the ground, trembling and groaning. "Are you alright?"

The man clutched onto Azizi tightly, his body quivering. "The cobra…"

Azizi looked at the cobra opening its jaws beside his ankle. Azizi quickly shifted away and removed his dagger. The cobra hissed as Azizi prodded the cobra back with the torch. "Go away! Leave!"

The cobra hissed and quickly swayed to the side around the torch. Azizi cut the snake as it lunged for his leg. The snake hissed and retreated towards the injured man on the ground.

"Help me! Help me!"

Azizi watched as the man backed away from the snake in terror. The teenager sighed with resignation. He ran for the cobra as the snake turned quickly. The snake lunged for Azizi. Azizi kicked a pile of bones at the cobra and brought the golden dagger into the cobra's scaly skin. The snake hissed and barred its teeth as it fell dead upon the ground.

Azizi sheathed the golden dagger and looked at the man leaning against the wall.

"Thank you! I cannot thank you enough!"

"Don't thank me," Azizi said with a growl. "You did not kill my parents. That is why I spared you. Go to a physician."

Azizi turned and walked towards the man laying on the ground. He looked at the man's injury. "You were bitten by the snake!"

The man nodded slowly. "I was."

"You should be dead. Why are you not dead?"

The man smiled at the teen. "Not all who are bitten by a snake will die. Those who are dead cannot die, but the suffering remains."

Azizi held the torch beside him, illuminating the man's sweat-covered face. "You are not dead. You are talking to me now."

"I am dead. I have been dead for millennia, cursed by the gods with an immortal life. I was to guard this chamber from Sekhmet's Evil."

Azizi tightened his grip on the torch. *So the pharaoh and Gahiji are still here somewhere. They must have continued through the corridor.*

"Did Lord Osiris condemn you?" Azizi asked.

"No, I was a priest of Horus. I devoted my service to my god in death as in life."

Azizi watched the man's body tremble with the venom. "My boy, do you wish to die?"

Azizi looked down solemnly. *When my mother was killed, I wanted to die with her. She was all that I had after my father's death. She loved me and cared for me. Since then, I have been sleeping along the reeds of the Nile, sleeping in an alley filled with death, and shivering in the night air. When I reach the Land of the Dead, the reeds of the Nile will be a comfortable mat. The alley will be a comfortable home filled with warmth and my family. I will no longer be alone.*

"I have no one to give my body offerings or even to bury me. I have friends, but you never know when one will die of extreme hunger or slain by my enemies."

"Immortality is a blessing and a curse, my boy. You never die. You watch your friends, your family, your village die. You live forever, wandering this world, locked in an eternal cycle of life, never knowing peace, and never knowing rest."

Azizi swallowed nervously. "That's awful."

The man clutched onto Azizi's arm. "Find the pharaoh ahead. Be careful, my boy. Find the pharaoh, Azizi Keket. Stop him."

Azizi looked at the fallen man with disbelief. "How do you know my name?"

"Prophecy has brought you to this place, my boy. You must stop the agent of Sekhmet. I was told a boy would follow the pharaoh into the heart of darkness. I have waited a long time for your arrival. I never expected one so young."

Azizi watched the man lay on the sand groaning, his fingers twitching from the venom. *Aneksi has always talked in riddles as long as I have known her. She always said I was special, too. The others in the streets call me the 'King of Thieves' now whenever they see me. Does this mean that Horus watches me?*

"Go, Azizi. Follow him."

Azizi stood with the torch and peered into the unknown darkness ahead. He swallowed nervously, feeling chills creep up his spine. He slowly approached the void before him. He held the torch ahead of him as he stepped between the confining walls. A rocky wall appeared before him as he slowly proceeded down the passage. He reached out timidly to touch it. The subterranean tunnel turned sharply to the right. Azizi's trembling hand touched the sharp, rocky wall beside him. His face covered with sweat as the passage seemed to close in on him. The air became thin.

The walls crept closer to him, blocking him from walking easily. His palms became wet as his chest was constricted by the rock. *I hate cramped spaces. I can handle darkness, but I cannot stand being confined. The tunnel curved to the left and further into the cliff. Osiris, guide me through here. Now I know how you felt when Seth nailed you into that coffin.*

The ground shook under his feet as he gripped onto the rock tightly. *What is the pharaoh doing?!* The loud, piercing shriek of a hawk returned. He released the walls as he held onto his ears. He grit his teeth against the pain echoing in his ear drums.

Azizi whimpered as he gripped his ears. The tremors of the ground threw him to one knee. His vision darkened as the ground rumbled beneath his knee. *Get up, Azizi! Get up! Remember what Darwishi's First Lesson: The strong stay on their feet!* Azizi lifted his head and struggled to his feet. He gripped onto the rockface, following the contour of the wall. *Keep moving. If the pharaoh finds you, he'll kill you here. There will be no witnesses.* Azizi opened his eyes and touched the sand at his feet. *Will Amsi coming looking for me if he knew my body was here? Would he bury me or leave me to rot in this passage?* Azizi sighed as he tightened his grip on the torch. *I only have myself. I can only rely on myself. It shouldn't matter to me if Amsi finds me.* He slipped through another passage which lead into a chamber filled with gold chests, precious jewels, and statues of orichalcum. Boxes of jewels lined the path to the next series of tunnels.

Azizi held his breath in astonishment of the wealth before him. He had stolen money from drunken men who had fallen unconscious on the road. He had dexterously untied money pouches from the belts of the Nobility. He had stolen bread and, on occasion, some sweet treats from the bakery. Nothing in his eight years of living on the streets had he had the chance to steal anything like this. Azizi looked among the riches and found a golden armband. With a grin, he slipped it onto his left arm. *I make this look good!*

His eyes glittered as he looked at a large blue sapphire sitting on a pile of gold coins. Azizi kneeled in front of the chest as his eyes worshipped the precious jewel. *Sweet Osiris, tell me I am not dreaming!* Azizi's brown eyes watched as the blue sapphire glittered in the light of the torch. *This would help feed Jamila and Giladi for years! They wouldn't have to worry about money or food again!*

Azizi reached for the jewel and let his fingertips glide longingly against the surface. With a shaking hand, he cradled the jewel in his palm. *I could be rich! I could become richer than the pharaoh! I could buy anything! I could be powerful like the Nobility!* Azizi's smile faded. He could become rich like the Nobles. Here was his chance, his ticket to freedom. *How could I consider becoming one of them? I see how they behave. I see how they treat others. I have longed for one day having enough to eat and a roof over my head. Now is my chance finally to acquire that which I have desired.* Azizi chuckled. *Can I see myself sitting in a villa with servants to wait on me hand-and-foot? Can I see myself sitting and dining on fish and antelope? It would make*

*me happy, but would that give me true happiness?*
*Sleeping beside the Nile may not be the best quarters for*
*a peaceful rest, but when I see the stars at night, and the*
*gentle glow of the moon, nothing can compare to the*
*serenity it brings. I make my bed under the stars and the*
*Eye of Thoth. As much as I would like things to be*
*different, I do not see that as making me happy.*

Azizi smiled at the gem. "I have to show the others the
riches of the gods!"

Azizi placed the jewel and several handful of coins in the
hidden sack under his black cloak. He dropped several
handfuls of gold coin into his bag. *This will help Giladi,*
*Sekani, and the others. I'm sure they'd appreciate a little*
*money for a very good dinner! I can come back for the*
*rest later.*

Azizi continued into the next series of tunnels as the fire
began to extinguish. The teen's face covered in sweat as
each breath became a struggle. The air thinned around
him as he walked down the path. *I must keep going.*

Azizi grit his teeth, determined to continue through the
dark tunnel. An archway appeared out of the darkness
ahead. Azizi stepped close to the archway. The golden
arch was decorated with hieroglyphics. The teen
examined the markings carefully. *If only Amsi taught me*
*how to read, this would be so much easier! Note to self:*
*have Amsi teach me how to read.*

"My pharaoh, you cannot do this!" Azizi heard coming
from inside the room ahead of him. "You cannot
desecrate the sanctuary of the gods! Please!"

Azizi ran through the archway and saw stairs leading down to the room below him. His hands touched the balcony as he looked into the chamber below him. A soldier was standing in front of an altar with his arms spread in front of the pharaoh. *That's the soldier who wanted to help Ferryn! Does he know what he is risking by standing against the pharaoh?*

Hamadi looked into Pharaoh Runihura's eyes. "I will not let you desecrate this sacred place!"

Runihura glared at Hamadi. "Be careful, Hamadi. You already have one foot in the grave. Do not make me push you in completely."

Gahiji narrowed his eyes as he held onto Akilah's wrist. "You foolish boy! You dare to stand in the pharaoh's way?"

"The relics of the gods are not meant for mortal hands!" Hamadi exclaimed loudly, his voice echoing through the large, sunken room.

Pharaoh Runihura lunged at Hamadi and wrapped his hands around Hamadi's throat. Azizi watched as the large hawk hovering above the altar blinked its eyes. Azizi's eyes widened in disbelief as the hawk looked at him and blinked his eyes. *Great Osiris! That bird is alive!*

Hamadi gagged as the pharaoh's grip constricted his windpipe. He grabbed the pharaoh's wrists.

"My pharaoh! Above you!" Gahiji exclaimed.

Runihura lifted his head as the hawk's talons reached toward him. Runihura removed his hands from Hamadi's throat and the hawk returned to its dormant state.

Hamadi sunk to his knees holding his throat and coughing. The pharaoh glared at the kneeling soldier and looked at the altar. Pharaoh Runihura opened the small chest sitting on the altar.

"Finally! I have gained the Scroll of Horus!" Runihura screamed in triumph.

Azizi watched as a brilliant, blinding light filled the room when the pharaoh opened the box. Azizi held his arms in front of his eyes to shield them from the radiant light. He grit his teeth against the painful brilliance as he heard the pharaoh laughing.

Pharaoh Runihura looked with a pleased grin as the light dissipated. "Nobody will be able to stop me!" the pharaoh said as he held the golden box in his hands.

*You shall find my relic!*

Azizi and Hamadi looked up at the hawk above the altar. Its eyes were glowing a fiery light. The hawk screeched loudly as it lunged its beak forward towards Gahiji. Hamadi lifted his head with a startled scream.

*This could get dangerous.* Azizi backed away towards the archway and ran from the room.

Gahiji swung his sword towards the stone beak as he continued to hold onto Akilah's wrist. Runihura placed the box under his arm as he ran for the stairs. The hawk saw the pharaoh's escape and opened its beak towards the pharaoh. Gahiji raced up the stairs towards the pharaoh. Hamadi looked behind him as the stone hawk quickly approached him and the General.

The ground began to shake under them as rocks fell from above. Hamadi ran from the room as the large bird missed his foot by inches. The passage shivered and quaked with their escape. Runihura clutched his stolen treasure tightly against him as he fled. A brilliant light shown behind them as they escaped.

Akilah screamed as the floor began to crumble beneath her feet. "Lord Gahiji! Hurry!"

Gahiji pulled the child along roughly, his fingers digging into her skin. "Those cowards who deserted us will pay for their flight!"

Hamadi turned his head as he saw spears flying from the sides of the walls. As they ran, the spears came closer. The light behind him illuminated the hallway as a series of harpoons raced their way towards them. The soldier's eyes widened as Gahiji grabbed him and turned him around the corner.

Azizi raced into the large room where the wounded man had disappeared. His feet carried him swiftly out of the cavern where he hid among the papyrus reeds at the entrance to avoid detection by the pharaoh. He watched the pharaoh and the others race out of the entrance as the rock collapsed, blocking entry.

Pharaoh Runihura breathed quickly as he held onto the golden box. Gahiji continued to hold onto the little girl's wrist as he fanned his sweating head. Hamadi leaned against the side of the cliff breathing heavily as he looked into the evening sky.

"That was a close call, my king," Gahiji said.

"Yes, too close," Runihura said, glaring at Hamadi. The pharaoh slowly approached Hamadi and removed his dagger. He stepped against the soldier and placed the blade against the soldier's throat. "Should you defy me again, should you stand against me, Hamadi, I will cut your throat. Do you understand me?"

"My king, I-."

Runihura pressed the blade against Hamadi's perspiring skin. "Do you understand me?" the pharaoh asked him, wild ferocity plain in his eyes.

"Yes, my pharaoh," Hamadi said quietly.

Runihura backslapped the soldier, sending him to his knees in front of him. "You should be happy that I am a man of patience."

Azizi watched from his hiding place as Gahiji approached the soldier. The Captain of the Guard kicked Hamadi in the stomach.

"He is the only soldier who remained. The others have fled. That is the only thing which has saved your head today, my boy."

Runihura turned his head to the path. The soldiers were waiting at the bottom of the path. "Those fools will regret abandoning me! I will make certain of that."

Runihura grinned at the box below him. "We must reach Edfû for the Scroll of Horus."

"I'm sure we will find a way, my dear General Gahiji." Pharaoh Runihura glared down the path towards his army. He grabbed the reigns of the horses and lead them down the rocky path. At the foot of the cliff, he looked with malice towards his army. "You cowards! You fools! How dare you abandon your great leader!" The pharaoh's lip curled in disgust. "You have all made a very dangerous…mistake."

Gahiji stepped beside the pharaoh. "My lord, should we make camp for the night? It is late."

Runihura looked up at the moon. "Very well," he groaned with annoyance. "No one is permitted to refill their water ration at the oasis. That is your punishment for your cowardice."

Azizi followed the pharaoh and his entourage as they fled the cliffs. He had hidden his horse from view among the rocky terrain some distance away from the pharaoh's sight. The pharaoh had made camp in the desert. Azizi kept his horse at a distance as he raced towards the oasis. Azizi lead his horse into the lush land in the middle of the desert. Azizi's eyes widened as a large smile crept onto his face as the moonlight cast a glittering reflection on the water. A lake was formed in the middle of the oasis. Palm trees and plants circled the fertile land. *I think I found my new home.* Azizi dismounted from his horse and walked slowly beside the water. He kneeled beside the water and scooped a handful into his mouth. When the warm liquid touched him, he licked his lips. He sipped from his hand with a contented sigh. He sat on the bank of the lake and looked up at the moon. The teen yawned as his body relaxed.

Pharaoh Runihura now has the Scroll of Horus. *He has the first item needed to gain immortality. I need to warn Aneksi when I return to Heliopolis. If only I could steal that box from the pharaoh! General Gahiji will keep watch. I know he will. Osiris, please keep me safe in my slumber.* Azizi laid beside the bank as he looked up at the stars. It's hard to keep my eyes open. *I must keep an eye out for the pharaoh.* Azizi yawned as he closed his eyes slowly. *I can't stay awake. Goodnight, mother and father.*

## XXXVII

### <u>My Friend or My Father?</u>

Amsi sighed as he leaned against the wall of the Kaemwaset family lands. The mid-day sun beat down on him as he looked towards the desert. Nakia and Nassar were standing beside him. Nassar's eyes watched the nearby Bedouin settlement closely. When Sumati passed along the edge of the camp, she turned to him and waved with a smile. The slave smiled and waved back pleasantly.

Amsi groaned as he skipped a rock across the grass. "Where is he?"

"I hope he didn't get lost in the desert," Nakia said, slightly fanning his master with feathers.

"I wish Azizi could be here for the celebration tonight. Tonight I will become an adult in the eyes of the Nobility."

Nakia looked down at his master. "I doubt your father would willingly open the doors and allow him entrance."

"I know he wouldn't, Nakia. But I'm certain we will have leftover food and I know he would appreciate some of it."

Nakia nodded. "It's too bad Issâm isn't here. He prepared the ointment for Baruti's Rite of Passage. Tabari helped him, I believe. It was so long ago."

"He-o, ah-ra," Nassar said happily as Amsi turned his head.

Zahra ran towards Amsi and smiled. "Greetings, Amsi. Did you have fun the other night?"

Amsi nodded. "Yes, I did. Qamra was a little slow the day after, but I don't think my father noticed. He had to go to the pharaoh's palace."

Zahra waved at the twins. "Hello, Nakia. Hello, Nassar."

The twins bowed their heads reverently. "Hello, Zahra," Nakia said with a smile.

"Tonight, my family is having a celebration. Do you wish to come?"

Zahra smiled. "We could dance again."

Amsi swallowed nervously as he noticed his fists were becoming damp. "Yes, absolutely."

"Am-i! Hor!" Nassar exclaimed as he put his hand on Amsi's shoulder and pointed towards the desert.

Amsi and Nakia turned their heads towards the desert to see a horse approaching. Amsi stood on his feet and watched the lone horseman approach swiftly. Zahra stood beside Amsi and watched as the horse approached the Al-Sakhir family land.

"Azizi!" Amsi exclaimed.

The horseman rode past the Al-Sakhir lands swiftly. Amsi sighed with disappointment.

"I hoped it was Azizi."

"Your friend?" Zahra asked.

Amsi nodded. "He left to search for the Zeniah Oasis. He hasn't returned yet."

Zahra looked towards the camp and tapped her mouth with her fingers in thought. "I could show you the oasis, Amsi."

"You know where it is?"

Zahra nodded. "Yes, I can show you."

Amsi looked towards the sky. "We should have enough time to search for it before the ceremony. Nakia, get the horses ready."

Nakia bowed his head. "Yes, Lord Amsi!" Nakia ran towards the stables.

"I hope you can come to the celebration tonight, Zahra."

Zahra smiled at Amsi and blushed. "Do you think your father will allow me to attend?"

Amsi smiled. "You are my guest. He should not turn you away if I willingly invite you. You could probably bribe him if you brought some money or some jewelry."

Zahra chuckled. "That can be arranged." Zahra looked towards the stable. "Do you think I could bring the twins, too?"

"Nassar and Nakia? They will serving the food, I believe. My father has told me that Qamra will definitely be there to serve."

Zahra shook her head. "No, I was talking about Sumati and Shera."

"I think Nassar likes Sumati," Amsi said with a mischievous grin.

"Nassar, do you like Sumati?" Zahra asked with a sly grin.

Nassar chuckled and lowered his head. He hid his eyes from Zahra and Amsi's eyes. "Ye-f."

"Sumati's been talking about you, Nassar. Shera likes Nakia. You can tell him that, Nassar."

Nassar giggled, nodding his head.

"I need to prepare my horse. I will be back shortly, Amsi!" Zahra said, turning and running towards her settlement.

Amsi watched with a grin as her long dress flowed in the wind behind her. Her long, black hair whipped behind her as she ran. He could see her beaded necklace fly side-to-side as she ran towards her horse. Amsi leaned against the wall with a grin.

*I keep watching her! What is wrong with me?*

"Nassar, why can't I stop watching her?" Amsi asked as he rubbed his sweaty hands against his white tunic. Nassar tapped his ear and shook his head. Amsi sighed and yelled loudly. "Why can't I stop watching her?!"

Nassar bent over and put his open hand close to the ground. He gradually straightened his body and put his open hand on the top of Amsi's head. "G-ow up. O-ger."

"Every time I see her, my hands become wet and I don't know what to say! It's as if my mind goes blank!"

Nassar snickered. "Am-i w-ove."

Amsi's eyes widened as he turned to Nassar. "I'm in love? No!"

Nassar nodded his head with a chuckle. "Ye-f!"

"No, no! It can't be!"

Nassar watched as Nakia approached with Hamza, Munir, and Hadi. "Ah-e-a! Am-i w-ove Ah-ra!"

Nakia grinned as he looked down at Amsi. "You're in love with Zahra, Master Amsi?"

"Me? No!" Amsi exclaimed, tightening his fists.

Nakia laughed. "You're blushing."

"No, I am not!"

"You are, too!" Nakia chuckled.

Amsi folded his arms defiantly. "I am not!"

"If you are, Master Amsi, that's great!  It's not a bad thing to fall in love."

Nassar watched as Zahra approached on her horse.

"Well, boys, are we ready?" the girl asked as she smiled at the teenaged boys.

Amsi grabbed Hadi's reigns.  "You are sure you know where this oasis is?"

Zahra nodded. "My people wander the desert.  We know where to find many places."

Nakia grabbed Hamza's reigns as the black stallion snorted. "Good boy, Hamza." Nakia pulled himself into the saddle as he watched Nassar mount Munir.

"Let's go, Chione!" Zahra exclaimed, giving her white horse a slight shaking of the reigns.

Amsi and the twins followed behind Zahra.  Amsi watched Zahra ride with expertise and grace.  Nakia raced ahead of them, cheering loudly with a grin.  Nassar dug his heels into Munir and coaxed the horse faster.

Amsi rode beside Zahra, watching the twins ride ahead of them.  Nassar and Nakia yipped and cheered as they leaned forward in their saddles.  "You would think they were born on horses," Amsi said.

Zahra smiled. "They seem to be very knowledgeable. Why did your friend wander into the desert if he does not know where he is going?"

Amsi sighed with a shrug. "Azizi goes where he wishes. He has no home or family and I've hardly seen him afraid of anything. There is only one thing that frightens him."

"Oh? What would that be? The dark?"

Amsi shook his head. "No, Azizi likes the dark. He's always lurking in the shadows during the day and he enjoys the cover that night brings. Azizi's always said that nothing can hurt him in the dark."

Zahra nodded. "The dark brings many dangers in the desert. The *Nuu* wander the desert. They have raided our camp twice in the desert. They claim to be searching for ancient relics."

Amsi's eyes widened as he turned to Zahra. "The *Nuu* robbed you?"

Zahra nodded again. "They claim to be looking for the pharaoh's rightful property. We told them we have no objects other than our crafts and our supplies."

"If I hear they did it again to you, I will hunt them down and take back anything that they take from you."

Zahra smiled. "Thank you, Amsi, but they are a dangerous people. They are under the pharaoh's command."

The pharaoh thinks that he can harass innocent people for no reason! How dare he intimidate Zahra and her people!

He will not get away with that! Amsi tightened his grip on the reigns. "That is not a reason to terrorize you."

"My father protects our people. We can defend ourselves, but the *Nuu* are many."

Amsi turned to Zahra. "Azizi and I have been trying to find these relics which the pharaoh seeks. We are trying to stop him, but it's not easy. I don't have any scrolls which speak of the prophecy. Azizi said someone called Aneksi has a number of prophecy scrolls."

"Have you ever met her?"

Amsi shook his head. "No. I have heard him mention her. We're trying to stop him."

Zahra reached out her hand and touched his arm. "Do you know what the pharaoh will do to you should he discover this?"

Amsi nodded. "Yes. Azizi and I know the consequences if we are caught." Amsi lowered his head and tightened his grip on the reigns. "The pharaoh killed Issâm. He was a generous old priest who kept the secret of Thoth and took it to his grave. The pharaoh and my father removed Nassar's tongue. I wish I could have stopped him, but I was only an infant."

Zahra looked ahead as Nassar and Nakia rode. Nakia leaned back in his saddle and tilted his head back with a loud laugh. Nassar's fist rose into the air as he leaned forward in the saddle.

"That must have been awful for him."

"Qamra told us Nassar nearly died from shock that night. They are my friends, Zahra. I don't approve of how the pharaoh treats them." Amsi shook his head. "He treats them both worse than wild dogs."

Zahra lowered her head. "We are labeled enemies of the pharaoh, but that is not true. We just yearn for a place where we can settle. Travel flows through our veins. Movement gives our lives meaning. We do not seek revolution. We simply seek peace."

Amsi looked at Zahra. "That is what Azizi and I seek, as well. We do not want to see the pharaoh obtain the items. If the pharaoh is a tyrant now without any immortal power, can you imagine him with the power of the gods at his disposal? He could bring an end to everything!"

Zahra looked at Amsi with worry on her face. "And yet you are determined to stop him, knowing that if you are caught, you would face torture beyond your wildest imagination? Amsi," Zahra said with concern. "Amsi, he could kill you."

Amsi wiped his sweaty palm on his white skirt nervously. "I know. He has already threatened me."

"Amsi, don't get yourself killed. You are a nice person. I like you."

Amsi swallowed nervously as he felt a drop of sweat course down his neck. "I like you, too, Zahra."

Zahra blushed with a smile and lowered her head.

Nakia smiled at his twin as they rode beside one another. "Isn't this great, Nassar?"

Nassar nodded with a smile. *I can't remember the last time I was allowed to roam free beyond the family walls! I'm usually kept inside the confines of the home. Nakia trains Master Amsi with his horsemanship and archery. My duties restrict me to the home where the master keeps a vigilant eye on my every move. He knows I cannot speak and he knows that I cannot hear. So, he knows I cannot say anything when he mistreats me. This is a freedom I have not experienced for a very long time. I'm glad I can share this with you, my brother.*

Nakia smiled. "Let me hear your battle cry, Nassar!" Nakia shrieked and yipped with a wide grin.

Nassar chuckled and growled angrily at the open desert ahead of them. Nakia laughed at his twin's battle cry. Nassar laughed with his twin as they continued to ride ahead.

Nakia's eyes widened as he saw a large object ahead. "My master! I believe something is ahead!"

"What is it, Nakia?"

Nassar narrowed his eyes. "A-Ree!"

Amsi raised an eyebrow. "A what?"

"It's a tree! I think we found it!"

Zahra nodded her head as she pointed ahead of them. "That is the Zeniah Oasis!"

"I wonder if Azizi is there!"

"Only one way to find out, Amsi," Zahra said with a smile. "Heya, Chione!"

Zahra's horse bolted ahead between the twins. Amsi smiled at her. *She's good. Really good.*

The twins followed Zahra into the oasis. Amsi arrived and looked around at the peaceful surroundings. The lake glistened in the mid-day sun. The breeze was warm as it blew through the several palm trees speckled across the tiny oasis.

Amsi looked around. "Azizi?"

Nassar dismounted Munir and kneeled beside the lake. He ran his hands across a patch of grass which had been pressed flat. "Ah-e-ah! Wook here!"

Nakia dismounted Hamza and kneeled beside his brother. He nodded his head silently. "Someone has laid here recently." Nakia pulled a blade of grass and sniffed it. "Azizi was sleeping here."

Amsi watched in amazement as Nassar pointed nearby to a patch of naked ground. The grass had been ripped from soil. Nassar talked to his brother using his guttural groans and signals. He pointed to the horse and made a motion to eat. Nakia nodded in agreement.

"Azizi was definitely here," Nakia said standing on his feet. "His horse ate a patch of grass over there." Nassar crawled along the ground on his hands and knees, sniffing the ground. The twin ran his hand lightly along the delicate blades of grass as he continued to crawl on his knees.

"Does he think he is a dog?" Zahra asked.

Nakia shook his head. "No, Nassar learned tracking skills from our father. He learned how to track prey through the jungle by the blades of grass and the depression of the soil." Nakia smiled proudly at his brother. "My father taught him well."

"I was wondering why he was acting so peculiar," Zahra said.

"He's trying to discern in what direction Azizi went."

Nassar put his ear to the ground and rubbed the grass with the palm of his hand. He lifted his head and jumped to his feet. He dashed through the foliage. Nakia followed him through the bushes to the sand of the desert. Nassar looked to the left and pointed towards his twin. "Hor-Cack!"

Nakia ran towards Zahra and Amsi. "There are tracks at the border! Follow me! Come, Hamza!" Nakia grabbed Hamza's reigns and pulled him towards the boarder. Amsi coaxed Hadi through the brush and stood beside the twins when he emerged from the oasis.

Zahra's eyes widened as her horse stood beside Amsi. "There must be a huge group of men!"

"Only one pair of tracks leads from the oasis," Nakia said. "Azizi is gone."

Amsi looked into the desert towards the direction of the tracks. Where is Azizi going? Did he encounter the *Nuu*? Was he running from them? If he did, did he escape?

"The desert sand will make it easy for us to track Azizi," Zahra said.

"Who knows where they went? We cannot spend the rest of the day wandering the desert. Master Amsi, you have your celebration tonight and if your father does not see you there, he will be very angry."

Nassar nodded emphatically. He poked his twin's shoulder and clenched his fist angrily. He pounded his fist angrily quick and hard.

"Nassar's right, he'll beat us if you are not attending."

"Nassar, can you track him?" Amsi asked.

Nassar nodded at Amsi and pointed to Nakia.

"Master Amsi, Nassar cannot wander alone. With our tattoos designating us as Kaemwaset's slaves, we cannot roam without permission," Nakia said.

Amsi looked into the desert. "If Azizi is in trouble, he needs help."

Nakia coughed as he covered his mouth. He gripped onto Hamza's reigns tightly as his frail frame trembled from the force of his cough. "Nassar could possibly go if I claim that he is sick and laying in the slave home. Maybe Karida or Laila can take his place."

Nassar nodded and pointed to his chest.

"What if you are discovered, Nassar? You'd be captured and dragged back to the Al-Sakhir lands by your wrists," Zahra said with concern.

"I would go, but I have to attend my ceremony," Amsi sighed. "I wish I didn't have to go. I'd rather make sure Azizi is safe."

*What do I do? I want to find Azizi and make certain he is not in the hands of the pharaoh. If the* Nuu *find him, they'll take him right to Runihura. My father would be irate if I did not attend my own ceremony. I would dishonor him. How can I choose between my friend and my father? Why must I choose?*

Nakia coughed again as Nassar stood and held his brother on the saddle. Nassar looked at Amsi staring blankly into the sand at his feet.

*Nassar is a good tracker, but my father would be furious if he were not serving the meal. Could I convince father that Nassar has taken ill and lies in the slave home? Nassar could track Azizi and make certain he's safe. I love my father and I want to make him proud, but I cannot ignore my duty to my friend.*

"Nassar, track Azizi. Return to the Al-Sakhir lands as fast as you can! I will find a way to explain your absence."

Zahra looked down at Amsi. "Is this the right choice, Amsi? You're sending Nassar into possible danger."

Amsi looked up at Zahra, his fists clenched tightly, his mind doubting the correctness of his action. "I cannot abandon my friend," Amsi said, his brow low. "He may be poor and he may be expendable in the eyes of my father and the king, but he is my friend. I won't let him face the jackals alone."

Nakia dismounted Hamza and stood in front of Nassar. He gave his twin a small smile as he put his hands on Nassar's shoulders. "Take care of yourself out there, my brother."

Nassar reached up and cupped Nakia's cheek with his right hand. "I wove you, Ah-e-ah."

"I love you, Nassar," Nakia said as he embraced his twin. Nakia rested his head against Nassar's chest as Nassar wrapped his arms protectively around him.

Nakia looked up at Zahra, swallowing nervously. "My brother is all I have left of my people…and my family."

Zahra leaned back in her saddle, looking sadly down at the parting twins.

Nassar kissed Nakia on the top of the head. "I wi-come back."

Nakia pulled back from the tight embrace with his twin. He nodded sadly. "I will miss you, Nassar. Please take care of yourself and return quickly."

Nassar looked down at Amsi and kneeled before his master. "I wi-come back, Ma-ger Am-i."

*Am I doing the right thing?* "Thank you, Nassar. Return quickly," Amsi said, placing a hand on Nassar's shoulder.

Nassar stood and mounted Munir. He looked down at Nakia and bowed his head. He shook the reigns and rode into the desert following the tracks.

"Your brother is very special to you," Zahra said with a smile.

Nakia nodded slowly as he watched his brother ride into the distance alone. "My mother always taught us a very important lesson. Always say 'I love you' when you leave someone close to you because that may be the last time you ever see them." Nakia wiped away a tear coming down his cheek. *Nassar, may the gods watch over you.*

## XXXVIII

### <u>Coming of Age</u>

Nassar tightened his grip on Munir's reigns as he rode quickly. His eyes scanned the sand as footprints and hoof prints intermingled in the sand. Nassar struggled to keep what little hearing he had sharp for *Nuu* and the thieves of the desert. Both would not hesitate to turn him into the pharaoh's guard for a profit. He would be returned to his master as an escaping slave, a crime punishable by whatever cruelty the master desired.

*I'm deaf and I'm mute. What else can they take from me? I do not fear death now.*

Nassar's knees clutched onto Munir's body as the horse continued to race through the desert, following the multitude of tracks. This was a large group of people.

Nassar's eyes widened as he saw something gold glittering in the desert sand. He pulled on the reigns tightly as Munir came to a stop. Nassar jumped off of the horse's back and kneeled beside the twinkling object. He reached down and plucked it from the sand.

*It's a gold ring with red, green, and blue gems. There's only one man who can afford this. Pharaoh Runihura is in this desert. I'm following his tracks!* Nassar swallowed nervously as he looked at the golden ring in his hand. *Azizi is following the pharaoh! The Nuu do not carry this type of wealth with them.*

Nassar stood and placed the ring on his finger. He mounted Munir and continued to ride, following the tracks. *Azizi's in big trouble if he's caught by the pharaoh. Master Amsi would want me to do anything to keep him safe. If I have to fight the pharaoh, I will. If I have to fight the gods, I will do it for Master Amsi and my twin brother. I will not disappoint Master Amsi.*

Nassar's eyes widened as tall pillars came into his view. A large temple slowly approached him, along with a tall arch flanked by statues of Ptah. The slave's eyes widened as he saw the multitude of people wandering the streets. Two soldiers stood outside the gates. They watched Nassar approach and crossed their spears as he rode towards the arch.

"Halt! What is your business here?"

Nassar looked at the soldiers glaring at him. He tightened his grip on the reigns as he looked into the crowded streets. I have to get through somehow.

"I haff get my ma-er's muvver."

The one soldier raised a curious eyebrow as he looked at the slave. "Speak clearly."

Nassar pointed into his mouth and shook his head. "I haff mo gung!"

"What is your business here?" the soldier asked again.

"Ma-er's muvver here."

The men exchanged confused glances and looked at Nassar. "What?"

Nassar nodded. "Ma-er ick."

The men uncrossed their spears and stepped aside. "Get going before we lose our patience with you."

Nassar bowed his head and rode through the archway quickly. He rode through the crowd, his eyes searching the crowd for signs of Azizi or the pharaoh. Nassar's eyes widened as he saw a group of soldiers marching around a corner. People were stepping aside to let the army through the road.

Nassar grinned triumphantly. He followed the army and turned his horse down a road. Nassar coaxed Munir down a narrow street to follow them. *I can't be seen by the army or the pharaoh.*

Four people stood in front of him as he made his way through the street. The four tall men smiled at him as they stood in front of Munir. "Move," Nassar said.

The men smiled quietly at him, pulling back their black cloaks to reveal scimitars.

Nassar's eyes widened in alarm as he moved Munir backward. He felt a sharp object pointed at his back and he tensed.

"Grab him," one of the men growled.

Nassar grabbed onto Munir's reigns tightly as the men swarmed him, grabbing at his white skirt and his arms. "Ge-off me!"

The men grabbed Nassar's arms and wrapped their arms around his waist. They pulled him off of Munir and threw him to the ground. Two men held his upper arms tightly. Two men grabbed his wrists, effectively immobilizing the thin slave's arms.

Nassar swallowed nervously as the leader smiled down at him. "I haff mo' momey."

The leader examined Nassar's fingers and saw the golden ring. The man smiled as he slipped it from his finger. "No money, boy? What do you call this?"

Nassar gasped as the leader placed a dagger's blade at Nassar's throat. The leader grinned seeing Nassar's fear. "You would lie to me, boy?"

Nassar slowly shook his head.

"We should cut your throat and send you to Merciful Ptah."

Nassar struggled against his captors as the leader backhanded him roughly. Nassar closed his eyes tightly as the leader grabbed his jaw and tilted his head backward.

"Thank you for the pretty ring. Tell Ptah that Harith sent you to meet him!" The leader placed the blade against Nassar's throat. He tightened his grip on the blade.

"Stop!"

The group turned their heads and saw Azizi standing nearby. Harith grinned as he stood straight, removing the blade from Nassar's throat. "What business do you have here?"

"Let him go."

Harith grinned. "He is our catch. This is our bounty," Harith said, holding the golden ring to Azizi's eyes. "Find your own."

Azizi's horse slowly approached the group of thieves. "You will let him go."

Harith smiled. "Kill the prisoner."

Nassar screamed as the men removed their scimitars. Azizi narrowed his eyes and removed his arm from his black cloak. He slid down a band of gold around his upper arm and revealed a tattoo.

"Wait!" Harith cried loudly.

Harith approached the young teen slowly and looked upon the tattoo. "That is the mark of Osiris."

Azizi glared at the man standing beside him and grabbed the rope tying the man's cloak. "Release him this instant before I get angry!" Azizi growled, kicking Harith backward.

"Release the prisoner."

The men released Nassar, dropping him on the ground. Azizi jumped off of his horse and ran to Nassar. He tilted Nassar's face upwards. "Nakia?"

Nassar shook his head.

"What are you doing here?"

"Fi-you. Maffer Am-i -ent me."

Azizi looked into Nassar's eyes. "On your feet. Get up."

Nassar stood on his feet and looked down at Azizi. Azizi turned to Harith. "He is a slave of my friend. You will not harm him."

"What is your name, child?" Harith asked.

"Azizi Keket."

The group of men exchanged glances and whispered amongst themselves. "You are the boy! You are the one who stood against the pharaoh!"

Azizi narrowed his eyes at the tall leader. "You were going to kill my friend!" Azizi punched Harith in the stomach hard. "Leave him alone!"

Nassar pointed to Harith's hand. "Ri-g, A-ee."

"Ring? Return Nassar's property!" Azizi grabbed the ring from Harith and examined it. "This is the pharaoh's ring." Azizi placed the ring on his finger and turned to Nassar. "I cannot lose the pharaoh. I'm following him to Edfû."

Nassar looked down at the young teen. "I go wiff you."

Azizi shook his head. "No, Nassar. If Kaemwaset sees you are missing, then he will be angry."

"Maffer Am-i want you -afe."

Azizi placed his hands on Nassar's shoulder. "Tell Amsi I am alright and I am tracking the pharaoh."

Nassar nodded slowly and bowed before Azizi. "Tank you, Maffer A-ee."

Azizi looked up at the evening sky. "It's almost night. Return to Amsi, Nassar. Harith," Azizi said, turning his head to the other thief. "I'm going to need a boat."


Imani stood in front of her son admiring him with a pleasant smile. Her hands were folded in front of her as Nakia smoothed Amsi's knee-length pleaded skirt. Nakia looked Amsi in the eye worriedly as he fastened golden cuffs around Amsi's wrists. The slave kneeled in front of his master and placed Amsi's fingers through golden rings adorned with diamonds and amber jewels.

Imani smiled at her son. "I have awaited this day, my son. Today the Nobility shall recognize you as a man worthy of overseeing his father's lands upon his death."

Amsi looked up at his mother as Nakia placed golden anklets around Amsi's ankles. "Mother, I do not wish to disappoint father, but I do not wish to follow the path he has set before me. I wish to follow my own path. I do not wish to marry Ife."

"You shall break your father's heart, Amsi. He has dreamed great things for you just as I have."

Amsi sighed with resignation. "What if I cannot manage my father's lands? I do not wish to follow in my father's footsteps. I'm sorry, mother."

Imani approached her son and placed her hands gently on his shoulders. "Your father wants to see you happy. I want to see you settled with a woman of good heart."

"Ife does not have a good heart, mother. You see how she treats Nakia and Nassar when she visits. She wants to separate Nakia from his brother and I see how she treats her own servants."

Imani looked down at Nakia. "Where is your brother? He should have been here to help my son prepare for the celebration."

Nakia swallowed nervously and looked up at his mistress. "My brother is running an errand for Master Amsi, my lady."

"Should your father notice his absence, he will not be pleased."

Amsi nodded. "Nassar is following my orders. He is my slave and he is doing what is told."

Nakia looked up at Amsi, his hands beginning to shake from Amsi's harsh tone. Imani nodded silently as she stepped back from her son.

A harsh knock sounded on the door, announcing Kaemwaset's entrance into the teen's room. Kaemwaset smiled at his son. "There's my young man!" Amsi's father put his hands on Amsi's shoulders. "Tonight I know you will make me proud. You have grown so quickly."

"Thank you, father," Amsi said blankly. I hope Nassar gets back soon. Azizi, are you alright?

"The Nobility are waiting in the Banquet Hall, my son." Kaemwaset looked down at Nakia, glaring at the slave. "You and your brother better not embarrass me tonight. Do you understand me?"

Nakia nodded and bowed his head reverently. "Yes, sir."

"Where is your worthless brother? Why is he not here, Nakia?"

Nakia swallowed nervously. "He is sick in the slave quarters, my lord. Qamra thought it best to leave him rest. Laila will be serving tonight in his stead."

Imani looked down at Amsi with a questioning glance. Amsi quickly shook his head for her not to question.

Kaemwaset leaned over to the kneeling twin and glared at him menacingly. "If I hear one word out of you other than 'Yes, master,' I will punish you severely. Do you understand me, you little useless boy?"

Nakia nodded sadly. "Yes, master."

Kaemwaset stood and smiled at his son. "Come with me, my boy!"

Kaemwaset put his arm around his son and walked him out of the room. Nakia and Imani followed close behind down the hall. Kaemwaset turned right and lead his son into the spacious Banquet Hall. Nobles in fine linen were clapping and cheering as their ragged slaves stood beside them, bowing their heads.

"Nobles of Heliopolis! Today we celebrate my son's journey into manhood! He has fulfilled the ritual and today we celebrate his passage into a new life! Drink, my friends! Eat, my humble friends! Celebrate! Enjoy yourselves and may we bless Rā for this day!"

Amsi and Kaemwaset walked to a long table lined with fish and various meats. Fruits, vegetables, and dates covered the table making Nakia's stomach growl with hunger. Amsi sat beside his father as Karida began to dance to entertain the crowd.

Laila kneeled before her father and placed a tray of dates in front of him. Amsi looked at his half-sister, watching her as she held a date up to him with folded hands.

"I have longed for this day, my son," Kaemwaset said with a smile. "I am pleased that you have grown into a man who will one day oversee my lands and my servants."

Amsi looked down as Nakia held a plate of lamb and cooked broccoli. Nakia closed his eyes and bowed his head as he presented the plate to Amsi.

"Master Kaemwaset, I present Lord Mahoma Re-Nefer and his beloved daughter, Ife Re-Nefer!" Qamra said with a bow.

Kaemwaset smiled as he stood. He walked past Laila and grabbed Mahoma's hands. "I am grateful for your arrival! You are my honored guests this night." Kaemwaset turned toward Amsi. "My son, come and greet your future wife!"

Amsi looked at Ife with a quiet groan. He slowly stood as she extended a hand with a smile. He walked past Nakia and hesitantly approached Ife. He took her hand and looked at it anxiously. *I do not want her as a wife. I don't love her.* "Charmed," Amsi said flatly.

Ife smiled and bowed her head. "Rā's blessings to you."

"Lead her to her seat, my son. She will sit beside you for eternity, so you should begin to forge that bond."

Amsi sighed as he lead Ife by her hand to the seat beside him. She sat on the golden chair beside Amsi and grinned at Nakia. "I'm glad that you brought him instead of his beast of a brother. At least I have something decent to look at while I eat." Nakia clenched his fist angrily behind his body.

Amsi returned to his seat as Mahoma sat beside Kaemwaset. He reached for the plate of lamb and took a piece slowly. "Thank you, Nakia."

Ife crossed her arms defiantly. "I have traveled a long way and I am not even offered a morsel on that plate? Nakia, feed me." Ife opened her mouth.

Nakia looked at her. *I'll feed you, alright. I'll shove it up your-.* "Yes, my lady," Nakia said as he placed a date inside her mouth.

Amsi watched as Ife chewed it. *Where is Nassar? Why is he not back yet?*

"It appears you did not spare any expense for your son's celebration, Kaemwaset," Mahoma said, holding a cup of wine.

"Today is not a day to count pennies, but blessings from the Sun God for showering his light upon us all."

Ife looked down at Nakia. "My feet are tired from the chariot ride. Come here, Nakia."

Nakia looked at Amsi, who gave him a quiet nod. Nakia turned to Ife. "Yes, my lady?"

"Get on your hands and knees!" she demanded.

Nakia slowly leaned forward on his hands and knees. Ife stretched out her feet, but only her toes could reach the kneeling slave. Ife narrowed her eyes and threw the plate of broccoli at Nakia. Nakia held his head as the bronze plate hit him in the back of the head. Kaemwaset and Mahoma turned their heads to see Nakia rubbing the back of his head.

"How can I put my feet on you if you are all the way over there? Clean up this mess and get us another plate of lamb and cake! You will return and kneel before me so that I may rest my feet!"

"Yes, mistress," Nakia said quietly.

"What was that, Nakia?" Ife growled.

Nakia turned his head, looking up at her. "Yes, mistress!" Nakia yelled loudly.

Amsi watched as Nakia stood on his feet and walked out of the hall. Nakia turned the corner and bumped into Qamra. Qamra saw him rubbing the back of his head.

"Nakia, did you hit your head?"

"No, Ife hit it," Nakia said quietly.

Qamra gave him a weak smile. Qamra kissed Nakia's forehead and caressed his cheek. "You poor boy."

"I have to go to Najam to get another plate before she hits me again. Has Nassar returned?"

Qamra shrugged. "I do not know, but Zahra is at the door."

Nakia gasped. "Ife is in there, too!"

"Go to Najam and get her food ready. I have to tell Master Amsi she is awaiting his arrival."

Qamra entered the Banquet Hall and bowed before Amsi. She leaned into his ear and whispered. Amsi's eyes widened. *She's here! I have to see her!*

Amsi stood and bowed to his father. "I must excuse myself, father." Amsi turned and walked out of the room calmly. When he turned the corner, he ran to the front door.

He opened the door and Zahra stood there with a smile on her face. Her body was wrapped in white linen with a sheer white veil over her hair. Blue sapphires and rubies were woven in wire through her hair. Gold bands sparkled on her wrist in the torchlight beside the door. She bowed her head.

"Hello, Amsi Al-Sakhir."

Amsi swallowed nervously. "Hello, Zahra. You are looking nice tonight."

Zahra smiled and tilted her head to the side. "You are very kind."

"Would you care to come inside?"

Zahra stepped into the reception hall and looked at the murals decorating the white walls. Her eyes went wide at the detail of the artistry. Candles were placed along the wall giving a gentle light to the darkness of the room. "Your home is very lovely, Amsi."

Amsi chuckled nervously as he looked at her in the candlelight. Shadows played around her shoulders as her face lit up with a smile. Amsi heard the sound of laughter and cheering coming from the Banquet Hall.

"Nakia is getting a plate of food for us now. Would you like me to escort you to the Banquet Hall, my lady?" Amsi asked with a smile, offering his hand to the smiling girl.

Ife smiled warmly. "It would be my honor, Amsi Al-Sakhir Ibn Kaemwaset."

Amsi took Ife's hand gently and walked her towards the Banquet Hall. Amsi walked beside Ife into the hall as his father laughed loudly with Mahoma. Ife's eyes narrowed at the girl walking beside Amsi. Her lip curled in disdain as she jumped off of her chair.

"Who is she?!" Ife exclaimed loudly, pointing an accusatory finger at Zahra.

Ife's body tensed as she walked quickly towards the couple. The people in the hall stopped their conversation and soon all eyes were upon Ife standing face-to-face with Zahra. "Amsi, who is she?!"

Amsi saw as rage burned behind the eyes of the other girl. He took a step backwards, but kept his hand on Zahra. "This is my friend, Zahra."

Ife crossed her arms angrily. "She's not even pretty! Why is she here?"

"She is my guest," Amsi said.

Ife chuckled as she leaned into Zahra's face. "You. Are. Not. Invited. Get out."

"Amsi invited me," Zahra said nervously.

"You are holding the hand of my future husband! Get your hands off of him!" Ife growled, shoving Zahra backward. Kaemwasct and Mahoma stood as they watched the girl shove her nemesis threateningly.

Amsi stood in front of Zahra. "She is my friend and you have no right to touch her!"

"I'll touch anyone I want! You are not my husband yet and I do not have to take orders from you!" Ife screamed at Amsi.

Amsi glared at Ife. "You do not mistreat my guests!"

Ife laughed, throwing back her head. "What can she offer you, Amsi? She doesn't look very rich with that cheap clothing. I offer you more than that harlot!"

Zahra glared at Ife and placed her hands on Amsi's shoulders. "I am not a harlot! Amsi invited me to his celebration! I would rather be poor than make a jealous, foolish donkey of myself in front of hundreds of people!"

Ife turned to her father. "Remove her from this place this instant!"

Kaemwaset narrowed his eyes and walked towards Amsi. "Why did you invite her, Amsi?"

"She's my friend, father! You invited your friends to my celebration and yet I was not permitted to invite anyone I desired."

Kaemwaset glared at Zahra. "What are you doing here, Bedouin girl? You are not invited into my home."

Zahra trembled as she stood behind Amsi. Her eyes widened at the large man standing before her. "Amsi, I think I should leave."

Ife smiled. "Leave before I beat you like I beat my servants!"

Zahra narrowed her eyes at Ife. "You do not frighten me."

Amsi took Zahra's hand and turned to her. "Let's go, Zahra."

Amsi slowly walked Zahra out of the Banquet Hall. He walked her to the front door and lowered his head. "I'm sorry about Ife."

"That is the girl you are intended to marry?"

"I don't love her, Ife," Amsi said, taking Zahra's hands tightly. "I don't want to be with her. She is a cruel, mean-spirited she-demon! I don't like her at all."

Zahra sighed and lowered her head. "You don't like her? But you are going to marry her, are you not?"

Amsi shook his head. "No, Zahra. I don't like her. I don't want her. You are a better friend to me than she and we just met!"

Zahra smiled slowly. "Do you mean that?"

Amsi nodded. "You opened your camp to me and my servants. Not once did you beat any of my slaves. You even tried to help me find my friend."

"So this means we are friends?"

Amsi nodded with a smile. "We're friends."

Zahra slowly opened her arms and hugged Amsi, putting her head on his shoulder. "I'm happy to be your friend, Amsi."

Amsi hugged her tightly, resting his head on her shoulder. "I will try to see you after the celebration tonight."

"Alright. Until later then, Amsi Al-Sakhir."

"Get out of my home, Bedouin vermin," Kaemwaset growled, standing in the entrance.

Zahra smiled at Kaemwaset. "Congratulations on your son's rite-of-passage. Good night."

Amsi watched as Zahra walked down the path towards the arch. "Father, that was not very nice."

Kaemwaset glared at Amsi. "If I see that boy you befriended here, I will hang him myself, Amsi-Al-Sakhir!"

Amsi turned to his father. "I do not want to marry Ife! I do not love her!"

"Love has nothing to do with marriage, Amsi! This marriage is about uniting our family lands!"

Amsi stood defiantly in front of his father. "I will not marry Ife!"

"You will marry Ife! I will see to it that you marry her, Amsi, even if I have to drag you to the temple itself!"

Amsi clenched his fists angrily. "I will not marry her! I refuse!"

Kaemwaset's eyes narrowed with fury. "You defy your own father for a marriage which cannot possible be fruitful and profitable?"

"I cannot myself by following the path you set before me! I cannot find pleasure in this world if I am watching my servants get beaten!"

Kaemwaset crossed Amsi's path and stopped at the top of the stairs. "My will be done, Amsi. You will take her as your wife or you will suffer not by my hands, but your own."

Kaemwaset walked towards the path to the archway. He saw Zahra illuminated by the torchlight of the slave house as she passed. Kaemwaset's angry footsteps dug into the ground as he watched her walk calmly down the sandy road. The land owner watched her pass the archway.

The man seethed with anger as he turned to the slave quarters. He is-sick in the slave quarters, my lord. Kaemwaset remembered Nakia saying. *It's time for me to check on how sick that boy has become.*

Nakia placed fresh lamb on the plate as Najam placed fresh dates on the plate. Nakia saw Najam smiling at him as she finished the plate. Nakia rubbed the back of his head as he opened the door on the floor. He descended the stairs to the cellar where the fruit and vegetables were stored. He grabbed an armful of fresh apples and emerged from the trap door, standing beside Najam.

"I hope I have enough dates for this celebration, Nakia. I'm beginning to run low."

The teen slave placed sliced bread on the plate. "I hope we have enough bread."

Nakia took a slice of bread in his hands and began to chew on it hungrily. His stomach rumbled with hunger as his teeth dug savagely into the food.

Najam chuckled. "Are you hungry, my boy?"

Nakia nodded with a smile. "Your bread is the best ever!"

Najam smiled. "You are very welcome, Nakia."

Nakia opened his mouth to take another piece when a rough hand grabbed his shoulder and spun him around. A large fist connected with his face, making him fall to the ground. Nakia dropped the bread with a painful groan.

"Where is he, Nakia?" Kaemwaset seethed.

Najam kneeled beside Nakia as Kaemwaset's foot slammed on the lower back of the thin slave. Nakia screamed as he rolled on his side and arched his back.

"Najam, step aside!"

Najam held out a hand in front of Nakia. "My lord, be careful! Don't hurt the boy!"

Nakia looked up at Kaemwaset through tear-filled eyes. "Who, my lord?"

Kaemwaset reached down and grabbed Nakia's throat. He pulled the boy to his feet and slammed his back against the table covered in food. Nakia gagged as the man's hands constricted his throat.

"Where is he, Nakia? Where is your twin?!"

Nakia's eyes widened as he looked into the furious face of his owner. Najam stood beside Kaemwaset and grabbed his wrists.

"You're strangling the boy!"

Nakia struggled for breath as Kaemwaset pressed harshly on his windpipe. Nakia opened his mouth to speak, but no words could come through the asphyxiating grasp of his assailant. Najam grabbed her master's cloak and pulled roughly, trying to separate Kaemwaset from his gagging victim.

Najam screamed loudly as she heard the wheezing, muffled whimpers of the suffocating boy. "My lord, you know Nakia has bad lungs!"

"He will tell me where his brother is hiding or I will kill him!"

Nakia's hands slowly released Kaemwaset's wrists as he started to become limp on the table. Kaemwaset grinned menacingly at the choking teen. He threw Nakia on the ground, watching the teen struggle for breath, holding his throat. Najam kneeled beside Nakia trembling on the ground.

"Where is he, Nakia? Tell me or I will strangle you again and this time I will not let go!"

Najam took Nakia in her arms and watched the teen tremble. His lungs wheezed as he held onto the cook tightly. "Breathe, Nakia. That's it. Take deep breaths." Nakia tensed as Najam caressed his cheek. "Good boy."

Kaemwaset hovered above Nakia with a smile. "He's not sick, is he, Nakia? Where is he?"

Nakia whimpered as he clutched tighter onto Najam. Najam turned his head to face her. "Focus on me. Breathe, Nakia. Good boy. Follow my lead." Najam took a deep breath and slowly released it. "Please, Nakia, breathe." Nakia wheezed sharply as he looked into Najam's eyes.

Nakia shook his head. *I can't breathe. Help, Najam!*

Kaemwaset grabbed Nakia, pulling the teen to his feet. "You insolent, defiant little rat!"

Kaemwaset pulled Nakia to the door on the floor. He threw Nakia down the stairs and shut the trap door quickly.

"My lord, don't do that! Please!" Najam pleaded.

Kaemwaset removed a key and shoved it into the lock angrily. "He does not get out," Kaemwaset said angrily grasping Najam's arm.

Nakia opened his eyes slowly, his breathing coming in sharp, struggling gasps for air. He looked up at the steps and saw some flicker of light through the trap door. Nakia struggled to his feet, but fell as his body went weak. The sound of a woman sobbing above him sent pain through his body. Nakia grabbed the step and pulled himself weakly to the top.

He reached up painfully and banged on the locked door. "Help!" Nakia scream sounding hardly above a whisper through his tight lungs. "Help!" Nakia tried to scream again as he banged on the trap door. "Qamra! Master Amsi! Mistress Imani!"

"Nakia," Najam wept on the surface as her hand grazed on the wooden door.

Nakia knocked on the locked door again as his head rested against the top step. His chest rose and fell sharply as he closed his eyes. The darkness was disorientating. The chill of the room stung against the cut on his forehead from the fall.

"Najam, I can't breathe," Nakia coughed as he sat on the step below the locked door. His hand touched the door. "Let me out. Please. Kaemwaset. I can't breathe. Qamra, please. Help me." Nakia's head fell forward on the step beside him. "Najam," Nakia whimpered as he hit the door with a punch expending the last of his strength. "Baruti. Get Father Baruti."

Najam stood and ran out of the kitchen. She ran through the garden, breathing heavily. Najam exited through the gate, running down the path as she grew alarmed at the condition of the trapped boy. Her body tensed at the thought of the suffocating boy locked behind the door. The cook fought back tears as she thought of the imprisoned boy dying on the steps, begging for his freedom.

"Baruti! Baruti! Help!" Najam exclaimed as she ran towards the slave home.

Najam quickly pulled aside the material of the entry way. Baruti looked up from the fire quickly as his children huddled beside him for warmth. "Baruti," Najam panted. "Come quickly!"

"Najam, what's wrong?"

"The boy, Nakia," Najam sobbed, tears falling down her face. "The boy needs your help, Baruti! He's trapped!"

Baruti gasped as he looked down at his children. "Stay here, both of you," the father said as he jumped to his feet.

"I want to come!" Meskhenet exclaimed.

"No. Stay here and wait for Nassar. Behave yourselves."

Baruti followed Najam towards the garden and through the gate. Baruti narrowed his eyes as he ran for the kitchen.

"The master choked him and threw him in the fruit cellar!"

Baruti ran into the kitchen and towards the trap door. "Is he still alive?" Baruti asked as he knocked on the cellar door. "Nakia? Nakia? It's Baruti! Can you hear me?" The desperate Baruti knocked hard on the door. Baruti swallowed nervously as silence responded. Baruti reached out slowly and touched the locked wooden door. "Nakia?" Baruti asked, fighting back tears at the possibility that the boy had died. Baruti leaned over and placed his forehead against the door. Najam heard Baruti sniffle and placed her hand on his back. "Lord Anubis, please do not take him," Baruti cried softly. "Nakia, please answer me." Baruti clenched his fists and punched the wooden door. "Nakia!"

"Baruti?" Nakia quietly asked, weakly opening his eyes from behind the door. "Help me, Father Baruti," the teen cried.

Baruti gasped and opened his eyes wide. He stared at the door, his fists tightly closed. "Nakia! I'm going to free you!" Baruti screamed, grabbing the handle of the door. He stood on his feet and leaned over, tugging harshly on the door handle.

Baruti and Najam looked at the cellar door as Nakia banged his shoulder into the door.

"Father Baruti! Help me!"

Baruti stamped his feet hard on the door. Baruti growled as he slammed his foot harshly on the locked door.

Nakia kneeled on the step, watching the door shake with Baruti's angry kicks. Nakia breathed quickly as he looked into the small, dark cellar. He shivered as he felt the walls close in on him. His eyes widened as he shifted against the mud-brick wall.

The shadows swirled around him as he peered into the looming darkness.

*Kelile! Ulan! Run!* His father called to him.

*Spare my boys!* His mother pleaded from the darkness.

Nakia's eyes widened and his body trembled as distorted images danced in the shadows. They smiled at him menacingly. They reached for him with bloody claws. They laughed at him.

Nakia drew his knees under his chin and tucked his arms against his chest. He closed his eyes tightly and hid his face from view.

Khentimentiu stood outside waiting for Nassar. He wrapped his arms around himself as he looked towards the arch. He sighed as he heard some laughing Nobles riding away in their chariots. The little boy watched as he saw Mahoma and Ife's carriage pass him. *Where is Nassar? It's not like him to be gone for so long. I hope he's not hurt.*

Meskhenet pushed aside the material and stood beside her younger brother. "Is he here yet?"

Khentimentiu shook his head as he wrung his hands nervously. "No, sister. I hope mother and father return soon."

The children turned their heads as they heard a scream of pain from inside the kitchen. Khentimentiu stepped closer to his sister and placed his arms around her waist. "What was that?"

Meskhenet heard the sound of footsteps on the path coming from the house. She put her hands on her brother's shoulders. "Khenti, get in the house."

"Is it the master again?"

Meskhenet saw a dark figure approaching. "Get inside, Khenti!"

Meskhenet pulled her brother into the slave home. Khentimentiu ran to the corner cowering behind his sister. Meskhenet narrowed her eyes at the material and clenched her fists, ready to defend her brother.

The material pulled back and Meskhenet lunged for the intruder. She pulled back her fist and jabbed it quickly into the man's bony side.

"Ah-w!" Nassar exclaimed as he looked down at the little girl. He caught her wrist as she tried to strike again.

Meskhenet pulled back her fist. "Nassar? Nassar! I'm sorry!"

"Wha oo hi-me?"

Meskhenet smiled and wrapped her arms around Nassar's thin waist. Khentimentiu squealed happily and wrapped his arm around Nassar's leg, hugging it tightly.

"Nassar! We're so glad to see you!"

Nassar smiled at the two children and pet their heads. "Heh-o, Mekhe-et and Khe-me-oo."

Meskhenet gasped as she clutched onto Nassar tightly. "Your brother needs you, Nassar!"

"Where Ah-e-ah?" Nassar gasped, holding onto Meskhenet's shoulders.

Meskhenet shook her head. "I don't know! Najam came in here and said he was trapped!"

"He might be hurt, Nassar!" Khentimentiu shouted.

"You no longer have to concern yourself with him," Kaemwaset said calmly as he walked into the house calmly.

Nassar turned to his master, moving the children behind him protectively. Khentimentiu cautiously peeked his head from behind Nassar. The little girl narrowed her eyes at her owner angrily.

"Stay away from us!" Meskhenet growled defiantly.

"Where mah bruffa Ah-e-ah?" Nassar growled.

Kaemwaset chuckled low in his throat. From behind his back, he pulled a bloody dagger. "I killed him."

Nassar looked at the bloody dagger in Kaemwaset's hand. A single drop of blood fell onto the wooden floor of the slave house. "Ah-e-ah," Nassar whispered sadly.

Khentimentiu's head lowered as she began to cry. Meskhenet growled and lunged at Kaemwaset.

"You murderer!"

Kaemwaset raised his dagger to strike the attacking little girl. Nassar lunged forward, grabbing Kaemwaset's arm tightly. Nassar threw himself against Kaemwaset, knocking the large man against the wall.

"Geh Fa-ah Ba-oo-ee!" Nassar screamed to the two children as they ran from the house.

Kaemwaset grabbed Nassar and threw him to the floor. "I killed your twin. Now it's your turn!"

Nassar moved his arm quickly as Kaemwaset brought the knife down quickly. The twin scurried backward as his master followed him. Kaemwaset's heavy foot kicked Nassar in the jaw, sending the twin falling on his back. Nassar screamed loudly as he felt a searing pain in his leg.

Kaemwaset removed the knife quickly. "Let's see you run now!"

Nassar rolled to the side and stood on his feet. With an angry growl, he shoved Kaemwaset against the wall and punched him in the face savagely. The bitter scent of alcohol wafted from his breath as he exhaled quickly.

Nassar punched Kaemwaset in the stomach, tears coming down his face. Blood trickled from Nassar's open wound. Kaemwaset reached out his hand and grabbed Nassar's throat.

"You are coming with me! Stop struggling this instant!" Kaemwaset held onto Nassar as he dragged the teen from the house. Nassar's punches struck at Kaemwaset's side as he was pulled towards the field. "I will make certain nobody finds your body! I will rid myself of you forever!"

Nassar screamed as he pushed against Kaemwaset. His leg burned with pain as Kaemwaset arrived at the edge of the field.  Kaemwaset held the tip of the knife against Nassar's throat.  The teen struggled to breathe as his owner's grip tightened.

"I will relish this moment," Kaemwaset smiled, pressing the blade against Nassar's throat and watching a thin trickle of blood begin.  "Now it's time to cut that throat, Nassar."

Nassar gagged as he drove his knee into Kaemwaset's back.  He kicked again as the man groaned in pain.  Nassar elbowed Kaemwaset hard in the side, making the man drop his knife.  Nassar elbowed the man again, making Kaemwaset release his grip on his throat.

The twin staggered backward, holding his throat as his right leg bled from the open wound.  Nassar turned and began to stagger towards the arch.

*Nakia is gone. There is nothing left for me here.*

Nassar breathed sharply as blood trickled from between his fingers. The warm blood from his open wound slipped between his toes as he walked.

*My brother is dead.  My precious Nakia is dead.  He was all that I had.  He was everything to me.  I love you, Nakia.*

Nassar breathed quickly as he was tackled from behind. Kaemwaset lifted the dagger over Nassar's back as the twin punched him from behind with a scream of alarm. Kaemwaset fell off of him as Nassar continued to crawl to the arch.  Nassar winced as Kaemwaset's foot crashed against his back.

Nassar curled himself into a protective ball as Kaemwaset kicked him again. Nassar closed his eyes as his body went limp. Kaemwaset grinned at the unconscious Nassar. He reached down and grabbed Nassar's wrist. The wrist dropped as he smiled. Blood from Nassar's neck and his leg pooled beneath his body. Kaemwaset casually turned and walked away.

Nassar opened his right eye, watching his master walk away calmly holding the bloody dagger. When his master was out of sight, he looked at the nearby arch. *I cannot stay here if he comes back.*

Nassar struggled to his feet and staggered through the archway. A bonfire from the Bedouin camp was lit beside the Nile. He held his neck as he staggered towards the water.

He winced in pain and gasped as his legs weakened beneath him. He fell onto the ground as his body began to shiver. He heard a startled cry sound from the Bedouin encampment.

Nassar breathed sharply as he felt a single hand caress his cheek lovingly. "Ah-e-ah," Nassar began to sob.

"Nassar?"

Nassar slowly opened his eyes and saw Sumati hovering above him. Sumati brushed her fingers against his cheek tenderly as he looked at her.

"He's been stabbed, Sumati! Move your hand, Nassar," he heard a young girl's voice say above him. He felt his arm being carefully moved. "Get Onfalia! His throat has been cut! Quickly!" Nassar felt a piece of cloth touch his throat. "Nassar? Can you hear me?"

"Ah-ra," Nassar whimpered as he reached up weakly towards her face.

Sumati took Nassar's hand and brought it to her breast. "Stay with us, Nassar."

"There's so much blood!" Shera exclaimed. "His injury doesn't look deep, thank the goddess!"

Zahra watched as Nassar's eyes began to close. "Nassar, no! Keep your eyes open!"

Nassar's eyelids fluttered as he began to whimper in pain. He watched through half-closed eyes as Sumati leaned down and kissed him softly on the lips.

Her hand cupped his cheek lovingly as she deepened the kiss slowly. Nassar returned the kiss as he felt a pair of hands on his leg. Sumati looked down at Nassar with tears in her eyes.

Zahra watched as Nassar's eyes slowly began to close again. "No! Nassar! Stay awake!"

Nassar closed his eyes slowly as he felt his body slowly go numb. *Nakia, my brother.*

"Nassar!" cried a desperate scream from somewhere far away.

Qamra kneeled beside Baruti as she looked at the lock. Najam buried her face in her hands as she cried quietly for the trapped boy. Baruti clenched his fists in anger. Amsi ran into the room, finding the slaves gathered around the door where one of their own had been confined.

"I'm not so good at this," Amsi said, bringing one of his mother's hairpins towards the door. "Azizi only showed me once."

Amsi kneeled before the lock and pushed the pin into the lock. He watched the lock closely, hoping to find the latch inside. "Don't worry, Nakia. I'll get you out."

"Hurry before the master arrives, Amsi," Qamra pleaded watching the gate of the garden.

"The twins helped me bake the bread. Nakia was always eager to help in the kitchen."

Baruti shook his head. "He's not dead, Najam. Hold on, Nakia."

Amsi heard the lock snap as he smiled. *Azizi would be proud of me! A child of Noble Blood can pick a lock like a Common Thief!* Amsi turned the circular knob and opened the door of the fruit cellar. Nakia was curled up in a fetal position below the door, shaking.

"Nakia!" Amsi gasped, putting his hand on Nakia's shoulder.

Nakia's head snapped up in alarm as he looked up at his master. "Master Amsi!"

Amsi took Nakia's hand and helped him out of the fruit cellar. "Nakia, are you alright?"

Nakia fell to his knees before Amsi and wrapped his arms around the other teen's waist tightly. "I saw angry spirits down there! You saved me! Thank you, Master Amsi!"

Nakia released Amsi as Baruti quickly grabbed him and pulled him against him. Amsi watched as the trembling Nakia was held in the other slave's muscular arms. Baruti caressed Nakia's head as Qamra kissed Nakia's cheek.

"It's alright, Nakia."

Nakia looked up at Baruti's smiling face. "Father Baruti? I tried to get out!"

"I know, Nakia. Take deep breaths."

The shaking teen looked at Qamra with large, pleading eyes. "Mother Qamra, has my brother returned?"

"Yes, he has returned," Kaemwaset said, standing at the entrance to the kitchen. Qamra wrapped her arms around Baruti and Nakia protectively. Amsi stood beside the cowering slaves. Amsi looked as his father's face bore a bruise. His clothing appeared disheveled as if he had been in a fight.

Kaemwaset held up a bloody dagger. "Nakia, your brother is dead. I killed him myself."

Qamra and Najam lowered their heads as tears fell from their cheeks. Baruti clutched onto Nakia tightly, unwilling to release the only surviving twin.

Amsi bit his lip sadly and looked down at Nakia, whose eyes were opened wide in shock. "Father, you had no need to kill him! I sent him on an errand!"

Kaemwaset watched as his son stood defiantly beside the slaves. "He may have been your body slave, but all of them belong to me. I choose their fate. Return to your ceremony, Amsi. Tonight is a night of celebration and it is impolite to ignore your guests." Kaemwaset turned and calmly walked away.

Baruti and the other slaves kneeled in silence. The man held onto Nakia tightly, cupping the boy's cheek in his hand. "Anubis will give Nassar a place of honor beside Osiris, Nakia."

"Nakia, I'm so sorry," Qamra whimpered.

"Nassar," Nakia whimpered.

Amsi watched as Nakia's eyes rolled up into his head and went as limp. Amsi touched Nakia's neck. "He fainted."

Baruti narrowed his eyes, seething in fury. "That man has no heart with which to be judged in the afterlife. He will regret the murder of that boy." Baruti grit his teeth. "I will see to it personally."

## XXXIX

### <u>Seige at Edfû</u>

Azizi kneeled on the tiny boat as Fath moved the oars. His eyes narrowed at the faint light ahead of them. Azizi gripped the edge of the boat tightly, thinking of the pharaoh's plans to obtain the Eye of Horus. "With the

Scroll of Horus, Fath, he can get his hands on the power of the Eye. He will have unbelievable strength and he may become physically unstoppable."

Fath looked into the distance as he heard the determination in the boy's voice. "The pharaoh has an entire battalion under his command. He has sympathizers wherever his feet tread. How do you hope to stop him with such opposition?"

Azizi sat in the boat with a sigh of resignation. He grabbed a piece of bread he had stolen from a cart before he left. "I don't know, exactly."

Fath chuckled quietly. "How do you expect a victory with strategic uncertainty, boy?"

"I'm going to stop the pharaoh, Fath! He wants to rule all for eternity! If he is mortal, his reign is only temporary." Azizi narrowed his eyes at the other thief. "Can you imagine a world where a tyrant can live for eternity? He will never die. He will only grow stronger and deadlier with each passing day. The world will turn into a desert and all life will end." Azizi sighed as he looked at the dark water's rippling surface. "He killed my parents, Fath. I watched them behead my mother when I was no taller than a reed of papyrus." Azizi lowered his head as he brushed away a tear. "I miss my mother. I won't let her fate befall anyone else."

Fath rowed the boat as he watched the boy closely. "You are very brave."

"Osiris gives me strength. I burn offerings to him every morning. I don't think what I'm doing has anything to do with being brave, Fath. I don't see myself as brave at all." Azizi turned to Fath. "I'm doing what needs to be done. I'm doing the right thing. If I'm captured by the pharaoh, he will kill me." Azizi nodded. "That frightens me. That makes me a coward."

"The brave can still be afraid, Lord Azizi. The difference between the brave and the coward is the brave control their fear. They do not give in to the terror in their hearts."

Azizi removed the golden dagger from under his black cloak. "So many people have suffered at the hands of the pharaoh already, Fath. If he were to live forever, this world would become one large graveyard. I can't let that happen."

"Even if it meant your death to achieve your goal?"

Azizi watched as the golden blade shimmered in the moonlight. "Yes. I would die if it was a requirement for my success."

"The King of Thieves' bravery is legendary, Azizi. Thieves from other towns told us of your birth. They said that the boy would bear the mark of Osiris."

Azizi wrapped his cape around his body. "The thieves of Heliopolis bear the same mark. It is hidden to retain our status as a secret sect."

"We bear the mark of Ptah, the god who created the world through thought. Osiris is honored in our town, as well, so when we heard of a follower of Osiris being the King of Thieves, we were told to welcome him."

Azizi touched the Eye of Osiris tattooed on his arm. "It was not an easy task setting my friend free. I can only pray that Osiris keeps my friends safe from Kaphiri in my absence."

Fath looked ahead at the pinpoint of lights in the distance. "Your friends speak well of you."

Azizi nodded. "I have saved many of them from Kaphiri's rage. A good thief has his allies and holds them close to his heart."

"A good friend could save you from the hangman's rope."

"A thief needs two sets of eyes: one of his own and one of his friend's at his back. I just wish I could have saved Ferryn. He did not deserve to die, but I know he lives in comfort now. When I die, I will enjoy the same blessings and be welcomed by the God of the Dead."

Fath looked up at the stars wistfully. "The Creator God will welcome all his faithful children. I cannot imagine a world where the pharaoh would be immortal. I have heard of the pharaoh's proclamations. The man has gone sick with Madness, my king."

Azizi laid himself on the deck of the small boat. He looked up at the sky with a tired yawn. "I will cure him. I will not let him succeed. I will fight him with the last ounce of my human strength."

Fath watched the teen's eyes close slowly and his head lull to the side in slumber. "I will wake you when we arrive at Edfû, my kingship."

Azizi opened his eyes quickly as Fath kneeled low on the deck of the boat. He gasped and pulled back quickly as Azizi pointed the blade at him quickly. Fath held up his arms. "My lord! We are here at Edfû!"

Azizi yawned and rolled onto his stomach, looking at the multitude of boats ahead of him. Fath watched in amazement as the large battalion of soldiers stepped off their boats. He grabbed his bow tightly in his hands. "Look how many of them there are, my lord!"

Azizi grabbed the hilt of his dagger tightly. "Get us into the reeds before the pharaoh sees us!"

Fath moved the boat into the reeds as Azizi and he disembarked. Azizi bent low among the papyrus reeds, holding his breath anxiously. Fath crawled behind him, his quiver strapped tightly to his bare back. He kneeled beside Amsi, peering out between the tall brush. The pair watched the soldiers disembark from their boats and form lines in battle fashion.

"The Eye of Horus is here?"

Azizi nodded quietly. "Edfû is the Holy City of Horus. No doubt, the temple and priests hold what is sacred to them. They will not let the Eye of Horus fall into the pharaoh's hands easily."

"The pharaoh is the Living Horus. Will they not see his arrival as the Coming of their God?"

Azizi gripped the hilt of his dagger tightly. "They will not welcome his visit if they know of the cruelty with which he rules and his abandonment of the rule of Ma'at. The pharaoh rules not with the hand of justice, but with the sword of bloodshed."

Pharaoh Runihura's eyes scanned the lines of battle-ready soldiers. He grinned as the soldiers stood before him, their weapons clutched tightly in their hands. "Today, we are to seize the Eye of Horus. Leave no stone unturned and leave no area unexplored! I will not tolerate cowardice! Any man who flees from battle will find an arrow in his back or a blade in the belly! Leave no creature alive until we find the Eye of Horus! I want the High Priest of Horus brought to me alive! He will know where to find the sacred relic!"

Fath gasped as he looked at the teenager kneeling beside him. "He's going to slaughter innocents for the sake of the Scroll of Horus?"

"I told you he is a butcher, Fath," Azizi whispered angrily. "Do you want his cruelty lasting for eternity?" Azizi shook his head. "We have to save the High Priest of Horus!"

Fath gripped his bow nervously as sweat formed on his hand. "We can't save everyone, Master Azizi!"

"Save anybody that you can. Take them to a safe place. No doubt the pharaoh will leave some soldiers out of the city to shoot any who seek to escape the carnage."

Fath swallowed nervously. "Young master, I don't think I can do this."

Azizi narrowed his eyes and turned to Fath. He grabbed the older man's arm angrily. "If we do not do something, everyone in that city will die!"

"For the glory of Sekhmet!" Runihura exclaimed as he lead the charge into the city.

Azizi watched as the guards of Edfû fell from the pharaoh's blade. Screams of terror pierced through the air as the soldiers flooded into the city.

"Get me an archer!" Azizi gasped.

Fath loaded his bow with an arrow and aimed for a soldier armed with a bow and quiver. He narrowed his eyes, focusing on the target and released the bolt. The arrow impaled itself into the archer, who collapsed on the sand with a scream.

"We're surrounded!" one soldier exclaimed.

Azizi emerged from the reed, his golden dagger clutched tightly. He ran towards the corpse to grab the bow and arrow when the soldier raised his sword. Azizi blocked the soldier's strike with his dagger and punched him in the stomach with his free hand. Azizi turned his wrist and sliced through the soldier's face. Azizi closed his eyes quickly as his first victim's blood splattered onto his face.

"It's the boy! Get him!"

Azizi grabbed the bow and arrow. How does Amsi make this look so easy? Three soldiers rushed towards him as two arrows flew out of the reeds. Amsi dropped the bow and blocked with his dagger again. The soldier kicked him in the leg, knocking off his balance. The soldier swung his sword low as Azizi jumped backward. The soldier's sword fell from above as Azizi sliced through the man's stomach with a quick slash of the blade. The man collapsed on the ground looking up at him.

Azizi breathed quickly as he heard the screams of women and children emerge from inside the city. Fath ran beside him and handed him the bow and quiver from the ground.

"You have never used a bow?"

Azizi shrugged his shoulders. "I have seen Amsi use it a few times. I can use it, but it's not my expertise."

Fath showed Azizi how to load and fire the arrows. "It takes practice," Fath said with a smile. The angry shouts of men rose from the city walls. "It appears the soldiers of Edfû are not going to let their city be taken without a fight."

Azizi smiled. "We have allies in them, then. Hurry, Fath, before there is not so much as a beetle moving within the city!"

Fath and Azizi ran towards the city gates. Fath unleashed arrows towards two soldiers battling a man with metal weapons. The two soldiers armed with clubs fell. Azizi looked at the soldier holding a spear.

"Who are you?" the man asked, holding his spear in front of him.

Fath narrowed his eyes. "We just saved your life and that is the gratitude we receive?"

"I am Azizi Keket! I am here to stop the pharaoh from obtaining the Eye of Horus. Can you tell me where the Eye is hidden?"

The soldier nodded as he lowered his weapon. "It is hidden in the Temple of Edfû! The Holy Priests of Thoth guard the sacred artifact!"

Azizi bowed his head to the soldier. "Thank you. Fath, get the women and children out of here! Clear a path for our escape if you can."

"Yes, my king!"

"You are going to rid our city of the soldiers of Sekhmet?" the soldier asked.

Azizi nodded with a grin. "An enemy of Horus is a friend of mine."

"May Horus, Avenger of his Father Osiris, bless you!"

"Find the survivors. Take them to the reeds beside the Nile and hide them. I will save as many as I can."

The soldier bowed his head. "Yes, my lord!"

Azizi bowed his head again and turned towards the temple. He raced towards the temple, burying a dagger in the back of the pharaoh's soldiers he encountered. He heard a scream from inside a mud-brick home. Azizi stepped through the door and saw a soldier cornering a mother and her young child in the corner. Azizi narrowed his eyes and lunged at the soldier quickly.

The soldier turned to Azizi and raised his club. Azizi blocked the club with his dagger and kicked the man into the wall. The mother kneeling on the ground held her child closely as the man kicked the teen backward as he ran towards him. Azizi swiftly flew his fist toward the soldier's face, punching him in the cheek.

"You think you are a man terrorizing a mother and her little girl? You are worse than a dung beetle!"

"You are the boy the pharaoh seeks!"

Azizi grinned. "You will not get the bounty on my head, I guarantee that!"

The soldier smiled. "I will be able to feed my family for eternity with the money I would get for your death, boy!"

The soldier removed a sword from his sheath and sliced towards Azizi. Azizi held up a chair as the blade sliced through the wood. The woman and little girl in the corner cried as they watched the soldier kick the fragments of the chair aside. Azizi grabbed an arrow from his quiver and jumped on the wooden table. The soldier sliced upwards as Azizi lunged at the man, knocking him onto the ground.

The teen straddled the man's chest. Azizi dropped the sword and pinned the man's wrist to the floor. Azizi growled as he stabbed the golden dagger through the man's chest. The soldier's eyes opened wide as he gurgled. His head fell backward on the ground as he laid dead.

Azizi panted heavily as he looked up at the mother holding her little girl tightly. "Are you alright?"

"Thank you! Bless you for saving my child!"

Azizi nodded as he looked at the dead man underneath him. "I want you to get out of the city and go to the reeds beside the Nile. There will be other survivors there. Go." Azizi looked at the sword and stole the sheath. "You will not need this anymore."

The mother brought her daughter into her arms and ran from the home. Azizi followed her out of the house and saw a soldier ready to deal a deadly blow to a priest of Horus. Azizi ran towards the man and stabbed the man through the back. The soldier screamed and fell to the ground beside the kneeling, shaking priest. Azizi kneeled beside the priest as the soldiers of Edfû battled around them. "Are you hurt?"

The priest grabbed Azizi's black cloak. "Save the High Priest! Please, whoever you are!"

Azizi nodded quickly. "I will. I'm going to the temple now. Flee the city and you will find a soldier who will show you to a safe hiding place."

The priest's eyes widened as he looked at the scarred cheek. "You are the Blessed Servant of Osiris! Our brothers of the Osirian order have told us of your arrival, Honored One!"

"I don't want worship, priest! I want you to flee the city! We have no time for prayer!"

The priest smiled at Azizi. "There is always time for prayer when it involves the Father of our God, Horus! Long live your Father!"

Azizi narrowed his eyes at the priest. "Stop praying and start moving! Hurry!"

"Yes, my lord!"

Azizi felt a tough hand grab the back of his cloak and pull harshly. "Here is the boy!"

The soldier pulled him to his feet as another soldier grabbed his wrists. "The money belongs to me, Mushin!"

"Leave!" Azizi screamed as the priest scurried away quickly.

Mushin pulled Azizi's wrists angrily. "He belongs to me, Teraj!"

Azizi looked down and stomped his foot hard on Teraj's foot. He grit his teeth and slammed his head against Mushin ahead of him. Mushin released his wrists as Azizi's balance wavered. He grabbed his dagger quickly, slashed Mushin's chest, and stabbed behind him, killing Teraj.

Azizi held onto the wall beside him as he held his aching head. Desperate times call for desperate measures. Praise Osiris that they were not wearing metal helmets like the soldiers of Edfû. Azizi pushed forward as he heard a girl scream from an alley. He turned his head and saw a soldier tearing the robe from a woman against a wall.

Azizi growled as he ran down the alley. The soldier turned his head as his scream rose into the air. The woman screamed as she saw the blade buried deep into the man's eye. Azizi kicked the man backward and watched as he fell, holding onto his empty eye socket. Azizi turned to the woman. "You must-."

The woman wrapped her arms around him, sobbing and trembling. She clutched onto him tightly as she wailed. "They came so suddenly! They killed my brother!"

"I'm sorry," Azizi said as he felt his feet become damp. His eyes looked down and saw the puddle of blood forming beneath him.

The young woman looked at him as she looked into his eyes. "Why are they here?"

"The Eye of Horus is their objective."

A tear fell down the young woman's cheek. "They killed my brother for a relic of legend?"

Azizi nodded solemnly. "I'm here to stop the pharaoh."

"Let me help you!"

Azizi shook his head. "No. You must get out of the city. Please."

The woman looked into Azizi's brown eyes; his face was dotted with blood. "Thank you for saving me." The young woman leaned into Azizi and kissed him on the lips softly. Her hand cupped his face lovingly as she moaned into the kiss. Azizi held the woman closely as he kissed her against the wall of the alley.

"Slaughter everyone in this city!"

Azizi opened his eyes quickly as he turned his head. "The pharaoh is nearby! You have to leave the city. Go to the reeds beside the Nile. A soldier will guide your way to safety."

The young woman smiled and kissed his cheek. "I owe you my life and you will be repaid handsomely."

Azizi smiled at the woman warmly. "There's no need to reward me. Go to the Nile."

The woman nodded reluctantly as she watched Azizi run towards the pharaoh. Azizi emerged from the alley and looked upward towards the Temple of Edfû. The pharaoh's sword slashed through a soldier's throat as he raced up the steps of the temple. Azizi narrowed his eyes and chased the pharaoh.

He fell forward as someone grabbed his leg. He looked down and saw a fallen soldier looking at him with desperate eyes. "Please save the High Priest of Beloved Horus!"

Azizi watched as the man released his grip with a strangled breath.

Azizi stood and raced up the steps towards the temple. A great staircase rose upward as two large marble statues of Horus greeted him at the top of the steps. Ahead of him, soldiers of the pharaoh and the High Priest of Horus battled. Screams of anger, alarm, and pain rose into the air.

I won't be able to get a good aim at the pharaoh through the crowd. Azizi raced up the steps, looking down at the battling men below. Azizi's face dripped with sweat as he watched the multitude of men fighting for their lives. He removed an arrow from his quiver and loaded the bow. He pulled backward, focusing on a single pharaoh's soldier. With a held breath, he released. The soldier fell to the ground with a cry of pain.

*I guess I'm not a bad of a shot as I thought!*

"Where is the Eye of Horus, old man?"

Azizi's eyes went to the front of the temple where a large statue of Horus was flanked by candles and an open gold box. The Gahiji was holding the High Priest of Horus against the altar with a sword to his throat. The pharaoh gripped his bloody sword tightly in his hand.

"Praise be to Horus, Avenger of His Father, Osiris! Fight, my men, with the strength of millions! Long live Horus!" the old priest called into the air.

Azizi watched in alarm as the pharaoh pierced the man's chest with his sword. "No!"

Runihura grinned. "Open the sanctuary. The god possesses the Eye."

Gahiji threw the dead priest to the ground and opened the door beside the altar. Gahiji entered the room and emerged later with a small sanctuary to the god. Gahiji kneeled before the pharaoh and placed it on the altar.

"Finally, the Eye of Horus shall be mine!" Pharaoh Runihura grinned as he opened the sanctuary. A brilliant light emerged from the open box. Azizi held his arms in front of his eyes as the blinding light shone around him.

Pharaoh Runihura took the Eye of Horus in his hand and grabbed the scroll with the other. The light diminished as Azizi watched the pharaoh hold the Eye of Horus into the air above his eyes. The pharaoh unraveled the scroll. Runihura grinned as he read from the parchment.

*The Power of Horus shall be mine*

*God-like strength shall be possessed for all time!*

*My enemies fall to their knees at my godly might!*

*Obey they my command and at my will do fight!*

*Eternal youth and strength shall time grant me*

*And at my word shall death swiftly flee!*

Azizi watched as the Eye of Horus glowed brightly. The Eye of Horus trembled in Pharaoh Runihura's hand. Azizi heard the pharaoh's painful, agonizing scream as the pharaoh's eyes began to glow with a radiant light. The teen watched as blood streamed from the pharaoh's eyes. The pharaoh fell to his knees before the body of the fallen cleric.

Azizi watched as Gahiji kneeled beside the pharaoh and placed a hand on the pharaoh's back. "My lord, what has happened?"

Pharaoh Runihura lifted his head to the ceiling with a menacing grin. The Eye of Horus had implanted itself into Pharaoh Runihura's eyes. The pharaoh blinked his golden metallic eyes with a menacing grin. "The power of the gods will soon be mine, Gahiji!"

*The pharaoh has obtained the power of Horus!* Azizi watched with horror as the pharaoh turned towards the combatants. The pharaoh extended his arms to the crowd.

"Hold your weapons, soldiers of Horus!"

Azizi watched in amazement as the soldiers of Horus stopped their fighting and held their weapons motionless. The soldiers turned towards Runihura and bowed to him on one knee. The pharaoh's soldiers watched in astonishment as the enemy kneeled with complacency. "What kind of magic is this?" Azizi asked himself quietly as he hid himself in the shadows above the pharaoh.

"Worship me," the pharaoh demanded with a satisfied grin.

"All hail, Pharaoh Runihura, Scourge of Heliopolis! Great is his mercy! Great is his power! Long may he reign in peace! His right hand is the hand of Sekhmet! His left hand is the hand of Ammut, Great Devourer of Souls. Great is He who tramples his enemies! Your desire is our command! Your words are as beautiful music to our ears. May we please you, our king."

Azizi watched wide-eyed in terror. "I think we have a very big problem here."

Pharaoh Runihura grinned as he looked at the kneeling soldiers. "Are you ready for your first command?"

"Yes, our king. Tell us what you wish of us."

Runihura grinned. "My enemies, I want you to kill yourselves."

Azizi watched as the men lifted their swords slowly. Azizi's hands trembled in horror as the soldiers held their swords to their chests. *No! Don't do it! Fight it! Fight the power of the gods!*

Azizi covered his mouth in alarm as the soldiers pierced their chests with their swords. Some soldiers slit their throats as they kneeled before the pharaoh. Azizi watched as blood crept from the bodies and pooled on the marble floor. The groans of men and the gurgling of severed throats rose into the air.

*May Osiris guide you all to eternal peace.*

Pharaoh Runihura grinned with satisfaction as the enemy soldiers laid motionless on the ground. His golden-metallic eyes blinked and glimmered in the candlelight of the altar. "Victory shall be mine at all costs, Gahiji. All hail the rise of Sekhmet!" Azizi watched as the pharaoh took a golden chalice from the altar and lifted the head of the dead soldier. Blood from the man's severed throat trickled into the cup. Pharaoh Runihura raised the chalice into the air. "May Sekhmet be praised!" Azizi watched in horror and disgust as the pharaoh drank from the cup of blood. *You will not get away with this, pharaoh. I promise you.*